"Most men avoid love like the plague," Tillie said.

She hated the resentment that laced through her voice. Liking even less Rexton's slow perusal, as though he could see the tiny fissures where her heart had cracked day after day, night after night until she'd feared it would shatter into nothing.

If he asked her about her marriage she was going to leap from the carriage and march home. Why had she even intruded on the conversation? She was the chaperone. Her role was one of silence and observation.

"Have you any advice for snagging a man's heart?" Tillie's sister asked Rexton.

He smiled. "Be yourself."

"But beware, sweeting," Tillie added. "For men seldom are."

"You haven't a very favorable opinion of our gender," Rexton said, his smile turning rueful.

"Prove me wrong, my lord."

"I may just do that, Lady Landsdowne."

By Lorraine Heath

LORRAINE HEATH

AN AFFAIR WITH A NOTORIOUS HEIRESS

AVONBOOKS

An Imprint of HarperCollinsPublishers

AN AFFAIR WITH A NOTORIOUS HEIRESS. Copyright © 2017 by Jan Nowasky. All rights reserved. Printed in the United States of America. No part of this book may be used or reproduced in any manner whatsoever without written permission except in the case of brief quotations embodied in critical articles and reviews. For information, address HarperCollins Publishers, 195 Broadway, New York, NY 10007.

First Avon Books mass market printing: June 2017
First Avon Books hardcover printing: May 2017

ISBN 978-0-06-239110-0

Avon, Avon & logo, and Avon Books & logo are registered trademarks of HarperCollins Publishers in the United States of America and other countries.

HarperCollins is a registered trademark of HarperCollins Publishers in the United States of America and other countries.

17 18 19 20 21 QGM 10 9 8 7 6 5 4 3 2 1

This book is dedicated on behalf of Karen Gibbs:
"To my mother, Joan Conner,
A woman who inspired my sisters and me to be the
independent women we are today."

AN AFFAIR
WITH A NOTORIOUS
HEIRESS

Prologue

From the Journal of the Marquess of Rexton

First son to a duke, I was born with a silver spoon in my mouth, to a life of ease and plenty. I never did without warmth, food, possessions, or love. But still, it was not a life without its challenges.

My mother, bless her, had survived the streets by thievery and cunning until fate bettered her life, brought her an opportunity to be a partner in a gaming hell. Fate intervened again. She met my father; they fell in love. They married.

But marriage does not always wash off the taint of one's past, and my mother's scandalous beginnings landed upon my shoulders. I was made to pay for her transgressions, for crimes of which she'd never been found guilty, as well as the audacity of rising above her station.

Away at school, small for my age, on numerous occasions at night, I would awaken to discover my head covered by a burlap sack as whispering bullies carted me outside, stripped me bare, and tied me to a tree. A sign was hung about my neck: son of a thief.

During rugby matches, I would find myself at the bottom of a scrum where the bruises left from random kicks and flailing fists to my torso were easily explained away as the price one paid for being involved in sports, rather than punishment meted out by those who saw me as less. I was trounced upon in darkened corridors. Assignments I worked to perfect often went missing before I could hand them over to the schoolmaster.

I bore these insults and transgressions in silence, never telling a soul, determined that the woman who gave birth to me would never know what price I paid for her acquiring the love she deserved.

Heir to a dukedom, I would one day have prestige and power, so these deliverers of "justice" were careful to keep their identities hidden for they knew they played a dangerous game, but the final move arrived sooner than expected when one summer I grew in height and breadth. I learned to fight back, with fists that were quick and hard. I boxed, I wrestled, and while my peers might not have come to respect my mother, they did in time come to respect me—or they paid a high price for it. Until the late night pranks stopped. The bruises appeared no more. My papers were left where they lay when I completed them.

Respect, it seems, is not granted by birth, but must be earned.

By the time I reached manhood, I was held in very high esteem indeed. My mother's past was but a fading whisper on the lips of those who no longer mattered.

Yet I was determined none of my children would be burdened with the sins of either parent. I would live my life above reproach, without scandal. And the woman I took to wife would be as pure as freshly fallen snow.

Chapter 1

"*A*llow me the honor of introducing Lady Margaret Sherman . . ."

"Allow me to introduce Lady Charlotte . . ."

". . . Lady Edith . . ."

". . . Miss . . ."

". . . Lady . . ."

The introductions of a new crop of debutantes became a blur of bright eyes, hopeful smiles, dangling dance cards, fluttering eyelashes, and waving fans. Yet Alistair Mabry, Marquess of Rexton, future Duke of Greystone, suffered through it all with gentlemanly aplomb, wishing to be anywhere other than where he was: his sister's infernal ball. Considering the mad crush of people who attended any affair hosted by the Duke and Duchess of Lovingdon, he was rather certain he wouldn't be missed—except by the mamas who considered him—at the age of nine and twenty— prime marriage material for one of their daughters, rather convinced he was in want of a wife despite the fact he had, on numerous occasions, indicated quite forcefully the opposite. His father was in good health. His mother had provided a spare, so Rexton was truly in no rush to become shackled.

He carried on polite conversations because Grace had asked him not to immediately disappear into the male-only domain of the card room. Once it became obvious senseless banter was all he was willing to grant, the ladies slowly drifted away like so many delicate petals on a summer breeze, dance cards minus his signature dangling from their limp wrists. Because he'd promised Grace an hour of his presence in the grand parlor and a mere forty minutes had passed, in order to stay true to his word, he wandered to a far corner populated with only ferns.

Watching the proceedings carried out before him, he couldn't deny that as much as he detested grand affairs, he was intrigued by the secretive games played, and it was to his benefit to remain in the good graces of the aristocracy because at some point, he would indeed be searching for a wife, one with an impeccable reputation, good breeding, and a penchant for staying out of the gossip sheets. While his own family had withstood numerous scandals, the process of deflecting censure was wearisome and he had no desire whatsoever to spend the remainder of his life serving as titillating fodder for the gossips. He'd made it a habit to be above reproach, which made him one of the more boring members among his family and friends, but it was advantageous to be considered dull. He wasn't scrutinized very closely which meant he was free to do as he pleased within the shadows. And within the shadows, life was never dull.

"Lord Rexton."

He turned slightly, having no wish to offend the older man. Garrett Hammersley, an American by birth, had embraced England as his own when he moved to London in order to oversee his family's fire-arms operations. Opening a factory in England had allowed them to claim the business as an international venture, which had added significantly to their stock value. Their subsequent wealth had given him entry into the more elite circles. Their paths crossed from time to time, mostly at the horse races. He was in pos-session of something Rexton coveted, and his recent attempts to convince the man to part with it had disap-pointingly failed. "Hammersley."

"Say, old chap, I was wondering if I might bother you for a tiny favor."

Rexton smiled inwardly. Favors usually came with a price. The question was: Would Hammersley pay his? "What did you have in mind?"

"My young niece, my dear departed brother's daughter, has just had her coming out. Unfortunately, I need someone to help wash off the blemish of her scandalous older sister. I was hoping you'd be willing to step up to the task."

Rexton knew the older sister only by reputation. Making quite the splash when she arrived in London a few years earlier, she'd caught the eye of the Earl of Landsdowne and their fairy-tale courtship had cap-tured the attention of most of Britain. A few years after they wed, she had engaged in a notorious public affair that had left Landsdowne with no choice except to divorce her, which had resulted in further scandal be-cause those in the aristocracy worth their salt simply did not divorce under any circumstances. Knowing what it was to be touched by scandal, he had empathy for the younger sister, but he rather suspected teaching her to box wasn't going to help her situation. "I don't really see how I can be of service."

Hammersley brushed his fingers over his thick sprinkled-with-gray mustache, twice one way, twice the other. "You are the most sought after bachelor in London, and have the respect of your peers. You're also known to have excellent taste in women and horses. If you were to show some interest in the girl—"

"I'm not looking to marry just yet." His compassion went only so far.

"No, no, of course not. I don't expect you to lead her to the altar. But if you were to dance with her, perhaps take her on an outing to Hyde Park, be seen with her as it were, it might serve to pique the other gents' curiosity. I'm certain once they take an interest in her, they will be charmed as she is a most charming girl. She has none of her sister's . . . flaws, shall we say?"

Flaws? The inability to remain faithful? To publicly cuckold her husband? To divorce a man whose lineage could be traced back to William the Conqueror? Americans certainly had a way of understating the faults of a calamitous woman. "I'm afraid you'll need to turn elsewhere for assistance on this matter; ask another gent."

"Damn it, man, no one else has your influence. The younger swells work to emulate you. They'll follow your lead. Take some pity on the poor girl. I promised my brother on his deathbed I would see her well situated, and she's enamored of the nobility."

"So was her sister from what I understand."

"In temperament they are nothing alike. Mathilda was always too strong-willed to be ruled. But Gina, bless her heart, is a shy wallflower for whom hope springs eternal. I have to do something to spark awareness of her. And I've deduced you're the ticket."

Tickets came at a cost. "A dance, you say, and an afternoon at the park?"

"Not much more than that, I should think. Truly, she's a remarkable girl."

But not one who stood out if Hammersley had to approach Rexton regarding generating interest in her. He wasn't quite comfortable with the notion of giving the girl false hope regarding his intentions, but if he kept his interest casual perhaps no harm would be done. "Once I dance with her, mamas are going to think I've announced my stepping into the marriage market. It's going to create some inconvenience as I'll be fending off ladies for the remainder of the Season, which has only recently begun."

"I'll make it worth your while."

But was it fair to the girl? He'd do all in his power to bring a quick end to the farce and find a proper gent for her. "Oh? How might you go about that?"

"Black Diamond. You can take him to stud."

"Thrice."

"Damn it, man, do you know how valuable that stallion is?"

"I do indeed." Since the Arabian had soundly beaten Rexton's best stallion in several races. "I want at least three progeny off him."

"Two."

Which had been Rexton's price all along. "Two it is."

"But not until my niece has a viable suitor. You have

to play at courting her until someone makes it a point to beat you."

That would be a further inconvenience, as he doubted many gents would even consider that they could beat him. His was one of the most powerful families in Great Britain. But to have Black Diamond breed with his Fair Vixen would be worth it. He had little doubt the mingling of those bloodlines would produce a champion. "Consider it done."

"Excellent. However, our agreement must remain between us gentlemen. I don't want her hurt, so if it becomes known to her, our bargain becomes null and void."

He was well aware ladies had tender feelings. "I would expect no less."

"Come along then, let me introduce you to Gina. Who knows? You might just decide she's the one for you."

He seriously doubted that, but he was a man, after all, and ladies did interest him. "Should that happen, it won't nullify our agreement."

"Absolutely not. It will simply make our arrangement all the tidier."

*M*iss Virginia Hammersley was so damned young. That was his initial thought upon being introduced to her. Her eyes were the color of a leaf bud in spring, sparkling with unbridled innocence. Her hair the shade of moonbeams. She was petite and willowy; he feared he'd easily break her if he were to ever bed her. It wasn't that he preferred sex rough, but he did enjoy it with a great deal of enthusiasm that left him and his partner damp with sweat and gasping for breath. He felt rather guilty for giving the young lady any hope at all that he was seriously considering her as the Marchioness of Rexton and future Duchess of Greystone.

The way her face lit up as though it had taken its place among the bulbs in the chandeliers when her uncle gleefully told her with an exaggerated whisper that Rexton had been most insistent upon an introduction hadn't done anything to quiet his misgivings regarding his deception. She wasn't the one for him. He knew that fact within five seconds of gazing at her hope-filled expression.

Still he was determined to at least strive to keep to his end of the bargain, for surely she would appeal to some gent. So he was moving forward with the arrangement for *her* sake and the good of the country. New blood as well as the coins she'd bring to someone's coffers was needed in the aristocracy. "I'd be pleased if you'd honor me with a dance," he said, as his lips hovered over her delicate hand after pressing a light kiss to the back of her gloved knuckles. Dear God, she was as fragile as one of the china dolls he'd recently gifted to his nieces.

Her laughter rivaled the tinkling bells that filled the air at Christmas. "As my dance card is thus far absent any signatures, I'd be pleased as well. I'm quite accomplished and would dearly love to put my lessons to good use."

They stood together, waiting for the next dance—a waltz—to start up. For the life of him, he could think of nothing interesting to say. He suddenly felt remarkably old, like a pair of well-worn boots that were incredibly comfortable but could no longer retain a shine no matter how hard the boot boy buffed at them with a brush. Perhaps he should have taken a wife sooner, when his age more closely aligned with that of the girls who were being debuted. They hadn't seemed so youthful last year or the one before, but they made him feel rather ancient now, a relic that wasn't quite as gleaming as it had once been. He couldn't help but believe she saw him in the same light as she seemed to be struggling for a topic as well, as though she recognized they had little in common other than presently inhabiting the same area of the ballroom.

"I've heard about your sister's balls for years," she finally said. "I must say it lives up to expectations. The duchess is such a gracious hostess."

"Grace was well tutored by our mother."

"Unusual for a lord to marry a woman who grew up on the streets, but I daresay when I was introduced to the Duchess of Greystone, I could certainly understand her appeal." His parents rarely attended balls any longer so their appearance at the Lovingdon ball was generally heralded as one of the few times they might make an appearance throughout the Season. Few knew the true reason behind their increasing absences.

"My mother is an incredible woman who rose above her beginnings," he said a bit more curtly than was polite.

"I hope I didn't offend."

At least she wasn't oblivious to his tone. He rather feared she might be. "Not at all. Having grown up with her during the entirety of my life, I take her for granted, and sometimes forget she was not always welcomed by the aristocracy." A small lie as he never forgot the impact her previous life had on his. Yet he held the girl blameless for the difficulties he'd endured during his youth. After all, she'd been on the other side of the Atlantic.

"I find your parents' story to be incredibly romantic."

"It is that, I suppose."

"I love romance."

Dear God, let the music begin as he was not romancing the girl. A dance. An outing to the park. That was it. If he couldn't get the gents interested in her by then—

Dash it all! He may have just agreed to sacrifice his entire summer to attending balls all for the want of a horse. However, he wasn't going to just give up if he'd misjudged the ease with which he could lure gents to her side.

The quadrille finally came to an end. He offered his arm to Miss Hammersley, aware her touch was featherlike, practically nonexistent, and escorted her onto the gleaming parquet dance floor. He couldn't deny she was quite lovely in an elfin sort of way. She had a gamine smile that never faltered during their dance. He was the worst sort of wretch for placing his racehorses above her. He consoled himself with the knowledge he'd spied a couple of gents giving her a once-over. And she was a graceful dancer. Those lessons were serving her well.

When the waltz ended, he began leading her back toward the chairs. "I wonder if I might call on you tomorrow afternoon and take you for a drive through the park." It couldn't hurt to allow all the swells to see her in his carriage.

"I'd be delighted, my lord."

"Say around two?"

"I'll be waiting with bells on. By the by, I'm staying at Landsdowne Court with my sister."

He blinked, surprised she lived in such close proximity to the notorious Lady Landsdowne. "Not with your uncle?"

"No. She's not welcomed within Society so my uncle carts me about, but he is a bachelor whose abode would not suit at all and so I reside with my sister."

"Then I shall see you at Landsdowne Court." Once they reached their destination, he again gallantly lifted her gloved hand and pressed a kiss to the back of it. "I shall count the hours."

He was going to burn in hell for that last remark. He didn't think it was possible for her smile to get any brighter yet it did. Shame pricked his conscience but he tamped it down. With any luck, by the end of the week the girl would have a hundred swains vying for her attention and Rexton would have Black Diamond.

He arrived promptly at two. He'd never been a slacker in any regard. Landsdowne Court was impressive from the outside, even more so from the inside with its cavernous entryway and stairs branching out on two sides leading to the upper floors. He wasn't certain how Lady Landsdowne had wrested the residence—which had been in the earl's family for at least a century—away from her husband, but her residing within these walls had resulted in another insult for which Society wouldn't forgive her.

Extending his card to the butler, he was surprised by the man's youth. "The Marquess of Rexton calling upon Miss Hammersley."

"I'll inform the countess. Allow me to situate you in the parlor."

The parlor was deep purple walls and furniture in various shades of white. He'd never realized white came in an assortment. Some of it was so pristine as to hurt the eyes, like snow captured in sunlight, some less so, more the ivory of tusks.

Rexton wandered over to the shelves beside the fireplace. Only half contained books. The others held wood, granite, and marble carvings of horses in various stances: leaping, trotting, prancing. Paintings of horses dotted the walls, a huge one hung over the fireplace. Obviously the room reflected the earl's love of horses. It must have pricked his pride to have had to leave all this behind.

Hearing the rapid patter of heels, he turned, completely unprepared for the hard kick his gut took at the sight of the woman striding toward him with such regal and uncompromising bearing. She held herself rigid and tall, with dignity and a daring that issued a challenge: mock me, mess with me, at your own peril. Nothing about her appeared youthful, yet he doubted she'd yet seen a quarter of a century.

She stopped in front of him, her blue eyes— shrewd, calculating, suspicious—slowly raking over him, taking his measure. Much to his annoyance, he found himself straightening his spine a tad, when he'd thought it was as straight as a poker. With hair as black as midnight, she in no way resembled her sister. This woman was no innocent. She didn't harbor dreams of love and romance. Poetry interested her not in the least. Pixie dust wasn't sprinkled about her. She was all strength and vinegar. She wouldn't break in his bed. He'd wager if anyone were vulnerable there, it would be he. She communicated quite effectively with her narrowed gaze that she would give no quarter.

"Good afternoon, Lord Rexton. I'm Lady Landsdowne. I don't believe we've ever been properly introduced."

No, they hadn't. He couldn't recall ever laying eyes on her. By the time he was occasionally making the social rounds she was persona non grata. "It's a pleasure."

Her smile, small and tight, indicated she knew he was lying. The décolletage of her burgundy frock was low enough to modestly hint at the swell of her bosom, only enough pale skin revealed to make a man's mouth water and his imagination to take flight, but the rest of her was covered as primly as a schoolmistress.

"It seems Gina slept in. She's preparing herself now. I'm afraid she might be a while. I'd offer to have the maid bring in tea but you strike me as being a whisky man." She walked over to a table sporting several decanters and winged a finely arched ravenblack eyebrow at him over her shoulder.

He didn't usually indulge this early in the day, but he'd welcome the heat of whisky at his throat to distract him from the other heated areas of his body. "Yes, please."

To his surprise, she poured whisky into two glasses. She handed him one, took the other, raised it slightly. "Cheers."

She took a sip and licked her lips in a manner that caused his gut to tighten, before walking over to the settee where she gracefully lowered herself onto a cushion. "Please make yourself comfortable."

He selected the chair nearest to her, studied her, and couldn't help thinking how quickly Landsdowne must have fallen for her. She was poised, graceful, and beautiful. The man would have preened with her on his arm. That she then betrayed him and her vows was beyond the pale. Little wonder people looked at her and expected the same of her sister. This woman commanded the room; she could not be without influence, and her sister was her vulnerable pupil. What lessons she must have taught her. And that tutoring was going to make his task all the more challenging.

"I'm actually rather glad we have this opportunity to speak privately," she said, brazenly holding his gaze. She might be American but her accent was refined—not the harsh brusqueness of her uncle's but neither was it quite British. "You may be aware that our father passed a little over a year ago, our mother some years before that. Gina's inheritance has been placed in a trust to be handed over to her when she marries or reaches the age of five and twenty. In either case, she will bring to her marriage a small fortune, all that was left to her, and the wrong sort of man could take advantage of that, take it as his own, leave her with naught."

"I have no need of a small fortune," he stated succinctly, feeling a need to defend himself even though he could care less about any girl's dowry. Based upon what he knew of her family's business, she was being modest concerning the size of the fortune she and her sister had inherited. "Reputation, not coin, is the currency by which I will measure the value of the woman I intend to take to wife."

Although she blanched, to her credit, she continued

to hold his gaze. "While you may claim money has no bearing, it still needs to be emphasized that much is at stake here. I'm quite aware you come with a respected title, position, and influence. However, my lord, if you seek to marry my dear sister, you must also come with your heart. You must not only convince her that you love her but you must convince me as well. I will not allow Gina to spend so much as an hour in a loveless marriage."

He had absolutely no interest in marrying the girl. Still, Lady Landsdowne's words irked. How dare she judge him or his motives when she knew him not at all. "I am quite the catch, *my lady*. Miss Hammersley would be damned lucky to have me as a husband."

"Modest as well, I see."

"Merely speaking the truth. I, on the other hand, need reassurances that she will not follow her sister's path to ruination and scandal."

Lady Landsdowne's chin came up and he suspected she had an urge to toss in his face what remained of her whisky. "If she marries a man who loves her, a man she loves, I believe that will be assured."

"You didn't marry for love?"

"I don't see that my feelings regarding Landsdowne are really any of your concern. However, I will admit my mother wanted me to have a title she could flaunt in front of her New York enemies. I was raised to obey my mother in all things. Landsdowne wanted a dowry. I provided that. A title never interested me."

"Yet you insist upon being addressed by yours." Another offense against the aristocracy for which she would never be forgiven, to have the title tainted permanently by her transgressions. Because of the embarrassment she had caused, Landsdowne had asked the divorce court to strip her of the title she'd gained through marriage to him. They'd ruled in his favor. She had appealed to a higher court—and won. Appalled by her cheek, people justifiably shunned her.

"I paid for the privilege of it. Quite handsomely since Downie took possession of my entire dowry. Besides, I knew it would irritate the devil out of him."

Her secretive smile made him want to grin but he refrained. His family wasn't without scandal but she seemed to relish it. He glanced around. "You seem to be doing quite well for yourself now."

"My father was not a man to fritter away what he acquired through blood, sweat, and tears. His fortune was vast. Certainly I shall never do without and I want to ensure Gina does not go without either, which is the reason it is even more imperative to weed out all fortune hunters."

He found it rather crass to be discussing money matters right out of the gate as though he was possessed of greedy fingers. Her opinion of him seemed to be as low as his of her. Her regard toward him was not deserved, and left a rancid taste in his mouth. "I was under the impression your uncle was responsible for her."

"He has the means to introduce her into Society which I do not. He and I are in agreement, however, that when it comes to her suitors, my opinion alone matters. He acts when called upon but in truth he has very little interest in either of us."

So the man was striving to get this duty out of

the way. Rexton couldn't fault him when he, himself, found balls and the social games that went along with them rather tedious.

"I am not naïve, my lord. I realize my divorce created quite the scandal, and I do not wish for Gina to pay the price. No doubt I should have waited until she was properly situated." She glanced away then, and he wondered what she was thinking. She brought her gaze back to bear on him. "But I didn't. Selfish on my part. But there you have it. I hadn't really thought things through—"

"I am given to understand you kissed a footman in front of guests." He couldn't believe he'd said it. To her face. His mother would be appalled.

Lady Landsdowne simply smiled, without joy but with triumph. "Yes. He now serves as my butler."

The one who had opened the door to him? The servant wasn't particularly handsome. Rexton found himself wondering at the size of the man's cock for surely he had to have offered her something worth her ruination. Or perhaps she simply enjoyed a bit of the rough. She wouldn't be the first well-placed woman to be attracted to those of the lower class. Still, he recognized he was behaving as though he came from the gutter. "My apologies. My words were uncalled for."

She took another sip of her whisky. "No apologies needed. I know I'm an object of curiosity and shame. However, I do not want my choices reflected upon my sister. I must know your intentions regarding her are honorable. To be quite honest"—she finished off her whisky, set her glass aside, and captured his gaze as though she intended to tame it—"I will kill any man who causes her any sort of hurt, no matter how mild or seemingly insignificant. I do not want her to shed so much as a single tear because of a man's heartless behavior."

Had she shed tears? He couldn't quite envision it. She was ice surrounded by cold steel.

"Have I made myself perfectly clear?"

The sharpness to her words, the challenge glistening in her sapphire eyes spoke loudly that she would indeed slay him if he did not rise to the occasion and meet her standards. He didn't particularly like the way his heart sped up and his chest tightened. He didn't like that he wondered what she would do if he got up, crossed over to her, caged her between his arms, and claimed her mouth. Good Lord, she was so much more appealing than the sister. She was spit and fire and unbreakable. Nothing about her was innocent. Something in her past, possibly her marriage, had honed her to a fine edge. He was fascinated, he was intrigued, he was—

"Apologies for keeping you waiting, my lord." Miss Hammersley fairly skipped into the room and suddenly she seemed more a child than ever. He could see her frolicking through fields of daisies. He doubted Lady Landsdowne had ever frolicked.

He shot to his feet and fought to keep his attention on Miss Hammersley rather than the woman he could see out of the corner of his eye. The contrast between the two was incredible. Woman . . . girl. Worldly . . . innocent. Tart . . . sweet.

Damnation if he didn't prefer tart. But tart wouldn't get him the stud. "You look lovely, my dear."

She smiled brightly, her eyes twinkling with joy.

His clothing suddenly felt tight, and he had a need to loosen his neck cloth before it strangled him.

"Your delay served us well," Lady Landsdowne said gently, "as it gave us the opportunity to get acquainted."

Tiny pleats appeared in the girl's delicate brow. "How is that you were not acquainted before? I'd have thought you of a similar age."

"During my youth I traveled extensively," Rexton said. "I didn't spend much time in London if I could help it." He decided not to mention he had no interest in the social scene and avoided it whenever possible.

She brightened once more. "How marvelous for you. I should like to see more of the world, I think. Will you take your wife traveling?"

"If it is her desire. But I must procure her first, and rituals must be followed." He set down his glass and walked toward her. "Miss Hammersley, my carriage awaits."

He offered his arm. Her face fell. "We have a bit of a problem there. My maid has taken a megrim and I've ordered her to bed." She looked past him. "Tillie, would you be so kind as to serve as chaperone?"

Tillie? An image of her, sweet and innocent, young and happy, indeed frolicking through meadows of daisies—before Landsdowne had taken her to wife—flashed through his mind. He didn't like it, didn't like it one bit. He glanced back in time to see the countess's calculating gaze travel the length of him. Christ, he had the urge to spread his feathers like a blasted peacock.

"I'd be delighted. It will give me the opportunity to

get to know the marquess better and get a sense of his true feelings toward you."

"He has no feelings yet," Miss Hammersley assured her. "We met only last night."

"Oh, I'm certain he's feeling something," the witch said with a smirk as she walked past him.

He was struck by the realization she smelled of lavender and orchids. She was also correct. He was feeling something—something that could lead to no good.

Chapter 2

$\mathcal{M}$athilda Paget, Countess of Landsdowne, couldn't deny that the marquess had excellent taste in horses. The two chestnut bays pulling the gleaming black open carriage obviously came from good stock. It had taken everything within her not to approach them and give them an affectionate pat when she first spied them. Just as now, it was with great difficulty she didn't reach across to Rexton, sitting on the seat opposite her sister and herself, to pat that muscular thigh of his outlined so provocatively by his taut breeches.

Damn if the man wasn't gorgeous with his golden curling locks and his blue eyes the shade of a winter sky promising snow and the need for warm fires. Her heart tripped over itself at the thought of this sensual and sexual man taking her sister to bed. With his heated gaze, he appeared far too wise, too experienced, too knowledgeable in the ways of women. He sat there like some large predatory tiger, considering how tasty a morsel his prey might be. She couldn't imagine him ordering a woman to simply lie still and endure what was to come. Nor could she imagine a woman being able to remain unaffected if he pressed those firm, full lips against her skin.

Something flickered in his heated gaze, and she was left with the uncomfortable sensation that he was able to read her thoughts, that he knew the errant path they traveled. Her cheeks warmed, and she cursed inwardly, jerking her gaze to the passing buildings as they made their way to the park. What was wrong with her to have such lurid images flashing through her mind? She wanted to spare Gina the shame of the marriage bed, even as she found her own skin tightening and something closely resembling desire coursing through her. She fully understood how any woman might fall at this one's feet. Or at least she assumed they might. His exploits certainly weren't reported on in the gossip sheets, so he was no doubt discreet in his affairs, unlike her previous husband. If Downie had been more circumspect, perhaps Tillie wouldn't have been required to stage an encounter that would force him, along with his obnoxious pride, to divorce her.

"You must have been a child when you married."

The deep voice shimmered through her, her reaction wrong on so many levels. Tilting up her chin, she met Rexton's gaze, surprised to see true curiosity reflected there. "I married on the day I turned nineteen."

"You can't have been married very long."

"Long enough to lose any semblance of youth." Three years. The process of obtaining a divorce had been a long, arduous, tortuous affair. Before its completion a little over nine months ago she had marked her twenty-fifth year. Reaching for her sister's hand, she squeezed it. "I know the trials and tribulations of marriage, which is the reason I will not let anyone who is undeserving of Gina marry her."

"And you've already deemed me underserving."

To her utter mortification, she had. This man would not do for her sister, would not do at all. He was far too mature, too knowing. She wasn't going to allow a man of such boldness and daring to have Gina. "To be quite honest, my lord, she is so innocent that I do think a less worldly man might serve her better."

"And you judge me worldly?"

"Are you not?"

A corner of his mouth hitched up slightly. "I've never had a woman complain."

She knew his thoughts were traveling the same path as hers—toward the bedchamber. It was all men really wanted once they had the dowry. Downie hadn't been able to get her out of her clothes fast enough. But then once he'd had her, he grew bored. Another truth she'd learned about men: they easily wearied of their bedmates. For them it was the lure of the conquest, but they had no desire to hold for long that which they had obtained. Greener pastures and all that.

Gina deserved a man who would stay on his side of the fence. Surely a deep and profound love could keep him there. She forced herself to hold Rexton's gaze. "You're not doing much to convince me that you and my sister would suit."

"It might be helpful if you shared with me the requirements you seek."

"So you can pretend to possess them?"

He held out his arms as though surrendering. "When it comes to the ladies, I have no reason to pretend. I have always found honesty in relationships to serve me well."

"Then you should have no fear of being found lacking while courting Gina."

He chuckled low, provocatively. "Being found lacking has never been a fear."

Before she could stop it, her gaze dipped to his lap, lower. She jerked her attention back to the passing scenery but not before she saw his satisfied smirk. No, he wouldn't do at all for Gina. Tillie would always see innuendo in his eyes, read it in his face, hear it in his voice. What did it matter? As soon as Gina was wedded, she suspected she'd never see him again.

"Why didn't you return to America?" he asked.

She hated the inquisition. He should be talking with Gina, not her. Yet she felt compelled to respond. "Gina adores England. I couldn't very well leave her here alone."

But she would leave . . . once Gina was married. Her sister didn't understand how much she despised it here, how difficult it was to live with the constant shunning and isolation. Another reason she needed to ensure the man who married Gina would be protective of her sister. Even as she had that thought, she couldn't imagine Rexton not safeguarding what he viewed as his. Perhaps he would make an excellent choice for Gina, after all.

"When I marry a man of position," Gina said, "everyone will have to welcome you back into Society, Tillie. Then we can attend balls together."

Reassuringly she patted her sister's hand. "I'm sure you're quite right."

But she saw the truth reflected in Rexton's blue eyes. Society would never welcome her back. She had moved into their circles only to bring mortification to one of their own. The divorce was bad enough but an affair with a footman . . .

Although, if she hadn't been seen kissing a footman, she wouldn't be divorced. Landsdowne had viewed her as property and the law had given him the right to do so. Her father had been too ill to help her get out of the unconscionable situation in which she'd found herself. Miserable didn't begin to describe it. So she'd taken care of the matter herself.

"I'm afraid I've never been one for keeping up with Society gossip. How long were you married?" he asked.

She gave him a pointed look. "I'm the chaperone. You really should be directing your questions toward the lady you're courting."

That wicked grin again, the one that said he knew what she was about, striving to deflect his attention away from her. "How long was your sister married?" he asked Gina.

Gina opened her mouth—

"That's not what I meant," Tillie responded quickly, with acerbity, not bothering to hide her irritation. "You should be asking Gina questions about herself. Or perhaps you're not truly interested in her, but in her money. In spite of what you say about not needing it."

He angled his head down slightly in acquiescence although she couldn't see this man bowing down before anyone. Even if he gave the appearance of giving in, she suspected he'd be working out how to get even, how to regain the upper hand. "You're quite right. Miss Hammersley—"

"Please, you must call me Gina. I hate formality."

"It can be rather tedious," he admitted.

"But necessary," Tillie said insistently. "Gina, you do not give a gentleman leave to call you by your Christian name until you have an understanding between you."

"The understanding is that he need not be so formal."

"It sends an improper message."

"And you would know all about improper messages, would you not, my lady?" Rexton asked pointedly.

"I would take care, Lord Rexton, if you wish to impress upon me your favorable merits when it comes to courting Gina."

He studied her for three full heartbeats during which time she suspected he was striving to determine if what he gained by pushing her was worth the price he would pay for doing so. Finally, he turned away from her. "So, *Miss Hammersley*, tell me what you value in a husband."

She'd won. She wondered why she took so little satisfaction in it.

"Someone who is kind, generous. Someone who makes me happy."

"What makes you happy?"

It was a good question, one Landsdowne had never asked Tillie. Although if he had, she doubted she would have said, "A man who is faithful." She'd thought it a given. She'd thought a lot of things a given. Devotion, attending affairs together, carrying on conversations during meals, always living in the same residence— not only during the Season when they were in London but throughout the year.

Gina gave a joyful sigh. "Pretty frocks. A generous allowance. Chocolates."

Tillie wanted to shake her sister. None of those things created happiness. Oh, they might lighten her mood for a few minutes but they didn't leave one happy for long. Chocolates disappeared, allowance dwindled, and frocks faded. Out of the corner of her eye, she watched as Rexton gave very little reaction, but he seemed equally unimpressed by her sister's musings.

"Surely you require more than that," he said flatly, without judgment or censure.

"I'm relatively easy to please."

"A woman shouldn't be."

His words surprised Tillie. Did he truly believe that? Did he not want a biddable female? What was the game he played? She gave up trying to appear as though she wasn't looking at him and stared at him directly. "Why would you seek to make your courtship more difficult?" she blurted, truly curious.

He shifted his attention to her. "Not more difficult. More challenging. There is a difference."

"She's offering an easy road. Why not take it?"

"Because it would bring me no pleasure."

That was when she knew the Marquess of Rexton was a man who liked to win, who thrived on competition. And who sought pleasure in all aspects of his life. Pleasure, and danger, and gratification. If he hadn't been born into the aristocracy, if he hadn't been born into wealth, influence, and privilege, if he'd been born into a hardscrabble life in America, he'd have been the sort to forge an empire, to carry others on his back, to stand his ground, to never back down. She was not at all pleased at the way that knowledge made it difficult for her to draw in breath, made her consider how fortunate any woman would be to stand beside him.

"What should I require, my lord?" Gina asked, obviously oblivious to all the messages the man across from her was sending, to the turmoil wreaking havoc within Tillie.

"Love."

He said it so simply as though it was easily given, easily received.

"Most men avoid love like the plague," Tillie felt obligated to point out, hating the resentment lacing through her voice. Liking even less his slow perusal, as though he could see the tiny fissures where her heart had cracked day after day, night after night until she'd feared it would shatter into nothing. If he asked her about Landsdowne, about their marriage, about her relationship with him, she was going to leap from the carriage and march home. Why had she even intruded on the conversation? Her role was one of silence and observation.

"Few men have grown up around the exemplary example I did," he said quietly.

The breath she didn't even realize she'd been holding eased out of her when he didn't take the conversation in the direction she'd been dreading.

"Do your parents love each other?" Gina asked.

"Immensely. They taught me to never take it for granted, that if you are fortunate to possess it, you nurture it. I daresay, my father goes to sleep each night pondering what he can do upon awakening to ensure my mother is grateful he shares her life."

"Does your mother do the same?"

"Love comes more easily to women, I think. It's more natural. Men have to work a bit harder at it, especially as we're not very demonstrative as a whole. So if you can snag a man's heart, Miss Hammersley, the frocks, chocolates, and allowance will surely follow. You need not insist upon them."

"Have you any advice for snagging a man's heart?" Gina asked.

"Be yourself."

"But beware, sweeting," Tillie added. "For men seldom are."

"You haven't a very favorable opinion of our gender," Rexton said, his smile rueful.

"Prove me wrong, my lord."

"I may just do that, Lady Landsdowne."

She did wish she'd kept her mouth shut as she'd never before had the sense she'd just issued an irrefutable challenge which he had accepted with a challenge of his own—and if she wasn't careful, she could find herself losing not only her pride but discovering her heart, too, had been part of the wager.

$\mathcal{H}$e had to quit engaging Lady Landsdowne, but he found her so much more fetching than her sister. She wasn't timid or shy, and she didn't retreat. But her eyes never sparkled and her lips never curved up into a genuine smile of joy; he had an irrational need to see both. Had she been as without guile as her sister when she'd married Downie?

As they entered the park, he became aware of her slight stiffening as though she were bracing herself for a blow to her midsection. Surely she hadn't avoided the park since her scandal. While Miss Hammersley fairly sat on the edge of her seat, glancing around eagerly, striving to determine who might be in the vicinity, Lady Landsdowne seemed to take great interest in the knot of his neck cloth.

He wanted her at ease again, wanted her comfortable enough to challenge him. Which was ridiculous. She was not the one to whom he should direct his interest. If he wasn't careful, she was going to advise her sister to cast him aside immediately. That would prove disastrous for Miss Hammersley. If the bachelors thought Rexton would dismiss the girl so easily after only one outing they weren't likely to give her much credence as a possible wife. He needed someone to take interest in her so he could pack up his courting manners.

He forced himself to focus solely on her and to keep the conversation relatively neutral so the sister wasn't interfering. They spoke of flowers and fauna and whenever he could work in a laugh he made sure it carried on the wind to gents trotting by on fine horses or in speedy carriages. He kept his features relaxed, and a pleasant smile on his face, portraying a man on the verge of being forever smitten. He was grateful Miss Hammersley was occupied with taking in their surroundings and didn't seem particularly affected by his feigned interest. He might have been insulted by her lack of attention, except vanity had never been one of his shortcomings. He was actually glad she wasn't likely to mistake his performance as true devotion.

He was rather certain, however, Lady Landsdowne could read straight through his efforts and decipher them for what they were. If her eyes narrowed any further, they'd be as sharp as a finely honed blade and might slice into him.

God, but she was protective, and he couldn't help but admire her for it. Those in his family had a penchant for caring for the less fortunate, for seeking justice, for striving to better living conditions. He could certainly see Lady Landsdowne carrying on the tradition with a fierce determination. He suspected if she discovered his true purpose, she'd flatten him with one solid punch. Or she'd try. He envisioned closing his hand around her fist before it met flesh, drawing her in, and claiming her mouth until he'd worked them both into a fevered tempest.

They'd been driving through the park for nearly half an hour before it dawned on him no one had stopped to speak with him. He became aware of gawks, glares, and frowns. They were garnering attention, but not the sort that served any good. He considered suggesting they stop and stroll through the green, but Miss Hammersley had begun to fidget as though taking note of the occasional glower. Unlike her sister, who held her head high and occasionally stared someone down.

"It's rather warm today," Rexton said casually. "I believe I've had enough of the park. What of you, Miss Hammersley?"

"It does seem a bit unwelcoming."

He leaned toward her. "People are jealous of my horses."

Her green eyes grew as round as saucers. "Truly?"

No, but still he nodded. "A few of the gents and I have on occasion raced. I always win. Not everyone is a good sport about it."

"Would you be a good sport if you lost?"

He grinned. "Probably not. I have a very competitive nature. I prefer to win."

"To be quite honest, I can't imagine you losing."

"On occasion I have. It keeps me humble and inspires me to work all the harder."

"This is you humble?" Lady Landsdowne asked.

He grinned at her because it seemed to irritate her when he did. "Decidedly so."

With a roll of her eyes, she directed her attention back to the greenery. He'd love to engage her in a match of wits.

"I don't believe I've ever competed in anything," Miss Hammersley lamented.

"You don't see seeking a husband as a competition?" he asked.

She shook her head, furrowed her brow. "No. I wouldn't go after a gent whom another lady wanted."

"Have you not heard there are no rules in love?"

"They are always rules, my lord. At least in my mind. Things I would not do for gain."

"Admirable." He instructed his driver to start back to Landsdowne Court.

Miss Hammersley sighed. "I believe, Tillie, I understand why you go riding in the park in the morning before anyone is about."

"It's much cooler, then, Gina. My horse prefers it."

And he imagined she did as well. Was she always striving to protect her sister from the truth of her dire situation: she was loathed among his peers?

They spoke very little on the journey back. When the driver pulled the carriage to a stop in the drive, Rexton leaped out and extended his gloved hand to

Lady Landsdowne. After a hesitation, she placed hers in it with assurance and certainty. Nothing delicate there, nothing that would break easily. He'd noticed it when he handed her up into the carriage, the way her warmth seeped through the kidskin to become part of his flesh. They were in close proximity as she descended the three steps to the ground and yet an immeasurable distance separated them, as though a wall surrounded her, one that could not be climbed over or breeched. She held herself apart, and he wondered if she'd done the same in her husband's bed.

After releasing her, he assisted Gina. He might as well be handing down a doll for all the effect she had upon him. Nothing vibrated between them. No heat arced. No awareness sparked. He'd think he had one foot in the grave if it weren't for the fact his reaction to Lady Landsdowne was so strong and unwavering.

She marched ahead toward the door, while Gina lagged behind, smiling up at him, her eyelashes fluttering as though she were striving to dislodge a speck of ash that had settled into the corner of her eye. She truly was too unknowing for him. Her sister had the right of it there, but he wanted access to Black Diamond more than he wanted to breathe.

"May I have a word in private, Miss Hammersley?" he asked quietly, and yet still Lady Landsdowne heard him. Her back went ramrod straight, when he'd thought it could go no straighter, and her slender shoulders stiffened as though someone had just walked over her grave and caused a shudder to course through her. She swung around, her features set in an impermeable mask.

"Keep it short," she ordered sharply before proceeding into the residence. Not ten seconds later the butler stepped out, standing at attention, his gaze boring into Rexton as though he suspected him of being up to no good. Not too far from the truth there.

Again Rexton found himself wondering what about the man had appealed to the countess. He was tall, trim, dark-haired but his features were so bland he wouldn't be noticed in a crowd of two. Did he possess a sense of humor? Did he cause her to laugh? Did he recite poetry in a mesmerizing cadence? Did he—

"My lord?"

He looked down to find the lass gazing up at him expectantly. Right. His focus was supposed to be on the younger sister, not the elder.

"I had a lovely time, my lord," she said with a sweet voice he couldn't imagine screaming out his name in rapture.

Why was he even considering these thoughts, comparing her to other women he'd known, to her sister whom he didn't, when he had no plans whatsoever to carry this courtship through to fruition? "As did I. I wondered if you might care to join me in my box tomorrow evening."

Her smile withered, her brow furrowed. "Your box? You live in a box?"

Was she serious? He hadn't judged her to be daft, but then neither had he truly conversed with her about anything complicated or of importance. He offered a teasing grin. "I have a box at the theater."

Her smile grew brighter, her eyes sparkling like jewels caught by the sunlight. "At the theater! I so love the theater! I'd be delighted to attend with you."

"Do you think your maid's megrim will have vanished by then?"

"I'm rather certain of it."

He didn't know why he was disappointed by the notion. Not having her sister about would make it easier to achieve his goal. "Then I shall be here tomorrow at half past seven." He took her hand, pressed a kiss to the back of her gloved knuckles. "I look forward to it, Miss Hammersley."

"In spite of what my sister said, I do wish you'd call me Gina."

He smiled. "My manners, it seems, are difficult to cast aside which would no doubt please my mother to no end."

"You are funny, my lord."

She was far too easy to please. "Until tomorrow, Miss Hammersley." He gave a brisk nod to the butler before striding to his carriage, leaping into it, and settling onto the leather bench. His driver immediately set the pair of horses to a trot.

Rexton was tempted to glance back to see if Lady Landsdowne was gazing out a window, but he didn't want to give her the satisfaction of knowing she was on his mind. He needed to quickly find someone for Miss Hammersley so he was free of her and had met his part of the bargain. Before her older sister drove him to distraction.

*P*artially hidden by the draperies, Tillie stood at her bedchamber window, gazing out on the retreating carriage. She was glad the man was leaving. He unsettled her in ways she didn't want to explore. He exuded sexuality in the same manner that the sun exuded heat—naturally, as though it had been created to do nothing else.

The jealousy that speared her when he'd asked for a private moment with Gina was entirely inappropriate. He was courting her sister, and Tillie certainly had no interest in him. She'd been married once and by God that had been a lesson in humility and subservience. Her opinion, her preferences, her desires had mattered not one whit. She much preferred having her independence, being completely in charge of every aspect of her life. Never again was she going to let a man have control over her.

Even as she had the thought, she understood Gina's desire to marry. Not every woman flourished in solitude. There was something to be said for being part of something, of someone. But only if it was the right something, the right someone. Otherwise, one was guaranteed naught but misery.

The door to her bedchamber burst open and Gina flounced in, spread her arms wide, and spun in a circle. "Isn't he wonderful!"

She flopped onto the bed and smiled up at the canopy as though it represented heaven. "He's so remarkably handsome and charming. And one day he'll be a duke and I shall be his duchess. How lucky I am!"

Tillie wasn't quite so certain. She crossed over, sat on the edge of the bed, and took her sister's hand. "Sweeting, you have to search beneath his chiseled nose and strong jaw—"

Gina bounced up into a sitting position. "You noticed?"

His features had been engraved into her brain as

effectively as they'd been carved into his face. "How could one not?"

"His eyes are such an incredible blue. I could become lost in them."

"That's the thing, Gina, you don't want to become lost when you're with a man. You need to keep your wits about you. With clever questions, you need to dig into his past, his present, his likes, his dislikes in order to determine what he's really about. Men put on a false façade when they're courting, especially when the lady in question is in possession of a fortune. At some point, you even need to make him angry."

Hard lessons learned.

Shock washed over Gina's delicate features. "Why ever would I do something as unpleasant as all that? If I'm not biddable, he'll move on to someone else."

"If upsetting him causes him to take his affections elsewhere then they never were yours to begin with."

"Is that what happened with you and Downie? You never talk about it."

And she never would. Marriage to him had been horrendous. He'd never struck her with his fists, but words sometimes cut deeper. "The man who courted me was not the man I married. It's important for you to discover all you can about the person you're marry-ing. Take this afternoon for example. He spoke very little to you. It's as though you were a prize he was showing off."

"I think he just didn't know what to say because we don't know each other very well."

That wasn't it. He and Tillie knew each other even less and yet he never seemed to lack for words where she was concerned. He hadn't settled for something as mundane as the shape or hue of a petal when he spoke with her. "Which means he should attempt to get to know you, all aspects of you, and I just didn't have the sense he was striving to do that."

All the exuberance drained from Gina, and Tillie hated that she'd burst her sister's bubble of happiness, but she couldn't stand the thought of her marrying a man who didn't appreciate her, who wouldn't treat her as kindly and as well as she deserved. Her mother had guided Tillie toward a title and nothing else. She'd never sought to counsel her on the ways of men, on how to best determine what lurked within their souls—whether it was for good or wicked.

"Do you think it's possible you made him uncomfortable?" Gina asked. "I did catch you glaring a few times."

"I doubt anyone makes the Marquess of Rexton uncomfortable."

"He does seem rather strong, doesn't he? Very sure of himself. I was left with the impression he wanted to be driving the horses himself."

Tillie smiled encouragingly at her sister. "Yes, I think you're correct there. He didn't seem to have the patience for just sitting. I actually think he would have preferred to be out riding."

Gina perked up. "I'll suggest that next time, that we go riding instead of in the carriage."

Again that tightening in her chest when she thought of her sister with Rexton. It was damned irritating. She wanted her sister to find happiness, and it was quite possible that Tillie had misread the marquess and his intentions.

"Just don't become so infatuated with the notion

you'll become a duchess someday that you forget you'll be married to the duke. Pay very close attention to the way he treats you, to the things he says, look for little signs that he's not being honest with you."

"Such as?"

So many things. Where to even begin? "His attention diverting to other women when he's with you. Talking at you and not with you. It's difficult really to explain."

Gina shifted around on the bed, took Tillie's hands, and squeezed. "You're so much wiser than I am, Tillie. You're right that I get so caught up in being with him that I don't pay as much attention as I should. I'm not objective because he makes my stomach do all these crazy somersaults. But you, you're objective."

Not so much. Not really. Especially as he made *her* stomach feel queasy.

"He's invited me to go to the theater tomorrow evening. Will you come with us? We'll tell him you're serving as my chaperone, which you will be, but you can also analyze him. Help me determine if he's the one."

Tillie shook her head. One afternoon in his presence was enough. "No, I don't think that would be wise."

"Why not?"

Because he caused her to grow warm, to wonder what his kisses might be like, if his lips were as soft as they appeared. He made her wonder what his hands looked like without gloves, what his chest looked like without a shirt, what his backside looked like without trousers. What his front side looked like as well. "I don't think I made him uncomfortable, as you insinuated earlier, but I do think I might be a distraction."

"Because he's drawn to you?"

Tillie shot off the bed and began pacing. "No, of course not. But he does know I'm judging him. I said as much before you joined us in the parlor."

"Then he'll probably expect you to accompany us. I need you, Tillie. I need your guidance. I don't want to make an awful mistake like you did."

Tillie brought her pacing to an abrupt halt.

"I'm sorry," Gina said quickly. "I didn't mean to say you made a mistake."

Tillie smiled softly at her. "But I did. Then I made it worse." And tainted her sister in the process. "Rexton requires a wife who is not stained by scandal. The reception we received at the park had nothing to do with his horses, and everything to do with my presence. In public, we must be separate and keep a distance between us if you are to have any hope at all of snagging a future duke—or any lord for that matter."

"That's hardly fair."

"But it is the way of things." Returning to the bed, she took Gina's hands and squeezed. "I want you to find happiness. Nothing matters more to me."

"I want you to be happy, too."

"And I will be. Once you are well situated."

Some minutes later, when Gina returned to her bedchamber, she rang for her maid. While waiting, she removed her hat and gloves before glowering at her reflection in the mirror. "Not as clever as you thought, are you?"

The rap on her door was faint. Her servant come to call. "Enter."

Annie came in and closed the door behind her. "Yes, miss?"

"Should Lady Landsdowne ask after your megrim, tell her it's fine now and thank her for her concern."

"My megrim, miss?"

Gina sat on the bench in front of her dressing table. "It is as I suspected, Annie. His interest in me is feigned." She had a feeling her uncle had put him up to it, although she wasn't certain what Rexton hoped to gain with his actions. Perhaps he was simply a kind man helping a friend. But he wasn't at all like the heroes in the romance novels she read. He didn't make her feel light-headed or grow warm or tingle anywhere that she ought not.

She was rather certain the same couldn't be said for Tillie. When she had met the marquess, she'd suspected that might be the case. And his interest in her sister wasn't feigned. That was obvious. Although Tillie might deny it, when Gina had walked into the parlor, she'd been nearly scalded by the heat generated between Rexton and Tillie. That's when she had decided that rather than sending for her maid to function as chaperone, she would ask Tillie to serve in the role.

It had been quite fascinating to watch the two of them verbally sparring, striving to get the better of each other. But if a man looked at Gina with a gaze as smoldering as Rexton's when his eyes settled on Tillie—

Well, Gina certainly would encourage his suit.

She knew Tillie well enough to know she would not do any encouraging when it came to the man, so it was left to Gina to guide her along. Her sister had been gravely hurt, suspected all men of being up to no good. Perhaps she was right. Or perhaps she needed someone like the Marquess of Rexton to help heal her damaged heart.

But because of Tillie's stubbornness, Gina was going to have to think of another ruse to get her sister to accompany her to the theater. It was going to take a great deal of ingenuity because she couldn't have her maid fall ill again. She feared when all was said and done, she was going to turn out to be a very poor matchmaker.

Chapter 3

*I*f one truly wanted to know what was going on in aristocratic circles then one went to the Twin Dragons, a gaming hell whose members were both male and female. Oddly the men gossiped far more than the ladies, but Rexton knew in order to discover if his courting of Miss Hammersley had been noticed and was being taken seriously that an evening at the card table in the main grand salon was likely to provide the answer.

He preferred playing in a private room where the stakes were higher, but for tonight he settled at a table with one lady and four other gents, one of them being the Earl of Landsdowne. He told himself he'd chosen that particular group because he wanted to get a sense of how Downie might react to his courting his former sister-in-law, wanted to ensure the man wasn't going to undermine Rexton's efforts to get Gina married to someone. But he had to acknowledge he was curious regarding what Downie might reveal about the woman he'd divorced. Maybe he'd even know why she'd taken up with the blasted footman.

He couldn't deny love was an odd thing. His family and circle of closest friends were a mixture of nobility and commoner, of the upright, the staunch obeyers of the law, as well as pickpockets, thieves, and swindlers. Therefore he understood the heart controlled destinies more than the head or social position. Still he could no more envision Lady Landsdowne with the butler than he could imagine himself with a Whitechapel whore. He had discerning tastes and he suspected the countess did as well. And here he was thinking about her again when he should be concentrating on her sister, on ensuring he met the terms he'd agreed to with Hammersley so he had access to the stud he wanted.

Or at that precise moment, considering he'd lost three hands in a row, perhaps he should focus on the cards he was dealt. Or ensuring Downie won. The earl tended to get a bit more verbose when Lady Luck was smiling down on him, so perhaps Rexton should continue to play haphazardly. In private, he tended to gamble with those who were very skilled at manipulating cards, at judging odds, and at reading the deck. So although it went against the grain, he began tossing away cards he shouldn't.

"Not having much luck tonight, are you, Rexton?" Downie finally crowed.

Rexton had forgotten how quickly the earl grated on his nerves. "No luck at cards tonight, it seems, but I have been having luck elsewhere. With a lady at least."

The solitary female at the table, Lady Edith Leland, to whom he'd been introduced the night before, lifted her twinkling brown gaze from her cards and smiled at him. "With Miss Hammersley, it would seem. I noticed her in your carriage at the park this afternoon."

He took a quick glance at his cards, tossed away two jacks. "Indeed. She honored me with her presence. She's quite a delight."

That two of the other unmarried gents at the table perked up with his comment gave him a sense of satisfaction. By night's end, he'd have the girl's dance card filled at the next ball she attended.

"Gina?" Downie scoffed. "I'd be careful there, old man. If she's anything at all like her sister, she'll be naught but trouble. You'll barely have her dowry in hand before she's sneaking off with a footman and doing her best to bring you down."

Rexton was tempted to tell him one night in his bed would be enough to convince her no footman, no other man, would satisfy her. But he was rocked with the realization he wasn't envisioning Gina in his bed but rather Lady Landsdowne. When he thought of her with Downie, he had a sick churning in his gut as though he'd eaten something rancid. "I'm quite certain I can keep her content."

Although when it came to Gina, he had no interest in keeping her at all. She was like a small fish to be tossed back into the pond for someone else—and now guilt was niggling at him for that unkind thought. He was not in the habit of being mean to women, thinking ill thoughts toward them, or taking advantage. He would redouble his efforts to find her someone more worthy than he was.

Downie exposed his cards, gave a satisfied smirk as those of the other players were revealed, before taking the chips from the center of the table with hands that appeared too soft. Rexton didn't want to think of them caressing Lady Landsdowne's stomach, shifting up to cup her breasts, circling around to cradle her backside. The man himself was handsome enough, even if his lips were so thin as to be nearly nonexistent. As the dealer began passing out the cards, Rexton heard himself ask, "I can't recall, Downie. How long were you married?"

"Three years before we separated and I petitioned for divorce. Although the time required to see me completely free of her seemed to pass as slowly as an eternity. These American girls are deuced spoiled, Rexton. Mark my words: you are better off with an English lass who knows her place and understands tradition."

Even from where he sat, he sensed Lady Edith teeming with indignation—or maybe it was himself bristling. He was accustomed to being surrounded by the strong women in his family. Their places had always been at their husbands' sides, if not a step in front of them. He imagined Lady Landsdowne— Tillie—as young and innocent as her sister, her blue eyes wide and filled with hope and promise, her smiles coming easily. It bothered him now to realize he'd not seen her smile, not a true smile. She'd given him a few sardonic twists of her lips, but nothing genuine, nothing joyful.

He exchanged only two cards. He was going to ensure Downie didn't win this hand.

"If I might be so bold, Lord Rexton," Lady Edith whispered, although her voice carried over the table, "I noticed the other lady in the carriage. That wouldn't have been the notorious heiress herself, would it?"

He gave her a hard look, one he'd practiced in his youth when he'd wanted to intimidate his younger brother, who had once told him his narrowed eyes reminded him of a finely honed rapier.

The poor girl blushed. "Lady Landsdowne, I mean."

"Indeed it was. She was serving as chaperone for her sister."

"Ha!" Downie exclaimed, loudly enough that people at other tables looked over at them. "Mathilda is hardly suitable for the role of ensuring a young lady behaves. She knows nothing at all about proper behavior."

"She served well enough," Rexton said. "Kept me on a short leash."

"Don't be a fool, Rexton. My former wife had no idea how to conduct herself in order to make me proud. To be quite honest, I was glad to be rid of her."

And I'm glad she's rid of you. The sentiment came fast, without thought, the protectiveness accompanying it surprising him. No, it was more than that. He felt a low simmering rage, slowly becoming cognizant that his free hand had fisted on the table so tightly it ached.

"I've never seen her before," Lady Edith said pensively. "She's quite beautiful."

"Beauty is as beauty does, my girl," Downie insisted. "I assure you nothing about that deplorable woman comes close to beauty. She is a conniving, vindictive whore."

Lady Edith gasped.

"Watch your language, Downie," Lord Somerdale said before Rexton could deliver a scathing retort while giving his clenched fist the freedom to deliver a solid blow to the offending man's jaw. "We have a lady present at the table."

"This is a gambling hell, not a parlor where tea is served. She can move elsewhere if she's offended."

"You can move elsewhere, Landsdowne," Rexton said in a low voice that shimmered with threat. Although in truth, he didn't want the man to leave the table, as it would make it more difficult to take his last farthing if he did. "Or you can remember that Drake Darling expects his members to behave with civility and good manners. Apologize to Lady Edith or take yourself elsewhere."

"You can't order me about, Rexton."

Rexton knew the smile he bestowed upon the man was somewhat chilling since Somerdale moved back slightly as though he expected a fist to come flying in his direction while the other gent began studying his cards as though they might run off if they weren't watched carefully. "Have you forgotten Darling is my brother?"

"Not by blood."

"By all that matters, so I'm compelled to remind you of the rules of this club. All I have to do is snap my fingers to have two gents come over and escort you out. Lady Luck might not smile on you as beneficently elsewhere. Now apologize."

Landsdowne glared at him for all of a heartbeat before turning his attention to the young woman. "Lady Edith, my sincerest apologies. Talk of my former countess always brings out the worst in me, because it was a very difficult time in my life. I hope you will forgive my slip of the tongue."

"Of course, my lord."

Being a generous sort, Rexton let Lady Edith win that hand. Then he took Landsdowne for every penny he'd brought to the table. The thing about being a member of a family of pickpockets, thieves, and swindlers was that one became very skilled at cheating without getting caught.

$\mathscr{D}$rake Darling could spot a cheater from a mile away. Standing in the balcony of the Twin Dragons, he watched with astonishment as his brother raked in his winnings, time and again, occasionally allowing the lady to take the hand but ensuring the Earl of Landsdowne never again felt the satisfaction of adding chips to his pile but rather was reduced to watching the wooden disks dwindle away.

He was accustomed to Rex using underhanded means in an attempt to prevent their sister from winning, but that was sibling rivalry, and Drake had yet to see Rex outsmart Grace. Drake had never known anyone—man or woman—with such nimble fingers. It was understood that when the family played cards, they were all likely to use questionable means to win. The object was not to get caught doing it. But on Drake's gaming floor, they were supposed to behave.

He made his way downstairs and out into the thick of the games, his stride casual while his mind whirled, striving not to judge or get angry until he understood the facts. As he approached the table where Rex sat, he watched as Landsdowne shoved back his chair and marched toward the library reserved for gentlemen who were in need of drink or conversation. The ladies had a corresponding library. When he'd decided to open his doors to the fairer sex, he'd recognized that private areas were needed for each gender so they didn't have to always display the best of themselves.

He was nearly to Rex's back when he heard him say, "Lady Edith, might I bother you to donate my winnings to your favorite charity?"

Another unwritten rule among his family and friends: ill-gotten gains could not be kept, but were to be bestowed upon someone in need or in a manner that benefited charitable works. So he'd been correct in his assessment: his younger brother had been manipulating the cards.

The lady beamed at his attention. "I would be most delighted, my lord, to see it put to good use. Your generosity is inspiring."

"Thank you, but it's the least I can do."

Truer words may have never been spoken. Drake curled his hand around Rex's shoulder. "Join me for a drink."

His brother didn't flinch. Merely met his gaze head on. When Rex was younger, he fairly worshipped Drake, but with age had come the realization that the lad his parents had taken in and raised as their own wasn't so very special after all.

Rex signaled for one of the nearby footmen to handle trading his chips for coin and instructed him to deliver the funds to Lady Edith. Drake might have thought he had an interest in the young woman except he'd seen him be as solicitous to any number of ladies, so he didn't think she meant anything special to his brother. If not to impress someone he might wish to woo, then why clean out another gent?

Drake didn't say anything until they were safely ensconced in his office, with the door closed and drinks in hand. "I didn't teach you to cheat so you could fleece my members out on the gaming floor."

Rex took a sip of the whisky, walked over to the widow, and glanced out. "He deserved it."

Drake sat on the edge of his desk. Black-haired and swarthy-skinned, he more closely mirrored a devil while his adopted brothers reminded him of angels with their blond curls and fair eyes. Yet at that moment, he didn't think he'd care to run into Rex in a darkened alley. "Care to tell me why?"

Rex shook his head, took another sip. "Was Lady Landsdowne ever a member?" Before Drake could answer, something seemed to have occurred to the marquess as he added, "Is she a member now?"

"She's not a member. I suspect she wouldn't like the chilly welcome she would be apt to receive." He shook his head slowly, even though Rex had yet to turn his gaze away from the night beyond the window and face him. "I don't recall her ever coming here while she was married to Landsdowne. Why the interest?"

Rex continued to stare at whatever was happening on the streets below. Another sip. A tap on his glass. A sip. "I'm not sure." He swung around, leaned against the wall, held Drake's gaze. "I met her today."

"And you started thinking with your cock instead of your head."

Rex laughed, downed what remained in his glass. "I'm not certain I was able to think at all. I'm supposed to be courting her sister."

Drake was glad to have been half sitting on the desk as he might have staggered back. Although it was high time his brother took a wife, he'd not yet expressed an interest in doing so. But then, Drake had planned to never marry. But that was eight years, four children, and countless rescued animals ago. His wife had a soft heart when it came to children and animals. And on occasion him. "Mother will be happy to hear that. She is in want of more grandchildren."

Rex scowled. "Between you and Grace she has more than enough. And I'm not going to marry the chit. I made a pact with her uncle to get the other lords interested in her. Apparently, they fear she will be as unskilled at honoring her vows as her sister."

"And what do you gain?"

"Two winners from Black Diamond."

Drake whistled. "You've wanted that horse for stud since you first saw him race."

"Indeed. So I'll play the besotted beau for a bit."

Frowning, Drake studied his brother. He wasn't an unkind man, but he was obsessed with the damned horse, with his racehorses overall. "Have you considered the girl's feelings?"

"I shan't be with her long enough for any true emotion to take hold."

"You can't control the heart."

"A week at the most. She'll have young swains falling over themselves to be with her. She'll cast me aside."

"Perhaps you shouldn't tell Mother or Grace about this plan."

"I had no intentions of doing so. As I said, it'll be over quickly enough. She drew the eye of a few gents when I took her to the park this afternoon. Tomorrow is the theater. One more ball, and it'll be done."

"I wouldn't be so sure. Take it from someone who knows from experience. Where ladies are concerned, the plans never go the way you expect they will."

* * *

*D*ear God, but she sat a horse well.

Rexton watched as Lady Landsdowne trotted a dark brown Arabian along Rotten Row. He'd arrived at six. She at seven. He didn't know why Gina's offhand comment about her sister riding in the early morning had stuck with him or why he'd felt a burning need to see her. Perhaps because his body was in urgent need of sexual release, although he wouldn't find it here. Better to tell himself it was part and parcel of his strategy to ensure Gina well situated, but the lie mocked him.

At this hour no one else was about. Daft woman hadn't brought a groom with her or even the blasted butler. What if she was accosted, what if some ne'er-do-well recognized quality when he saw it and decided he'd like a taste?

He set his gelding into a gentle gallop, following a path he knew would intercept hers. She must have heard him approaching, because she brought her horse to a halt. When he was near enough to do the same, he found himself staring at the business end of a very small pistol, clutched tightly in her gloved hand, her gaze uncompromising and harsh. Apparently the woman saw to her own defense and didn't require assistance.

"Lady Landsdowne." He spoke calmly, evenly, the way he might to a skittish filly. "It would be a shame for your sister to lose her solitary suitor so shortly after acquiring him."

"Would it?"

He wasn't reassured that she sounded quite doubtful. "Indeed. I assure you that she would mourn my passing. A great many women would, in fact, mourn my passing."

"I hope you are not counting me among them."

"I would not be so presumptuous." Although the truth was: he did hope she would feel a bit of sorrow at his leaving this world.

"I do suppose bringing Gina sorrow would defeat my purpose in wanting to see her happy." She slipped the pistol into a pocket in the skirt of her riding habit. "I don't recall seeing you here in the mornings before."

"To be sure, I'm certain you haven't. I don't usually make it a habit to get up at such an ungodly hour, but I was curious regarding the report you delivered to your sister after our afternoon in the park."

"My report?"

She sounded thoroughly confused when he knew she wasn't. "Come now. I'm certain you outlined my good qualities and what you might have perceived as my . . . bad."

"Not arrogant, are you, to think we would spend time discussing you." It was stated, not asked.

"I'm simply rather convinced I was the topic of conversation once I delivered you home. I shall make it easy on you and share what I believe you told her. How's that?"

She shifted in the saddle and he wished she wasn't buttoned up so tightly in her forest green riding habit. A bit of white lace peeked out from her cuffs and above her collar. He wished they were at his personal estate where they'd have room to gallop madly over the flower-dotted meadows. He had no doubt she would give him a good race, that her hat would go flying off, her pins would come loose, her hair would tumble down. He longed to see it cascading along her back, over the horse's flank. A vision of her without clothes suddenly flashed before him. Lady Godiva—he had no doubt Lady Landsdowne would rival her in beauty.

"I would indeed be very much interested in what you believe I relayed to my sister, but alas I have finished with my time in the park and must be home."

"I'll escort you."

"Not necessary."

"As a gentleman, I must insist. Besides, it is certain to put me in your good graces."

"Do you not think you are there now?"

"I do not." He knew he wasn't. She looked at him like she wished she'd squeezed the trigger. "Please, Lady Landsdowne, in spite of what you might think, I do wish to ensure your sister's happiness. Knowing what you are telling her about me could aid my cause and in the end, yours, as I believe you want the same thing for her. And I fear we got off on the wrong foot."

Smart man, the Marquess of Rexton, to understand the influence Tillie had over her sister. "To be honest, I don't recall your name on my tongue a single time after we returned to Landsdowne Court."

His darkening gaze dipped to her mouth and she did wish she hadn't mentioned her tongue. To make matters worse, she now envisioned it parrying with his in physical intimacy rather than with words. She suspected, for reasons which eluded her, that those marvelously shaped lips of his would urge hers into parting so he could deliver a kiss so all encompassing, so deep, that she would feel it in the soles of her feet. Even now, within her boots, her toes longed to curl. She had to be free of him, and quickly. "Escort me if you wish. But I shan't disclose what I said to Gina regarding you. Musings between sisters are for sisters only." She nudged her mare forward, disliking that she took satisfaction in his guiding his horse until it fell into step beside hers.

"I suspect you waxed on for some time regarding my handsome features," he said.

She scoffed. Arrogant man. They always thought—

"I doubt either of you has ever known a man of such perfection."

Her musings came to a sudden stop as though they'd hit a brick wall. His tone was more teasing than anything, perhaps a bit self-deprecating. Was it difficult to be as good-looking as he, to have women falling at his feet whenever he came near?

"We did have a time of it not swooning in your carriage yesterday afternoon."

She wished she hadn't said anything, had kept quiet, because he delivered a smile that very nearly caused her to fall out of the saddle. It wasn't fair a man of such perfection should exist.

"You were charmed by my wit and exemplary manners."

Enough of this. She wasn't going to be enchanted. "I did question why you asked so much of me and not her."

"No one enjoys an inquisition."

"Yet you seemed determined to put *me* through my paces."

"You seemed the one better able to withstand the attention. Has she never had anyone court her before?"

She didn't want to be taken in by the true concern she heard in his voice. "You are her first. As I found the waters difficult to navigate at the tender age of eighteen, we decided it would serve her better to wait until she was nineteen."

The faint light of morning allowed her to see the calculations running through his mind. She was rather taken aback that he was still striving to discern information regarding her—her present age of twenty-five, perhaps—but then she was the more interesting of the sisters, although she recognized that particular fact was not complimentary. It was only her scandal that made her noteworthy. He seemed to have finished his sums, satisfied with his answer. She wasn't going to inquire regarding his conclusion, because she didn't give a fig whether he'd gotten it correct or not.

"Did you dissuade her from attending the theater with me this evening?" he asked.

"I did not. I have surmised you are not the correct gentleman for her, but I also sense you will do no harm."

That devilish grin again. She should hate him for the ease and smoothness with which it arrived. He was a man completely comfortable around women. No doubt because he'd known more than his fair share—intimately.

He opened his mouth, closed it, shook his head. "I was going to say you don't know me well if you believe any woman is safe with me." He seemed somewhat abashed. "It is second nature to flirt, but the truth is, you are correct. I would not intentionally cause her harm. She is a delightful girl. I enjoy her company."

He might have said he was speaking the truth but somewhere within the words he'd woven a lie. She was rather certain of it, although she couldn't quite pinpoint exactly what it was but there had been a slight change in his inflection, something to indicate his guilt. Or perhaps it was simply that her time with Downie had made it so she could never completely trust a man to be wholly honest.

"What sort of chocolates does she prefer?" he asked.

"You should ask her."

"That would ruin the surprise, would it not?"

What a disloyal sister she was because she didn't want him sending chocolates, didn't want him wooing Gina. "Ones with soft centers. Strawberry."

"And yourself?"

"I don't fancy chocolate."

"What do you fancy?"

It was the quietness of the morning that made it seem he was asking something entirely inappropriate, like a preferred position for coupling, or how eagerly she liked a kiss delivered. Why was it that he caused her mind to travel to the gutter? "I don't see *that* being knowledge you require to effectively win over my sister."

"Ah, but you've already told me the way to your sister's heart lies through you."

"It lies in the way you treat her, in the care you give her." They'd reached the small stables at the back of her residence.

He had the audacity to wave away the groom who had come out to assist her. He dismounted in a smooth movement of muscles and sinew that caused her clothing to shrink until she could scarcely breathe. Without a word, he placed his hands on her waist. They spanned the expanse of it. Large hands, capable hands. She'd felt the strength in them the day before as he'd assisted her into and out of the carriage. She did wish she wasn't so taken with them, that she couldn't imagine them stroking breasts and caressing thighs.

He tilted his head up, his gaze latching onto hers. Against her ribs, her heart throbbed, and she wondered if he could feel the vibrations through his gloved fingers. She curled her palms around his broad, sturdy shoulders. It was like grasping steel. She doubted this man possessed an ounce of fat. He was lean, but firm.

He lifted her down slowly, so slowly she could have counted his eyelashes, the folds in his neck cloth, the buttons of his waistcoat. If she'd been able to look away from the blue of his eyes.

"I do hope you will speak well of me to your sister and will not dissuade her from stepping out with me."

Her feet were on firm ground now, her mind less so. He had yet to remove his hands from her waist. She would have stepped back but her horse was in the way. A little. Not completely. There was room. For some unfathomable reason, she didn't want to make use of it. "Rest assured, you will at least have her in your company tonight."

"I ask no more than that."

His hands fell away. She could finally breathe. Strange how she thought it an unfair price to pay in order to be free of his touch.

"You should have a groom escort you on your morning ride. You never know when you might cross paths with a scoundrel."

As she had this morning, no doubt. Reflexively, her hand went to her pocket where she kept her small gun. "I can take care of myself."

"Are you truly skilled with a pistol?"

"Deadly so. Firearms is the family business, after all. My father taught me how to shoot when I was six."

"Then I shall be grateful you didn't demonstrate your talents this morning."

"As you should be because I did consider it."

He smiled as though he enjoyed sparring with her, liked the challenge of it. That was so very unnerving as it had been a good long while since a man had enjoyed her company—and she his.

He tipped his hat. "Good day, Lady Landsdowne." He'd taken a mere three steps when he turned to face her. "Will you be acting as chaperone this evening?"

"No. Gina's maid will serve in the role."

"Is she young?"

"What does it matter?"

"In my experience, young servants are often intimidated by those of rank." He slowly lifted a shoulder, lowered it. "I know many a gent who has managed to elude less watchful eyes for a bit of mischief."

"Yourself included, I assume."

He merely smiled, the scamp.

"I assure you Annie knows her duties and will see to them," she said pointedly.

"I'm certain you're correct."

She watched him easily mount his beast and trot away. It wasn't fair he should look so marvelous riding—riding, walking, sitting, damn him.

She should warn her sister off. The man was far too dangerous. He could easily capture Gina's heart and then she would have to spend the remainder of her life knowing other women yearned for him. For how could any woman not want to be with a man of such confidence and charm?

That charm was a problem. She could easily envision him directing it Annie's way, convincing her to be less diligent in watching the couple—and Gina with her hopeful heart would see it as an adventure to scurry off to some darkened corner of the theater for a kiss, a kiss that if discovered could ruin her reputation and her future. Blast the man. He was too smooth. She didn't trust him.

She marched through the gardens, into the residence, and up the stairs. With a balled fist, she knocked on Gina's bedchamber.

"Come," her sister trilled.

Opening the door, Tillie stepped into the room. Gina sat at her dressing table, her maid holding up Gina's hair in the midst of styling it. Yes, Annie was far too inexperienced to handle the likes of Rexton. "I'll be attending the theater with you."

Gina's eyes widened and she grinned broadly. "Wonderful! What changed your mind?"

"I simply decided you were correct. I need to observe Rexton in order to determine if he will do right by you."

"I'm so relieved. Annie has never been involved with men. She knows little of their ways."

Whereas Tillie knew far too much.

$\mathcal{R}$exton knew he was a scoundrel, a rake, a rogue with his attempt to manipulate Lady Landsdowne into accompanying them to the theater this evening. He didn't know why he wanted her there. Her presence didn't serve his purposes. He needed to focus on the girl, not the woman.

Guilt over his using Gina for his own gain prodded him to stop at the confectionary shop where he purchased a dozen chocolates with jellied strawberry centers to be delivered to Gina later in the morning. Even though he wasn't seriously courting the young woman, he'd had no business seeking out her sister in the park. If they'd been spied together, it wouldn't have gone well for either of them. Her reputation would have been blackened further because no one would have deemed their encounter innocent. His being involved with the sister of the woman he was supposedly courting would have brought into question Gina's appeal as a prospective wife.

He knew the uncle well enough to know he wasn't a fool. Their arrangement had to be followed precisely. Hammersley wasn't going to give up the stallion unless Gina had a viable suitor. It might be worth it to determine who would make a viable suitor.

The problem was he liked the girl well enough and he didn't want to saddle her with someone who wouldn't appreciate her, was more interested in her money than her. He cursed Lady Landsdowne for making him care, for making the task more challenging than it needed to be.

With the chocolates ordered, he rode his horse to a less affluent part of the city. Dismounting, he dashed up the steps and pounded on the door of a modest townhome. It was opened by a man who was two inches taller and a bit wider than he. His bleary-eyed look told Rexton he'd woken him up.

"What the devil are you doing here?" Jamie Swindler asked.

"I have some excess energy. Thought you might help me burn it off."

Jamie scrubbed his hands through his thick, dark hair. "I had a late night in Whitechapel. I'm in need of sleep."

"Come now, constable. You need to keep your fighting skills sharp. Can't have the degenerates taking you down."

"You have a point, I suppose. Let me have some coffee first." Jamie was always in the mood for a solid round of fisticuffs.

Half an hour later, they were in the garden behind the house, shirts off, boxing gloves on. When Rexton had needed to learn how to fight in order to deal with the bullies he encountered at school, his friend had served as his sparring partner when Jamie's father, James Swindler the elder, had given him lessons.

Now Rexton jabbed at him. Jamie feinted to the left, delivered a glancing blow to his shoulder as Rexton jumped aside.

"What's her name?" Jamie asked as he circled around, bouncing on the balls of his feet.

"Who?" Another jab, another miss.

"The woman you can't have."

The blow to his midsection nearly had him dropping to his knees. The statement had momentarily stunned him, and Jamie had taken advantage. Not that he blamed him. He'd have done the same. He straightened. "Why would you think that's an issue?"

"Because you usually burn off energy with a willing female. I'd also wager you saw her this morning. You're decked out awfully fine for an early morning ride. Your handsomest horse is tied out front. Your nails were recently buffed, probably within the last few hours."

"All of that only signifies that I'm a gentleman."

Much to Rexton's irritation, his friend arched a dark brow. "And you smell of lavender and orchids. You either took her flowers or you were close enough for her scent to latch onto you."

"You're deuced irritating, you know that?" He swung. Jamie ducked.

Then his longtime friend had the audacity to laugh. "So I have the right of it?"

"You're wasted as a constable. You should be an inspector at Scotland Yard."

"Have to earn my way up the ranks."

"Your father could put in a word for you."

"I want to do it on my own."

"I have to admire that." His gloved fist made contact with Jamie's ribs, sending him two steps backward.

"You took me off guard with a compliment," Jamie said. "So tell me about her. Why isn't she giving in to your charms?"

"I haven't directed them at her. She and I wouldn't suit. She's a woman of scandal."

"That won't do for a future duke."

"It's more than that. Scandal can touch the innocent." He landed a blow to Jamie's shoulder, jumped to the side as Jamie retaliated. "I don't want my children to have to learn to fight."

"For good reason. They might be as bad at it as you."

He smiled at that. He wasn't as skilled as Jamie but then he wasn't spending his nights dealing with thugs. "So make me stop thinking about her."

Jamie accepted the challenge with glee.

$\mathcal{S}$itting on the bench at her dressing table, staring at her reflection in the mirror, Tillie was not particularly pleased with herself, with how much she was anticipating the outing to the theater. It had been so very long since she'd attended a play. As she was in the role of chaperone, she'd considered dressing modestly but her vanity got the better of her. It would be her first foray into the public realm at an evening event, and she intended to make a splash, to hold her head high, and to weather whatever censure might be tossed her way.

The rap on her door caused her heart to hitch because she knew what the hollow echo portended. Taking a deep breath, she gathered up her lacy shawl and stood. With a final glance at her reflection to ensure she was as put together as possible, she walked out.

Annie stood in the hallway. "Miss Gina wanted me to alert you that his Lordship has arrived. She's already gone down to greet him."

Of course, she had. Gina had absolutely no patience, which hinted that she might fall quickly in love. Life had yet to season her, and Tillie was desperately afraid her sister was in for heartache down the road.

After taking six steps down the stairs, she nearly tumbled down the remainder when she caught sight of Rexton, standing in the foyer in his finery, smiling broadly at her sister as though they'd just shared an intimate joke. In his evening attire, his black swallowtail jacket and waistcoat, his pristine white neck cloth knotted perfectly, his top hat in hand, he was devastatingly gorgeous. How could Gina not fall for him when he had the ability to stir to life portions of Tillie she'd long thought dead?

He made her wish he was waiting on her, that she was not consigned to scandal and chaperoning, that she had not made choices in her youth that now relegated her to dark corners where the unacceptable could be ignored. She had no doubt she would receive many cuts direct tonight, could only hope that Gina being seen on the marquess's arm was going to serve as an effective buffer against any damage Tillie might cause.

Then his gaze swung up and landed on her like a physical presence, a heated caress that traveled along her cheek, her throat, her bared shoulders. Never before had she felt such a powerful force, and she was grateful a myriad of steps separated them. If she were any nearer to him, she might combust into flames.

As she gathered herself together and began descending the steps, his gaze never wavered. Rather he watched her, and she was left with the distinct impression he was considering charging up the stairs, taking her into his arms, and carrying her off to bed. Or maybe that scenario was merely her own wild, chaotic desires.

What in God's name was wrong with her to have such unwelcoming and entirely inappropriate thoughts? This man was interested in her sister. That she, herself, was unequivocally and against her will drawn to him was unconscionable. Perhaps she should claim a megrim and let Annie accompany the couple.

But this morning the rogue had given her cause to doubt the maid's ability to keep him in hand. She would not see her sister compromised. Tillie's attention would not wane, and she would ensure Gina's reputation remained pristine.

"Tillie, don't you look lovely!" Gina said with such enthusiasm and kindness that Tillie deeply regretted every sensual contemplation she'd had as she traversed the stairs. "Doesn't she, my lord?"

"She does indeed." He still didn't look away from her, and she rather wished he would.

"Look, Tillie. His Lordship brought me a flower bracelet. Isn't it gorgeous? I've never seen anything like it." Gina was holding out her arm. An orchid was secured to her wrist with a black velvet ribbon.

Touched by the small kindness, she smiled at her sister. "It's very unusual and very kind of his Lordship."

"I'd been led to believe the maid would be accompanying us; otherwise I'd have brought you one," he said.

Angling her chin defiantly, she held his gaze, feeling a need to challenge him because his presence warmed her entire body. "It appears Annie is suffering another megrim." She was not going to admit he'd caused her to doubt the maid's ability to protect Gina from his possible naughtiness. "Besides, one does not bring a gift for the chaperone."

"You hardly appear the chaperone."

"Trust me, my lord, I shall be ever alert and ensure no shenanigans occur under my watch."

"I would expect nothing less." His words didn't quite match the challenge in his eyes, as though he were contemplating testing her. No doubt her wanton musings placing thoughts in her head again. He'd made no untoward advances, was standing there like a perfect gentleman. Too perfect.

"We should be off, shouldn't we?" Gina chirruped.

"Yes, of course," Tillie responded, grateful something had broken the mesmerizing spell she'd fallen into. Rexton had a way of drawing her into a vortex of confusing emotions. If he was doing the same for Gina, her sister was handling it much better, as though she hardly recognized the man breathed sensuality in to the room with every breath.

Rexton offered Gina his arm and escorted her to the door. The butler opened it, and Rexton stepped aside, indicating Tillie should precede them.

"The chaperone follows," she told him.

"Not when she's a lady." His tone indicated he was offended on her behalf.

She wanted to argue with him. She didn't need him standing up for her, but her throat knotted up with the realization he was the first, other than Gina, to defend her position, to show her any measure of respect since the ill-fated night when she'd been caught "practically crawling up a footman." Her father had been so blistering mad at her that he'd seldom spoken with her after reading the account in the gossip sheets. He'd never asked why she'd done what she had, why she would have risked public censure and ridicule rather than remain in her married state. Divorce was for the weak. A woman of any substance would have tolerated marital discord and simply moved into another wing in her residence, assuring the couple retained mutual respect for each other while each person went on his or her merry way. Her uncle had fallen in line behind his brother and not hidden his censure of her. Now, she could do little more than give a brisk nod before carrying herself over the threshold and into the night, hating herself for wishing she was the one on the marquess's arm rather than her sister.

*H*e wasn't going to feel guilty because she'd taken the bait, because he was glad to have her here.

She was beautiful. As they moved slowly through the theater following the crowd toward the stairs, Rexton fully understood why Landsdowne had wanted her for his wife. He suspected it had little to do with the dowry she brought to the arrangement, even if the earl was in desperate need of funds. It was her regal poise, the grace with which she moved, the way she held herself with pride even as people turned away from her.

It was fascinating to watch those around them striving to give her a cut direct while not offending him when he was standing so near to her. He halfway wished she, rather than her sister, was on his arm, as it would communicate loudly that she was under his protection. He wished he'd arranged for close friends to approach, to engage her in conversation. He didn't like that she was viewed as a pariah.

"Take my arm," he ordered Lady Landsdowne quietly. Gina was already clinging to his right, her gaze darting around with delight as though she'd never before been in a theater. Perhaps she hadn't. But her interest in the surroundings had her failing to notice the scornful looks tossed her sister's way.

With her finely arched eyebrows meeting in a crease, Lady Landsdowne jerked her attention to him, clearly confused by his request.

"Going up the stairs can be treacherous with so many about," he said. "Even for a chaperone."

She gave a slight nod, before slipping her arm around his. He didn't fail to notice the gratitude that sparked in the blue. Nor did he fail to notice the tiniest of tremors cascading through her. Damn, she was courageous. She was here to protect her sister from the transgressions he'd hinted at this morning, but still to put herself through this—it spoke not only of devotion but of love.

Why hadn't those emotions transferred to her marriage, to Landsdowne? And why was it that he found himself far more intrigued with the countess than with her sister? Why was he drawn to her bared shoulders? Why did he want to take his mouth on a journey over them, feel their silkiness, and taste them? Gina's gown revealed smooth, alabaster shoulders, and yet they interested him not in the least. Was it because he wasn't truly seeking her as a wife?

He'd often lusted after other women he had no desire to marry. Both of these women were forbidden. Gina because of her innocence. The countess because of her notorious reputation. Yet at that moment, he knew if he could have only one in his darkened box, he would have chosen the countess, her reputation be damned.

He couldn't recall ever wanting a woman so much, and yet he couldn't identify exactly why she appealed to him. It was obvious she neither liked nor trusted him. But when he'd seen her on the stairs, for an insane moment, he'd considered rushing up them so he could take her in his arms.

Once they reached his box, he drew back the curtain and escorted them inside. He assisted Gina in sitting, turned to assist Lady Landsdowne—only to find her already seated in a chair on the row behind. "Come and sit beside your sister."

"I'm the chaperone. This will suffice."

It occurred to him that perhaps she preferred the shadows to the front of the box where people might be better able to stare at her. "Ladies sit in the front, gents in the back," he stated succinctly.

"And if I were the maid?"

"You're not the maid."

"I'm perfectly fine where I am."

"I'm certain your sister will enjoy the performance more if you're sitting beside her."

She angled her head like a dog striving to decipher its master's command. "Why will she not enjoy it if you are sitting beside her?"

"Because I detest theater."

She jerked her head back as though truly surprised by his words. "Then why bring her?"

"Because it is what a gentleman does."

"You're giving her false expectations regarding how you will treat her." Her tone was harsh and angry, leaving him to wonder what false expectations Landsdowne had delivered.

"How so?"

"You'll bring her to the theater while you're courting her but not after you're married to her."

Had Landsdowne done that? Treated her one way before the marriage, another after? "I have a box for which I pay handsomely so it is always available. Without question, I'll bring her to the theater after we're married if that's what she wishes." He nearly groaned in frustration. Why the devil had he said that? He wasn't going to be bringing her to the theater after she was married because she was going to be married to someone else. Thank God, Gina didn't seem to have heard him as she was leaning forward, looking over the balcony at the patrons below, clearly more interested in whom she might recognize than any ludicrous conversation he was having with her annoying sister.

Lady Landsdowne narrowed her eyes, leaving him with the impression she saw him as being no better than a dung beetle. "Easy enough to make a promise before you're married."

Her voice was a harsh whisper as though she would flay him if she could. She sat in judgment when she knew nothing at all about him, about how hard he strived to be good and proper. It was deuced irritating to think she might be painting him with Landsdowne's brush.

"I'm not in the habit of being other than I am. Nor do I go back on my word." He lowered himself until his face was even with hers, taking perverse delight in the widening of her eyes. "Nor am I sitting on the front row whilst a lady sits behind me. So you can either sit beside me back here or move up to sit beside your sister. But rest assured, madam, your obstinacy will not sway me from my course."

She looked as though she was considering the benefits of spitting at him. Finally she rose in a rush that had her skirts rustling and her breasts very nearly skimming along his nose before he leaped back. "I thank you for the kindness." Although she didn't sound at all grateful. Rather she sounded quite put out with him. He didn't know why he took satisfaction in that. Perhaps her anger would dampen his lust toward her, as he'd seldom had to deal with a woman's fury and wasn't particularly keen on dealing with it now.

Only once they were settled, and he was behind her, he realized her wrath served to dampen nothing at all. He couldn't even admit to being put off by it. Instead he marveled at the fire and suspected she brought the same ardor to her bed.

He stared at the length of her neck, imagined trailing his mouth over every inch of exposed skin, lapping along her nape, past her shoulders. Unfastening her gown until he could reach the dimples above her backside. Did she have dimples? He rather suspected she did. The thought caused him to grow so hard that he very nearly groaned.

Suddenly the curtains were flung aside and footsteps sounded as his brother rushed in, then staggered to a stop. Rexton came to his feet, hoping the ladies didn't turn around. His hopes were dashed, but it appeared they were taken with the intruder rather than noticing the bulge evident in his trousers.

"You're using your box," Andrew said in a tone one might use to greet someone who had risen from the dead.

Rexton had spoken true. He wasn't fond of the theater but most ladies were so it behooved a gentleman to have a box handy for when a lady might need a bit of wooing. His brother often made use of it, usually accompanied by a bit of silk, but this evening he was alone. "Yes, it is my box after all."

But Andrew seemed not to have heard him. His attention had shifted to the ladies. "My, my, looks as though you're planning to have double the fun later tonight."

"Watch your tongue, Andrew. These are ladies."

"My apologies. I just didn't realize—"

Before his brother could complete a thought that might reveal he wasn't truly in the hunt for a wife, Rexton said, "Lady Landsdowne, Miss Hammersley, allow me to introduce my younger brother, Lord Andrew Mabry."

Andrew took the countess's hand, bent gallantly over it, and pressed a kiss to its back. "Your beauty exceeds expectations. It is a pleasure."

When Lady Landsdowne smiled tightly at Andrew, Rexton fought the urge to shove his brother over the balcony.

"A pleasure, my lord."

Moving past her, he gave the same attention to Gina. "I'm honored."

"As am I, my lord."

"You are the sort about whom poems are written."

Rexton rolled his eyes, while at the same time seeing Lady Landsdowne's lips twitch with amusement at his brother's atrocious flirting skills. He wondered why she found fault with his own wooing talents, why she was so suspicious of them—perhaps because she could see right through him, knew he had no real interest in her sister whereas his brother's attention was merely harmless flattery.

The lights began to dim, the curtains were drawing aside, and only then did Andrew release his hold of Gina's hand. He looked at Rexton. "Mind if I join you?"

"Not at all." But he forced his brother to glide past him to the seat behind Gina because Rexton had no plans to give up his view of Lady Landsdowne.

"The notorious heiress," Andrew whispered. "What the devil are you doing with her?"

Rexton was beginning to hate that moniker. He had yet to see the countess exhibit any sort of notorious behavior, not that he wouldn't like to. But what he had in mind involved them both naked and rolling around on satin sheets, limbs tangled, his mouth doing wicked things between her thighs while hers was doing equally tawdry things between his. "I'm with Miss Hammersley. The countess is merely serving as chaperone."

"The girl doesn't seem your usual fare."

He did little more than offer a withering glare. Their voices might be low but he suspected Lady Landsdowne had exceptional hearing. Gina was obviously enthralled by the play. He doubted she could repeat a single sentence that had been uttered.

With a shrug, Andrew gazed forward, giving up on his inquisition. Rexton leaned toward him. "As you're alone, I assume you're involved with an actress."

"Not certain I'd call her an actress, but she is quite skilled at standing on the stage." As the spare, Andrew had never been as discreet with his affairs as Rexton was. Someday Rexton would be forced to take a wife in order to provide an heir. Andrew claimed he would remain a bachelor until he drew his last breath.

Rexton looked the performers over. He knew his brother's tastes leaned toward the buxom. "The blonde?"

"The red."

Whose breasts were very nearly spilling out of the bodice of her costume. His brother did enjoy flamboyant attention-seeking women. He wondered if Lady Landsdowne had once fit into that category. But since her divorce she'd very much lived the life of a recluse, avoiding Society. Although that didn't mean she avoided the scandalous parts of London. Perhaps she flourished there.

Suddenly he found himself curious regarding exactly how she did spend her time. Had she a lover? She was young and obviously had needs her husband had failed to meet. Was she still involved with the butler?

He certainly hadn't detected any heated glances, stray touches, or lingering about in each other's company. The butler was either extremely disciplined or their affair had ended long ago. He'd wager on the latter as he was extremely disciplined and he had yet to remove his gaze from the slope of her enticing neck and the tantalizing spot where it curved into her shoulder. It was unsettling, how badly he wished to place his mouth there.

In the future, he would not taunt her into serving as chaperone. Otherwise he was likely to go mad with wanting.

*T*illie tried to focus on the play, but she was incredibly aware of Rexton sitting behind her. Why the devil hadn't he taken the chair behind Gina? Or better yet, beside her. Then Tillie could observe him rather than being the one observed. And she was fairly certain she was being observed. Her nerve endings tingled as though he was scraping the edge of his perfectly aligned white teeth along them.

How was it that a man so fair could create such dark images? She could so clearly envision herself with him at the back of the box, lost in the shadows, his mouth trailing along the column of her throat, skimming lower until he dipped his tongue into the narrow valley between her breasts. Her nipples puckered tightly as though he'd closed his mouth around them.

Whatever was wrong with her? She was supposed to be an observer.

It was his blasted fragrance that had circled her in the coach. He smelled of rich earth and leather and whisky. His scent was purely masculine, and she suspected all him. No perfumes, no colognes, no civility. When he'd spoken in the unlit coach, his deep voice sent shivers through her, and she'd imagined him whispering naughty things in her ear as he rode her hard and fast. Oh, dear God, he was courting her sister. All these thoughts were inappropriate. It would be so much easier to send them all to perdition if he hadn't offered her his arm.

She'd seen the compassion and kindness in his eyes. He'd recognized how difficult it was for her to be surrounded by all the censure, and he'd lent her his strength. He should have been mortified to have to endure her notorious presence at his side. Instead, he'd plowed through the crowd with seeming pride and pleasure, quelling any hostile reactions with an icy glare that would have sent a shiver scurrying down her spine if it weren't for the fact it was being delivered on her behalf.

Or perhaps it was on Gina's behalf. He certainly had no reason to strive to protect Tillie. On further thought, his reaction had to be an attempt to spare Gina any embarrassment. He had to care for her sister a little; otherwise he wouldn't be spending time in her company. She may have misjudged him and his motives, his ability to love. She felt a strong urge to apologize for doubting him—and yet something still niggled at her.

He was certainly kind enough to Gina, had patience with her, spoke with her, and yet something about his actions didn't ring true. In spite of his hints this morning that he would strive to escape the bonds of a chaperone, he wasn't drawn to Gina. Perhaps Tillie's presence accomplished what she'd hoped and kept him tethered to gentlemanly behavior. But she doubted it. The man exuded too much sexuality to be easily bound by convention. She suspected after returning them home, he'd end the night in the arms of some beautiful woman. She didn't particularly like the jealously that shot through her with that thought. These were the sort of musings Gina should be entertaining, the reactions that rightly belonged to her sister. Not to Tillie.

If Gina were thinking about the marquess at all, Tillie would be surprised. Her sister appeared to be completely absorbed in the play. Not once did she glance over her shoulder to give her escort a teasing grin. When Downie had been courting her, Tillie had been barely able to go a minute without looking at him. She'd been so concerned about Rexton's interest being genuine perhaps she should have questioned if Gina favored more than his good looks and title.

Maybe she was judging harshly. Perhaps the play was enthralling, and she'd simply failed to be captivated by it because she was far too aware of the man sitting behind her. She heard the rasp of his clothing when he shifted in his chair, fought not to realize it would sound similar when it was being removed. It was as though a thread had been woven through her and was being pulled tighter and tighter. At any moment it was going to snap. What made it worse was the realization that a caress would loosen it. A long slow stroke that traveled from the nape of her neck to her ankle. Leisurely down. Even more leisurely up.

She'd always thought Downie had killed any semblance of desire that resided within her. How awful at that moment to find it sparking back to life, more powerful and zealously than she'd ever experienced it before. She truly thought she might go mad, considered excusing herself to take a brisk walk outside in the cool evening air—but she was the chaperone and couldn't abandon her sister when two gentlemen sat in the box.

Although what sort of mischief could they get into when others could see them? It wasn't as though they were encased in total darkness. She leaned toward Gina. "I need a bit of air."

Her sister turned her attention from the stage. "Are you feeling unwell?"

"Simply a bit too warm."

"Shall I go with you?"

"No, I won't be long."

With a nod, Gina returned her focus to the performance. Tillie rose, feeling a bit self-conscious when both gentlemen did as well.

Rexton took a step toward her. "Is something amiss?"

"I need a moment. Do behave while I'm gone." No doubt, he'd think she was going in search of the ladies' necessary room. But when she stepped into the dimly lit hallway, she merely leaned against the wall, closed her eyes, and inhaled deeply. Why did he have to unsettle her so? Why did all these inappropriate and lascivious thoughts have to scurry through her mind like naughty children intent on mischief?

His interest resided with Gina. That Tillie was remarkably aware of him was beyond the pale. That her nerve endings tingled without him touching her, that her skin grew warm as though he'd placed his lips in the curve of her shoulder, that her lungs fought for air, while her stomach quivered—

"Mathilda."

Her eyes flew open at the deep voice, and she found herself staring at one of Downie's contemporaries whose age resided somewhere on the other side of thirty. A couple of inches taller than she, he was slender, not bad looking. "Lord Wickham, it's Lady Landsdowne to you."

He gave her a laconic smile. "Come now. A woman with your past can hardly stand on formality."

"The courts granted me the use of the title. I shall have it used."

Slowly, he raked his gaze over her. "The divorce did not diminish your beauty."

She had no idea what one had to do with the other. "I should return to the box."

She made to move past him and he blocked her path. "Surely you cannot fault an old friend for wanting to spend a few minutes in your company."

Friends did not abandon during a time of need. Not that she'd ever held him in such regard. He'd danced with her on occasion, flirted with her before she'd married. But they'd never taken a turn about the garden or conversed on anything of consequence. "I'd be hard pressed to identify us as friends. Acquaintances perhaps."

"I'd like for us to be more." Coming nearer, he placed his forearm on the wall, his gaze locking onto hers. Her heart spiked but she refused to be intimidated or run. Although she did wish she'd brought her pistol.

"I don't see that happening." She was rather pleased that she sounded so calm when her body was tensing with each passing breath. "Please move away."

He stayed where he was. "You have no reputation to protect, and I am in want of a mistress."

"I'm not certain your wife would appreciate that."

"She'll never know."

"The wife always knows. Now step aside."

"You don't really want that." The smile he gave her indicated he thought himself irresistible. He lifted his ungloved hand, moved it toward her cheek—

"Touch her and I'll break your fingers one by one."

Wickham jerked as though he were a marionette whose strings had been yanked. It was strange how the breath seemed to whoosh into her lungs—whether it was because Wickham was no longer hovering near or because Rexton stood there like an avenging angel.

* * *

Rexton was rather disappointed Wickham had heeded his warning. Breaking fingers and then tossing the lord over the balcony had a certain appeal. He wasn't accustomed to harboring such uncivilized thoughts but when he'd stepped into the hallway and seen the man looming over *Tillie*, Rexton had experienced an irrational urge to do harm—swiftly and with malice. He'd been standing there long enough to hear the cad's proposal and her rebuffing of it. He wondered if she'd have accepted if the gent weren't married. Based upon her pale features, he didn't think so.

"This doesn't concern you, Rexton," Wickham had the audacity to spout.

"Afraid it does, old chap. Lady Landsdowne is with me this evening."

Wickham narrowed his eyes. "Rumor is you're courting the sister."

"Miss Hammersley would never forgive me if I allowed anything untoward to happen where Lady Landsdowne is concerned. I heard her ask you politely to leave off. If you're wise, you'll return to your box . . . and your wife."

"Or you'll break my fingers?"

He grinned slowly, confidently. "With enthusiasm."

"There's still the street in you."

"Insult my mother and I'll break your jaw."

Wickham spun on his heel, marched down the hallway, and disappeared into his box. Rexton heard Lady Landsdowne's breath come out on a rush as though she'd been holding it.

"Would you really have broken his fingers?" she asked, her brow pleated, her gaze on his.

"I don't make threats idly."

She bobbed her head. "Thank you for that then."

She made a move toward the entrance to his box. Curling his hand over her shoulder, he wished he wasn't wearing gloves, wished he could feel the silkiness of her flesh against the roughness of his palm. "You should take a moment to gather yourself."

Her chin that reminded him of the bottom half of a heart came up a notch. "I am gathered." Her chin dipped a fraction. "But a bit unsettled. Still, I don't think I should leave Gina alone with your brother."

"He's not going to take advantage of a woman in whom I've shown interest." He knew that to the depths of his soul.

With a slight nod, she walked over to the railing and gazed down into the fairly empty lobby. He eased up beside her, not as near to her as he'd like. He couldn't feel the warmth of her body, but her lavender and orchid fragrance still wafted around him, teased his nostrils.

"What made you step into the hallway?" she asked quietly.

I was worried. For her to leave her sister unattended, he'd sensed something was amiss, but it probably wouldn't do to let her know she occupied his thoughts far more than Miss Hammersley did. "I just needed a bit of air. Do gentlemen often accost you?"

"It was hardly an accosting. But men—and ladies for that matter—do tend to make assumptions regarding my character based on my past actions." She gave him a pointed look. "Don't you?"

He had, but she was unraveling the tapestry he'd woven regarding the sort of woman she was. She was capable of great love, showered her sister with it. He found himself envying anyone to whom she might give her heart. "It cost you dearly to accompany us tonight."

"You're referring to the flagrant hatred cast my way when we walked in. I'm immune to it."

Only she wasn't. But still she'd held her head high, her shoulders back. "Gina seems unaware of the difficulties you face when you venture out in public."

"She believes in goodness, that people aren't deliberately cruel. I prefer she maintain that optimistic outlook."

"Were you like her before you married?"

She looked away, glanced down. "I don't know if I ever was quite that hopeful."

He wondered if he'd been in search of a wife years ago, if he'd met her, courted her, if her life might be different now. He had a strong urge to guard her against the unkindness of others, even though she wasn't his to protect or care about.

She spun around. "We should go back in now, before Gina begins to worry."

He couldn't say he was surprised to see Andrew had moved up to sit beside Gina. His brother enjoyed women, all women, but he knew Andrew wasn't taking advantage. Andrew glanced back, started to rise, but Rexton signaled to him to stay as he was. He leaned toward Lady Landsdowne. "No sense in disturbing your sister."

With a nod, she allowed him to assist her in sitting on the row behind. He took his place beside her, which was where he'd wanted to be all night. She intrigued him in a thousand different ways and possessed a dignity he could not help but admire.

He found himself wishing she was the one Garrett Hammersley had asked him to court.

$\mathscr{A}$t least with him sitting beside her, she couldn't erroneously imagine his gaze was focused on her. When she looked at him out of the corner of her eye, she could see his attention was directed forward, away from her. Still being this close to him made her all the more aware of him.

His kindness in the hallway after her encounter with Wickham had nearly brought her to tears. It had been so very long since anyone besides Gina had shown her true concern. If she were honest, she couldn't claim Downie would have threatened to break fingers on her behalf. He'd never been the jealous sort. She wasn't even certain he'd been jealous of her encounter with the footman. Furious, yes. Embarrassed beyond reason, yes. Mortified, certainly. His pride had taken a blow. But his heart bruised? She doubted it.

She couldn't ascertain why Rexton had made the threat. He wasn't interested in her. Was it merely because of her relationship to Gina? Would he extend his protection of her sister beyond Gina to encompass Tillie? She didn't want to like him for it, but she did. Still she was bothered he'd come to look for her at all, that in doing so he'd abandoned Gina. Not abandoned her entirely—he'd left his brother to keep her company.

She was striving to find fault with him because of her own reactions to his nearness, because of this damned awareness of him that plagued her. His scent circled about her and eased into the marrow of her bones. She wanted to reach out and squeeze Rexton's gloved hand where it rested on his muscular thigh. She wanted him to reach out and take hers. When his hand had curled over her shoulder, she'd felt the warmth as though he wasn't wearing gloves. She was actually glad to have him sitting nearer to her. Which was unconscionable.

What if she'd worn her favorite gown—not because of pride as she'd surmised—but because secretly she'd wanted him to notice her? She wouldn't overtly attempt to steal away a man who was showing interest in Gina—but what if there was a horrible part of her willing to do it covertly?

The man drew her attention and held on to it like a conqueror who would relinquish none of the lands he held. The irony was that he didn't realize the effect he had on her—and that she didn't have the same effect on him. Which was all good news for Gina. Rexton appeared to be loyal, but Tillie knew all too well that appearances were deceiving.

Thank God, the curtains finally closed. Clapping enthusiastically Gina leaped to her feet. Tillie followed suit even though she had no idea if the performances were worthy of such exuberance. It didn't matter. The thing was at an end, and she'd finally be free of the confines of the small box, the nearness of Rexton. Even the thought of facing all the censorious gazes brought her no apprehension. She'd wade through hell for the chance to escape his nearness in a way that didn't make it obvious she was running away.

Smile wide, Gina swung around. "My lord, that was wonderful. Thank you so much."

His grin was a bit self-mocking. "I had nothing at all to do with the performances."

"But you brought us, allowed us to sit in your box. That was so very kind of you."

"It was my pleasure. I don't think my box has ever been graced with such beauty."

"I can attest to the truth of that," Lord Andrew said. "I daresay I regret I have other plans and must dash off."

Reaching out, Gina touched his arm. "Thank you, my lord, for keeping me company when my sister and your brother needed a bit of air."

"It was my pleasure, Miss Hammersley. I do hope our paths will cross again."

"As do I, my lord."

He nodded toward Tillie. "Lady Landsdowne."

Then he was gone, but she could see speculation in Rexton's gaze as though he were contemplating his brother's words, suspected something was afoot. He returned his attention to them. "I'm in no rush to weather the crowds. Perhaps we should give them a chance to thin out."

"That would be lovely," Gina said. "I rather felt as though I were trapped in a coffin when we were making our way here."

He waved his hand over the chairs. "Make yourselves comfortable."

"I'd rather stand," Tillie said. Standing gave her a bit of distance from him. "But ceremony be damned. You needn't remain on your feet."

"I welcome the opportunity to stretch a bit."

And she had the unsettling feeling he knew exactly why she wasn't placing her bottom on the cushion: because she didn't want to be so near him that she could inhale his fragrance.

"Did you enjoy the play, my lord?" Gina asked.

Had she not noted his comment earlier when he'd referenced detesting plays? Truly, she needed to speak with her sister about paying more attention to what was said. She couldn't be responsible for translating all of Rexton's musings or identifying their purpose.

"I enjoyed the pleasure that wreathed your face as you watched the performances," he said smoothly.

His words seemed sincere, which left Tillie feeling like an utter nincompoop for believing for even a moment she'd been able to sense him watching her. Why would he have any interest in a woman with her reputation? He came from one of the most powerful and well-respected families in Great Britain. He, himself, was free of scandal. His behavior was touted as an example for the younger lords to follow.

Having her in his presence probably turned his stomach. He tolerated her because he had a care for her sister. She was silly to believe it was anything else.

That he hadn't exhibited any unkind tendencies toward Tillie was evidence that she should welcome him as a suitable suitor for her sister. And yet Gina seemed far too innocent for a man of his experience. He might not have been caught in any scandals but she doubted he was completely without sin.

"Perhaps we can come again," Gina said.

He laughed softly, as though amused.

"Gina," Tillie chastised. "One does not invite oneself on an outing with a gentleman."

"Then how will he know I'm interested? He might be too shy to ask otherwise."

"I doubt his Lordship possesses a shy bone in his entire body."

"Been paying a good deal of attention to my body, Lady Landsdowne?" he asked in a soft purr that would have been inappropriate under any circumstances but particularly so in the presence of her virginal sister. "Think you know all aspects of me, do you?"

A whirlwind of heated air seemed to consume her. She'd once been in the desert. She'd felt cooler then. "When you speak, please consider my sister's innocence."

"I'm not that innocent," Gina declared.

Tillie snapped her head around to give her sister a warning look. Men applauded women who were unknowing in the ways of men and fornication. A shame really. Although understandable. While she had the experience, she couldn't quite bring herself to sit Gina down and have a frank discussion with her regarding what would occur on her wedding night. "You're more innocent than you probably think."

"I know about men's bodies. I've seen statues."

"They are hardly the same."

"I don't know. When I first met Lord Rexton, I rather envisioned him posing for Michelangelo. That he could have served as the inspiration for David. Didn't you?"

"No! Absolutely not!" She was horrified Gina had spouted such nonsense, more horrified that she had indeed had the exact fleeting thought that Gina had voiced. "Young ladies do not say such things."

It didn't help matters that Rexton was chuckling. "That would make me rather ancient, Little One."

She was struck with the realization he had a pet name, an endearment for Gina. Horrible sister that she was, Tillie felt it like a stab in her chest.

Gina's eyes widened. "Would you pose in the nude for an artist, my lord?"

"Gina, do not ask such personal questions," Tillie chastised. She did not want images of Rexton in the buff filling her head. She did not. She did not. She did not. "You are going to cause his Lordship to reconsider his courting you."

"Lord Andrew told me men enjoy a bit of the naughty."

"Not in a wife!" She glared at Rexton. "You should not have left your brother alone with her."

"I doubt he did any real harm."

"No harm at all," Gina piped up. "We only talked."

Thank God for small favors although what they'd talked about was apparently inappropriate. Rexton seemed to be enjoying this exchange far too much. They needed to leave before Gina said anything else untoward. "I believe the crowd has dispersed sufficiently. We should be off."

Rexton stepped back, indicating Gina should precede him. Her sister headed for the draped doorway. Tillie had taken only a step when he placed his hand on her arm, stilling her actions. She glanced back at him.

"For any woman who asked, I would pose in the nude, artist or no."

And there were those damned images she didn't want crowding into her mind. She glared at him. "You're incorrigible. Hardly the sort of gentleman I want for my sister."

That salvo sobered him and he bowed his head slightly in acquiescence. "You're right to take me to task."

"She truly is innocent, my lord, and we should both

be glad of it." Gathering her skirts, she marched into the hallway. Gina was waiting. When Rexton joined them, he offered only Gina his arm. Thank goodness as Tillie would have refused it, no doubt embarrassing him and herself. But she didn't want to feel that firm arm because it made her think of other firm things. She trudged ahead. As they were descending the stairs, she heard Gina say, "I did feel rather sorry for your brother, my lord. If not for us, he would have been forced to watch the play alone. That's rather sad."

"I assure you, Miss Hammersley, he would not have minded."

When they reached the lobby, Tillie said, "He's probably involved with an actress, Gina."

"Truly?"

Waiting until her sister caught up and fell into step beside her, she said, "You're a bit more innocent than you realize, Gina."

"Imagine the stories she could tell."

Yes, Tillie was rather certain the Greystone spare was with the woman for the stories. Over Gina's head, Rexton met Tillie's gaze, his eyes dancing with mirth. While it might be funny in one way, in another it worried her to distraction.

Take care with her heart, my lord.

He grew somber, as though he'd read her plea in her eyes. She should have taken satisfaction in the fact he was so attuned to her. Instead it made her realize that never before had she been able to communicate so effectively with a man. And here, she could do it with the last man she cared to.

* * *

$\mathcal{D}$amnation but he needed a woman. After delivering the ladies to their residence, he'd been able to stay in his retreating coach for all of five minutes before banging on the ceiling to signal to the driver to stop the conveyance. As soon as it halted, he leaped out. "I'll be walking, Mick. Carry on home."

"Yes, my lord."

He'd had two women in his coach, yet the fragrance of only one tormented him. Lavender and orchids assailed his nostrils, stirred his desires, made him as hard as a rock. He inhaled deeply a breath of London air that didn't seem to help clear his lungs. It was as though her scent had woven itself into the very fabric of his clothing, the essence of his skin, and made its home there.

Allowing his long strides to lead him toward he knew not where, he soundly cursed Lady Landsdowne. Tillie. He longed to catch glimpses of the girl she might have been. Tonight her defenses had been up. He'd wager half his fortune that if pressed she would be unable to describe the story that had taken place upon the stage. Although she could bluff her way through by telling him anything at all—the tale of a princess and a pirate falling in love—and he wouldn't be able to call her on it as he'd never taken his attention from her.

Which was the reason his body was thrumming and aching with need. Need that would go unsatisfied, because as he slowed his steps he admitted he didn't want just any woman, he wanted her.

The very last thing he should desire because she wasn't the one who would give him access to the stallion. She wasn't the one upon whom he was supposed to shower his attentions. She was a woman with no morals, no honor, no decency. No discreetness.

He damned his cock to hell for not giving a bloody damn.

I need a man.

She couldn't recall ever having that particular thought before, but as she sat in her nightgown in the plush chair in the sitting area of her darkened bedchamber the litany echoed through her mind.

I need a man.

But even as the words served as a sinful siren, she knew not any gent would do. Only Rexton. The gloriously beguiling man whose mere presence kept her warm and on edge.

She'd been on this earth a mere quarter of a century and she was living as though her life were over, secluded away as though she could infect people with some strange disease. As uncomfortable as it had been going to the theater, she'd still felt a measure of triumph. She'd survived. She wanted to attend more plays and have more interaction with people. It wasn't a possibility here in London, but once Gina was situated, she could return to New York. She'd never planned to stay here. The memories were too unpleasant, the people equally so. But she'd promised her father she would see to Gina's happiness. Had vowed to her mother she would do all in her power to see Gina married a titled gentleman.

She wanted to help Gina find the right man to wed. She wanted nothing more than she wanted her sister's happiness. Rexton didn't suit. She knew that deep within her heart, but what could she point out as an example of his unfitness? His dazzling blue eyes? How when they twinkled with mirth they made her want to laugh when she couldn't remember the last time any man had caused her to feel anything beyond unhappiness?

His broad shoulders that called to a woman to snuggle against them? His sturdy arms that provided support? His smile that came so easily as though he was skilled at warding off troubles?

That he noticed things like cuts, even when they weren't directed his way? That he had served as her champion when he could have left her to languish in humiliation as Downie had done? Although she did have to give Downie credit for not making his humiliation of her public. But it had flourished in the private corners of their lives.

She couldn't imagine Rexton treating his wife with anything other than respect. Even knowing her past, he'd never thrown it into her face. He treated her with deference as though it were her due. Even when he said naughty things he shouldn't, she couldn't seem to think of him in a bad light. If anything, she was the one in need of chastisement because she couldn't seem to escape the image of him posing nude.

Which was the very reason she needed a man. Tonight. This very moment.

While she had no basis for her certainty, she did not doubt he would be an exceptional lover. If he could send desire dancing through her veins without even touching her, what the devil would it feel like to be caressed and stroked by his large sure hands? What sensations would be stirred to life if his mouth traveled along her throat? If he suckled on her breast, a breast that ached for a touch as it never had before?

Her nipples were hard, her breasts heavy with want, with need. And it was Rexton's fault, damn him. She couldn't stop thinking about him, couldn't stop envisioning the pleasure it would bring her to take his full lower lip between her teeth and draw it into her mouth, to release it and dart her tongue between his parted lips. To hear his groan, to feel the rumble of his chest.

Even as she cursed him, she cupped her breasts, flicked her thumbs over the taut pearls that ached for something she couldn't deliver. It was wrong, so wrong to have these thoughts, to be encouraging these sensations, to be touching herself in a sensual manner, imagining his hands, his tongue, his mouth bringing her pleasure in a myriad of ways.

It was wrong, so wrong, to slowly gather up her nightgown until it was pooled at her hips and she could feel the cool air gliding over skin she never exposed. She rested her hands on the inside of her silken thighs, the tips of her fingers creating tiny circles. She'd never done this before, never teased herself. Even now she didn't feel as though she was the one doing the teasing. It was him. The Marquess of Rexton.

He was the one calling to the wanton in her, the one setting her on edge, the one tempting her, demanding she reach for release. Slowly, hesitantly, she parted the folds, surprised by the heat, the dampness, the sensitivity that greeted her. She'd never been so bold but neither had she ever been quivering with such need for release.

Closing her eyes, she saw him standing before her, his shirt gone. Although she'd never before seen his bared chest, she could envision quite vividly how Rexton might appear. Gloriously. Everything firm. Everything taut.

Slowly, she stroked, pressed, circled around the sensitive area. She imagined him going down to his knees—

The rapture came swift and hard, her screech an unexpected sound she'd never before made. Quickly she lowered her nightgown, having a ferocious need to hide the evidence that anything untoward had occurred within her bedchamber, within this chair.

Good Lord. Obviously she couldn't serve as an objective observer when the man caused such exciting stirrings within her.

Her chaperoning days were definitely behind her.

Chapter 5

Everyone had expected Rexton to attend the Lovington ball. But his appearance at the Ashebury affair caused a few startled glances to be cast his way, a few mothers to smile with glee, and a few additional ladies to be introduced to him. He used the occasion to mention offhandedly to the mamas that he found Miss Hammersley to be charming. With any luck those with unmarried sons would nudge their offspring toward her in an effort to thwart Rexton's perceived plans to court her. He'd seen it happen before. The matrons of the *ton* could teach a general or two about strategy when it came to dividing and conquering. If he were truly courting a lady, he'd be a bit more discreet, concerned with protecting her reputation, but he was in a hurry to see his part of the bargain completed.

Not that he didn't enjoy Gina's company. But he was having a devil of a time stopping her sister from haunting his thoughts. His body had never suffered through such unfulfilled need, yet he could work up no enthusiasm for any other woman. He enjoyed sparring with her, teasing her with inappropriate suggestions. He liked the way she stood up to him, called him out on his improper behavior. And here he was, thinking of her again when his focus should be on Gina. He hadn't rushed up to her immediately, but once the mothers had veered away, he'd retreated to the shadows, striving to get a sense of who was and wasn't here, who would make a good catch for Gina. Knowing Lady Landsdowne's exacting standards, not just anyone would do. He needed someone with a title, a modicum of wealth, and a sterling reputation. Someone capable of falling in love. He did like Gina enough to care that she was happy.

"What are you up to, Rex?"

Turning on his heel, he gave a sardonic twist of his lips to the former Miss Minerva Dodger, who had broken a good many hearts when she'd fallen for the Duke of Ashebury, and effectively taken her immense dowry off the marriage market. Because he considered her more family than friend, had spent a great deal of time in her company since her father and his mother had been pals on the streets, he was aware she knew him better than most and was terribly skilled at judging men. It was one of the reasons fortune hunters had failed miserably when courting her. "I have no idea to what you're referring."

"Liar." Her directness was one of the reasons bachelors had been more interested in her money than her. As much as he liked her, even he often found that particular aspect to her character irritating. "You've never before attended one of my balls."

"Yet you continue to send me invitations so I thought it high time I did." And he'd known Gina would be in attendance because Garrett Hammersley had sent

Rexton a note alerting him that he'd be escorting his niece to the affair.

Narrowing her eyes, Minerva gave her head a subtle shake. "No, something is going on. I've heard rumors that you've been seen escorting Miss Hammersley about."

He raised his brows in innocence. "Is she in attendance tonight?"

"You know damned well she is."

"Then I'll give you more fodder for gossip, as I'm going to dance with her. Feel free to confirm that she— and not your much talked about affair—is the reason I'm here."

She gave him a scorching once-over. "Why?"

"I beg your pardon?"

"Why are you showing an interest in her? She doesn't strike me as your type."

"She's a lovely girl." He realized too late that he'd said it too defensively, and Minerva, who was too sharp by half, picked up on it. Her mouth thinned into a disapproving straight line.

"Lovely doesn't suit you."

"And you know what suits me, do you?"

"She's too genteel and gentle. I don't think she's weak necessarily, but neither do I believe she'd ever stand up to you."

Unlike her sister who had no qualms whatsoever in striving to keep him in his place. "Perhaps I want biddable in a wife."

"You'll be miserable."

Damnation, of course, he would. He didn't want someone who looked at him as though he hung the moon and stars. He didn't want a wife who didn't challenge him to be better, who didn't look at him as though he were up to no good when in fact he was. "I'm simply testing the waters of courtship."

"She could get hurt."

He knew that fact which was the very reason he was striving to take such care. It had been three nights since he'd escorted her to the theater. He'd sent her flowers and more chocolates, but he couldn't accomplish his goal if he ignored her completely. "For God's sake, Minerva, while you've stood there putting me through an inquisition on matters that are none of your concern, three gentlemen have approached her. Last week, I was the only one to dance with her. My attentiveness to her makes others wonder what hidden gem I've discovered."

"So you're doing it as a favor to her?"

"In a manner of speaking, yes. Now, leave off. I know what I'm doing."

"For her sake, I shall hope so. For yours as well. I'd hate to be forced to beat you up for not being sensitive to a lady's plight."

He'd heard rumors she had a very wicked knee that could fell a fellow. "Why don't you go bother your husband?"

Her smile lit her eyes. "Trust me. Ashe never sees me as a bother."

Of course he didn't. The man was ridiculously in love with her. Although Rexton had to admit Minerva deserved that sort of devotion. All women did. Still, she wasn't going to make him doubt his plan.

No, Gina was going to do that herself with the bright smile she bestowed upon him as he approached her when there was a break in the music. Two dances had seen her with partners, chaps younger than he and more suited to her. But would they meet with her sister's approval? That was the question. Strange how he was more interested in pleasing the countess than Gina.

"My lord," she chirped. It wasn't natural for a woman to always be so happy. It wasn't natural for him to be grumpy because she was joyful. He wasn't upset with her, but Minerva was correct: he would find no peace with someone like her as his wife. He didn't want discord, but neither did he want someone with whom he was always in agreement.

"Miss Hammersley, I wondered if you'd honor me with a dance."

"I'd be delighted, my lord, although my card isn't nearly as empty as it was the last time you asked. I've had four other gentlemen show interest." She extended the card dangling from her wrist.

Scribbling his name, he said as offhandedly as possible, "I didn't notice your sister here."

"My maid is serving as chaperone tonight. It's one thing for Tillie to accompany me to a public park or theater, but she wouldn't intrude in a private home when she wasn't invited."

Of course she wouldn't, and she wouldn't be invited, not even by the generous and rule bending Duchess of Ashebury. Unless he'd asked. He wished he'd thought to ask. On the other hand, he didn't relish the notion of witnessing all the glares and cuts direct she'd have received.

"It doesn't seem quite fair, though, does it?"

He shifted his attention back to the young lady. Little wonder Minerva didn't think they'd suit. He'd always think of her in a brotherly manner, a sister to be protected from scoundrels and rakes. "What's that, sweetheart?" he asked, wishing he'd refrained from using an endearment when her eyes sparked with pleasure.

"That she's not welcomed, yet Downie is."

The earl was here? Rexton wondered if he could lure him into the card room so he could lighten his pockets a bit further.

"I realize a divorce is scandalous, but he is divorced as well."

He gave her a sympathetic smile. "A bit more than a divorce is involved."

"But he was a beastly husband." Her eyes widened and she pressed a small, gloved hand to her mouth. "I shouldn't have said. Tillie would be horrified by my words. She never speaks ill of him."

The rage that shimmied through him made him want to punch something—or someone. "Did he strike her?"

"Not to my knowledge but there are other ways to make a person feel less or unworthy, aren't there? I think she was rather mortified she had judged him so incorrectly, which is the reason she's guiding me. So I don't make a similar error in judgment. The thing is, people can hide things from you, and then how are you to know?"

Like he was hiding his true reason for giving her attention. Something of his guilty thoughts must have crossed his features because she reached out and placed her hand on his arm, squeezing lightly.

"Not to worry. I've assured Tillie your intentions are honorable."

If he wasn't careful, in order to get the horse, he was going to have to marry the girl. He gave her a sardonic smile. "Does she believe you?"

"I'm afraid not, but you mustn't take offense. Marriage to Downie taught her one thing: no man is to be trusted."

Him least of all at the moment. He was grateful the music started up so he didn't have to contemplate that unsettling realization for long.

After leading her onto the dance floor, he took her in his arms and swept her around the room. She was graceful, but he suspected her sister would be more so. He imagined her smiling up at him. She wouldn't have to gaze up as far because she was a few inches taller than Gina. He couldn't seem to stop comparing the two of them.

"Does your brother ever attend balls?" she asked.

He frowned. "Andrew?" He shook his head. "Hardly ever. It is his intention to remain a bachelor for the remainder of his life."

"Do you resent that you have responsibilities and he doesn't? That you must marry?"

"Because not marrying wasn't an option, I've never really considered having a life without a wife."

She gnawed on her lower lip. "I've been told by numerous mothers that I shouldn't take your attentions seriously. That you would never marry an American."

The mothers were supposed to prod their sons in Gina's direction, not cause her to doubt his intentions. "I'll admit I've always favored English lasses, but that doesn't mean I can't be won over by an American."

Her laughter tinkled around them, and he found

himself wondering how her sister's laughter sounded. Damnation, he had to focus.

"I'm so glad Tillie got to go to the theater with us. I'm not certain all men will be as accepting of her as you are."

"You are her sister. I would not expect you to have to choose me over family."

"You are a rare find, my lord."

"You humble me, Miss Hammersley."

"Gina."

The music began to drift into silence.

"Will you dance with me again before the night is done?" she asked.

"I will indeed. The last dance." To show the mothers they knew not of what they spoke—even though they did.

He escorted her back to the maid. While he was in the mood for a stiff drink and a game of cards, he stayed in the grand salon and watched Gina from afar, striving to determine if any gent had more than a passing interest in her.

"Rexton."

He glanced over at the man who'd approached. "Hammersley."

"Care to join me in the garden for a cheroot?"

"I'd be delighted."

They found a spot far from the terrace where the shadows were thick and they weren't likely to be over-heard. Hammersley had the manners to wait until their cheroots were lit and they'd both taken a couple of puffs before saying, "I expected the girl to dance every dance tonight. I may have misjudged your influence."

Misjudged his older niece's notoriety more like. Rexton slowly inhaled, blew out the smoke. "I'm not yet done. Another outing or two, one more ball . . . finding the right gent takes time." While he'd thought he'd be done within a week, he was rather glad to discover he wasn't.

He welcomed another excuse to visit with the countess.

*T*illie loved the scent of freshly turned earth. Or she had before it had begun to remind her of Rexton. She shouldn't be so displeased with the man. He'd managed within the space of a week to bring acceptance for Gina—and for that Tillie was grateful.

She'd felt guilty that Gina's Season had begun with hardly any notice or fanfare, while she, herself, had burst onto the scene like someone novel who should be embraced simply because of her uniqueness. She was American, which made her intriguing, beautiful which made her acceptable to the gentlemen, an heiress who came with an immense dowry to be followed with an untold fortune that she would inherit upon her father's death which made her alluring to every lord with an estate in need of upkeep. She'd been as enamored of the aristocracy as Gina was. And that infatuation did not work in her sister's favor because it made her blind to the practicalities of marrying into the peerage. Which made her think Rexton was perfect.

She'd waxed on for an hour on his qualities when she'd returned from last night's ball. He was such a graceful dancer, such a delight to converse with. Such a gentleman to bring her a spot of lemonade while warning her off regarding the lord with whom she'd been dancing. Gina speculated it had been jealousy that prompted his warning. Tillie didn't think so.

He wasn't enamored of Gina. She was rather certain of it. Oh, his eyes twinkled when he spoke to her, but they didn't warm as though he wanted to draw her in and hold her close. The tone of his voice was gentle, but he spouted no naughty whisperings that caused Gina to giggle. If he did, surely her sister would tell her. She had shared that during their final waltz, he'd spoken about the fine weather they were having. He'd hinted at a picnic. But the details of the weather? The sun, the slight breeze, the occasional rain? Hardly flattering conversation.

He should have complimented her eyes, her hair, her gown. He should have hinted he wanted to remove said gown.

She drove the trowel into the ground with such force she was fairly certain the gloves were not going to prevent her from blistering. Just because she dreamed of him rasping near her ear in exquisite detail how he would slowly undress her did not mean it would be appropriate for him to do the same with Gina. Poor innocent Gina would no doubt swoon on the spot— regardless of how many nude statues she'd ogled. Even now, Tillie was having a difficult time drawing in air as images of him peeling off her stockings caused heat to course through her.

When it came to Gina, he was a gentleman. The last thing Tillie wanted was for him to be a gentleman to her. She cursed soundly. He was interested in her sister. She shouldn't be thinking about him at all except in the context of behavior that proved he would love and care for Gina as she desired.

Out of the corner of her eye, she saw a shadow move in and she knew—*knew*—to whom it belonged because she felt his gaze like a physical caress. The hairs on the nape of her neck rose up and pleasure spiraled through her simply because he was so near. What the devil was wrong with her? She'd learned the hard way that men were disappointments. She certainly had no wish to fall under the spell of another. Especially this one who seemed to turn her inside out without even trying.

In spite of the small tremors of awareness coursing through her, she slowly and calmly peered out from beneath the wide brim of her gardening hat to see the Marquess of Rexton standing there, legs spread akimbo as though he stood on the deck of a roiling ship. He must have given his hat to the butler because it was nowhere about and the wind was having its way with his blond curls. She wanted to remove her gloves and have those silken strands wrap around her fingers and hold her captive. Never in her life had such wanton thoughts tormented her, and she seemed powerless against them forming. Which was the reason, no doubt, that her tone came out tart and short. "My lord, I don't recall inviting you out into the garden."

"To be sure, Lady Landsdowne, you didn't. I've come to call on your sister, but apparently she's still abed. I asked the butler to direct me to you so I could leave a message for her with you."

"And that would be?"

He had the audacity to crouch beside her, and his scent won out over the freshly turned earth. It was richer, warmer, and seemed to call to every purely feminine point she possessed. She couldn't help but notice the tautness of his breeches, the firmness of his thighs. She'd seen the evidence that he was a fine horseman. She imagined those thighs controlling the horse, controlling her. Damn it all.

"Does Miss Hammersley always sleep so late?"

"My sister didn't return from the ball until the wee hours in the morning, so I think her sleeping in is justified. It's a bit too early for a social call," she castigated.

He grinned as though tickled by her chastisement. She didn't want to make him smile or laugh or be delighted. That would be Gina's honor and joy.

"As I was out and about, I saw no harm in stopping by." His gaze shifted to her hand gripping the implement as though it were the only thing that held her in place. "I've never known a lady to work in the garden."

"My gardener tends to most of it. This is just my little patch of whimsy. There is no rhyme or reason to what I plant, and I seem to have more luck with weeds than blossoms but I prefer it to needlepoint." Why had she gone on about that? What would he care?

"You didn't attend the ball last night."

"I wasn't invited."

He looked at her as though she were a puzzle with a missing piece. "Would you have gone if you had been?"

She honestly didn't know. A part of her didn't want to be cowed, wanted to attend wearing a bright red dress so she couldn't be overlooked. Part of her wanted to hold her head high and meet those gazes head on. "I see no point in speculating on hypotheticals. I shan't be invited to a ball."

"You underestimate my influence."

He said the words simply, without braggadocio. She liked him for it, realized he was a man who owned his influence to such an extent he didn't need to boast about it, didn't need to be cocky. It was what it was. "Perhaps you didn't notice at the theater, but I make people uncomfortable."

"I wasn't uncomfortable." His easy tone made her wish she'd known him before she met Downie, before Rexton had taken an interest in Gina.

"My presence wouldn't serve Gina well."

He studied her, studied her flowers, the bee that was buzzing around, pollenating. And she found herself wondering if he'd ever pollenated anyone. She'd certainly not heard of him having any bastards. She'd wager her fortune he wasn't a virgin, but she was unaware of any rumors associating him with anyone. Which meant he was very discreet, that his lovers would never be found out. Why the hell did her mind keep traveling toward sex?

"You love your sister very much," he finally said.

"Of course I do. I'd do anything to see her happy." *Even steer clear of you.* "Wouldn't you do the same for your sister?"

He chuckled. "I don't have to. That's Lovingdon's job, and he apparently excels at it."

"And if he didn't?"

He grew somber. She didn't like the way his gaze roamed over her face as though he could read every unhappy moment in her life in the lines and creases that hadn't been there on the day she wed. "I'd beat him to within an inch of his life."

"She's very fortunate, then, your sister." She'd not meant to travel this road or to have this conversation.

"If you'll give me your message for Gina, I'll see that she gets it."

"A question first. Do you know if she's ever been to the Twin Dragons?"

"She hasn't, no. I hear it's a rather fascinating place."

"It is. I thought to take her there for dinner tonight. I'll stop by at seven. If she's not interested, no harm done. I'll simply go on without her."

"I'm rather certain she'll be joining you. She enjoys new experiences."

"And do you . . . enjoy new experiences?"

The question was laced with innuendo. She shook it off. The intimation was only in her mind. He wouldn't risk insulting her when his interest was Gina. So why did he continually ask about her preferences? He should state his business and move on. She should answer his question and not read more into it than existed. "Obviously, when I was younger that could be said of me. I kissed a footman after all." She didn't know why she'd said it, why she felt a need to remind him of her reputation.

"Curiosity prompted your actions, then?"

"Among other things."

Reaching out, he closed his hand over hers where it clutched the digging implement. They both wore gloves and yet it felt like there was no leather serving as a barrier to their skin.

"You're strangling this poor little spade."

She meant to merely scoff, but the sound came out rather mocking. "It's a trowel. I take it you don't garden."

"Creating beauty is not my forte."

Was he implying that he found her little patch of

ground beautiful? What she created brought her pleasure but she'd never known anyone else to give it
much notice. She stared at him for the longest time,
marveling that he still held her hand as though reluctant to give it up. Would he hold Gina's with the same
care, offering her comfort and strength while doing
so? Would he gaze into her eyes for long moments as
though lost within their depths?

Would Gina notice his long, spiky eyelashes and
their burnished shade? Would she see the darker blue
circling the pale blue of his iris? Would she yearn
to reach up to brush back the curling locks that fell
over his brow? Would all the sounds surrounding her
fade away until all she heard was his breathing as she
waited for the rough timbre of his voice to soothe her?

She loved her sister dearly but there were times
when she was a bit flighty, when she didn't seem to
appreciate all she held, all she possessed. Would she
appreciate this man?

"You should loosen your fingers a bit," he said quietly, "before you cause your hand to ache."

She didn't like being ordered about, but his words
were delivered as more of an entreaty than a command, as though he held true concern for any discomfort she might suffer. She didn't want to deem him
worthy of her sister, but he was making it difficult not
to acknowledge that he might indeed be a fine catch.
"Will you put her wants ahead of your own?" she
heard herself asking in a voice that didn't quite sound
like her own, that rang hollow as though it had traveled from a great distance, down a long tunnel.

Slowly his fingers unfurled and her hand did
indeed ache, but only from the loss of his touch.

"I shall do all in my power to ensure she is happy."

"She requires more than chocolates and theater and waltzes."

"Hence the invitation to dinner." He unfolded that tall, lean marvelous body that kept invading her dreams. For a moment she'd almost allowed herself to be lured into believing she should encourage Gina to accept his suit, but still something nagged at her. Perhaps it was merely her own wants and desires.

Standing there, he gave a quick tug on his gloves as though they'd somehow fallen out of favor. "By the by, the invitation includes you. She'll have a better time if you're there, so don't disappoint."

Before she could let him know she had no interest in going, he was walking away. She almost darted after him to alert him that he couldn't order her about like that. But she didn't want to get into an argument that might cause him to rescind the invitation. Even as the thought of going out in public again caused a small measure of panic, she couldn't deny her curiosity about the private club that catered to London's elite.

Jabbing the trowel into the dirt, she cursed soundly for lying to herself because much to her mortification, she was anticipating another evening in his company.

Will you put her wants ahead of your own?

Lounging in a chair in his father's library, Rexton found himself wondering: Had Landsdowne not done that for his wife? Not put her wants first? Every time he was in the company of Lady Landsdowne, he found himself wanting to know more about her: her life before her marriage, during it, after it. Had she always spent time nurturing flowers? What other hobbies did she enjoy?

"It's quite a risk," his father said.

He nodded. One afternoon a week, he visited to discuss the status of their estates, the profitability of their various income streams, how to diversify, how to ensure profits. More and more, the duke was turning the reins over to him. He enjoyed the challenge of it—

Enjoyed the challenge of Lady Landsdowne. He hadn't given her time to decline his invitation and he suspected she'd bristled as he'd walked away. He was halfway surprised she didn't dash after him and smack him on the head with that little trowel. He'd been a fool to take her hand, hadn't wanted to release it once he had. If he hadn't thought she'd object, he'd have removed her glove . . . and his own.

"Andrew requires a larger allowance," his father said casually.

"Without question." Skin to skin. Hers would be as smooth as silk. He had no doubt. Her long, slender fingers would be on display during dinner. If he could determine a way to accidentally touch them—

"I was thinking ten thousand a month."

"Reasonable." Perhaps he should tell her the truth, acknowledge he had more interest in her than in Gina, that Lady Landsdowne occupied his thoughts for the greater part of each day and every night.

"We shall be bankrupt by the end of the year."

Nodding, he tapped his fingers on the arm of the chair. Although with the truth, she might cast him out for his deception and he would lose not only a chance at the stallion but at Lady Landsdowne. Was it worth the risk of losing the horse to gain her? But in what manner could he have a woman of her notoriety? Certainly he couldn't marry her, but an affair might not be out of the question. She'd engaged in at least one. Why not another—with him?

"Rex?"

The tone wasn't one he'd been the recipient of since he left school. It jerked him out of his reveries, and he snapped his attention to his father. "Sir?"

"The idea of bankruptcy doesn't bother you?"

He glanced around the various sitting areas and the shelves lined with books. "Who's going bankrupt?"

"I just said we were."

Why would his father believe that? "We're solvent. The estates' incomes have dwindled a bit but we have other businesses. We're in remarkably good shape."

"What of Andrew's ten thousand pounds a month allowance?"

Obviously he hadn't paid nearly as much attention as he'd thought. Lady Landsdowne was affecting every aspect of his life. "I'd never agree to that amount. It's ludicrous. Not to mention a reckless dispersal of funds. I hate to say it but Andrew would fritter it away. He isn't completely irresponsible, but he hasn't yet found a purpose to his life." He was a year younger than Rexton, but he'd never been asked to do anything more than live the life of a gentleman—like most spares.

His father leaned back in his leather chair. "I've been tossing out ridiculous statements and you've agreed to them all. You weren't listening to a word I said, were you?"

He was embarrassed to admit, "Not really, no. But

I've thoroughly studied the ledgers and the reports. I'm confident we're faring well. My meeting with the estate managers tomorrow gives me no concern."

"What does? What causes this unusual distraction when I usually have your full attention?"

What indeed? He couldn't tell him the truth when Rexton knew he would find fault with it. He'd worked so blasted hard his entire life to ensure he didn't disappoint his parents. "Have you ever wanted something so badly that you use questionable means to acquire it?"

"Been cheating at cards when playing your sister again?"

He chuckled. If only it was that innocent. Was he being unfair to the girl to be giving her attention when his intentions weren't serious? Perhaps he should simply admit the truth. Yes, Lady Landsdowne would certainly fly into his arms then.

"What made you decide to court Mother?"

His father looked somewhat surprised by the notion, as though he'd never given it any thought. "I'm not quite certain I ever really did court her. Not properly anyway. Our paths just seemed to cross on occasion and when they did—" He lifted a shoulder, dropped it, looked away. "I took advantage. Then one day I realized I loved her."

He again looked in Rexton's direction, but he wasn't certain how much his father could see. For a good portion of his life, he'd been losing his eyesight. It was nearly gone now. "Have you met someone for whom you care?"

"I don't know how I feel about her exactly. She vexes me. Intrigues me. But I know we would not suit. She has none of the qualities I would seek in a wife."

"Where I was concerned, neither did your mother. But she possessed all the qualities I could love. In the end, that won out."

"I don't love her. I don't even know if I like her."

"What of these questionable means you referred to? Is she behind them?"

"No, she's innocent of that." The problem was there were too many things of which she wasn't innocent.

Chapter 6

$\mathcal{T}$onight she would be a respectable chaperone. She would fade into the woodwork, observe, and make a mental list regarding Rexton's suitability. To discourage Gina from falling for the fellow, Tillie needed specific examples. And if she approved of the match—she needed to burn samplings of his exemplary behavior into her mind so she could torment herself with the images of his love for her sister so she, herself, would cease with all these horrendous fantasies of him doing wicked things to her that tormented her throughout the night. She hadn't slept soundly since the blasted man had come into their lives. She stepped into the hallway—

The high-pitched shriek had her jumping out of her skin and her heart racing.

"What have you done to yourself?" Gina squealed. The abject look of horror on her usually joyful face alerted Tillie that she'd accomplished her goal of ensuring no man would find her the least bit enticing. If Rexton ignored her completely, perhaps her stomach would stop its irritating and continual fluttering whenever he was near. "You resemble a ghoul."

"Not that bad, surely." Her black dress buttoned to her chin and her wrists. Her maid had pulled her hair back into a severe, tight bun that caused her skin to feel taut as her high cheekbones hollowed out to dominate her face.

"At the very least someone in mourning."

She gave an ineffectual tug on her black gloves. They were fitted as tightly as possible and not going anywhere. "As any well respected chaperone should be."

"This won't do at all." Sweeping past her, Gina rushed into Tillie's bedchamber.

With a roll of her eyes, she followed. Her sister was at her wardrobe, pulling out one gown after another and stuffing it back into place as though it offended her. "Gina, a chaperone shouldn't draw attention. It was a mistake I made at the theater. I should have dressed in a less striking manner so as to be overlooked. When people notice me it only serves to reinforce we're related, which serves you no good."

"But we're going to the Twin Dragons, and while I've never been, I have heard people talk about it. One must wear one's finest." Holding up a plum gown, she swung around. "Especially if you wish to be extended an invitation for membership."

"Why would I want that?"

"So you have something to do in the evenings, other than haunt this place."

"I enjoy haunting this place." A lie. She'd wanted it because Downie had loved it so. She'd wanted to take something he'd treasured because he'd taken something precious from her. While the manor had been in Downie's family for a century, it wasn't included in his entailment, and he'd been willing to part with it for a substantial sum, much to his mother's horror. At the time, Tillie had taken satisfaction in her reaction. Although in hindsight, she feared she'd been rather petty. "Besides as I mentioned, a chaperone shouldn't be noticed."

"Well, you're going to be noticed in *that*. Dreadfully so. If you don't want to draw attention, then you must blend in." She tossed the gown onto the bed. "That one will do nicely. Call for your maid and have her do something with your hair while she's at it. Pulling it back that tightly makes it appear as though you haven't had a bite to eat in a year."

"It's not that severe."

"It's awful."

All the better then. She wouldn't imagine she felt Rexton's gaze roaming over her because she could reassure herself he wouldn't even look at her. "Gina, sweeting, what I wear is unimportant. Rexton's attention will be on you as it should be—"

"So you've noticed he looks at you."

She was stunned by the pronouncement. She'd imagined it, but that was her own wantonness rearing its ugly head. "He can't ignore me completely without being rude."

"Perhaps," Gina said nonchalantly. "However my doubt is all the more reason you should be at your best. If he has a wandering eye, then he's not someone I want, is he? Play the tart tonight. Let's test his devotion to me. The gaming hell is perfect, because people don't really behave there, do they? It's all wickedness, so you can be subtle and it won't be obvious what you're doing. I don't want you to try to steal him away—as I can't compete with you."

"Don't be silly. I'm no competition for you. You're pretty, young, enthusiastic. You're wildly fun while I much prefer quiet and solitude."

"Well, you won't get much of that this evening, I'm sure, not based upon what I've heard of the club. Now prepare yourself for an exciting night of adventure."

Tillie shook her head. "I haven't time to change. He'll be here any minute—"

"I'll entertain him in the parlor. It's not as though we're on a schedule. We arrive when we arrive."

Tillie hated to admit Gina was correct: Rexton needed to be tested. She wouldn't be blatant about it, but the club would be the perfect place to observe all the nuances to Rexton's characteristics. How much he drank. How much he gambled. Was he reckless or disciplined? How much attention would he pay to her if she were as her sister suggested: somewhat tartish?

"All right, but ensure your maid is in the parlor with you. I don't trust Rexton not to take advantage."

Gina beamed. "Splendid. Although I daresay I wouldn't object if he took advantage. He's just so magnificently delicious."

The jealousy that speared Tillie with the thought of Rexton kissing her sister took her by surprise, causing a sharp pain in her midsection which nearly caused her to groan. Her reaction was inappropriate, shameful. Gina was obviously infatuated with the marquess. Tillie had to quell her own interest and her own wicked thoughts. "Perhaps the maid *and* Griggs should be in the parlor with you," she said pointedly.

Gina merely laughed. "Not to worry. I won't let him misbehave. I won't be forced into a marriage."

"Jolly good for you."

As soon as Gina had skipped from the room, Tillie called for her maid. How different her life would be now if she'd had someone on hand to point out Downie's flaws. She glanced over at the plum. It wouldn't do. If temptation was the goal, she needed to go with the red.

*R*exton didn't much like the disappointment that hit him when he walked into Landsdowne Court to discover Gina and her maid waiting for him rather than the countess. She'd rebuffed his overture. He should have been relieved, as he needed to focus his attentions on getting the eligible Miss Hammersley aligned with a suitable gentleman.

He liked even less the relief that hit him when the lady he was supposed to be courting apologized for her sister's delay and offered to keep him company in the parlor with her maid serving as chaperone while they awaited the tardy one's arrival. He didn't like being drawn to Lady Landsdowne, he didn't like that she haunted his nights, that he thought of her more than was practical or that those thoughts usually involved naughty and lascivious activities occurring on satin sheets within midnight shadows.

Although Gina had invited him to sit, he was wound up in a way he'd never been before. He needed to pace or ride or box. Instead he took up a post beside the fireplace as though the hearth were in need of defending, might spontaneously ignite at any moment if he weren't standing guard. It was the deception making him antsy because the young woman peered up at him as though he were the answer to every dream she'd ever possessed. He was a fine catch. He knew that. Titled, wealthy, influential. He was the sort American heiresses flocked to England in search of. He'd lost some friends to their charms. As for himself, he preferred the English rose and when the time came that he was actually on the hunt for a wife, he would go with a woman who understood proper behavior and avoided scandal.

Even as he had the thought, he knew he was judging Gina unfairly, painting her with a brush that rightly belonged to her sister. Gina had done nothing to deserve his censure. He couldn't fault her for wanting an English lord when so many were idolized because of their impeccable manners and good breeding. He knew a few American men, and while he enjoyed their company, he couldn't deny they were a rough lot. Her uncle was a prime example. He worked hard, drank hard, played hard. Ironically, when it came to his nieces, however, he wanted things easy. Let another gent take the necessary actions to see the girl wed. For the price of a stud, Rexton had been willing. Was still willing. He just wished the girl didn't always look so pleased to see him.

"Might I offer you something to drink, my lord?" she asked sweetly, and he knew her sister would have already had the whisky poured and in his hand. Would have joined him, her gaze never leaving his as she sipped, challenging him to find fault with her actions.

"No, thank you."

"I'm certain Tillie won't be much longer."

"We have no schedule."

"That's what I told her when she was concerned about you having to wait."

"She was concerned?" Of course, she would be. She wasn't concerned about him in particular, simply the bad manners of not being ready on time.

"She doesn't like to be a bother."

Then she shouldn't have had a quite public affair with a manservant. Although he did have to wonder: if she'd been married to him, would she have strayed? Did he possess the wherewithal to keep a woman such as she happy, content, and at his side? It was strange to realize he'd have embraced the challenge of it.

"I think she rather feared her tardiness would taint your opinion of me," Gina said.

"I'm not in the habit of judging people based upon their familial relations."

Her cheeks pinkened, and he imagined her sister's blush would be a darker, richer hue. He suddenly wanted to see Lady Landsdowne blushing, wondered if the flush would travel over every inch of her skin. Did she even have it within her to blush?

"That's obvious, my lord. Otherwise you'd have never shown me any attention. Most men aren't as open-minded. They viewed me as unsuitable before I even attended my first ball."

Telling her the truth, that he'd given her attention because of a damn stallion's seed, was likely to bruise whatever self-esteem she had remaining. He cursed himself, cursed her uncle. He was going to find himself married to the girl if he didn't give up his obsession with being in the company of Lady Landsdowne and begin searching for a replacement suitor in all earnestness. He'd been lax in his endeavors because Gina gave him access to Lady Landsdowne. Would the countess be open to his attentions if he wasn't courting her sister? "I believe gents are coming around. You had a bit more attention at the ball last night."

She batted her eyelashes at him. "Did it make you jealous?"

Not one iota but he couldn't confess that. Before he could respond with some flirtatious harmless comment that neither confirmed nor denied any jealousy on his part, Lady Landsdowne swept into the parlor in a sea of red silk taffeta and satin that stole his breath, his reason, his attention. His vision narrowed until no one else occupied the room. It was only the two of them. He'd thought her beautiful before. At that moment, he realized a new word needed to come into being to describe her because every descriptive word in his vocabulary was insufficient. She was beyond striking, beyond gorgeous.

"Forgive my tardiness," she stated matter-of-factly as though completely unaware of how easily she could mute a man.

He would forgive her tardiness, forgive her anything. He would wait until the end of time for her.

Bloody damned hell! What was wrong with him? She was dressed to seduce. She was a woman who had brought an earl to his knees and then a blasted footman. Who knew how many men had followed? She comprehended what she was about. She was testing him, testing his devotion to her sister. If he wanted the stallion, he was going to have to ignore Lady Landsdowne, imagine her dressed in unflattering widow's weeds. At least for tonight, at least until he turned the girl over to someone else. "Not to worry. The one who holds my interest was here. That's all that matters to me."

The words came out so smoothly that perhaps he should consider the stage. He forced his legs to go in the direction of Gina, smiled at her, and offered his arm. "Shall we be off?"

For a moment, she seemed confused by his attention; then she smiled brightly. "Yes, absolutely. I'm quite looking forward to dinner."

"Dinner is only the beginning," he assured her.

"Oh?"

"It shall be a night for enjoying vices." As he walked past Lady Landsdowne, her lavender and orchid fragrance wrapped around him, and he was keenly aware he wouldn't be indulging in all vices. He already knew insisting she join them was a mistake, and yet he couldn't seem to regret it.

*O*pulence didn't begin to describe the dining room of the Twin Dragons. They'd used a door that allowed them to enter without passing through the gaming floor. When Gina had expressed disappointment at not seeing the more interesting aspects of the club, Rexton had simply laughed and promised her, "In due time."

Tillie didn't like the way his satisfied laughter caused pleasure to ripple through her, as though the sound was for her and her alone when in truth he'd directed it only at her sister. A liveried footman escorted them to a white cloth-covered table in the center of the dining room. That surprised her. She'd expected something a bit more intimate and shadowed where more secretive flirtations could occur, but then with her in tow, he wasn't going to be able to get away with much so perhaps he simply wanted people to see the lovely lady who decorated his arm.

That was the impression she had, anyway. He was showing Gina off like some sort of prize he'd won at a country fair. Which she knew was totally unfair of her. He was doing everything right, behaving properly. She shouldn't find fault with it. And yet, she did.

The gorgeous crystal chandeliers hanging from the vaulted ceiling did not give off much light. A tall candle burned in the center of the table, and she had to look over the flame to see him because he sat opposite her. Gina sat between them. Rexton was turned her sister's way, leaning toward her as though he found her discourse on Jane Austen the most fascinating conversation he'd ever experienced, yet every now and then he slid his eyes toward Tillie and in that second, his gaze shifted from interested to smoldering. She told herself it was an illusion caused by looking at him through the flickering candle flame, and yet the heat that swamped her had nothing at all to do with a burning wick. It had everything to do with the way he could make her feel as though his true interest resided with her.

Then his eyes were back on Gina, and they seemed to cool, as though he were indulging a favorite cousin or sister. Was it just wishful thinking on her part, and why would she wish for his attention? If she could steal him away from Gina, then he wasn't deserving of her sister—but was it worth hurting Gina to determine the truth, even though Gina had asked her to do precisely that?

She'd expected to be a good judge of his character; yet the emotions somersaulting through her only served to confuse her. Taking a sip of the excellent wine he'd procured for them helped calm her nerves and dulled her awareness of those surrounding them.

Suddenly he reached out and moved the candle aside.

"What are you doing?" she asked.

"It obstructs my view, makes it more difficult to include you in the conversation."

"You don't have to include me. All your attention should be on Gina."

"Not tonight. You're here as my guest. It would be rude to ignore you completely."

"I have no objection to your rudeness."

The smile he gave her called her a liar. "But you're judging me, and my suitability. Inclusion would make your job easier. Besides I'm curious. Do you agree with your sister that Mr. Darcy truly exists, that he was in fact a gentleman, a neighbor, whom Miss Austen favored but their love went unrequited?"

"I'm quite surprised you know who Mr. Darcy is. Have you ever read *Pride and Prejudice*?"

"I have. My sister was quite fond of the story when she was younger. The mischievous minx informed me that if I ever wished to win a lady's heart I needed to follow Darcy's example. Being young myself, and of a romantic bent, I was open to searching for the magic potion that would entice ladies to flock to me. I found him to be rather pompous."

He had read a book in order to appeal to ladies? Did he not realize he had a natural charisma that could not be found between leather covers? That no doubt flourished between silk ones. "He is rather . . . prideful. Although he has his reasons, and in the end, he quite charmed Elizabeth, didn't he?"

"But was he based on fact? Was he indeed Austen's unrequited love?"

She glanced over at Gina, whose expression for some unfathomable reason was hopeful. "I suppose it makes the story more appealing to believe he did exist."

"Do you find unrequited love romantic?"

"I find it tragic."

"But I suspect there is a good deal of it," Gina said. "Especially among the aristocracy. Your lot seldom marries for love, do they, my lord?"

He gave her an indulgent grin. "More often than not other considerations are placed above love."

"Will you marry for love?" Tillie asked pointedly.

"Did you?"

The trap had been set, and she'd taken the bait, blast him. "We're not here to discuss me."

"Why not? My mother often says when one marries, one marries into a family. It seems I should know as much about you as I do of Gina."

Gina's eyes rounded, her lips parted slightly, at the hint he might indeed be offering marriage in the very near future. Rexton seemed not to notice as his gaze was homed in on Tillie and she feared he'd witnessed her stomach dropping to the floor with his pronouncement, his possible unintentional admission that he was seriously considering Gina for the role of future marchioness. Of course he was. He wouldn't be courting her otherwise, wouldn't have escorted her to the theater, wouldn't have invited her to dine with him this evening. She didn't know why she and her sister were having such odd reactions: disappointment on her part, surprise on Gina's.

"In considering your decision, my lord, all you need to know about me is that I shall scarcely be in your lives. Once Gina is married, I shall be returning to New York." She would begin her life anew there, leave behind this wretched existence.

Silence stretched between them. It was the only indication that her words had taken him off guard. His features seemed to be set in stone. Nothing moved. Not an eyelash fluttered, not a tick in the muscles below his sharp cheekbones, not a tightening of his chiseled jaw. Finally he leaned back as though coming to some resolution regarding her and directed his attention to Gina. "Were you aware your sister was leaving?"

Lips pressed together, sadness reflected in her eyes, Gina nodded. "Although I don't know why she can't stay here. People tonight don't seem to be glaring at her as much as they did at the theater."

"The glares have nothing to do with it," Tillie lied. They had something to do with it, but not everything. "I've never been happy in this country."

"So you've stayed only for me?"

Leaning across, she squeezed her sister's hand and smiled. "Small sacrifice. As for the people surrounding us at the moment, they probably want to be noticed as little as we do. This is a den of vice after all."

"A respectable den of vice," Rexton pointed out.

She arched a brow at him. "You are aware that respectable and vice don't go together very well."

He grinned, and she wished she didn't take pleasure in being the one responsible for lightening his mood. "You have a point, but there are much worse places where vice occurs, where a man can lose not only his purse but his life."

"Frequent those places do you?"

"Let's just say I'm aware of them. Ah, it seems our main course is arriving."

They'd already enjoyed a vegetable soup as well as crabmeat smothered in a shrimp sauce. The beef tenderloins the waiter placed before her smelled delicious. String beans and potatoes were set on a separate plate beside the first. Tillie wasn't disappointed with her first bite, nor was she surprised when Rexton ordered a second bottle of wine. She didn't usually indulge so much, and it was making her a bit lightheaded, but she was also enjoying the sensation.

"You'll avoid those darker places once you're married, won't you?" Tillie asked casually, not about to let him get away with the simple answer he'd given.

"I suspect there's a good many things I'll avoid once I'm married," he said equally casually.

"Other women?"

He wasn't quite so stony faced this time when he met and held her gaze, but she didn't think he was analyzing how best to answer but rather he was striving to determine what had prompted her question, trying to read something about her into it.

"Tillie," Gina said, clear exasperation in her voice, "I know you have my best interests at heart, but can't we just enjoy the night without putting his lordship through his paces?"

Only then did she realize she was being insufferable. He'd invited them to dinner, was being pleasant—willing to discuss Jane Austen when she suspected he'd rather discuss Mary Shelley—and had already indicated she was to enjoy herself. "My apologies, my lord. I tend to be overprotective where Gina is concerned."

"No apologies needed. I suspect I'd have been the same if I'd been in the country when Lovingdon was courting my sister. I daresay, he and I would have enjoyed a bout or two of fisticuffs."

"Where were you, my lord?" Gina asked before Tillie could.

Once more, he gave her an indulgent smile. "Traveling the continent with my brother."

"I suspect you had a jolly good time together."

"It was memorable."

"Will you share some of your adventures?"

And just like that, Gina carried them away from any conversation that would cause tenseness around them. Tillie couldn't help but think that Rexton was born to weave stories as his deep voice carried them through the canals in Venice, the Sistine Chapel, the Coliseum, vineyards, and the Alps. When she'd come to England at the age of eighteen, she'd considered it a marvelous adventure. She'd traveled to Paris in order to have her gowns made, but she'd never traveled beyond that. He made her yearn to see the world.

He made her long to see the world with him.

*I*t was for the best that she was returning to America after her sister married. *No, the bloody hell it wasn't.* Sipping on his wine, he wondered why he'd even had the thought that he'd prefer her in America. He wasn't courting Gina—even though he'd inadvertently implied several times during the course of the evening he was in serious pursuit of a wife.

And a woman who had been unfaithful to her husband, was divorced, and had insulted the aristocracy by insisting she be addressed by her title was certainly not a contender for the position of Marchioness of Rexton, future Duchess of Greystone. Rexton had too much respect for his family and his heritage to bring such a fallen woman into their midst. But that didn't mean he didn't contemplate bedding her. He did—every second of every moment he was in her company.

"That was lovely," Gina said as she set down her fork after finishing off the chocolate cake she'd requested for dessert. Lady Landsdowne had declined dessert and joined him in a brandy instead. She seemed to enjoy the flavor, and he envisioned her relishing all sorts of dark pleasures. "Everything was delicious."

He wondered if Gina ever complained about anything, if she ever grew angry, if she ever threw a tantrum. She was the most pleasant, docile, accommodating woman he'd ever known. He should be enthralled. He should, as Hammersley implied, decide she was the one for him. She was pretty enough. Bedding her would certainly be no hardship. Yet he could work up no enthusiasm for being in her company, thought he would expire from boredom if he took her to wife. He hated those thoughts, hated that he couldn't treasure her as she deserved to be treasured, wondered if something was inherently wrong with him for finding himself irrevocably drawn to her notorious sister.

Christ, the things he would do with Lady Landsdowne, if given the chance. He would argue with her, he would tease her, he would tickle her. He would chase her, both of them stark naked, through his residence. When he caught her he would kiss her head to toe, front to back. He would take her slowly; he would take her quickly. He could take her gently; he would take her with enough enthusiasm they might break the bed. Hoping none of those thoughts traveled over his features, he finished off his brandy. "I'm glad you enjoyed it. The night is still young. Care for a little gaming?"

"I'd love to give it a try. What say you, Tillie?"

She appeared uncomfortable but then for most of the evening she hadn't been completely relaxed, although the second bottle of wine seemed to have helped some, the brandy more. He wanted to see her when her walls weren't up, when she seemed not to have a care, the way she'd been in the garden before she'd discovered he was watching her.

"I'm not certain that's wise," she said. "We're likely to lose our shirts."

He'd once played a game with a couple of ladies where clothing had been wagered. He wouldn't mind a hand or two with her. He'd play honestly—probably. "I'll put up the blunt."

"Why would you do that?" she asked. "In exchange for what?"

"You are a suspicious wench." He wondered if she'd been so before her marriage. He rather doubted it. "I'll fund you both so you enjoy the night. Say, a hundred pounds each."

"That's rather generous."

"It's more than rather. It's incredibly generous," Gina piped up. "It'll be no hardship for us to pay our own way, however. I don't mean to be vulgar but we both inherited a grand sum when Father passed."

"Shh, Gina," Lady Landsdowne said quietly. "You shouldn't speak of your inheritance."

"Why not?"

"Because it could influence a man into charming you when all he wants is your money."

"My wife's money will remain her own," Rexton said, feeling a need to defend himself. "My father felt the same. My mother brought a fortune with her, and he never touched a penny."

"Your mother was an heiress?" Gina asked.

Shaking his head, he laughed. "No, she was a book-keeper." He waved his hand in a gesture to encompass all that surrounded them. "And a partner in this establishment back when it was known as Dodger's Drawing Room. Vice is a lucrative enterprise. Now, let's go add to their coffers, shall we? As the odds of winning are against us."

He shoved back his chair, stood, and assisted Gina while a footman stepped forward to help Lady Landsdowne. He wished he didn't envy the servant his role.

Gina looked up at him. "I don't know any wagering games, my lord."

"We'll give several things a try until we find something you enjoy."

"I suppose you know every game there is," Lady Landsdowne said.

"And then some." Even though Gina clung to his arm as he led them into the gaming area he was far more aware of Lady Landsdowne walking on the other side of her sister. "Not to worry. You shouldn't get much censure here. Although Drake is very particular about who is granted membership—and they are all upper class—they are a largely tolerant sort."

"Then Downie's membership has been terminated has it?" the countess asked.

Damnation. He'd forgotten about her idiot husband and his friends. "Once people realize you're with me, they won't give you any trouble, even if their allegiance rests with Landsdowne."

Gina came to an abrupt halt. "Perhaps you should escort her in on your arm. I can walk beside her."

That would undermine his plan. In order to spark others' interest in Gina, he had to give the impression that she was his mark. "One on each arm," he suggested. "As we did at the theater."

"I'll be fine," Lady Landsdowne said.

"Must you be so stubborn?" he asked.

"The ladies are the worst and there aren't going to be that many here, are there?"

"There will be some," he assured her.

"*Some* I can handle perfectly fine."

He knew that for the lie it was. She could handle them *all* perfectly fine. She'd been doing it at the theater before he'd come to her aid. He liked that she was strong and relied on herself. But that didn't mean he wouldn't have minded her relying on him just a tad. "Very well. Onward."

As Lady Landsdowne charged ahead he could feel the hesitation in her sister. He leaned down. "Not to worry. I won't allow anyone to disparage her."

"Thank you, my lord. She puts on a brave front and would go through hell for me. I just wish I could make things easier for her."

"We must all live with our decisions, Miss Ham-mersley."

"Even when they're forced on us, my lord?"

"Even then."

Still he was left to wonder if Lady Landsdowne would have made different choices had she been his wife.

*I*n the end, Rexton insisted that their first foray into gambling be on him. He made the offer at the roulette table in such a manner that it would have been ungracious for Tillie to argue against it, especially as several people were eyeing them with curiosity. It took her only a few minutes to determine there was no point to the game other than to hand over money. Whether she placed her chips on a number, a color, or a line, she always seemed to get it wrong.

Gina had a bit more luck, was very vocal with her wins, squealing her pleasure. When she lost, she simply said, "Next time." And went about putting down more chips.

Naturally, Rexton was guiding her sister as though he knew a secret about the wheel, as though he could look at it and determine where the little ball would land long before the wheel was spun. He'd offered to assist her, but she'd pointedly declined. She didn't want his gloved hand closing around hers and leading it to the numbers. She didn't want him whispering his magic into her ear. She didn't want him so near that his earthy fragrance drowned out all the other smells. She didn't want him drawing her attentions when she was striving to get a better sense of the place.

He, however, seemed incapable of not leaning in

and saying in a low voice, "If you believe you'll lose, you'll lose."

"Are you insinuating my mind controls the ball?"

"I'm saying there is more to gambling than simply placing a bet."

"I suspect everyone at this table believes they'll win."

"And they will." He rocked his head from side to side. "Now and then."

"Yet I've failed to even once."

"Because you don't believe at all, because you don't want to be here."

"This game requires no skill," she said defensively, trying not to take it personally because she had yet to experience the thrill of a win.

"Perhaps you would prefer cards. There are several games. Some require more skill than others. We could start with one that requires only being able to count to twenty-one."

She wished he wasn't so close that looking into the blue of his eyes was like swimming in a vast ocean, one in which she could so easily drown and not care. He needed to return his attention to Gina. An insult should work. "I suspect you cheat at cards."

His devil-may-care grin left her wanting to feel it pressed against the pulse at her throat. "Depends whom I'm playing."

So much for causing him to lose his patience with her. He leaned in nearer, those luscious lips brushing against her ear, his voice a low intimate hum. "When I play against Landsdowne, I take him for every far-thing he has."

Pulling back quickly, she stared into his eyes, searching for the truth of his words. It was there, clear and concise, but somber as though he'd done it as a means of defending her honor, as though he were aware that her husband had brought her as much dishonor as she'd brought herself. Only he couldn't know that. He couldn't know the truth of her circumstances, the reality of the farce her marriage had been.

She wanted to look away; she needed to look away. Instead she wondered how he would react if she rose up on her toes, wound her arms around his neck, and kissed him. Would he be horrified, would he push her away, would he proclaim his undying devotion to Gina?

The truth was she wouldn't be kissing him as a test of his loyalty to Gina. She would be kissing him because she selfishly wanted to experience passion, and she was rather certain that Rexton could deliver it in spades. Without guile, she licked her tingling lips. His eyes darkened. And she had the titillating notion that he might snatch her up and plant his mouth on hers. Gina would be mortified, her Season ruined. A woman publicly scorned.

It was hellish enough to be scorned in private, behind closed doors, but to be so in public would be a humiliation from which her sister might never recover. Not to mention that being kissed in a gaming hell beside a roulette wheel was not going to bring Tillie any closer to redemption. No matter that ladies were probably often kissed within this establishment. Wickedness thrived here. It was the reason people came.

"Can you direct me to the necessary room?" she asked, her voice strangely steady as though she'd somehow managed to disconnect it from the remainder of her quivering body.

He blinked, seeming to emerge from some sort of spell. Was Gina correct? Could Tillie lure him away from her sister's side? Did she want to? Turning slightly, he pointed. "That hallway leads to a host of rooms for ladies only. I suspect you'll find it there."

"Thank you." She eased around him. "Gina, I'm going to the necessary room. Would you care to join me?"

Her sister didn't take her gaze off the spinning wheel as she shook her head. "Not while I'm winning. I don't want to change my luck."

"I won't be long."

Without looking back, Gina lifted her hand, waved her fingers. "Take all the time you need."

If she took all the time she needed, she'd be gone until dawn. As she walked away, she could feel his gaze on her, wondered why it was she seemed unable to escape her awareness of him. Just knowing he was in the same building as she was enough to have her nerve endings rioting. It was bothersome.

She forced herself to concentrate on her surroundings. The crystal chandeliers hanging from the vaulted ceiling. The various gaming tables. She considered stopping to observe the play at each one as each game was unfamiliar to her. She was rather certain she could figure out the generalities but it would be so much more pleasant to have Rexton whispering the rules in her ear. The man's deep, husky voice could make the most mundane tantalizing. And here she was thinking about him again. At least her nerves had settled a bit, so he'd no doubt taken his gaze off her.

She was surprised that few gave her a passing glance, and those who did proceeded to do little more than raise an eyebrow. Perhaps she should have considered that here where sin ruled, she'd be more welcomed. Seeing so many people smiling, laughing, enjoying each other's company brought home exactly how lonely she'd been for so very long. Her friends had abandoned her. Her acquaintances had crucified her. She'd been the fodder for gossip and disdain. Only Gina had remained loyal. Her sister deserved a special sort of happiness, and Tillie suspected Rexton could provide it. She needed to be more open to the possibility of his becoming her brother by marriage. Needed to put her own biases aside. As well as her lust-filled musings. No doubt her interest in him was simply because he was the first man of any consequence to spend time in her company.

Perhaps she should consider visiting the notorious Nightingale Club where ladies of quality could find a well-heeled gentleman to keep them company for the night. It would be something to consider. It might do something to settle her body's heightened sensitivity. Although she'd never found it particularly enjoyable to suffer through a man's groping. Perhaps it was simply better to endure the shame and guilt of seeing to her own needs. A private affair with herself would certainly remain secret.

Shaking her head at so ludicrous a notion, she entered the corridor where the lighting was a bit dimmer. Never before had she spent so much time considering the various aspects of bedding. Oh, before she'd married, she'd certainly contemplated the act, speculated about everything that might be involved. Her wedding night had done little more than dull her enthusiasm for mating rituals. Making love was certainly an inappropriate description for what occurred in the marriage bed. Downie—

"Well, if it's not the notorious heiress."

Spinning around at the ominously delivered words, she found herself facing one of Downie's most trusted friends, hatred and disgust burning in his eyes. "Lord Evanston, it was my understanding this area was reserved for ladies."

"But then you're not a lady, are you? You're a *whore.* As such, you should be treated as one." He took a menacing step forward.

She couldn't rush past him, so she turned, hiked up her skirts, and ran.

*C*hrist, he was failing his mission. Instead of implying with word and deed that he was infatuated with Gina, he was constantly giving attention to her sister. The temptation of her was something he'd never before experienced. He was drawn to women, but he'd never been obsessed with wondering how they might taste or feel or sound when passion took hold, rolled through them, conquered them. He was strung so tightly, was so distracted that if he sat down to play cards, he'd probably lose every hand. He'd not be able to count the cards, to determine what remained to be played. Fortunately, Gina was not becoming bored with roulette. Probably because she was having a string of wins. If he didn't know it was impossible to influence the wheel, he'd think she'd figured out a way to cheat.

Glancing over his shoulder, he looked at the hallway into which Lady Landsdowne had disappeared. He probably should have found a woman to accompany her, to assure she found her way. When Drake had opened the club up to women nearly a decade earlier, he'd introduced the renovated place to London with a night where the entire establishment could be viewed by either gender. Rexton had been curious about what the private areas for only the women offered. He recalled a room for cards, a library with spirits, a chamber mostly made up of fainting couches. But those rooms were accessed via a corridor that veered off from the main hallway. Might she get lost in the warren?

"Is something amiss, my lord?"

He looked back at Gina, her brow pleated with fine lines. He was no doubt worrying for naught, but he couldn't seem to shake off the unsettling thought that she'd been absent too long. He'd seen the disgust at the opera. He'd noticed less of it here, but then those within these walls were often skilled at not showing what they felt—the ability to hide one's feelings and thoughts came in handy when playing cards. "I'm going to go make sure your sister's all right."

Her brow furrowed more deeply. "She's in an area where only ladies are allowed. Should I go?"

As though this slight girl could fend off someone if trouble were afoot. Although what sort of trouble could Lady Landsdowne get into? A lady pulling on her hair perhaps? On the other hand, he had run into some vicious women on occasion. And there had been the incident in the hallway at the theater. "No, I'll see to it. Don't leave this spot."

"I won't."

With a nod, he turned on his heel and strode quickly and with purpose to the corridor. As he traversed it, he remember it was a jagged journey to a door that opened to the outside so women could come and go as they pleased if they wished to retain a bit of discretion when it came to vices they might enjoy. Men would never see them, learn of their visits. Not unless they ventured into the areas where both genders mingled.

He came to the split in the passageway and was about to turn down the one that led to the chambers when he heard a struggle coming from the opposite direction. His heart leaped in his chest. He took off at a dead run. Even if it wasn't Lady Landsdowne, someone was in trouble. When he careened around a corner, he saw that it was indeed the lady for whom he was searching.

She was pressed against a wall, her arms behind her, no doubt shackled at the wrist by the tall, broad man's powerful hand, his other large hand cupping her chin, holding her face tilted toward his mouth as he tried to connect it with hers while she moved her head as much as she was able to avoid him. She was attempting to kick him, to break free, but her heavy skirts were hampering her movements. Yet still she fought.

And Rexton saw red, crimson, scarlet.

Mine roared through his head or maybe it even roared out of his mouth because the man looked back over his shoulder. Evanston. Rexton grabbed a handful of clothing near the lord's throat, tore him away from Lady Landsdowne, and directed three hard, quick jabs into Evanston's face. He was aware of the popping and snapping of cartilage and bone, the spurting of blood before he threw the man, whimpering and groaning, to the floor.

"Get the bloody hell out of here before I kill you." His voice was low, shimmering with restrained violence.

Evanston didn't argue. He merely scrambled to his feet and, holding both hands over his face, ran.

"Coward," Rexton spat after him. He turned to Tillie. He couldn't think of her as Lady Landsdowne at that moment because there was no sign of the haughty, prideful woman who had greeted him that first afternoon at Landsdowne Court. All he saw was her vulnerability, her wide frightened eyes, her chest heaving with her labored breathing. "Are you all right?" He shook his head before she could answer. "No, of course you're not. Are you hurt?"

She blinked at him. He could see her trembling. "Are you hurt?" he repeated a bit more gently.

"You . . . you . . . hit him. Three times."

"I'd have hit him more but touching him was beginning to make my skin crawl. Did he harm you?"

Tears began to well in her eyes. "You didn't think I deserved it, for being an unfaithful wench?"

"A man pawing at you? No woman deserves that, regardless of her behavior." He tore off his glove and tenderly cradled her cheek. "Do you have pain anywhere?"

Slowly she shook her head. "No. I just . . . I couldn't push him away."

"He's a big lummox, but you shouldn't have had to. He shouldn't have been anywhere near you."

The tears that had been hovering vanished. She took a deep breath, once, twice, three times. He couldn't seem to help himself: he skimmed his thumb over her silky cheek, all the while watching the movement, mesmerized by it as though he'd never before touched a woman. What was it about her that made her so different?

"Why are you here?" she asked, bringing him back to the present, to the situation. He lowered his hand.

"I was concerned. You were gone too long."

"So you left Gina alone?" Her obvious displeasure irked.

"I left her in the company of others. She'll be fine." He noticed the rip in her gown then, and the anger rose up anew. He should have hit Evanston at least three more times. "You not so much. Your gown is torn. You can't return to the main area looking like that. I'll see you to one of the ladies' lounges, then fetch Gina. We'll go out through this door."

She rolled back her shoulders, angled her chin, and somehow managed to look down her nose at him. "I can find the lounge myself. You need to return to my sister's side."

The haughty Lady Landsdowne had returned. Damn it all. Why the hell did her actions make him want to kiss her all the more? "Ah, bugger it."

Once more he cradled her cheek, only this time he lowered his mouth to hers, relishing the plumpness of her lower lip, the taste of brandy—

She shoved on his shoulders, and he reluctantly relented, taking two steps back.

"What are you doing?" she demanded.

"Giving into temptation and kissing you, obviously."

She narrowed her eyes, her lips tightening with disgust. "You're like all the others, no loyalty, no allegiance. Naught but lies, deception, and false devotion."

He didn't much like being bundled with such an

unfavorable lot, liked even less acknowledging that she was well within her right to find fault with him. He was no better than the other two men he'd witnessed with her. "Accept my profuse apologies. I have no excuse for my behavior except to admit that I have been drawn to you from the moment you walked into your parlor and offered me whisky."

She appeared even more horrified. "Yet you continued to call upon my sister? You are the worst sort of blackguard. Your courtship of my sister has come to an end. We'll find a hackney and make our own way home."

She brushed by him with righteous indignation. He didn't blame her, and he knew the next words probably weren't going to gain any favor with her, but still he grabbed her arm. She swung around, her fist landing with a wallop on his shoulder that he rightfully deserved.

"I'm not courting your sister."

Jerking her arm free of his hold, she glared at him. "I beg your pardon?"

He heaved a frustrated sigh. "I was never courting her, not seriously. Your uncle asked me to give her attention because he thought it would cause the other lords to take an interest in her."

With her hands fisted at her sides, she took a step toward him, and he, for some inexplicable reason, felt compelled to take a step back. Perhaps it was the fury burning in her eyes. "Do you have any idea what this is going to do to her? She thinks you're her knight in shining armor. She waxes on about your looks, your virtues, your kindness as though you are a god." She punched him again. "You bastard! You will shatter her heart, and I will be left to pick up the pieces." She hit him again. "You're despicable!"

"I wasn't giving her that much attention," he offered ineffectually in his own defense.

"Why give her any at all? What did my uncle promise you?"

It seemed rather trite when compared with the possibility of shattering a girl's heart, and yet he'd gone this far in revealing himself for the scoundrel he was. No sense in holding back now. "Black Diamond for stud."

Her ugly and hideous scoff echoed with retribution. "I can promise you that you will never damned well get that. You will fetch Gina from the gaming room, you will escort us home, and once there you will tell her the truth of your dastardly deceit." She spun on her heel and began marching away from him.

"Where are you going?"

She swung back around. "To find a room where I can wait for you. You are correct. I can't go out onto the gaming floor with a ripped bodice." She shook her head, and he could make out tears welling in her eyes again. "Damn you!"

Watching as she stormed away from him, he knew she was right. He was a complete and utter ass. His confession had caused him to lose any chance of obtaining Black Diamond for stud.

But more, he feared it had cost him Lady Landsdowne.

Chapter 7

*R*exton had never been more disgusted with himself. While he'd questioned his fake courtship of Gina, Lady Landsdowne had managed to drive home the possible damaging consequences of what he was doing. It had never been his intent to cause Gina any hurt. He'd convinced himself that finding the proper gentleman for her would absolve him of any wrongdoing. It had helped matters because she'd not seemed particularly besotted with him.

He had to face the reality he'd behaved badly and that behavior had put Lady Landsdowne beyond reach. Not that he had a clear idea regarding what their relationship might have been had he caught her. Her reputation coupled with her desire to return to America indicated anything between them would be short-lived. Although now it wouldn't exist at all.

As Rexton approached the roulette table, he noticed Andrew standing beside Gina, talking, laughing, pointing to where she should place her bets. She seemed to be having a jolly good time, and he loathed himself because he was going to ruin her evening.

"Andrew," he said quietly, placing his hand on his brother's shoulder.

"Rex." Andrew stepped back, giving him room to get nearer to Gina. "I was just giving Miss Hammersley some tips on wagering."

"Lord Andrew is ever so clever," she said, smiling brightly. "He always seems to win."

Especially with the ladies. He wasn't very discreet with his affairs. Rexton grinned at the chips stacked in front of her. "You seem to have done well for yourself while I was away."

"I'm having a marvelous time." She glanced past him, furrowed her brow. "Where's Tillie?"

"Resting in one of the parlors." He leaned down and whispered, "I wondered if you might like to see something that very few have: a view of the gaming floor from the balcony."

She looked over her shoulder and up, a smile spreading across her face, before she turned back to him, her eyes sparkling like emeralds. "You can get me up there?"

"There are benefits to being related to the owner."

"What about my winnings?"

He signaled to a young man dressed in livery. "Collect Miss Hammersley's winnings. I'll pick them up later."

"Yes, m'lord."

Rexton stepped back, indicating she should follow.

She touched Andrew's arm. "Once again, my lord, thank you for keeping me company while your brother was seeing to other matters."

He lifted her hand, placed a kiss on her gloved knuckles. "Once again, Miss Hammersley, it was my pleasure."

Andrew was an incredible flirt. Rexton might consider him a possible suitor for Gina if his brother hadn't vowed quite emphatically and on numerous occasions to never marry.

"Good night, all!" she chirped, waving at the others gathered around the table. He wondered if any of the other gents in attendance might take an interest in courting her. Strange how he took no satisfaction in the thought. He'd wanted to find someone who would appreciate her.

After offering his arm, he led her away from the roulette wheel.

"Should we see if Tillie wants to join us?" she asked as they strolled around various tables.

"I'd prefer to have a few moments alone with you." If she had pinned her hopes on him as her sister indicated, he wanted to break the news to her gently while giving her a special memory so she might think less harshly of him.

"It sounds as though I might be in want of a chaperone, that my reputation might be at risk."

To his surprise, she wasn't teasing, but appeared a bit worried. "The people here don't usually worry about chaperones, and I assure you that I intend to be a perfect gentleman."

"I don't know whether to be grateful or disappointed." She fluttered her lashes at him teasingly. He was a fool not to be taken in by her amusing mien and lightheartedness. Not bothering to respond, he removed a key from his pocket and used it to unlock the door that led to the offices and some private rooms where the games involved a great deal of money exchanging hands. She preceded him into the darkened hallway.

"I suspect people get up to some mischief here," she whispered.

"They can. This way." He led her to a set of stairs where the shadows were thicker. He had the ungentlemanly thought that if he brought Lady Landsdowne here, he'd be taking advantage, his heart would be speeding up with anticipation as they ascended the stairs, his skin would be tingling with desire as he pulled back a curtain and directed her onto the balcony, his entire body would be thrumming with need as he stood behind her and watched as she leaned over to gaze on the floor below.

What a silly girl she was to come here with a man alone, to not realize she was at his mercy. He had an urge to shake her and warn her that she was taking a risk, that she should never allow a man to get her alone. At the very least a man was going to steal a kiss. He might even ruin her.

The women with whom he kept company had nothing to lose. This sweet, innocent lass had everything to lose. He didn't know whether to explain the ways of men to her before or after he bruised her heart.

"You can see everything, everyone, from here," she said in wonder. "If I owned this establishment, I believe I'd spend a great deal of my time up here, just looking out over my domain as though I were some emperor or something."

"Drake Darling does just that. As did the owner before him."

She swung around, leaned back against the waist-high wall, and held his gaze with a challenge that surprised him. "But I don't think you really brought me up here so I could look out over the floor."

Perhaps she wasn't quite as obtuse regarding the dangers as he'd surmised. "No. That wasn't my purpose in secreting you away." He'd expected if he gave her something most people never saw, it would ease his guilt. It didn't.

Crossing her arms over her chest, she arched an eyebrow. "If you try something untoward, I will scream."

He couldn't seem to stop himself from grinning. "I'm not going to try something untoward." Taking a deep breath, he slowly released it. "Miss Hammersley—"

"Gina," she interrupted, no doubt wanting to remind him that their relationship had moved beyond the formal, that they were in a courtship where things could be a bit less proper between them. Only they weren't in a courtship. She just didn't know it yet. Perhaps he should have waited until he'd returned her to her residence but up here everything seemed less stark.

"Gina." Where to go from there? He was unaccustomed to struggling to find the correct words when he was with a lady. But then he'd never been dishonest before. He hated himself at that moment. "You are a lovely girl." He should simply tell her that he was a cad. "Pretty, charming . . . amiable . . . delightful . . . witty . . . funny . . ." *What else?*

"Are you going to list every adjective in your vocabulary?"

If need be to soften the blow. "I want you to understand, to know, I find you remarkable."

"But we do not suit."

The air rushed out of him. She stated it as fact, without even a modicum of disappointment reflected in her tone. "You mustn't take it personally."

"Oh, I don't. Not at all. I'm thrilled you're drawn to Tillie."

If he were standing where she was, he might have fallen over the ledge and onto the floor below. "I beg your pardon?"

With a laugh, she pointed at her face with her middle and forefinger. "I have eyes, my lord. And they work rather well. It was quite obvious that day in the park you were far more interested in Tillie than you were in me. To be quite honest, I was rather relieved as I knew when we were introduced that your courtship would lead nowhere."

He stared at her. No woman had ever rejected him. No woman had ever failed to be attracted to him. "I don't understand. I'm not an ogre. I'm titled. One day I'll be a duke. My coffers overflow. I—"

"You come with some wonderful traits, my lord, but you don't make my heart sing." She smiled brightly. "But it is funny you're striving to convince me now that I should want you when you're trying to tell me you don't want me."

"It's not that I don't want you. It's that—"

"You want Tillie."

He cleared his throat. "I might have an interest in your sister but . . . what are your objections to me?"

"For one thing, you are so old. You must be at least a decade older than I."

She had a point. Had he not possessed a similar thought when he met her? "What gave away my interest in your sister?"

"The way you look at her. The heat in your eyes. My God, on more than one occasion, I thought you might burst into flames." She gave him a gamine smile. "I am not as ignorant or uninformed in the ways of men as Tillie would believe."

He narrowed his eyes. "Yet you continued to accept my invitations."

She nodded quickly. "Yes, so you could spend time in her company. That is why you asked me, isn't it? Although I don't quite understand why you continued to pretend to be courting me once you met her. I suppose because Society doesn't accept her. You can still pretend to court me if you like."

How exceedingly generous of her. Moving forward, he leaned down, folded his arms over the railing, and gazed out. "That would be unfair to you. You may have caught the eye of a few gents over the course of our time together."

"But Tillie is so lonely, so miserable here." She moaned softly. "I suppose my marrying is the kindest thing I can do for her."

Then England would be rid of her. He'd be rid of her. Glancing over his shoulder, he could see the seriousness in Gina's expression. "She wouldn't want you to fall on your sword for her."

He knew that. Unequivocally. She would not have others make sacrifices for her. Strange how he found himself contemplating everything he might be willing to give up for her. As though he had any hope of her returning his interest after what he'd done.

She gave a wistful sigh. "Sometimes things are so complicated. I didn't notice people glaring at her, but I suppose some were. I suppose that's why she sought solace away from the main salon."

Where these two sisters were concerned, he seemed to be taking all sorts of missteps. "Actually, her bodice got torn."

Her head gave a little bob as though the words were foreign to her. "How the devil did that happen? A hem I can understand, but a bodice?"

"Lord Evanston managed to corner her and take some liberties. I was able to stop him before things went too far." Although they'd gone further than they should have. The man never should have touched her.

"The beast!" She slammed her fist into his shoulder. What was it with these American women smacking men about? "Why didn't you tell me immediately?"

"She's unharmed—"

"She's not, and you're a dunderhead if you think any woman would be after having her gown torn by any man at all. Take me to her at once."

Spinning around, she was marching away before he realized her intentions. He rushed to catch up. Lady Landsdowne had seemed so strong, so in control, he hadn't considered she was more shaken than she appeared. Blast it. He should have stayed to comfort her, to offer a shoulder. The thought of her somewhere in tears had his chest tightening. She might be done with him, but he wasn't yet ready to be done with her.

*S*he found a room populated with fainting couches. Fortunately no one was there to disturb her as she settled onto one of the plush lounges. Her trembling began anew, and not because she was reliving her encounter with Evanston but rather she was thinking about the kiss that Rexton had bestowed—or had begun to bestow before she'd shoved him away.

She'd almost given into it, welcomed it, parted her lips to give him full access to her mouth but she'd remembered Gina . . . she couldn't betray her sister in such a vile manner. Then when he'd confessed he hadn't been courting Gina at all—his behavior was reprehensible. All because he wanted access to a horse's cock.

Tears threatened; she buried her face in her hands. Tears because of the horror she'd endured in the hallway, the yearning that Rexton instilled in her, the heartbreak he was going to bring to Gina. She should have gone to fetch her sister—her torn gown be damned. If he hurt Gina's tender feelings before Tillie was close enough to comfort her sister, she was going to make him pay in ways he couldn't imagine. In ways she couldn't imagine if she was honest about it because she truly didn't know how to go about getting even with him. It had been different with Downie. She'd known his excessive pride was his weakness. She had yet to determine any weaknesses on Rexton's part—other than his desire to possess Black Diamond.

"Are you all right?"

At the softly spoken question, Tillie jerked her gaze up to find two ladies who looked remarkably alike staring at her with identical furrowed brows. Their hair was a blond, paler than any she'd ever seen, almost white. Their blue eyes showed true concern. Tillie nodded. "I'm fine, thank you."

"You've torn your lovely gown," one of them said as she settled on the lounge, her hip nearly touching Tillie's. "And you have a scratch on your shoulder. What happened?"

Her eyes held Tillie's in an almost trancelike state.

She wanted to lie, make an excuse, tell them to go away. Instead she heard herself say, "I was accosted."

"Who was the gentleman?" the woman asked with insistence and a tightening of her features.

"If he accosted her then he was no gentleman now, was he?" the other asked. "Who was the damned bastard? We'll have him routed out and—"

"Lord Rexton already saw to him. Quite satisfactorily if I'm honest."

"Beat him to a bloody pulp, did he?" she asked with a twinkle in her eye.

"Close enough."

She tilted her head, studied Tillie shrewdly. "If Rex is coming to your defense then you must be Lady Landsdowne. I've heard he's been keeping company with the notorious heiress."

"Actually he's been keeping company with—" She stopped. Gina was going to be mortified that people had noticed him courting her. And then to be tossed over. She couldn't allow that to happen. The man was going to have to continue to court her sister until someone else was willing to step up to the role.

"With?" the woman prodded.

"My sister. I've simply been serving as chaperone."

"Would you like my sister to mend your frock?" the one sitting beside her offered. "She always carries around her sewing kit for emergencies."

"Indeed I do," she said as she began riffling through her reticule.

"I couldn't trouble you."

"Oh, it's no trouble." She held up a small leather case. "I'm very skilled. Move aside, Scout." As she replaced her sister, she said, "I'm Skye, by the way."

"You have correctly discerned who I am, but you must call me Tillie." She didn't know why at that moment she didn't want to be associated with Downie at all.

"It's a very lovely gown," Skye said. "When I'm done here, you'll be able to wear it again as no one will be able to tell that anything was ever amiss."

She couldn't see herself wearing it. Too many memories associated with it. All the inappropriate thoughts she'd had regarding Rexton. How she'd begun to think he was a different sort of man, one worthy of Gina—one worthy of herself. She'd started to like him, to have hope that he could prove not all men were beasts.

A shiver went through her as she remembered Evanston grabbing her, clawing at her.

"Don't think about what happened," Skye said kindly, and Tillie realized she probably felt the shudder go through her.

"However, if you'd care to give us the name," Scout said, "our brother is a constable. He likes nothing better than bashing heads."

"Not while he's on duty, naturally," Skye added. "But on occasion, he and Rexton make the rounds through Whitechapel, warding off ne'er-do-wells."

That explained the speed and ferocity with which his fist had made contact with Evanston's face. "They roam the streets, looking for trouble?"

"Not looking so much as not running off when it crosses their path."

"They've a bit of the uncivilized in them," Scout said.

Rexton certainly seemed uncivilized when he let

his fist fly—and when he'd taken her mouth. She did wish she wouldn't grow warm with the reminder of how soft but talented his lips had seemed during the short time they were upon hers.

"Well, if it's not the Swindler twins."

Tillie jerked her attention to the door, not at all pleased with the momentary gladness that swept through her at the sight of Rexton. She was angry with him, and yet his presence was a welcomed relief.

"Oh, Tillie!" Gina rushed past him and fell at her feet, with a swath of skirts circling her, and took Tillie's hand. "I heard what happened. Are you all right?"

"No worse for wear."

"Hello, Rex," Scout and Skye said in unison. Obviously their relationship with Rexton was more intimate than she'd realized if they addressed him so informally. She didn't like that she wondered exactly how intimate they might have been.

"What sort of mischief are you getting into now?" he asked.

"Just mending a frock," Skye said, patting Tillie's shoulder before moving away. Gina immediately replaced her, squeezing Tillie's hand in reassurance.

"It was our pleasure to meet you," Scout said.

"I appreciate your assistance," Tillie told them.

"We're sorry the assistance was needed," Skye said. "Rest assured Drake Darling will not be at all happy there was an incident. Are you sure you don't want to tell us who the fellow was?"

"I'm taking care of the matter," Rexton said.

"I rather thought so," Scout said. "I just wanted confirmation."

"You could have asked me."

"But it's so much more fun to vex you."

Yes, they certainly were more familiar with him than Tillie had thought. As they were leaving, they stopped and said something to Rexton which made him laugh easily. She wondered at the exact nature of their relationship, diligently fought back the envy that wanted to raise its ugly head. The two ladies quit the room, and Tillie took some unwanted and unwarranted consolation in the fact he didn't watch them go, but rather returned his focus to her with an intensity that implied she'd never not been the object of his attention.

"Shall we be away from this place?" he asked quietly.

"Yes, let's," Gina said, jumping to her feet before plopping back onto the lounge. "If you're up to it. We can wait a bit longer so you can recover."

"I'm perfectly fine." To prove her point, she rose to her feet. He stepped nearer as though to assist, and she held up a hand. "I don't require your support."

If she didn't know better, judging by the sorrow that crossed his features, she'd have thought she lanced his heart. "Let's be off then," he said quietly.

He didn't offer Gina his arm, and Tillie might have chastised him for it, but she saw no point in making him give her sister more reasons to believe he favored her. Not that Gina was likely to give up her stranglehold on Tillie's hand. He escorted them to the door, swung it open, and led them onto the street.

A gentleman decked out in the Dragons' livery stood there. Rexton spoke to him, and the man dashed off.

"He'll fetch our carriage," Rexton told them, his gaze wandering over her in search of evidence that she'd spoken false regarding her well-being.

"You seem awfully tense for someone who claims to be unharmed," Gina said.

"It'll be explained when we get home."

"Has it anything to do with the fact Rexton isn't courting me?"

She jerked her attention to Gina. "You know?"

She nodded. "He told me before we came for you. I'm all right with it, Tillie. To be honest, I figured out rather early on that his interest is in you."

"He has no interest in me."

"But he does. Ask him."

She was going to do no such thing. "I have no interest in a man who would show such blatant disregard for a young lady's feelings all for want of a horse."

"A horse? Which horse?"

"Did he not tell you?"

"I thought to spare her feelings with the particulars," he said, irritation lacing his voice. Why was he irritated? It was Gina who had been wronged—and Tillie as well for believing him to be better than he was.

"Black Diamond," Tillie said curtly, holding Rexton's gaze.

"But you love Black Diamond. Why would you part with your favorite horse?"

"I wouldn't, but Uncle promised him to the marquess for stud."

"Wait." Rexton stepped forward. "Black Diamond belongs to you?"

Tossing back her head as her stallion often did, she

angled her chin haughtily. "Now you know why you shall never *ever* have him."

$\mathscr{A}$s the coach rattled through the late night streets, Rexton was of a mind to pay Garrett Hammersley a visit. Surely the bargain had been made in good faith, and he'd have convinced his niece to honor its terms. Although now it was a moot point, but had he known the truth, he'd have been more honest in his dealings with Lady Landsdowne from the beginning. He'd have at least ensured she understood and agreed with the role he'd assumed in her sister's life. Instead he'd honored Garrett's request to keep the arrangement between the gentlemen. He'd assumed Lady Landsdowne would not approve of the plan and would tell Gina—which would have nullified the pact.

The interior of the coach was thick with silence, interrupted occasionally when Gina patted her sister's hand in reassurance.

"I feel fairly certain we should all be able to remain friends," Gina said quite naïvely, but then she didn't know about the kiss he'd attempted to steal in the hallway shadows.

That she'd seen through to his interest in Lady Landsdowne was a bit unsettling. The countess had given no indication she was aware of it. The kiss had seemed to take her by surprise. For the briefest span of time, he'd thought she was going to return his kiss with equal fervor—but the fervor she'd unleashed had been a fury he couldn't help but admire. She'd been worried about her sister. Always Gina came first. He wondered if Lady Landsdowne ever put her own wants and desires ahead of anyone else's. She'd married a titled gentleman because her mother had wished it. When was the last time her own wishes had been fulfilled?

"Friends are not dishonest with one another," she said sharply, and he imagined her striding through a classroom with a ruler in hand, ever ready to rap knuckles. Assumed she'd gladly rap his at the moment.

He'd hold out his hand to her if she asked. He'd thought he'd be able to control the situation, the girl's emotions, what she felt toward him. No doubt because he'd always been able to control his own emotions. Except where Lady Landsdowne was concerned. From the moment she strode into the parlor, he'd felt like a train that had skidded off the tracks and lost sight of its destination. It had never occurred to him Gina would develop a tender regard for him when he wasn't developing one for her. He'd known that feelings and their intensity weren't always reciprocated in kind, but until this evening, he'd never experienced the full measure of the knowledge.

"It seems Uncle is more to blame for putting his Lordship up to it," Gina said in his defense. It didn't make him feel any better that this sprite of a girl was defending his abhorrent behavior.

"If a man comes up with a plan to rob someone, and another gent offers to help, they are equally guilty of the crime."

"That's a drastic analogy there. What were we thieving?" he asked.

"My stallion. Gina's innocence."

"I wasn't going to take her innocence."

"You led her to believe you had an interest in her—"

"But I never followed him down the path," Gina said. "No harm was done."

"The absence of harm does not make it right. I shall be speaking with Uncle on the morrow."

Rex would love to be a fly on that wall, to watch her deliver a set down in all her glorious fury. "Perhaps we should speak with him together since he made an offer that in all likelihood he might not have been able to deliver."

"I can promise you it would not have been delivered."

"Why the deuce allow everyone to believe he owned the horse?"

"Because I am so reviled. I feared for the stallion, feared someone might seek to harm him."

He heard the truth in her tone. And the pain. The words sliced into him as though she'd delivered them using the finely honed edge of a knife. He'd thought he had an understanding of her life, of what she suffered. He realized he hadn't a clue. Gazing out the window, he wondered if she might have had an easier time of it if she'd simply poisoned Landsdowne in order to be rid of him.

The carriage rolled to a stop. The door opened. He leaped out and then reached back for her. She turned her nose up as though he'd offered her offal. With an understanding sigh, he stepped back and allowed the footman to assist the ladies in exiting his carriage.

Gina gave him a sympathetic smile before rushing to catch up with her sister who was marching up the steps. Rexton took them two at a time.

"I truly meant no harm." They both swung around to face him, one smiling, one glowering. "It was my intent to help Miss Hammersley find the most compatible suitor available for her. I'd not have shackled her with some miscreant."

"We can do without that sort of help," Lady Landsdowne said tartly before turning sharply for the door.

"I'm sorry things didn't work out, my lord," Gina said softly.

"You will find someone worthy of you."

"I wish the same for you."

"To be honest, Miss Hammersley, I am not searching."

"Pity."

"Gina!" Lady Landsdowne called from the doorway. "We must abed."

Damnation, the last thing he wanted in his head was an image of her preparing for bed, crawling between the sheets. Still, he waited until Gina was safely inside and the door slammed shut.

He dashed down the steps. When he reached his carriage, he shouted up to the driver, "To Whitechapel!"

He wasn't in the mood for civilization this night. He wanted hard drink, debauchery, and decadence.

He bounded into the carriage and found himself surrounded by lavender and orchids. He cursed soundly. Why hadn't he been honest with Lady Landsdowne from the beginning, when his first glimpse of her knocked the breath out of him?

*H*e awoke with his skull threatening to split in two and his body aching. Never before had he slept on such an uncomfortable bed. He smelled coffee. Nectar of the gods. He needed some. Then perhaps the sledgehammers pounding his brain would still.

Forcing open one eye, he found himself staring at a

pair of black boots, well worn, but polished to a sheen. What were they doing standing upright on the bed?

As he opened his other eye, his view expanded and he realized they weren't on the bed. They were on the floor.

And so was he.

Bloody damned hell.

With a groan, he slowly pushed himself up. His head protested, his stomach roiled.

"It awakes," the wearer of the boots, sitting in a nearby chair, called out.

Rexton held up a hand. "Don't yell."

Jamie had the audacity to laugh, which only made matters worse. "I didn't. Shall I whisper?" he asked in a lower voice.

"Please," Rexton croaked. Then he curled and uncurled his fingers over and over. "Coffee."

Jamie handed over the mug. Rexton put the clay to his lips, grimaced, and gingerly touched his fingers to the swollen and tender corner of his mouth. Lovely. He drank slowly, cautiously. He'd never felt so ill in his life. He would pray for instant death except if delivered, it meant he'd never again set eyes on Lady Landsdowne. Why was he worried about that? He was never going to see her again, and if he did, she would turn her back on him. Give him a well-deserved cut direct.

"How did I get here?" he asked through a mouth that felt like it was filled with sawdust.

"You don't remember?"

He squinted at Jamie who looked far too happy for whatever god-awful time of day it was. "I went to a couple of pubs."

"Our paths crossed at The Ten Bells. You were three sheets to the wind by then, searching for someone to fight. I pretended to accommodate—did have to jab you in the mouth when you started to announce I was a copper."

Rexton touched his lip with his tongue. "They don't know?"

Jamie shook his head. "Long story, don't ask. Anyway, once I got you outside, I dragged you here."

"And left me on the floor like rubbish?"

"Do you have any idea how big and heavy you are?"

Rexton pushed himself back until he was leaning against a chair. He was beginning to feel better. He suspected Jamie had put something in addition to coffee into the mug. "I'm not as big and heavy as you."

"You didn't seem to mind the floor." Jamie leaned forward, planting his forearms on his thighs. "I know you enjoy a glass of good whisky but I've never seen you so wrecked. What happened? Has it anything to do with the lavender and orchid lady?"

Rexton shook his head, no longer feeling as though the room was spinning. "Don't think I want to know how you came to that conclusion."

"You kept mumbling lavender and orchids."

His laughter was harsh, self-mocking. "She isn't to be."

"Why?"

"She discovered the truth. Let's leave it at that."

"Sounds as though you like her."

"She's strong. I always thought my mother and Grace were strong—but I think she has them beat. She's American. Scandalous. Her past has touched her sister, would touch her children if she stayed here.

Children shouldn't have to suffer because of the sins of their parents."

"So you were drinking to forget her. Did it work?"

"Think it just got me a busted lip."

Jamie chuckled. "Be glad that's all you got. Dressed as finely as you are, I'm surprised I didn't find you robbed, with a knife in you."

"As you said, I'm a big fellow."

"You are that. Want something to eat?"

Rexton shook his head. "No, I should be off. I appreciate you looking after me."

"Let's not make a habit of it."

"I won't." He forced himself to his feet. He hadn't been drinking to forget Lady Landsdowne. He'd been drinking because he'd known he'd never forget her.

Chapter 8

"*Y*ou offered Black Diamond to the Marquess of Rexton?"

Tillie had barged into her uncle's study with the question more a statement leading the way. While leaping out of his chair from behind his desk, he had the good graces to look abashed.

"He told you? He was supposed to keep it to himself."

"Last night a situation developed which caused it to be known to me. Whatever were you thinking to make such an arrangement? Black Diamond belongs to me."

His jacket was draped over a chair. He hitched his backside onto the edge of the desk, the buttons of his waistcoat straining to gain freedom. "I figured you'd indulge my whim. You want your sister to be happy, don't you?"

"You should have discussed it with me first. You didn't because you knew I would find fault with it." She marched over to the window and gazed out on the townhome's small garden. As a bachelor, he didn't require much room. He spent his money on indulgences such as rich foods and fine spirits. Hence the abuse to his buttons. "You demeaned Gina and her value in the process."

Coming to stand beside her, he offered a glass of whisky. She took it, sipped.

"No one was dancing with her," he said quietly. "I have no wife to introduce her about, no lady friend to take her under her wing. What was I to do? Ignore the longing in her eyes, not notice the overly bright smile she projected whenever a gent walked within a foot of her? We're Americans, not highly regarded to begin with. Then add to that . . ."

His voice trailed off, but she heard the words as though he'd delivered them with a blow to her midsection: *your scandal.*

"I promised your father I would see you both well situated. I don't worry about you. Marriage forged you into a formidable woman. But Gina—you cannot deny she is not yet made of firmer stuff. She wants marriage and children. She deserves them. She wants to marry into the aristocracy." He shook his head. "I admit to not understanding this obsession with the upper class but I intend to see she is not disappointed by life."

"We can never guarantee that, no matter our actions."

"But we can strive to meet our goal, and not look back, doubting ourselves because of inaction."

Taking another sip, she wished she didn't love this man, wished she didn't appreciate what he was striving to accomplish. She knew love spurred his actions. "Why Rexton?"

He lifted a heavy shoulder, dropped it as though it carried a great weight. "I know him. Through racing and gambling. I know he's not a drunkard, he's not in debt. He seems to exercise moderation when it comes to vices. He claimed not to have any interest in marriage presently, but I thought once he met Gina, he might change his mind. And if he didn't, being seen in his company would be a boon for her. There isn't an unmarried woman in the aristocracy who doesn't vie for his attention." He looked down at his shoes. "Does Gina know about the arrangement?"

"Yes."

His grimace and whispered curse made Tillie soften toward him a bit.

"Did she take it hard?" he asked, true concern and remorse edging his tone.

"No. As a matter of fact, she claims to have no interest in him at all. She accepted his invitations because she was playing matchmaker, striving to pair me with Rexton."

Her uncle scoffed. "That was jolly stupid. Rexton is heir to a dukedom. He isn't going to marry a woman with a scandalous past. No aristocrat is going to do that. The only hope for you, my dear girl, is to get thee back to New York."

The truth of his words hurt. Not that she'd ever considered she could mean something to Rexton. "I'm well aware."

She spun away from the window and walked to the fireplace, suddenly feeling quite chilled. The new location helped not one iota as no fire burned upon the hearth.

"Don't take offense, Mathilda. You know I speak true."

"I know." But dreams were seldom based on reality. It was what made them dreams. "So you will accompany her to the Claybourne ball next week and not strike deals with any other gentlemen?"

He released a labored sigh. "Perhaps we should hire a matchmaker."

She faced him. "I don't think that's necessary. She's been seen with Rexton. I know she danced at the last ball, and a couple of gentlemen were eyeing her last night. Without the marquess hovering around her, perhaps someone will take steps to press his suit."

"I detest balls."

"And I detest England, yet here we both are—for Gina's sake. We must see her happy. We made promises, did we not?"

He nodded. "Yes, all right."

"And do not offer my stallion to anyone else."

"He wanted Black Diamond badly. With a little negotiating, we could no doubt convince him to marry her."

"I fear that would only lead to misery." For everyone involved.

A week passed, and she couldn't stop thinking about him. He was constantly in her mind, in her dreams as vividly as though he were actually in her bed. It irritated the devil out of her that she'd begun to scour the gossip rags—which she generally avoided because they had focused on her lascivious tale far longer than necessary—but she was desperate for any news of what he might be doing. It didn't reassure her when she found no mentions of him at all.

What was he? A blasted saint?

It was even worse that she paced the parlor, sipping whisky, her gaze constantly drifting to the clock, as she waited for Gina to return home from the Claybourne ball. Guilt pricked her conscience because she wasn't truly interested in what sort of success her sister may have had at the affair. Rather she was hoping for some little tidbit about Rexton. What he might have worn, how he might have looked, with whom he may have danced.

She felt like a jealous shrew, although it wasn't really jealousy she felt. It was loneliness, sharper than she'd ever experienced—soul deep, as though Rexton had been physically torn from her. It was ridiculous, not to be tolerated. She'd fought not to enjoy his company and lost. She'd battled against not being drawn to him and had gone down in defeat. She'd rebelled against being conquered and found herself captivated all the same.

Damn the man. It would be so much easier to discard him if he hadn't sent Gina a bouquet of roses along with a letter encouraging her not to settle for less than she deserved: a man of the highest caliber. As though he weren't.

She finished off her whisky, poured some more. Without question he wasn't. A man of the highest caliber wouldn't have pretended to be courting her sister, wouldn't have risked breaking her heart. It didn't matter that Gina had claimed to have no real interest in him. The potential for heartache had been there. Tillie was all too familiar with how fragile the heart could be.

At the echo of the door opening, she finished off her drink, set aside the glass, and hurried into the foyer, catching Gina just as she reached the stairs. "Did you have a lovely time?"

Her sister swung around, smiled. "You didn't have to wait up for me."

"I wanted to. Come into the parlor, we'll have a drink, and you can tell me everything about your evening."

"There's not much to tell," Gina said, "although I'd dearly love a spot of brandy."

After the drinks were poured, and they were sitting in opposite chairs, facing each other, Tillie asked, "I suppose you saw Rexton."

Gina took a slow sip before saying, "Actually I didn't. He wasn't there."

"Are you sure?" She couldn't imagine it. "I didn't think he'd be so cowardly as to avoid you."

Her sister giggled. "I don't think it was that. Apparently he's rather scarce when it comes to balls. We may have overestimated his influence." She held up her wrist, her dance card dangling from it. "I danced only twice tonight."

"It's not the number of dances that matters, but rather how much interest your partner shows."

"One dance was with the host. While his attentiveness seemed genuine and he was incredibly polite, I have it on good authority that the Earl of Claybourne very much adores his wife. I also assume said wife would relieve him of his family jewels if he ever strayed."

She couldn't help but smile at that. She knew the Countess of Claybourne, had spoken with her on numerous occasions when she'd been accepted by Society. "There is that. The woman is no wallflower. But then how could she be when she tamed the Devil Earl? And your other partner?"

"The second son of a second son who seemed rather taken with the rumors regarding my inheritance."

The disappointment hit her and she sank back into the chair. "But you were making such progress."

"I think because people noticed I had Rexton's interest, and now I don't seem to have it, so there is speculation regarding the reasons behind his setting me aside."

Tillie rose to her feet in a rush and began to pace agitatedly in front of the fireplace. "Damn the man to hell. He didn't set you aside. You set him aside. Why must the woman always be blamed for everything?"

"I'm not certain he's to blame—"

She came to an abrupt halt and glared at her sister. "If he hadn't given you attention to begin with, you wouldn't now be the object of gossip. Something unflattering is bound to be in the newspapers tomorrow." She gave her head a hard shake. "This is my fault. I should have anticipated the message his absence would send."

"Don't be silly, Tillie. You can't keep blaming yourself for my failure as a debutante."

She could and she would. If she'd stayed married to Downie, she could have ensured her sister was accepted by Society. If she hadn't wanted the temptation of Rexton removed from her life, Gina's matrimonial prospects wouldn't have disappeared. She'd acted far too hastily and impulsively to both circumstances, caring more for her own sanity than her sister's well-being. She'd taken Gina under her wing when their mother died. Now the responsibility was even greater with their father gone.

Taking a deep breath, she returned to her chair, lifted the snifter of brandy, and swallowed a good portion of it. "I shall see the matter set to right."

"How are you going to do that?" Gina asked, concern and worry etched clearly in her voice.

Tillie finished off the brandy, set the glass aside.

"What are you going to do, Tillie?" Gina drew out the question as though she were in no hurry to hear the answer, as though she already knew she wouldn't like it.

"Not to worry. I won't do anything foolish." But it was high time she made use of her scandalous reputation. Otherwise, all she'd suffered was for nothing.

Chapter 9

The Nightingale Club
Tonight at 10

*R*exton stared at the note his butler had just delivered. It wasn't unusual for him to receive a missive such as the one he held—his membership at the club was widely known among those who knew of the place and in his youth he'd frequented the establishment quite often—but he'd grown weary of married women and widows in want of brief affairs. He was also accustomed to the notes being signed, or at least offering a hint as to whom he would be meeting for a rendezvous. "Who delivered it?" he asked Winchester now.

"Some scruffy lad. He wore no livery, and I didn't see a coach or carriage about. The boy knocked at the servants' door, handed it over, and scampered away as though fearing a hangman's noose was about to drop about his neck."

Rexton didn't recognize the handwriting. It was neat, precise, and definitely feminine. He'd once received a letter written with a masculine hand—a gent trying to determine if Rexton had been having an affair with his wife. He'd wisely not gone to the club that night.

The Nightingale had been established years before as a place for unhappy women to find a moment of happiness. Usually he had an inkling as to whom he'd be meeting. The flirtation usually began elsewhere, but of late the only woman who'd garnered his interest was Lady Landsdowne.

He tapped his fingers on his desk. Was it possible she was summoning him? He nearly laughed aloud. She'd be glad to never set eyes on him again.

Like some besotted youth, he went to the park every morning before the lark trilled hoping to catch sight of her, but he always left disappointed. If she was still going for morning rides, she was doing it elsewhere. He wasn't even certain if he saw her that he'd approach her. She'd no doubt put that pistol she carried to excellent use.

He'd written three letters of apology only to tear them up because the correct words of contrition failed him. How did one go about making amends for such atrocious behavior? He'd considered flowers, sweets, and jewelry. But he couldn't envision any of those things softening her toward him.

He avoided balls because he didn't want to converse with women. He avoided the Twin Dragons because he had no interest in being in the company of other men. He avoided the pubs because it had taken him two days to recover the last time he lifted a tankard. He was becoming a hermit. His reclusiveness made no sense whatsoever. For a dozen years now, women had come and gone through his life with ease. He never regretted when the lady moved on, never ached with a need to see her again. He'd enjoyed her company while they were together but it had never been more than mutual pleasure for a time—and they'd both known it was only for a time.

It was different with Lady Landsdowne. Perhaps because their parting had not been amicable, had not been of his choosing. With her, he regretted so many moments, so many lost and missed opportunities to get to know her better, to explore all the intriguing facets to her of which he'd only caught glimpses. He had a hundred questions he wished he'd asked, a thousand answers he'd have liked to obtain. And a million kisses he'd have enjoyed experiencing.

It didn't help matters that he'd instructed his housekeeper to have the vases throughout the residence filled with lavender and orchids. He'd thought the scent would bring him solace. Instead it was like being flayed day after day.

"Will there be anything else, my lord?"

He'd become so lost in regrets that he'd forgotten the butler was there. "No, that'll be all. Wait." He had to admit his curiosity was piqued. If it was her, he couldn't let the moment pass. "I'll be going out this evening. Have the carriage readied at half nine."

"Yes, my lord."

His man left. Rexton got up, went to the sideboard, and poured himself some whisky. His hands were shaking. He could be wrong. It might not be her. If it wasn't, he'd simply offer his regrets.

His harsh laughter echoed around him. What the devil was wrong with him to turn aside a willing woman?

The hell of it was, though, that there was only one woman he wanted. He wasn't willing to settle for any other.

*W*hen all was said and done, he had his carriage readied earlier and arrived at the Nightingale Club with twenty minutes to spare. Sitting in a plush chair in a corner of the dimly lit parlor, sipping whisky, he observed all the little trysts taking place. It was an unwritten rule that a seated gentleman was meeting someone, a standing gent was fair game. Women wearing masks to protect their identity and reputation chose their partners from among the unmasked men. Obviously women were more circumspect when it came to bedding—they wanted to know who they were approaching, who they were enticing, who they would eventually invite to join them between the sheets. Men were generally here simply looking for a tumble. All were sworn to secrecy regarding who they saw here, who they met.

When the ladies arrived they changed into a silk sheath. None wanted to be identified later because her frock had been spotted at the Nightingale Club. For some in his world the club was merely myth. For others it was a dark secret. Throughout the years it had flourished and although it was only spoken of in whispers, somehow those who needed to know of its existence discovered it.

He wondered if Lady Landsdowne had visited. He imagined her here, searching for a lover for the night, for more than a night. He'd never been approached by her, never taken her up the stairs to the bedchambers where couples could rut to their heart's content. Anger sliced through him with the thought of her with one of these gents. Some of them were young and randy, others older. A widower or two. Some married. Most unattached.

Gina had the right of it. The aristocracy seldom married for love. Mistresses and lovers were commonplace. Like Downie, Rexton wouldn't tolerate his wife having affairs. He expected, would demand, faithfulness and loyalty. He wouldn't dishonor his vows and would insist upon the same consideration in return. He certainly wasn't going to contemplate taking to wife a woman who had already proven she didn't have the moral character to honor her promises. And here he was thinking of Lady Landsdowne again.

He changed his mind. No matter who had set up this rendezvous, he was going to bed her. He needed to exorcise the blasted countess from his thoughts— once and for all.

A woman, draped in purple silk, strode hesitantly into the parlor. Her purple and white mask covered three-quarters of her face. Generally ladies provided their own masks. The object served as their identifier so once an introduction was made it didn't have to be made again. Some men wanted to avoid certain women. Easy enough to turn a woman away before they arrived at a bedchamber if a man could identify her by her mask.

Rexton had never been with this woman, had no recollection of ever seeing her here. But her hair, cascading like a waterfall over her shoulders, was gloriously dark. A woman of her height, her slender form had invaded his dreams for far too many nights now. Without conscious thought, slowly he rose to his feet, viscerally aware the moment she spied him, the moment her blue gaze—he knew it was blue even though the mask cast her eyes in shadow—landed on him. She stopped walking, but didn't look away. She licked her lips, full ruby lips that he was fairly certain he'd only been given the chance to taste for a heartbeat.

If he was incorrect, if she wasn't here for him, some poor sod was going to be introduced to his fist before the night was done, because it no longer mattered who had sent the missive, who had wanted to meet him—

All that mattered was that she—Lady Landsdowne—was standing before him.

*S*he was aware of him, felt his gaze on her before she saw him. She'd been afraid if she signed the missive he wouldn't come. Or perhaps she'd been afraid he would. It terrified her—how badly she wanted him, how glad she was to see he was here, waiting for her.

A dozen times she'd reconsidered her plan. She knew it was reckless, and yet what did she have to lose? She'd lost everything that mattered: her reputation, her pride, her respect. She'd lost her influence. She'd lost her ability to ensure Gina was happy.

Without her sister's happiness, she'd lose her opportunity to return to America, to begin to rebuild her life. Her sordid reputation was unlikely to follow her to New York. She'd never been accepted into the Knickerbocker Society—which was the reason her mother had so desperately wanted her to marry a lord, to be a lady, to possess a title. She doubted being a divorced woman with a title was going to get her into that Society now. But she would hold grand affairs for the newly-monied. She could create for others what she and her mother had longed for: acceptance based solely on one's self.

Whatever she did tonight, whatever she did for the next few nights, was not going to alter her long range plans. Nothing she did here was going to be packed into her trunks and carted back to New York. What happened next was strictly for the present, completely for Gina, to ensure she had the life she dearly wanted and deserved.

He had yet to move toward her, was merely waiting, his eyes burning into her. He had to know who she was, had to know why she was here. At least he'd reacted as though both those things were true. It was unnerving to finally be on the cusp of doing something so wicked, of being with a man who could totally destroy her if she wasn't extraordinarily careful.

She felt fairly naked in the flimsy silk she was forced to wear, suspected he'd probably disrobed her with his gaze. No petticoats, corset, or chemise served as protection. No layers separated her skin from the silk. Her nipples had reacted to his heated gaze as though he'd closed his mouth around them and sucked hard. She'd imagined it too many times as she'd moved restlessly beneath the covers. Dear God, she was trembling like a leaf in the breeze. She may have made a ghastly mistake in coming here, but she was too stubborn to turn tail and run.

Instead, she took a deep breath and forced her legs to walk forward. He, drat him, moved not at all. Perhaps he was too mesmerized by the way the silk seemed to undulate over her body with each step, the way it clung, leaving no doubt she wore nothing beneath it. She could see the advantage as it failed to hamper movements. It was more nightdress than frock, and a man could get at what he wanted rather quickly. Although, he could also get at what he wanted sooner if he'd take a step nearer.

When she completed her lengthy sojourn, she wasn't quite sure how to greet him, how to ensure they progressed to the next step. Directness was no doubt warranted, and the order of the night. "You received my missive, I see."

Although in retrospect hers could have been one of a dozen, two dozen, three.

"You're late."

He didn't sound particularly put out but rather curious. She glanced over at the mantel. No clock. She supposed this wasn't the sort of place where people worried about time. "Not by much, I'd wager."

"Four minutes."

"You were counting?"

"Wouldn't you be disappointed if I hadn't?"

"But I didn't sign the note. You couldn't have known who sent it, couldn't have known who you were waiting on." She suddenly hated that he was here, that he had shown, that he hadn't cared who had sent it. She was a fool to think he wanted anything other than a tumble. It didn't matter to him who the lady was. He had lust that needed to be slaked.

He leaned in, his lips brushing over her ear, his breath stirring the strands of her hair that she'd left unbound. Everything within her stilled, waited, as though she were the prey, and he the hunter about to pounce. "I'm anxious to know if I guessed correctly."

How silly she was to think he would be able to see through the mask, that her eyes, hair, form would give her away. He hadn't paid nearly as much attention to her as she'd thought. Perhaps she'd misjudged his interest. Perhaps in the end, he'd dismiss her out of hand, and she'd be left feeling foolish.

"I've secured a room," he said, in a lower, throatier voice. "Shall we make use of it?" When he drew back, his eyes held a challenge as he extended his hand. His bared hand. His large, bare hand.

Her own was equally bare. Skin to skin. She wanted to spin on her heel and simply lead the way, wanted him to follow like a lapdog, but he wasn't one to be subservient. She needed something from him and that required she stay on his good side. She placed her hand in his, watched as his long, thick fingers slowly closed in a way that spoke of absolute possession. Anyone watching could not doubt that he had just claimed her for his own.

She'd expected him to drag her from the room like some Neanderthal. Instead, he set a leisurely pace, shortening his strides so she could keep up easily, giving the impression they were equals in this endeavor. But they weren't, and he'd soon realize it. He had more experience, more knowledge, more confidence.

When they reached the stairs, he swept her up into his arms. She hated the tiny squeak that escaped. She was grateful he was close as she latched on to his lapel with one hand, her other arm curling around his broad shoulders. She could feel the strength in his arms. He carried her up to the landing as though she weighed no more than a summer cloud. Down one hallway, then another. She could hear moans and cries escaping through the closed doors.

When they reached a room at the end of a hallway,

he set her on her feet, removed a key from his jacket pocket, unlocked the door, and swung it open. Easing past him, she walked quickly inside, stopping short at the sight of the bed—the reason people came here. She didn't turn when she heard the door close with a hushed *snick*, didn't move as his soft footfalls brought him nearer, hardly dared to breathe when she felt his fingers at the lacings that secured the mask to her face. It loosened, began to fall. He caught it, then tossed it onto a nearby chair.

Gathering up her resolve, she spun around, caught unawares by the heat and want she saw reflected in his eyes.

"Thank God, it is you," he rasped before taking her face between his hands and lowering his mouth to hers.

He sounded truly grateful. Her feminine side told her to luxuriate in it, but too much was at stake. She would allow him to have this, but only this. They needed to come to an understanding before things went further. Her marriage had been on Downie's terms. This, whatever *this* with Rexton turned out to be, was going to be on hers.

Although for a fleeting moment, she feared it might turn out to be on his. How could she think, plot, scheme when his tongue was tenderly coaxing her lips to part, when they obeyed his insistent command without even asking her permission. When he was then stroking that very same tongue over hers, parrying with it as though they were engaged in a fencing match, coming in for the touch, retreating, encouraging her to take a stab. He tasted of something dark and rich, whisky probably. He tasted of wickedness, desire, and untold passions. He was an intrepid explorer, leaving no aspect of her mouth unsurveyed, encouraging her to return the favor.

She did so gladly. Running her hands up into his hair, smiling inwardly as the curls wrapped around her fingers, holding her as he eventually would. For the briefest of moments, she felt young and innocent again, untouched, with her life unfolding before her and all her dreams waiting to be realized.

He drew her in close, so close it didn't matter that he wore clothes and she wore naught but flimsy silk. She could feel the hard length of his cock against her belly, could feel the rumble of his chest against her breasts as he growled, could feel the power in his hands as he skimmed them up her back and down, cupping her buttocks, and pressing her harder against him.

She had an insane urge to scramble up his body, to wrap her legs around his waist, to unfasten his trousers, set him free, and slide down over him. Right here, right now, standing in the center of this room. She was close to exploding, just as she was every night when she thought of him touching her. What was it about him that brought out such extreme wantonness? He made her yearn to be exactly what all of London whispered she was: notorious, scandalous, indecent, disgraceful.

But in spite of everything, in spite of the way he called to her, she wasn't here for this. She was here for something far more important. With a great deal of effort, and regret, she tore her mouth from his. They were both breathing heavily and harshly.

His eyes boring into hers, he waited, as though conceding the next move was hers, that she was the one who would set the pace. He was accepting her as an equal. It was an odd realization, seeing the need etched so clearly on his features, to feel it thrumming through his tense body, and to know he recognized she required more than lust satisfied.

"You need to court Gina again," she forced out on a rush.

The stunned expression on his face was almost comical, made her want to laugh, only there was nothing humorous in this situation. "I beg your pardon?"

His hold on her had loosened, and she used the opportunity to step away from him, beyond reach of those magnificent hands and talented lips. She didn't want to consider how truly incredible it might be to tear off his clothes and allow his entire body to have its way with hers.

"At least pretend to be courting her, as you were. The gentlemen have ceased to give her attention. I fear they believe you found fault with her."

He plowed his hands through his hair and stared at her as though she'd gone mad. "You set up a meeting *here* to discuss my courting your sister?"

"I wanted someplace neutral, someplace where our coming together wouldn't be observed. I'm willing to honor your original bargain with my uncle and ensure you have Black Diamond for stud."

His laughter was harsh, dark, a little frightening in its intensity. Turning on his heel, he walked over to a table, splashed whisky into two glasses, and brought her one. She did hope he didn't notice how her hand was trembling when she took it. His gaze never leaving hers, he dropped into a chair. She eased over to the one opposite him and settled into it.

"How many times have you visited here?" he asked.

Not exactly the question she'd been expecting. "Three."

"Twice before tonight then."

She nodded. "Yes."

Sipping on his whisky, he seemed to mull that over. For some reason, the mulling irritated her. "And you?" she asked pointedly. "How many times have you been here?"

"I didn't keep count. Although I've never spotted you, you must have seen me somehow. Otherwise, you wouldn't have known I knew the whereabouts of this establishment and could in fact meet with you here."

She had seen him. A few years ago. The first time she'd come. She'd been skirting the shadows of the hallway, working up her nerve to enter the parlor, when she'd seen him walk out of it with a woman on his arm. She'd stayed where she was until they disappeared up the stairs. "Your point?"

"This isn't the sort of place where people come for a *conversation*. I think you chose this establishment because you hoped for more than that."

"I selected it because it gave me more control of the situation. With a mask, no one will have recognized me. No one will know we are talking instead of—" She waved her hand toward the bed.

"Fucking?"

The crudity of the word was like a punch to the stomach. Was that how he had viewed the kiss? As a prelude to *that*? Passion and desire had been no part of it. Had it been all lust and animalistic baser instincts? At that moment, she hated him, hated herself. "Do you want the stallion or not?"

"Not."

The word was delivered like a shot from a rifle. Succinct. To the point. And had taken her completely by surprise. She was familiar with his racehorses. Had seen them run at various racetracks. Had even wagered on them a time or two. "But Black Diamond mated with one of your mares is certain to give you a winner. I don't see that pretending to court Gina is much of an inconvenience. You were willing to do it before—"

"I'm still willing to do it. But now the price has changed."

"What do you want in exchange?"

"You."

Chapter 10

$\mathscr{H}$e was fairly certain that within the annals of horseracing history would be a footnote that indicated the Marquess of Rexton had been a complete and utter fool. When given the opportunity to breed one of the fastest and finest stallions in existence with his mare, he'd tossed it aside in favor of his cock.

Tillie—after the searing kiss they'd just shared he could no longer think of her in so formal a manner as Lady Landsdowne—stared at him with wide eyes and slightly parted lips. Damn but he was anxious to explore that mouth again. He didn't know if he'd ever tasted anything so sweet.

"Me?" she asked finally, as though insulted. She glanced over her shoulder at the bed. "There I suppose." Swiveling her head back around, she glared at him. "You want to fuck me."

He regretted now his choice of word earlier. He'd been keenly disappointed her reason for meeting him wasn't the one he'd expected, that they weren't already tangled in the sheets, lost to wild and untamed passion. "I want to have an affair with you."

Again, she seemed surprised by his words. Did she think he was going to be content with one night, one coupling? Was that her usual method? Once with a gent before moving on? Once with a footman—within her residence by all accounts; once with a couple of gents here? The jealousy that ratcheted through him with the thought of any of those men touching her might have doubled him over if he weren't sitting.

"An affair," she repeated as though testing the word on her tongue.

"And not here." He'd taken other women within these walls, but he didn't want to bed her here. She was somehow different, in ways he couldn't fathom or explain.

Her delicate brow furrowed. "Why not here?"

It gave him hope that she was considering his proposition. "It's too tawdry."

She tilted her head to the side as though the angle would allow her to decipher his meaning better. "But you've been with other ladies within this establishment."

And she'd been with other men. Perhaps that was part of it. But more, he wanted with her something he'd never had. "I see no need for the games played within these rooms. I reside alone. You can come to my residence in an unmarked carriage—or I can send mine for you. Wear a hooded cloak. If someone figures out it's you, it's not as though your reputation will be sullied."

"There is that, I suppose." She took a swallow of whisky, tapped the glass. "Although I don't want you bragging that you're fucking me."

Damn these Americans for their boldness. An English lass would have been shocked, but never repeated the word once, much less carrying on so. "I'm not going to be fucking you."

She raised a finely arched brow. "Is that not the purpose of an affair?"

"I apologize for using the crass word in your company. I shouldn't have. It was ungentlemanly and you are undeserving of such language. Trust me, when we are done, you'll be glad to have been in my bed. Nor will I be bragging to anyone about it. It doesn't serve your sister well if we're not discreet."

She nodded. "She above all is my concern. When you escort her somewhere, I will come to you the night following."

"That's fair." He would be doing a great deal of escorting.

"However, there will be no complete consummation until she is betrothed."

He narrowed his eyes. "It's not an affair if we're not—" He bit back the word he wanted to use. "If I'm not buried inside you."

"Once you have that, what assurances do I have you will work diligently to see she is settled with a proper gentleman?"

"My word and my honor."

"Yes, well, I've had another lord offer me his word and his honor. Little good either did me."

What did she mean by that? What had Landsdowne done? "You were the one who was unfaithful."

She lifted a shoulder, dropped it back down. "If you want a complete coupling, those are my terms."

"I want more than once, so I don't find those terms agreeable. But I understand your concerns. A counteroffer." He leaned forward, elbows digging into his thighs. "Are you familiar with Fair Vixen?"

A tiny pleat appeared between her brows while she seemed to be scouring her memory. Finally she nodded. "I've seen her race." Realization seemed to dawn as her eyes widened. He wanted to see pleasure reflected in the blue. "You want Black Diamond for her."

"I do indeed. If I don't uphold my end of the bargain, if I abandon this quest to find a match for your sister after you and I have been together, I forfeit my most prized mare to you."

She blinked, studied him. "That would no doubt make me the most expensive whore in history."

"Damn it, Tillie. You're not going to be my whore and I shan't treat you as such. You can't deny there's an attraction between us. If I say no to helping you with Gina, are you truly going to walk out of here without making use of that bed that's only a few yards away?"

She shot to her feet and walked over to the window. She wasn't foolish enough to stand before the glass, but took a position so she was hidden from view by the pulled-aside drapery, but still she could see out. He contemplated staying where he was, but he loathed the distance between them. When he reached her, he didn't touch her, although he longed to with a need that was close to a physical ache.

"There's no shame in desire, in wanting intimacy," he said quietly.

"Society would disagree."

"Society isn't going to know." Slowly, so very slowly, he touched a finger to a bared spot on her shoulder, drew a tiny circle on her skin, felt a shudder ripple through her. "Tell me I'm wrong; tell me you don't go to sleep at night wondering what it might be like between us."

She shook her head. "You're not wrong. But these terms, they feel degrading."

"They merely extend what otherwise might have been only one night."

"If you discover . . . if you're disappointed . . . if one night is enough for you."

It wouldn't be. He trailed his finger down her arm, back up. "Then you acquire Fair Vixen."

As though her limbs were controlled by the slow steady movement of the minute hand on a clock, she unhurriedly turned to face him. "If Gina is not settled by Season's close, our arrangement will come to an end at that time. I can't have you striving to undermine your own efforts just to keep me about."

"I would not be so underhanded." The words were a lie of course. If they were half as compatible in bed as he suspected they would be, he was going to take his time seeing her sister set. Although it was also possible he'd have no control over it at all. He couldn't stop a gentleman from falling in love with her quickly, nor could he prevent gentlemen from not wanting her at all.

"Fair Vixen becomes mine at that time."

He couldn't help himself. He barked out his laughter. The cheek on her. Damn but he couldn't wait to have her in his bed. "I beg your pardon?"

"I need to ensure you are working diligently to see to her happiness. So there must be a cost to you if you fail."

He heard the hesitancy in her voice, as though she feared she'd pushed him too far, had demanded too much. He wondered how it was that she failed to comprehend her worth, how badly he wanted her. She could have asked for his entire stable, and still, he would have said—

"I agree to your terms."

Chapter 11

*S*itting at the breakfast table the following morning, Tillie couldn't believe he'd agreed to her outlandish terms. He was either very confident or very foolish. She knew the value of his mare. He wouldn't part with it. He'd find a suitable match for Gina, even if he had to step into the role himself.

No, after being in his bed, she wouldn't allow him to marry Gina. She could hardly fathom she was on the cusp of having an affair or how very much she was anticipating it. He'd had the right of it: she'd chosen the Nightingale Club because she had been willing to fall into bed with him.

Her reputation was ruined. No one here would ever marry her. When she returned to New York, it was quite possible someone there would be willing to take her to wife. But he never need know about her affair. And if she didn't marry—shouldn't a woman have some memories to carry with her as her hair turned silver? She suspected Rexton would give her memories to eclipse any others that might come along.

She looked up as Gina strolled into the room. "Good morning."

Her sister smiled at her. "You look happy this morning."

"I have some splendid news. Prepare your plate and I'll tell you all about it."

Setting aside the newspaper she'd not been reading because her attention kept drifting to Rexton, she waited on tenterhooks while Gina took various offerings from the sideboard before joining her at the table. A footman approached and poured her tea, then refilled Tillie's cup. She added two lumps of sugar, stirred, and wondered how many lumps Rexton liked with his tea. How much would she learn about him during the coming nights?

"So what's the news?" Gina asked.

"Lord Rexton will be taking you for a ride in the park this afternoon." They'd worked out the details for the first outing before they parted ways last night. She'd been disappointed he hadn't attempted to kiss her again, had acted as though he were barely interested in her. But then if he had kissed her, she didn't know if she'd have been able to resist luring him into that bed. Why was it she was constantly thinking of his taking her?

"He's going to start courting me again?" She shook her head. "Or pretending to as he was before?"

"It will be as it was before. Not a true courtship. He's going to give you attention until you have a viable suitor, and is going to work diligently toward that end. I have no doubt you'll be betrothed before Season's end."

"How can you be so certain?"

"I just am."

Gina narrowed her eyes. "What have you done, Tillie?"

Worked to make amends. She'd spent so much of her youth thinking only about her own yearnings and desires. Now her sister was paying the price. But still she didn't want Gina to know the true cost of what she'd arranged. "I met with him, spoke with him. We came to an understanding."

"Which is?"

Gina, who always seemed so sweet and unassuming, could be doggedly determined when she set her mind to it. "I offered to put the arrangement he had with Uncle back into play." Not entirely a lie, even if that wasn't the final agreement.

Gina nibbled thoughtfully on the corner of her toast. "So you and I shall be going about with him again."

"My absence will serve better. I don't need to observe him with you as we now know his attentions were never true."

"But other gentlemen's might be. I still require your opinion."

"I'll observe when they call on you here."

Gina skewed up her face into a very unattractive pout. "He likes you, you know. Something could come of that."

He lusted after her. It was a very different thing. And something was going to come of *that*. She was rather ashamed by how much she was anticipating it. "I've alerted a groom to have your horse readied at two. He'll also accompany you."

"I still think you should be there as well."

"It's completely unnecessary."

*U*nfortunately, the Marquess of Rexton did not agree.

He'd arrived early, so early that Gina was not yet ready. He had to have known she wouldn't be. He'd then had the audacity to insist a servant fetch Tillie to keep him company while he waited in the parlor. She'd been a bit miffed by his high-handedness and had gone to join him simply to set him straight that they might be on the brink of having an affair, but he didn't own her, she wasn't going to come at his beck and call.

She'd arrived to discover keeping him company hadn't been on his mind at all. But rather he'd anticipated that he'd have to convince her to join them.

She didn't like at all that he'd made himself perfectly at home, had poured them each a glass of whisky, and now enjoyed his in a lazy manner, one shoulder pressed to the fireplace mantel, his gaze never leaving her as he swallowed the amber brew. And all she seemed capable of thinking was: I know what it tastes like on his tongue.

"My presence doesn't encourage people to approach her," she stated succinctly, her fingers tightening around her own glass, a defensive maneuver because they wanted to advance and brush from his brow some of the locks that were in danger of falling into his eyes.

"Is that what you want for her? Someone who is going to ostracize you?"

"This entire exercise has nothing at all to do with

me and everything to do with Gina. We must do what is best for her."

"Best for her is to display her loyalty to a family member whom Society shuns."

"It links her with me. That has been the obstacle to her having a grand Season all along. People shall assume she will follow my path, that she wishes to marry for a title, will not honor her vows, and will find herself divorced and cast aside. It must be evident we are nothing alike."

"When people get to know her, they will realize that."

She didn't know why the words hurt. Probably because it confirmed that he believed the truth of her scandal, that he didn't know her at all, that he didn't realize she had once been as innocent as Gina. But then she didn't want him to know her. It would make things easier when their affair came to an end.

"Meanwhile," he continued, "you underestimate the curiosity factor. People will want a closer look at you. They'll approach."

"They didn't before."

"They were too shocked. Or timid or wary. Their reasons don't matter. I guarantee at least six approach today."

She scoffed at his arrogance. "Not even one will speak with her."

"Care to make a wager? If I'm correct, you'll come to me tonight instead of tomorrow."

"And if you're wrong?"

"What would you like?"

The first thing to flash through her mind involved his mouth doing wicked things to hers, but that would no doubt happen tomorrow night. She thought about asking to ride Fair Vixen. She could envision the joy that would surround her galloping over hills with that horse beneath her. But it seemed a trivial thing to bargain with when he had handed her the opportunity for power. "Tomorrow night when we are together, I will be in charge. You may only do as I command."

The grin he bestowed on her was so wicked, so full of promise that for a moment she forgot how to breathe. "You want me to be your slave?"

Squaring her shoulders, she tossed back her head. She had fantasized about him too much, about what he might do to her. She didn't want to be as disappointed as she'd been on her wedding night; she didn't want him not to live up to her expectation. "Yes."

"I'll accept the wager."

She blinked in surprise at the notion he wasn't put off by the possibility of her ordering him about. The confidence he possessed, the surety in himself to not be threatened by the prospect of not being in control made him all the more appealing.

"You overestimate the power of my presence in the park," she told him.

"You underestimate the sway of my influence."

"I suppose we shall see who is correct."

"Indeed, we shall. Although I must confess you make me regret I shan't lose this wager."

"You are too arrogant by half."

"You like that about me."

Damned if she didn't. His overconfidence was very different from Downie's. Her former husband had been insufferable with his, but Rexton seemed to use his for teasing and occasional self-deprecation.

"Off with you now," he ordered. "Ready yourself. The park awaits."

*W*hile Rexton waited for her to prepare for their outing he stood at the window in the parlor, gazing out, and mulled over their latest wager. Although he was more than willing to play the part of slave, he preferred for them to be equals. Still he wondered at her request, what had prompted it, what her experience with Downie and the other gents might have entailed.

When both ladies finally joined him, he discovered he had eyes for only one. No matter how much he tried to appear neutral, he was drawn to her more strongly than he'd ever been to anyone else. With his own horse in tow, he escorted them out to the stables where their mares awaited.

A groom led Gina's horse to some steps and assisted her. Rexton merely closed his hands possessively around Tillie's waist, relishing its narrowness, imagining it in his hands with the cloth gone, and hoisted her into the saddle. He didn't fail to notice the way her gloved hands had folded around his shoulders for support, the deep breath she'd taken that caused her breasts to skim along his chest. Damnation, if things at the park didn't go as planned, if he lost this wager, he'd go insane with wanting before tomorrow night.

He was reluctant to release his hold on her, considered moving her to his horse, to have her nestled between his thighs, riding with him. He tried to convince himself that it was only the physical aspects of her that he yearned to explore but the truth of it was that she fascinated him in all ways. Her sister knew the truth of his courtship so he no longer had to solely engage with her, he didn't have to flirt or feign interest. Certainly, he wasn't going to be rude and ignore her, but the three of them could now have honest dialogues.

Still, riding between them, he waited until they neared the entrance to Hyde Park before asking, "So, Gina, what is it that you desire in a future husband?"

For some odd reason, she looked around him to her sister, waited several heartbeats as though seeking the answer, before turning her attention back to him. "I would like to marry into the aristocracy as it is a world with which I'm very comfortable. I prefer a husband who isn't desperate for my money. What else should I want, Tillie?"

He didn't think it was a good sign when a woman had to ask another what she sought in a husband.

"Kind. Generous. He should make you laugh."

"So she should marry a jester?" he asked.

Tillie gave him an oh-you-silly-man look. "Don't be daft. But they should have the same interests, the same outlook on the world. They should find joy in each other. Joy often leads to smiles and laughter. Surely you have known women who made you laugh."

He considered. "My sister. A couple of friends." But in truth, no one he'd ever bedded. Perhaps that was the reason the affairs had lasted such a short time. The sex had been good, but beyond the bed there had been little to recommend them. Conversations were brief, words seldom exchanged except for those designed to titillate.

"I think it would be splendid to be friends with my husband," Gina said. "We'd enjoy each other's company a bit more I think."

"Were you and Downie friends?" he heard himself

ask, hating the words even as they'd poured out of him. He didn't want to bring up her former husband, certainly wasn't jealous of the man who'd lost her, although he did find himself wondering if he'd have been able to hold on to her. He would have been kind and generous to her. Would he have made her laugh?

"We were nothing," she said quietly, before applying her crop to her horse's flank and trotting ahead.

He was about to urge his horse forward when Gina said, "She doesn't like to discuss him. You'd be better served not to ask her questions about Downie."

He glanced over at her. "You've discussed him with her?"

"Discussed is a bit of a stretch. I've managed to glean a little information. She's far too secretive for her own good. But then I suppose that's what happens when you've been terribly hurt. You tend to build walls."

Then she, too, was racing off to catch up with her sister. He was torn. He didn't want to know about her life with Downie—and yet he did. He also realized he was an absolute cad, grateful she had implied Downie had never made her laugh. If he had to tickle her from head to toe, her joyful giggles were going to be ringing in his ears when all was said and done.

He urged his horse into a trot. The ladies had slowed so it didn't take long to catch up. As he neared he determined they were engaged in serious conversation—but it came to an abrupt halt when he was within hearing distance, leaving him with the distinct impression he'd been their subject. He didn't much like that he found himself hoping at least one of them had been espousing upon his good qualities—whether it was Tillie striving to justify why she'd turned once again to him to assist with securing a proper husband for Gina or Gina seeking to convince Tillie that she'd be a fortunate woman indeed if Rexton gave her his attentions.

On the other hand, he was rather certain Tillie hadn't shared with her sister the precise terms of their arrangement. Any decent woman would find it horrifying. He was rather gratified Tillie couldn't be described as decent.

"Ladies," he announced as he pulled up on Tillie's left side, deciding not to separate the sisters. "We must stay together if you wish for my influence to have any bearing."

Tillie gave him a hard-edged glare. "You should be on the other side of Gina, so it is clear where your interest lies."

"My *pretended* interest. Let's be clear when it's only the three of us."

"But it is not only the three of us. The park is bursting at the seams with visitors this day. They need to see you showering Gina with attention."

"And they will once our visitors are on their way."

A faint crease appeared between her brows. "Visitors?"

"My influence alone is not enough to awaken widespread interest in Gina. We must rely on others. Halt your horses, ladies." He was surprised they did so quickly, without argument. If he was discovering anything at all about American women, it was that they didn't like to be ordered about.

He grinned at his sister and her husband as they approached on matching bays. The Duchess of Lovingdon had a style about her that extended to the animals in her life. Everything matched. "What a surprise running into you here!" he exclaimed.

Grace scowled at him, no doubt because he'd joined them for breakfast that morning and asked her for the favor she was now delivering. With a warm smile, she turned her attention to Tillie. "Lady Landsdowne, it's been a while. If I may say, you're looking well."

She seemed surprised by the kindness in his sister's voice. "Thank you, Your Grace. I'm pleased to say I'm doing quite well. I hope the same may be said of you."

"Quite well indeed. The duke wouldn't have it any other way."

"You're very fortunate."

"As I'm well aware." Grace turned to Gina. "Miss Hammersley, I do hope you enjoyed yourself at our ball the other evening."

"It was a magnificent affair, and one I shall always remember with fondness, as I became acquainted with your brother there."

"Don't let my brother fool you, Miss Hammersley. He is a scoundrel."

"I believe you're confusing me with your husband," Rexton said.

Grace smiled, a bit of wickedness in her eyes. "Scoundrels have their uses."

"Once a scoundrel, always a scoundrel," the duke said. "But then we do make life interesting for the ladies, don't we, Rex?"

"Indeed." And he planned to make life very interesting for Tillie later tonight.

"Hate to chat and dash," Lovingdon said, "but we're expected elsewhere. It was a pleasure to cross paths with you ladies."

"We must get together for tea sometime," Grace said. "There is a lovely new establishment called The Royal Tea Palace where my friends and I take tea on occasion. You must join us some afternoon."

"We'd be delighted," Gina chirped. "I've heard the place is exceptional."

"I find it so. I shall see about sending an invitation around in the near future, shall I?"

"That would be lovely."

"Good day to you then."

He waited until the duke and duchess were beyond hearing before leaning toward Tillie and whispering, "Two down, four to go."

*T*he scoundrel! The rogue, the rake, the . . . cheater!

"Family does not count," Tillie informed him with every bit of haughtiness she could muster.

He grinned as though she were a simpleton. "Our wager had no conditions on it, other than six people would approach us. The Duke and Duchess of Lovingdon will have been noticed, stopping to speak with you. They did have another engagement. We almost missed them because of your dillydallying earlier."

She wanted to reach out and tweak his nose, then wrap her hand around his neck and bring him in for a kiss. She had little doubt he was going to win the wager, that four more people would be giving them attention before their time in the park was done. "I do not dillydally."

A ridiculous thing to say when she had indeed taken her sweet time, taking pleasure in making him wait—as a sort of punishment for insisting she accompany them.

"It's not doing my reputation any good for people to see the two of you arguing," Gina said, impatience and perhaps a bit of embarrassment woven into her tone.

"You're right," she told her sister. "We should carry on."

Five minutes hadn't passed before another couple approached them. She recognized the couple. Mr. and Mrs. Drake Darling. While his wife had every right to be addressed as Lady Ophelia, when she had married her husband, she'd made it clear, with an announcement in the *Times*, she was casting aside any ties to the aristocracy. She was an equal with her husband. While some might have thought she was lowering herself in Society, it was quite obvious the lady had an elevated position at her husband's side. After all, the owner of the Twin Dragons was known to be ridiculously wealthy, had been raised as an equal within the Greystone household, and was acknowledged as the Marquess of Rexton's brother.

Darling removed his hat. "Lady Landsdowne. Miss Hammersley. I am led to understand there was a bit of trouble when you were at the Twin Dragons the other night. I'd like to extend a complimentary membership to you both to make up for the unpleasantness you suffered."

Tillie jerked her attention to Rexton. Who had he told? What had he said?

As though reading her mind, he said quietly, "He doesn't know the particulars."

"Lord Evanston, however, has been banned from the club," Darling added. "Hopefully, the canceling of his membership will put your mind at ease that you'll not be bothered should you visit again."

She knew Rexton had been responsible for the man's ousting. But Evanston wasn't the only friend Downie had in his pocket. "I appreciate that, but not everyone welcomes me."

"Send word 'round when you're of a mind to visit," Mrs. Darling told her. "I'll accompany you. Once it is seen you have my support, none will bother you within those walls."

Darling chuckled. "No one wants to suffer my wife's wrath. And within the Dragons, she is queen."

"To your king," Gina chirped.

"I am merely her dragon slayer."

"And a fine one he is," Mrs. Darling said, reaching out and squeezing his hand. "The past may shape us, Lady Landsdowne, but it need not control us or our destinies."

Tillie found herself wondering what in Mrs. Darling's past had shaped her. She'd met her years ago when she was Lady Ophelia. A haughtier woman she'd never known. Her marriage had changed her. Or perhaps there was more to it.

"My sister and I appreciate the offer of the membership and the accompaniment if needed. Although you may come to regret it, Mr. Darling. It seems Gina has considerable luck when it comes to games of chance."

Unlike Tillie who was very close to losing today's wager.

Darling smiled confidently, the grin of a man who knew he wasn't going to lose, not in the end. "I'll take the risk."

They spoke for a few more minutes, nothing of any

importance. When they went on their way, Rexton held up four fingers.

"Don't gloat," she ordered.

"Don't be a sore loser."

"You might not get the six."

He got eight. The Duke and Duchess of Avendale, traveling in a cabriolet, visited with them for a while. They were followed by two lords the marquess had not arranged beforehand to approach them. Apparently, Gina was being noticed whether or not she realized it. Perhaps Tillie hadn't needed to seek Rexton's assistance after all, although she was hard-pressed to regret the decision.

As she watched the exchange, the ease with which her sister flirted, she felt an ache in her chest because Gina didn't have a dozen swains swarming around her.

"There'll be more."

She glanced over at Rexton. Why was it he seemed to always know what was on her mind? Because he had a sister, because she had shared her hopes and dreams with him? She didn't want him to be sensitive, understanding, kind. "You cheated."

"I'd already confessed to doing so at cards when it was to my benefit. So you knew going in to this arrangement that I have no morals when it comes to gaining what I want."

And he wanted her. That thought should not have pleased her so much. "You're also impatient. I don't see that one more night would have made such a difference. It would have simply increased the anticipation."

"Any more anticipation and I'm likely to explode the first time you touch me."

She was likely to do the same. Not that she was

going to admit it. The man's self-esteem was great enough as it was. "Are these gents viable candidates?"

"They'll both inherit earldoms. Will that make your sister happy?"

She shook her head. "She's too young to understand exactly what she needs. Unfortunately we don't always realize what we need until we've gained what we don't."

"You're speaking from experience."

Not a question. A statement, filled with sadness. "I was a silly girl indeed."

"Was he the only one who courted you?"

"The only one I cared about. My mother and I fought. She wanted me to marry a duke, to be higher up on the social ladder. But Downie was so dashing and so gentlemanly. I was quite swept away."

"Did he make you laugh?"

It pleased her that he'd paid attention to her comments regarding what one should look for in a man. Because of that, she decided to be honest. "Not once. Our courting rituals don't really allow us to get to know someone before we marry. A shame, really. I think the Nightingale Club exists because a lot of couples are unhappy."

"But you got out of your unhappy arrangement."

She nodded. "It cost me. It's cost Gina. That I regret. I should have waited."

"If you had, you wouldn't need me now."

She wasn't quite certain that was true. She had the horrifying thought she'd always needed him, always would.

He leaned toward her, his voice low, seductive. "To be quite honest, while it makes me a cad, I'm rather glad you do. I spent a week striving to determine how best to apologize to you so I could have you back in my life. The need is mutual, Countess."

He straightened, turned his attention back to Gina and her admirers, as though he hadn't just delivered words that held the power to devastate her. As the air backed up in her lungs, Tillie didn't know what to say, how to respond. Downie had needed her money, but she couldn't claim he had ever needed *her*.

She was not going to fall under his spell. She was not going to read things into his words that were not meant. He needed her in his bed, but he didn't need *her*. Yet she couldn't quite dismiss the absolute gratefulness that had woven itself through his voice and actions when he'd removed the mask and confirmed it was indeed she in the bedchamber with him. His obvious joy had thrilled her, elevated her self-esteem that had been beaten down for far too long.

He kept his horse beside hers as though there was no shame in being seen with her. But then he'd acted that way from the beginning. She'd assumed because he wanted to impress on Gina he wouldn't be rude to her sister; but now she understood his actions spoke of his kindness and his own willingness to buck Society's conventions. She was beginning to think even having his family approach today had more to do with her than Gina.

The gents finally departed, and they began making their way home. None of them spoke, each lost in their own thoughts she supposed. Her mind traveled to what was to come. She suspected his did as well. She could feel his gaze coming to bear on her time and time again, as though he were measuring her worth.

Or perhaps he was calculating how long it would take him to divest her of her clothing.

When they reached the stables, he dismounted, strode over to her, and wrapped his hands around her waist. Tonight they would be at her waist with no cloth between them. She placed her hands on his shoulders. Slowly, he lifted her up, brought her down. But when her feet were firmly set on the ground, he didn't release her. Rather he held her gaze, seemed to be studying her, considering something.

"If I were a gentleman," he finally said, "I would admit to cheating and forfeit the bet. For both our sakes, I'm damned glad I'm not. I'll send a carriage 'round at half ten."

"Eleven. Gina tends to stay up late. I want her abed before I leave, so she is unaware of my little outing."

"As you wish."

He released his hold on her, swung up onto his saddle, and was trotting away. She, too, was damned glad he was no gentleman.

Chapter 12

*S*he wasn't accustomed to having to sneak about her residence, but she didn't want to awaken Gina, whose room was three down from her own. The possibility of being caught, however, added a tantalizing edge to the night, even though discovery was incredibly slight as all the servants were abed. When she'd arranged to be found kissing the footman, she'd been nervous, terrified that her plan wouldn't work.

She wasn't terrified tonight. She wasn't even nervous. It was true the night might not go as she'd planned, as she hoped, might be naught but disappointment and leave her to face further unsatisfactory nights but the number was limited. She'd been wise enough to ensure their association ended on her terms. She could suffer through anything for a specified period of time. Her marriage to Downie had taught her that.

Slipping out the front door, she locked it behind her. The gleaming black carriage was unmarked as were the driver and footman, neither wearing livery, but rather dressed as vagrants with heavy black coats.

Battered broad-brimmed hats shaded their faces from the glow emanating from the nearby lampposts. The footman opened the carriage door and handed her up. She was halfway through when another hand took hold and assisted her to the bench. The dark, earthy fragrance of the other passenger calmed her nerves as nothing else might.

"I didn't think you'd come personally," she said.

"I wasn't about to leave your safe delivery to others."

His rich, deep voice washed over her. It was ridiculous how much she enjoyed the smallest things about him. His fragrance, his voice, his presence. His care for her safety.

"I take it you managed to slip out with your sister unaware of your departure," he said as the coach lurched into motion.

"She's a sound sleeper once she drifts off. I do need to be back before she awakens."

"I'll have you back hours before anyone stirs."

It wasn't going to be a very long night then. She'd expected to be in his company until near dawn. Shoving back the disappointment, she looked out the window, or wanted to. Curtains obstructed her view. Such a clandestine adventure. She wouldn't have thought to draw the curtains. She supposed she should be grateful he had more experience at these sorts of situations than she did. But she was hard-pressed to see it in a favorable light, to know she was one of many.

"You seem to be quite skilled at carrying on an illicit encounter," she said. "I suppose you've brought a good number of women to your residence."

"You'll be the first."

His answer surprised her. She tried to read the truth

of his words in his face but he was lost to the shadows. She could barely make out his form, which was a bit of a disappointment. She did so enjoy looking at him. "I'm honored."

"You should be."

"Why no one before me?" She wasn't quite certain what she wanted him to say. That she was special. That she was different. That she mattered.

"It complicates things. I generally take my pleasures at the Nightingale. The women visit the establishment for one reason, and I'm happy to accommodate."

"The masks are a bit of a bother, though, aren't they? Have you ever discovered yourself with a woman you didn't fancy—once the mask was removed?"

"I have. Although it wasn't so much I didn't fancy her but rather I knew the taking of her would leave us both with regrets and a good measure of guilt."

"Since the ladies make the selections, I'm certain she was disappointed."

"No doubt, but revenge is a two-edged sword. It cuts both ways. And her selection of me was based on her wanting to hurt someone else."

So he had some lines he wouldn't cross, even in the pursuit of pleasure. She liked knowing that facet to his character. "Does it make you feel cheap? Standing there, waiting to be chosen?"

"Unlike the ladies, the gentlemen pay a hefty purse for membership. So, no, I do not feel at all cheap."

She hadn't been aware of that aspect to the club. It was no doubt necessary in order to maintain the place. There would be costs after all. She didn't want to consider how much of her dowry might have gone to Downie's membership.

"Do you not consider these ladies amoral?" she asked.

"I assume women have urges the same as men."

She wondered what he'd think to know that before meeting him, she'd had very few. Now the ones she did have were distracting and unsettling. She was grateful for the mundane conversation. It kept her from reaching for him. "Why do you suppose it is that men are not flung aside when they engage in sordid behavior and yet ladies are? No one cares which men are standing around at the Nightingale, whether they be bachelors or husbands. Yet women must seek to hide their identity, must strive not to be caught."

"Because women are so much better than us."

"We're not so different."

"I beg to differ. We'll compare our differences before we're done and be glad of them."

His grin flashed in the darkness. She almost laughed. Almost. Yes, their differences were one of the reasons she was here. Loneliness was a poor excuse when the truth revealed she was rather anxious to explore every facet of him that wasn't the same as hers.

He'd had the right of it. She had chosen the Nightingale because she'd hoped to leave there with more than his cooperation regarding Gina. She was rather glad they hadn't consummated their arrangement the night before, that she could pretend his taking her to his bed in his bedchamber signaled he wanted something special with her.

Silence eased around them, creating an intimacy within the darkened interior. Her nerves were beginning to stretch thin with the waiting for their arrival, for the moment when she would find herself in his arms, his mouth on hers. While she wasn't virginal, she wasn't certain her experience would be a match for his. She did hope he'd turn out to be kind if she mucked things up.

"I'd have thought your residence was closer," she finally admitted.

"We're not going to my residence."

That pronouncement surprised her. "Where are we going?"

"Someplace I think you might enjoy."

Would she not enjoy being in his residence, in his bed? "Is it a secretive place?"

Another place of vice, of sin. Perhaps even of depravity.

"The place itself isn't secretive but it does hold one of my secrets."

Dear God, she didn't know why the words sounded ominous, as though she might be on the verge of learning something about him she'd rather not know. "Perhaps you should tell me about it."

"Better to see it, I think."

"Will it change my opinion regarding you?"

"Difficult to say. Depends what your opinion is."

"I don't like secrets." Downie had been full of them, and each one had sliced into her heart, her self-esteem, her confidence.

"I'll wager an additional night with you—one not due me for escorting Gina somewhere—that you'll like this one."

"And if I don't?"

"Then you shall have a night owed to me where you will not have to come to me."

She wished he'd asked for another sort of payment. She didn't much like how easily he wagered nights she feared might become special to her. Obviously they meant little to him, like the coins he so easily wagered at the Twin Dragons. Still she refused to show any vulnerability, had learned it was always preferable not to let the hurt surface. "I accept the terms."

"Splendid."

The carriage was traveling along at a fast clip. Daring to lift aside the edge of a curtain, she peered out. Buildings, but not residences, whipped by. She wasn't familiar with this portion of London. Nothing appeared recognizable. "How much longer before we arrive at our destination?"

"Half an hour perhaps."

Time enough for a kiss or two. She released the curtain. It fluttered back into place. "I'm not quite certain what to make of this . . . adventure. I'm beginning to wonder if you've lost interest in me, now that you know you can have me."

"I assure you, I have not. I would cross over and take you in my arms this very minute except it would mean you'd arrive rather disheveled, possibly with all your clothing pooled on the floor."

She'd never heard such need, such desire woven through a voice. It pleased her no end. With him, she had a feeling she might live up to her reputation of being notorious. "I thought you a man of discipline."

"Not where you're concerned, apparently."

She watched as the shadowy outline of him moved forward. "Make no mistake, Tillie, I want you in my bed. But tonight is the result of a wager won, not a condition met. I'm not going to take advantage of it." He shrugged. "Not entirely. I have your company and for now that is enough."

If she was a silly eighteen-year-old girl who had just come to London, she might think he was courting her, wooing her, striving to win her over with a slow seduction. Their arrangement gave him what he wanted—what she wanted as well if she were honest. All he had to do was take it. That he wasn't caused something inside of her to ache in a way most welcome. When she was twelve, she'd fallen from her horse, broken her arm. The pain had been immediate, sharp, unbearable. Like her divorce from Downie. But as she'd begun to test it, she'd experienced an ache that had felt remarkably good because it had signaled a healing.

She rather felt that way now, as though her cracked and splintered heart was being granted hope of a healing.

Before she could give the matter any further thought, the carriage came to a halt. Thank God, as she didn't want to explore these unwanted feelings and sensations. She was not letting the man get anywhere near her heart.

The door opened. Rexton disembarked, then handed her down. They both wore gloves. She wished they didn't.

The glow from the streetlamps revealed a monstrously large but relatively plain brick building. An enormous sign proclaimed Durham Amusements.

Such an innocuous name for the sort of wicked amusements she suspected were housed in a place on the outskirts of the city. Although she saw no one else about, it was obviously opened to customers this time of night. She imagined peep shows, orgies, decadence, and other sinful activities. Rexton's secrets: he dabbled in the pornographic.

He offered his arm. "Shall we?"

She should emphatically state "No!" She should return to the carriage, make clear she didn't approve of such debauchery. But her curiosity got the better of her. She'd heard whispers about these places, had overheard Downie speaking with his friends about them. Rexton couldn't force her to participate, but to have a look, to confirm the goings-on was tempting beyond measure, could prove interesting and educational. A woman was wise to be as informed as possible, something she'd learned a bit too late. With her knowledge, she could write a letter to the *Times*, alert the constabulary. Perhaps she could bring about some good.

With a jerky nod, she placed her hand on his arm. "I'm not familiar with this place."

"Few people are. It took considerable research on my part to find it."

He began leading her toward the massive door. Two doors actually, and she imagined the dissolute streaming in during the late hours for surely this sort of decadence only occurred after good folk were abed. "Do you come here often?"

"Every couple of weeks. I'm fascinated by what transpires inside."

She wished she didn't know this about him, didn't want the details of his life to sully her opinion of him. It was always impossible to know everything about a person. How could she ensure Gina didn't end up with a man of perversions?

He rapped loudly on the door. Waited. Laid his hand protectively over hers where it rested on his arm as though he sensed it—along with her—might take flight.

Finally a tall, burly man opened it. His thick brown beard hid most of his smile. "My lord."

"Mr. Durham, I do appreciate your making special arrangements to be open to us tonight."

"The blunt you paid me, my lord, ensures I'll open anytime you so wish."

Was he paying for private entertainments? If so, she didn't have to worry about being spotted or recognized.

"Allow me to introduce my friend Miss Tillie," Rexton said.

She appreciated the fact he was giving her some anonymity, that she would be able to deny ever being within the walls of this audacious establishment.

Mr. Durham touched two fingers to his brow. "Welcome, miss. Do come in."

He stepped back.

With a deep breath and steeling herself against the naughty sights that might greet her, Tillie launched herself over the threshold and came up short as the fragrance of freshly hewn wood and newly applied paint assailed her nostrils, not unpleasantly so, but definitely overwhelmingly so. Not surprising as sawdust and wood shavings littered the floor. The cavernous structure was a woodworking workshop. No more than that.

In the far left corner was a gloriously beautiful carousel with an elaborate canopy that she could only describe as a work of art. The horses, in different colors and various poses, were lined up along the circular platform. She couldn't imagine the amount of time, effort, and dedication that had gone into making something so exquisite.

"You make roundabouts," she said in awe, abashed and pleased that the expected nefarious undertaking had turned out to be something that brought naught but delight into lives.

"Indeed we do, miss. Would you care to see the one we're crafting for his Lordship?"

She turned her attention to Rexton. His eyes were glinting with amusement and mischief. To her mortification, she suspected he might have discerned the path her mind had traveled before they'd walked through the door, was rather certain he'd been deliberately mysterious with his answers in order to surprise her. "You're having one built?"

"For the family estate. For my nieces and nephews to enjoy."

"I would like to see it, yes."

"This way then, miss, my lord."

Rexton offered his arm. She took it, feeling as though he were escorting her through a magical place. They passed tables where blocks of wood were in various stages of carving: a head here, a body there, legs over there. She was amazed by the amount of work that each horse took to shape, assemble, paint.

"Each of his carvers specializes in some part of the animal," Rexton said quietly.

"You've watched them work."

"For hours. As I mentioned, it fascinates me to observe as a block of wood become a work of art."

That wasn't exactly what he'd said. Fascinated, yes,

but he'd stopped there, allowing her mind to wander down wicked passageways. She adored carousels but never in a million years would she consider having one created for her personally. That he had thought to have one made for the children in his family touched her in ways that left her reeling with grand emotions she'd not felt in a good long while. What sort of man was he to give so much thought to what might bring joy to children?

As they neared some horses supported in containers, Mr. Durham said, "Watch your skirts, miss. Some of the paint is still wet."

She didn't care about getting paint on her clothing, but she was concerned she might ruin the fine artistry. The craftsmanship was incredible, with intricate detailing that must have taken hours to accomplish.

They reached an area where a small carousel, about half the size of the one she'd first spotted, was on display. Only two animals were positioned on the platform: a lion and a tiger. Nearby rested a bear, a giraffe, a camel.

"It's a menagerie," she said in awe. She'd never seen the like. Every roundabout she'd seen had included horses, some an occasional bench.

"I thought the children would grow bored if they were all ponies," Rexton said. "A dozen animals will circle the platform when it's completed. Mr. Durham has created a system of mechanisms so we can crank it up and it should circle around for a bit before it comes to a stop."

"It's a unique and wonderful gift." She looked up at him, could see how pleased he was with the work that had been done. How unusual for a man to care so much about a child's happiness. "I'm sure they'll enjoy it very much."

He gave her a self-deprecating smile. "It's a selfish endeavor. My hope is that it will reduce the number of requests I receive for rides upon my back."

He played with his nieces and nephews, gave them attention. She couldn't recall any fun memories with her uncle. Before she'd grown up, he'd often repeated the adage that children were to be seen and not heard. He took it quite literally. He looked but he never held. He spoke at but never with. Her opinion and interests were never explored. "They're very fortunate to have you as an uncle."

"Careful, you'll make my head swell."

She very much doubted that. Glancing around, she saw the body of a brown horse. Nearby was the head, adorned with a bridle of delicate red roses. "Fair Vixen, I assume."

"As close as possible."

"Do you really deck her out in roses?"

"No, but my niece informed me I should, that it would make her feel more a lady."

"Wise girl, your niece."

"Mr. Durham is almost finished with her. But she requires one more thing. A secret. I thought perhaps you would do the honors."

She furrowed her brow. "Pardon?"

"Explain to her please, Mr. Durham."

"Aye, sir. See here, miss?"

She walked over to the body of the horse, aware of Rexton following her. Mr. Durham was pointing into the neck.

"That little hollow space remains when the head is

fitted on. It's considered good luck to leave a message inside."

"But no one will ever see it."

"Which makes it the perfect place for secrets," Rexton said near her ear.

"I don't know about that, my lord," Mr. Durham said. "The weather will take a toll on this handiwork. It might need repairing someday. The note could be discovered then."

"But we shall be long gone. Think of the stories that will be woven around the mysterious words left behind. Words left by lovers, perhaps."

They were going to be lovers, soon, so very soon. "Will you write a note?" she asked. "Dare to reveal a secret to the gods of amusements?"

In acquiescence, he dipped his head slightly.

"But we shan't look at each other's," she insisted. "The secrets must remain secrets."

"I would have it no other way."

"You can't cheat, sneak back here and have a look."

His devilish grin did funny things to her stomach. "On this matter, I will not cheat. We'll place our confidences in Mr. Durham's keeping and he'll seal up the horse tonight, before we leave."

She nodded, although she feared she might be proven a fool for putting to paper what she was thinking. But there was a deliciousness to it, to knowing she could put into permanence words that no one would ever see—at least during her lifetime. "All right then. I don't see how any harm will come of it."

"Have you something upon which we can write, Mr. Durham?" Rexton asked, moving away from her.

"Bits of foolscap over here, my lord. You can tie it off with string."

She couldn't help but believe Rexton had discussed all this with Mr. Durham in advance, before he'd brought her here, as everything was laid out on an exceedingly clean and organized table. After dipping pen in inkwell, she composed her note, rolled it up, and wrapped a piece of string around it to secure it. She walked over to the horse and carefully placed the revelation that caused her heart to pump wildly into the small hollow of its neck, wondering what stories might be woven around it if it were indeed discovered years hence.

Rexton dropped his contribution inside. He winked. "Did you write something naughty?"

"Wouldn't you like to know?"

"I would, yes."

She shrugged nonchalantly. "Pity then as I shall never tell."

"Aren't you curious about what I wrote?"

More than she'd ever admit. "Not particularly."

He leaned in. "Little liar." Then he watched her as though searching for something. "Mr. Durham, would it be possible to give my lady a ride on your carousel while you're sealing up our secrets?"

"Absolutely, my lord."

She knew her eyes widened. "The roundabout works?"

"It does. He keeps it as an example of his craftsmanship." This time instead of offering his arm, he closed his hand around hers. "Come along. His is only horses, but each one is different. You can select the one you like best."

She chose a white prancing horse with a red rose carved into its bridle. Rexton lifted her onto it so she was sitting almost sidesaddle. Clutching the pole, she noticed the gears overhead beneath the canopy. "That's elaborate."

"I suspect you've never ridden on one quite like this. Mr. Durham enjoys tinkering."

The man to whom he'd alluded emerged through a door from what appeared to be a small room in the center of the contraption. "Ready, my lord?"

"Yes, Mr. Durham."

"Aren't you going to get on a horse?" she asked Rexton.

"Places too much distance between us."

Mr. Durham disappeared inside. The roundabout gave a jerk before slowly starting to move. He came out, dashed over the platform, and leaped to the floor. "It'll go until it runs out of steam."

He headed back to where their secrets waited to be sealed, leaving them quite alone.

The horse she sat upon began to gradually rise. It peaked, then slid down. Back up—

It was almost like being in a steeplechase—not nearly as thrilling but exceedingly joyous. It caused an incredible lightening of her heart, as though her life had yet to be touched by disappointments and disenchantment.

"There," Rexton said quietly, his bared hand— when had he removed his gloves?—cradling her jaw, his thumb touching the uplifted corner of her mouth. "That's what I wanted to see. Your smile."

She couldn't look away from him, from the way his eyes studied her lips as though he'd never seen anything quite as enchanting, as remarkable.

"I've never seen you smile before. Not from pure pleasure. It's lovely." He lifted his gaze, held hers as though he might never release it. "I knew it would be."

The wonder in his voice, the gladness of it signaling his joy at seeing her smile touched something deep inside her, something she'd thought locked away forever.

"A roundabout makes one feel carefree." Although unable to breathe apparently, as she sounded rather breathless. However, it could have been because she was noticing how rough the edges of his fingers were, how delicious it might feel to have them gliding over the sensitive skin of her breasts, circling her nipples, pinching them.

He scraped his thumb over her lower lip. "Did he steal them from you? Your smiles?"

She didn't need to ask to whom he was referring. "I don't want to talk about him. Not when we're together. All of that is best forgotten."

"Tell me he deserves it and I shall see him ruined."

Her stomach tightened with the knowledge he would do that for her. No one, not even her father, had ever wondered if the blame for her actions should have been laid at Downie's feet. She shook her head. "He doesn't deserve ruination."

He studied her as though he suspected her of lying.

"I was a silly girl. I'll say no more than that. Don't ruin this moment by pressing for more."

"I want your smiles. I want your laughter."

"I want your kiss." She'd never been so bold as to state what she wanted when it came to what transpired between a man and a woman.

His eyes darkened. He moved in. The damned horse

carried her away. Brought her back. His lips touched hers for only a fleeting moment and then they were again separated. Up and down she went. A touch. A separation.

The ride began to slow. The horse lowered and stayed where it was. Rexton placed his hand behind her head and guided her toward him, opening his mouth to hers. He didn't need to prod her this time, didn't need to entice her into parting her lips. She wanted to taste him fully, to stroke her tongue over his, rough velvet to rough velvet. Her position on the horse put her just a little higher than him. She liked the angle, the way he bent his head back, how easily she could scrape her fingers through his hair. She did wish she'd removed her gloves, but she didn't want to stop now to do so. She simply wanted to remain lost in the sensations coursing through her.

With his mouth alone he elicited sparks of pleasure that danced along her nerve endings. She couldn't imagine how marvelous it would be when his entire body was involved. With his hands clamped around her waist, he slowly slid her off the wooden horse and held her aloft as though she were spun from moonbeams. Quarter inch by tormented quarter inch, he lowered her to the platform, her body pressed to his so she was aware of buttons and bulges.

Drawing back, he pressed a kiss to her chin, her temple—and held her there, his harsh breath rasping against her ear as though he'd dashed up a towering hill. "I told Mr. Durham we would be only an hour."

With her face pressed to his chest, she could hear the thudding of his heart. "We should be off then."

"Yes."

Leaning away, he reached down and took her hand. "You may have well ruined roundabouts for me. I won't be able to look at one without thinking of you."

She couldn't recall anyone offering her such a beautiful sentiment. And she wouldn't be able to look at one without remembering the night she might have fallen a little bit in love with him.

He wanted to hold her, kiss her, take her to his residence and make wild, passionate love to her until dawn. Instead he sat opposite her in the coach because he didn't intend to take her quickly or like a savage—and he wanted her so badly he wasn't certain he could restrain himself.

Her smile . . . her smile had unmanned him.

"Your own children will play on that roundabout," she said quietly, gazing out the window.

He'd drawn the curtains aside. The inside of the carriage was dark. No one was going to be able to make out their features. His coachman and footman weren't in livery. They'd actually embraced the notion of going on a clandestine outing. He'd left disguising themselves to them. They'd done a remarkable job. "I suppose they will, yes."

"Gina is correct. You're getting up in years. You can't put off marriage much longer, not if you want a young wife."

He wondered what she was thinking, why she was discussing his future. "I may have already missed the mark on that. Do you know what my first thought was when I was introduced to Gina?"

She turned her head to look at him. "That she was beautiful?"

"That she was a child. To be honest, I can't see myself with any of these debutantes. They have no life experience. They're all innocent and naïve and . . . they're not women." But she was a woman. She wasn't innocent. She had experience. A great deal of experience.

"Why the footman?" he heard himself ask. It was ridiculous to be envious of a servant, and yet he was. Outlandishly so.

She looked back out the window. "I was lonely. And he was kind."

He wanted to ask in what manner, what had he done precisely. Because Rexton would duplicate it. Whatever she required, whatever she needed. Again, ludicrous thoughts as he wasn't going to emulate the actions of another man. He'd never felt the need to imitate. "Kind in what way precisely?"

Damn it! Why couldn't he let it go?

He heard a short burst of harsh laughter.

"It's difficult to describe. You're accustomed to servants showing you deference. Ours had little ways of implying—with tones or the upturning of a nose or questioning a request—that I wasn't quite up to snuff. I was American. What did I know about what was right and proper?"

"You should have sacked the lot of them."

She turned back to him and as they passed a streetlamp, the light caught her small, sad smile. "I wasn't allowed to. Downie's mother, the dowager countess, was still in charge. She lived with us. The day after we were married, she was waiting for me at breakfast, determined to ensure I had done my duty the night before. I suppose she was going to

deny me sustenance if I hadn't admitted to endur-
ing the unpleasantness in the bedchamber without
complaint."

"Was it unpleasant?" While he'd never taken a
virgin, he knew discomfort, possibly pain, could be
involved.

"Not overly much. I was inexperienced. My mother
had told me nothing. All I knew about the act of breeding I learned watching horses, so I was a bit nervous. I
suppose all brides are. Anyway, his mother informed
me I was to see to my duty posthaste and deliver a son
to my husband. A daughter would not be tolerated. I
was to produce boys. Only boys until we had an heir
and a spare. Then perhaps a daughter would be welcomed."

He tried not to read things into what she hadn't
said. It wasn't his place to pry but he did wonder if
Landsdowne had been patient, gentle. Still he let the
topic return to what she was willing to discuss. "We
do seem obsessed with gaining our heirs," he said
quietly. "Although I don't think my father would have
objected if Grace had been born first."

"But I wasn't married to your father. And it's a bit
difficult to get with child when your husband leaves
you at the country estate for long stretches."

"Leaves you? You mean alone?"

"With his dragon of a mother. He had matters to
see to. I never learned her name."

Downie had been having an affair? Why the bloody
hell would he do that when he had Tillie? She said
she'd been lonely, the servant kind. Christ, Rexton
would not have left her for a single night, a single hour.

He certainly wouldn't have gone to another's bed. "Did you love him?"

"I thought I did. I wanted to. I wanted to marry for more than a title. Perhaps I was merely in love with the idea of being in love. I look at Gina sometimes . . . and have difficulty believing I was ever that young. Six years separate us, but there are times when it seems we are separated by a century." She released a bitter laugh, looked back out the window. "Only a little while ago, I said I wouldn't discuss him and now I've gone on and on."

He was torn between being grateful at having a clearer understanding of what her life might have been—the reasons behind her decisions—and wishing he'd remained in blessed ignorance. He didn't like thinking of her being unappreciated. "He was undeserving of you."

"His mother and sister thought he deserved better than me. His sister treated me as atrociously as his mother did. My dowry helped her become the Countess of Blanford. Would the earl have given her the time of day if Downie hadn't used a portion of what I brought to the marriage for *her* dowry? Yet she never had a kind word. When she discovered me with the footman—the look on her face. It wasn't horror but triumph because she knew she would be rid of me. And I was glad of it." Her gaze once more landed on him, and he felt the weight, the intensity, of it. "What of you? Surely not all your relationships ended happily?"

"I have nothing to rival what you experienced." But she'd been open with him, more open than he suspected she'd ever been where he was concerned. "There was a girl. Her name was Emmaline. She sold flowers near the school. I was fifteen and fancied myself in love. She stepped out with me one evening. Lifted her skirts for me." Now he was the one to glance out the window. They were nearly to Landsdowne Court.

"She was your first," Tillie said quietly.

"No, actually. She would have been but the lad with whom she was living showed up with some of his mates. Because I was all agog at what she was offering, I didn't notice them until it was too late. They beat the bloody hell out of me, took everything of value, stripped me bare. Do you have any idea how difficult it is to get about the city when you're not wearing a stitch of clothing?"

"Whatever did you do?"

Looking at her, he was glad to hear the interest in her voice, the underlying shimmer of laughter she refrained from releasing. He hadn't wanted to end the night with her melancholy, thinking of her past. He shouldn't have asked about her marriage, the footman, or Downie. He wouldn't again.

"Hid within some bushes until it was full dark. Then cautiously began making my way back to school. Stole a blanket from somewhere, some trousers that were too large from someone's clothesline. I never saw her again. She no doubt saw me as an easy mark. I should have known better, considering my mother's past."

"What if the lad hurt her for carrying on with you?"

He shook his head. "No, she was laughing too much for that and I overheard him praising her ingenuity as his boys pummeled me." He leaned forward. "But I learned that I can't judge other people based on someone else's actions. The next time I fancied myself in love with a girl, she provided more pleasant memories."

"Fancy yourself in love a lot, do you?"

He grinned. "When I was younger, yes. But with age has come more discerning tastes, at least where my heart is concerned."

The carriage came to a stop. She raised the hood on the cloak over her head.

The door opened. He made to exit. She touched his arm, stilling him as effectively as if she'd suddenly appeared before him like a brick wall. "Where are you going?"

"To escort you to the door."

"I don't need people to see you."

"My hat will shade my face. Besides, there is a good distance between your residence and any other. I doubt anyone is looking out this time of morning. I'm not going to let you traipse off by yourself as though I haven't a care for you."

Chapter 13

His words—*a care for you*—echoed through her thoughts as though he'd proclaimed his love. But care was a far distance from love. She couldn't insert meanings that had no bearing into his words. Her heart was balancing precariously enough as it was, wanting more from him, knowing she could never acquire it. She could never be more than his mistress, more than the woman with whom he had an affair.

He was destined for a dukedom. He required—deserved—a woman above reproach.

She constantly reminded herself of that fact as she made her way through the following day and evening, as her nerve endings grew taut with each passing hour that brought the clock nearer to the stroke of eleven. She suspected she'd get no reprieve tonight. But then she didn't want one. She wanted him, wanted them together.

With the hood of her cloak already covering her head, she was standing at the front window in the foyer when she saw the carriage approaching. She was out the door and down the steps before it stopped. The footman opened the door, assisted her inside.

And he was there. His scent and his warmth wafting around her. His presence bringing such gladness. She almost told him that this day had been the longest of her life, but experience had taught her to be cautious with her heart, her hopes, her dreams.

"I thought the night would never get here," he said, his voice a low thrum in the darkness. "How did you occupy yourself today?"

"I worked in the garden." Not a single weed had survived her thorough search. In need of distraction, she'd become lost in her endeavors. "Read." Held a book more like. "You?"

"Met with estate managers. Visited a friend. Did a little boxing."

"Did you get hurt?"

"No, he went easy on me. Mostly we danced around each other. But I had a lot of energy to work off."

"I do hope you saved some for tonight."

"I saved a good deal for tonight."

The carriage drew to a stop. She raised the hood on her cloak just as the door opened. Rexton exited, then reached back to help her disembark. He tucked her hand into the crook of his elbow.

"I suppose your servants are discreet," she said, as she glanced up at the massive manor.

"They are." He led her up the wide stone steps. The door opened. A footman who stood at attention nearby had obviously been awaiting their arrival.

As she averted her eyes, she was grateful for the hood. She caught sight of the sweeping stairs, wished they didn't make drawing in air so frightfully difficult. Now that the moment was upon her—

She became aware of Rexton unfastening her cape, drawing it and the hood away from her, handing it over to the servant. Here no shadows hovered; light in the chandeliers allowed her to see him so clearly. The blue of his eyes, a strong jaw recently shaved if the smoothness of it was any indication. She licked her lips.

"You're nervous," he said, his voice low.

"It's been a while." A while since she'd been alone with a man for the purpose of intimacy. An even longer while since she'd wanted to be.

"I've something to show you."

She dropped her gaze to his crotch. "I'm certain you do."

His deep laughter echoing through the foyer made her smile.

"Are all Americans as blunt?" he asked.

"Only those of us with notorious reputations."

"I like that you're not a shy miss."

She was grateful he couldn't see what not being so was costing her. She wanted this, wanted to be with him, but a part of her wanted to retreat, wanted to ask him not to go too quickly, to give her time to adjust to the notion she might be desirable.

Again, he tucked her hand into the crook of his elbow and began leading her down a hallway, not up the stairs as she'd expected. Paintings of horses dotted the walls.

"You do love your horses," she mused.

"I do indeed. I find them to be gorgeous in their

simplicity, noble in their endeavors. A horse will race his heart out for you. What of your parlor? Are those various representations of horses displayed there your doing?"

"Yes. I admire them as well. I suppose we have that in common."

"We have a good deal more than that."

They reached a parlor or perhaps it was a lady's library. A wall of shelves contained books and assorted vases. The chairs and sofa were covered in pastels that surprised her.

"You favor pink?"

"My mother had a hand in decorating this room. My tastes lean toward the dark. She wanted someplace to sit that wouldn't leave her melancholy when she visited."

"I met your mother once. She was very kind."

"I find her so."

He led her to a set of double doors. After opening them, he escorted her into a garden. Roses and other blossoms long closed for the night scented the air. The glow from two lanterns revealed a blanket spread over the ground, a wicker basket, a bottle of wine, glasses, and plates.

"We're having a picnic?" she asked, the very last thing she'd expected.

"I'm a firm believer that seduction begins before one nears a bedchamber."

She looked up at him. His mother wasn't the only one who was kind. She'd deduced he wouldn't make a good husband for Gina. Now she felt rather guilty about her assessment, worried she might have caused her sister to lose out on a lifetime of happiness with a man who might have appreciated her. "I may have judged you harshly, my lord."

"Because you didn't think me suitable for your sister?"

She nodded, hating that she'd been so obvious in her disregard for his attentions.

"We're not suited, Gina and I. I much prefer a woman who views herself worthy of a great deal more than pretty frocks and chocolates."

Two of the items Gina had claimed would make her happy.

Drawing her in, he lowered his mouth to hers and took with a slow and steady insistence that curled her toes, melted her knees, turned the secretive place between her thighs into liquid desire. Did he really think after delivering a searing kiss that they were going to sit on a blanket, sip wine, and converse about the weather or the stars? Although she had to admit if she saw one arcing across the sky, she might very well find herself making a wish that somewhere in America she would find a man who would cause her to feel as this one did: treasured, adored, desired.

He growled once before stepping back with a harsh curse directed at himself and his lack of restraint. She'd never let him know that his ability not to resist her stroked her ego, lifted her self-esteem. He grabbed her hand with an abruptness and lack of gentleness that spoke to the tension rampaging through him. She was awful to take such delight in it.

"Let's sit, shall we?"

Let's not hovered on the tip of her tongue. Part of her wanted to admit there was no reason for all this. That she was well and truly seduced already. That she was anxious to go to his bedchamber, to lie in his bed. Part of her craved the wooing that had been so absent from her marriage, wanted to savor these moments, knowing everything would change once he possessed her, once he obtained what he sought. She would be his in ways she feared, in ways he'd never comprehend or understand. There was a difference between men and women, in how they viewed such an intimate act. He could partake in it without involving his heart. She wasn't certain she could. "Let's," she whispered, before stepping onto the blanket and lowering herself to the ground.

He didn't know why he was of a mind to woo her. They had an arrangement. He could have raced up the stairs, dragging her behind him, and she couldn't have complained or objected. He could have tossed her onto the bed, lifted her skirts, and taken her and she couldn't have faulted him. They had an agreement. They had terms.

He hated everything about the reasons that had brought her here.

But he was too selfish, wanted her too badly to send her away, to return to the original bargain and take the damn stallion for stud. She'd given herself to others, to her husband, to a damned footman, to some lucky sod or two at the Nightingale. She wasn't pure or moralistic or particularly selective when it came to bedding. Yet, he wanted her to be all that—for him. He wanted to be all that for her.

He set out the cheese, olives, and fruit. He poured their wine, raised his glass in a salute. "To a night neither of us will soon forget."

She lifted her glass, bowed her head, sipped. Her fragrance drowned out the blossoms that scented the air.

"During our arrangement, you're not to go to anyone else's bed."

She jerked her gaze up to his, her eyes wide. He hadn't meant to sound so commanding. But the thought of her going to anyone else after being with him turned his stomach, caused his skin to crawl, made him want to hit something.

"I expect the same consideration from you," she said tautly, equally as commanding.

"Why would I want anyone else while I have you?"

"I could prove a disappointment."

Tillie despised the silence stretching between them, taut and frayed, as though he were mulling over the real possibility that when all was said and done he wouldn't find her to his liking. That sometimes it was better to possess the dream than to hold the reality. She wished it were afternoon, that they were wreathed by bright sunlight, so she could look more deeply into his eyes, could discern what he might be thinking. Finally, he shook his head, cupped her cheek with one large strong hand.

"Not bloody likely."

Then his mouth was on hers and it was like there had been no end to the kiss he'd given her before they'd lowered themselves to the blanket, as though no time had passed since his lips had last glided so provocatively over hers. But time had passed between one kiss and the next. She tasted the wine more strongly on his tongue, could feel the coolness of the night air on the nape of his neck as she clasped her hand around it. Could feel the tension radiating through his body as though he'd found no respite in the delay, in the conversation, as though he'd been torturing himself striving to give her a bit of civility when he was naught but barbarism and savagery, yearning for her with an intensity that she was rather certain had never been directed her way.

She gloried in it. In the way he eased her down to the ground, the way he nibbled on her throat and bared shoulders before returning his mouth to hers with a feral growl that spoke of untamed passions. He called to the wildness in her, the unruly longings that she'd banked because her husband had declared any sort of enthusiasm or excitement as unseemly in a wife, more suited to a harlot.

But tonight she didn't care if she behaved as a doxie, if Rexton found her vulgar. Tonight was for her fantasies, needs, and wants to be fulfilled. And if he claimed her lacking, to hell with him. They could do away with their nightly trysts, but he would have to help with Gina or turn over Fair Vixen. She knew he would never give up his mare.

So Gina's future was safe, secure, no matter how tonight went, no matter how much Tillie writhed as Rexton's hands skimmed over her, no matter how she whimpered wanting more from him, no matter how firmly she brazenly pressed her body against his and urged him to take her: here, now, on the blanket with the moon looking on—and any number of neighbors with a spyglass.

"To hell with the seduction," he rasped. "You seduced me the moment you strolled into the parlor and offered me whisky."

She'd offered it to him because she'd needed it for

herself. When she'd seen him standing there, in his golden glory, so beautiful, so devastatingly masculine, she'd wanted to turn tail and run. The shock of her immediate attraction to him had caused her to tremble. The whisky had been for her, to calm her pounding heart, to silence the vixen residing within her skin who had begun whispering "Want!"

He shoved himself away from her, leaving her forlorn and miserable, pushed himself to standing, reached down, pulled her to her feet, and lifted her into his arms. His strides were long, quick, purposeful as he headed for the house. She rested her head on his shoulder and began toying with the buttons on his shirt.

"Why do men wear so much clothing?"

He laughed. She truly loved his sound of merriment, of joy. For the life of her, she couldn't recall ever hearing Downie laugh. But then she'd never been carried in his arms or rushed to a bedchamber as though he might expire if he didn't get her there quickly, as though without her he would cease to exist.

What a silly girl she was to read so much into his actions when he might only be seeking release for his swollen and aching cock. Perhaps any woman would do. Perhaps she wasn't so special. But it didn't matter because at that moment she was the one in his arms.

"Women wear so much more—and it's much more cumbersome to remove," he lamented.

"You can rip it off," she said dreamily.

"Then how will I get you home?"

She had the insane thought she never wanted to go home, never wanted to return to the mausoleum in which she lived, the residence she had claimed out of revenge, mistakenly thinking that it would bring her satisfaction.

Into the manor they went, up the stairs. By the time he charged into a bedchamber—his, she assumed—she'd unknotted his neck cloth and mussed his hair until he looked rakish and uncivilized. The door had barely closed with a *snick* before her feet were hitting the floor and his mouth was claiming hers with a hunger that equaled her own. Unlike the kiss last night, this time she was inches lower so he had to dip his head. She liked the way he curled his arm around her, brought her in closer to his body. She loved the way he was undoing lacing and ties without ever removing his lips from hers or his tongue retreating from its enthusiastic engagement with hers.

This, she thought wildly, this was how kisses should be—full, bold, fervent. They should steal the breath, weaken the knees while at the same time reawakening, inspiring, rekindling passion until one felt incredibly alive, ignited, aware of every small touch, every nuanced stroke.

When his mouth left hers, the fire in his eyes caused heat to rampage through her. With quick sure hands, he worked to remove the clothing he'd unfastened so expertly. She refused to consider how much practice he might have had elsewhere to achieve what he did with such proficiency. She was not a virgin, untouched, without experience.

She recalled how awkward and clumsy she'd been the first time, how shy and afraid. She was grateful not to be his first, grateful to be the beneficiary of all he'd learned. Her clothing became a discarded pool on the floor, and she fought not to cover herself from his excruciatingly slow perusal. The heat in his eyes burned hotter, the corners of his mouth curved upward.

"My God, but you're beautiful."

He began tearing at his own clothes, and she could do little more than watch as his glorious chest was revealed. Oh, yes, marble sculpted much as she'd imagined it. His boots, stockings went. Then his trousers.

Her breath caught, suspended, rushed out. With trembling fingers, she touched his sternum before pressing her palm flat, splaying those fingers out. "You're equally beautiful."

"You're wrong but I'm not going to ruin things by arguing with you." He pulled her close. Skin to skin from shoulder to toes. Warmth and silk. Coarse springy hair. Heat. A throbbing as his cock pressed against her belly. A rumbling of chest against her breasts as he growled low and deep.

He began marching her backward, never taking his mouth from hers, his hands never ceasing their stroking of her back, her shoulders, her hips as though with her legs moving various parts of her felt different. Perhaps they did.

He felt different. His buttocks bunched and tightened as he walked. She loved squeezing them, stroking them. Gliding her hands up his back, sliding them down. She imagined she could feel the individual muscles doing their work as he guided her toward the bed.

The backs of her thighs hit the mattress. He drew back, lifted her up, and placed her on the sheets as though she were a piece of hand-blown glass to be carefully set on velvet to avoid breaking.

He covered her body with his, heat against heat,

hard steel against soft silk. He was so much larger, he fairly swamped her, yet she felt no fear, no panic. He'd made her smile again. She suspected he was going to make her smile a great deal more before the night was done.

He nipped at her shoulder, kissed her collarbone, trailed a series of butterfly-light kisses over her breasts. "Spread your legs," he ordered, his voice deep and gravelly.

She did as he bade.

"More."

She obeyed. He eased into the space she'd created. He kissed his way down her belly before sitting back on his heels, his gaze not on her eyes, her face, her breasts, but lower, much, much lower.

"You're not looking at me there," she whispered, horrified by the thought she was so exposed. Why had they not dimmed the lights? Why wasn't he already joining his body to hers?

"I am. And I'm going to do much more. I'm going to lick it."

"No." She tried to close her legs but he was in the way.

He curled his hands around her thighs. "Don't struggle. I won't do anything you object to, but I think you would like it."

He released his hold on her legs and used his fingers to gently spread the folds open as though unfurling a rose. "Such a pretty pink." Over the opening, he stroked a finger. When he held it up, she could see it glistening.

"So wet," he said. "Do you ever touch yourself there?"

Now he held her gaze? When he asked such a personal and impertinent question?

She wanted to lie but there had been too much dishonesty in her other relationship. "Yes." It came out as a scratch, like fingernails scraped over a slate.

"Do you think of me when you do?"

Still he held her gaze. She nodded.

"Do you peak?"

She bit her lower lip, not wanting to acknowledge the truth with words or movement, although she suspected he knew it.

"I do," he said quietly, leaning forward and kissing one of her lower ribs. "When I think of you and stroke myself, I come swift and hard." Still he did not look away from her eyes. "I fear I will do so tonight, when I am buried inside you, when your notch closes around me, hugs me tightly, threatens to strangle my cock. When you are so slick and I like a rock and we move in tandem. I fear I will not be able to wait for you—no matter how hard I try. If you were any other woman I would distract myself with sums, but I don't want to think of anything except you, of what it feels like to be inside you."

She had ceased to breathe, to think. If he touched a finger to her now, it would come away drenched. Her nipples had hardened; her stomach was quivering. Poetry would not have sounded sweeter to her ears.

"I want you to come before me, Tillie. Allow me to lick you, sweetheart."

The deep yearning reflected in his low voice was her undoing. He truly wanted this—for her. A shudder of pleasure rippled through her. A croak escaped her lips. It was meant to be yes, but it sounded like desperate desire, unbridled longing. Yet apparently he accurately interpreted it, because he shifted until he was stretched out on his belly, his face positioned between her thighs. He lowered his head.

The first stroke nearly had her catapulting off the bed. Had she ever felt anything so sublime, so wicked, so marvelous? He made a sound deep in his throat as though he were feasting on a delicious morsel. Was he possibly enjoying this as much as she was?

There was no part of her that didn't feel touched by him, that wasn't curling. Clutching the sheets, she released a little mewling cry, embarrassed that it had escaped.

"That's it, sweetheart. Make all the noises you want."

"I feel a need to scream."

"Then scream. There's no one to hear."

He wouldn't judge. She knew that. She looked down at the blond curls, the strong hands cradling her hips, the broad shoulders keeping her legs spread wide. Everything she'd experienced before tonight told her that she should have been mortified by this intensely personal encounter—

Yet she'd never felt more treasured, more loved—no, not loved. They did not love each other. But she did feel adored. Appreciated. He could have taken his pleasure without worrying about her, without seeing to her needs. But he hadn't.

She combed her fingers through his soft curls and surrendered.

To the remarkable sensations that his efforts elicited. To the fire that burned, to the glorious unfolding of pleasure in its purest, most basic form: uncivilized, feral. She couldn't control the scream, the arching of her back, the wracking of her body that overtook her as splendor engulfed her.

Never before had she experienced anything like it. She was left lethargic, gasping for breath, barely aware of his moving up to hover over her.

Then his eyes met hers. Reaching up, she cradled his beautiful face. "Take me."

"With pleasure."

He glided into her smoothly, her body stretching to accommodate him. She lifted her hips and he sank deeper with a groan, his arms closing around her as his hips pistoned, fast, hard, sure. She'd thought it impossible, but the pleasure began building again, tighter, more intense.

She clutched him, buried her face in his neck, pressed her mouth against his skin as the cataclysm overtook her, overtook him. The force of his release nearly slammed her into the headboard. If he hadn't been holding her so tightly, she'd likely be unconscious now. She was fairly close to that, to not being able to think.

Smiling, she held on to him, wishing this moment would never have to end.

*S*he'd never simply lain there afterward, snuggled against a man's side, his arm around her, his fingers lazily stroking and circling over her upper arm. It was a devastating moment to realize what she'd never truly possessed, what she might never possess for longer than a few nights, for however long this affair lasted. She rather regretted now that she'd insisted they'd be done by the end of the Season.

"I was never intimate with Griggs," she felt compelled to confess. She needed him to know how truly unique, how special it was that she was in this bed with him. She was keenly aware of his stilling.

"Griggs?"

"The footman who is now my butler."

He shifted slightly, his arm coming away from her, as he rose up on his elbow and looked down on her. Even though his hip rested against hers, she wished she'd held silent, that she hadn't disturbed the lethargic spell that had encased them.

"People witnessed you kissing him."

She nodded. "But it was never more than a kiss. And only that once." She'd gone this far. She might as well go all the way. "I was so terribly unhappy. As I mentioned, Griggs was kind, because it was his way. He had no romantic feelings toward me, and I had none toward him. Our relationship was distant, but respectful. In the beginning, when I was learning my way around, he would cover for me if I made a mistake. I came to trust him. So I asked for his assistance, to help me stage a situation in which we'd be caught kissing. I promised him he'd always have a position in my household if he would do me this one favor. Public humiliation was the only way to force Downie into divorcing me."

"You wanted a divorce?" His tone implied he found the notion inconceivable. Most did. The shame of it, the embarrassment it brought. It signaled failure, loose morals, lack of loyalty.

"Desperately. I'd asked him for over a year, pleaded with him to end the farce of our marriage, but he had too much pride to go through something so scandalous. So I created a scenario that was more ruinous, one that allowed him to garner sympathy."

"You made him look a fool."

"I was the fool." In so many ways.

"The men you met at the Nightingale . . ." His voice trailed off, but she knew he was asking a question, wanted details.

"I didn't meet men at the Nightingale. Other than Downie, you're the only man I've ever been with."

"But you knew of the place. Its location isn't known by many. Most don't believe it even truly exists."

"Something was amiss in our marriage. I knew that. He was so distant. I thought the fault was mine. He invariably left me alone in the country. When we were in London for the Season, he would often go out at night. We'd been married a year. I was all of twenty and growing more despondent, because I couldn't determine how to make him happy, how to please him. So one night when he left, I followed. I'd heard rumors of the Nightingale Club, but I thought it was myth.

"I was standing in the shadows, trying to determine if I should go in and confront him, worried that perhaps it wasn't what I thought, perhaps it was much worse. A woman approached. 'Is it your first time, love?' she asked. 'I'll show you how it's done.'

"She escorted me inside, introduced me to the matron who kindly took me under her wing, loaned me a mask, arranged for a servant to help me change. They thought I was in want of adventure. I walked into that parlor and saw a woman sitting on Downie's lap. They were laughing. Somehow that hurt worst of all. He never laughed with me. To be quite honest, I can't remember him ever smiling at me once we were married. I could do little more than stand there like an idiot and watch as she slid off his lap. He stood, tucked her beneath his arm, escorted her from the room and up the stairs. He looked as though he anticipated being with her. Coming to my bed was always a chore."

He grazed the backs of his fingers along her cheek. "He couldn't have seen bedding you as a chore."

"'Just lie still and endure it,' he said on our wedding night. So I did. Still, I always dreamed it could be so much more." Reaching up, she cupped her palm over his jaw, feeling the slight tickling of his stubble. He'd shaved before he retrieved her, but his beard was making itself known. "Tonight for the first time, it was what I'd always believed it could be."

"Christ, Tillie," he growled before taking her mouth with an urgency that alerted her this time they would not go slow.

*S*he hadn't been unfaithful. She didn't have a taste for the rough, hadn't been bedded by a footman, soon to be butler. She hadn't had affairs. She'd sacrificed her reputation, her standing, her place in Society for a chance to be free of Landsdowne. She'd forced a life of solitude, an absence of friends, onto herself.

He adored her for it. For not staying with the unfaithful bastard, for recognizing she deserved better, for using whatever means necessary to free herself.

For taking a chance, for being with him now.

When he had promised her only this: running his hands and his mouth over every inch of her body. He loved every aspect of her. The roundness of her breasts, the arch of her back, the dimples in her backside. Tiny, but there just as he'd envisioned them.

He entered her with a sure thrust, up to the hilt, and pumped hard and fast. Threading his fingers through hers, he carried her hands over her head, held them there, held her gaze. "Don't close your eyes," he ordered.

He wanted to see the fires of passion burning within the blue. Her hard nipples grazed his chest with each movement, her thighs bracketed his hips, her knees pressed against his sides. Her sighs and moans filled his ears, echoed through the chamber.

He wanted this every night, every morning, every afternoon. Never before had anything felt so right. She was made for him, and him alone. It didn't matter that she'd had another. It mattered only that she was here now, with him.

He would not think about her leaving Britain; he wouldn't contemplate that this was not forever. He would give her memories to take with her, and she would leave memories with him behind. For above all else, he wanted her happy.

"Rexton," she rasped, her eyes holding his even as she rolled her head from side to side, as her fingers tightened on his.

"Fly, sweetheart. I'll follow."

Her cry was the sweetest he'd ever heard. Then he kept his word.

*T*illie understood at long last why Juliet argued with Romeo that she'd heard the nightingale and not the lark. She didn't want her time with Rexton to end, for dawn to creep over the land, to awaken all sleeping things, to bring with it the reality of her life. In his carriage, he held her against his side as though he, too, were reluctant to let her go.

"I would apologize for my rudeness in not letting you sleep," he said, his voice a low lullaby in the rocking carriage, "but I suspect you'd view it as insincere."

They'd drifted off a couple of times, although not for long. But even during sleep-filled moments, she was acutely aware of the long length of his body pressed against hers, his chest to her back, his leg draped possessively over her hip. There was security in that position. She'd never wanted to be a possession, yet she couldn't deny that she relished being possessed—by him, at least. She didn't belong to him, not truly, not for more than a few weeks anyway. Yet she liked the idea that at this particular moment she was his, and he was hers.

"I acquired more sleep than I expected—or wanted," she assured him. "I'll sleep the remainder of the morning, probably well into the early afternoon."

"Mmm," he murmured, nuzzling her neck. "Do you know how good you smell right now? You smell of sex, a little sleep, and me."

She felt the blush rising over her cheeks. He smelled of her mixed with his scent. It was a glorious fragrance.

"I'm half tempted to have the carriage return us to my residence," he said.

"How would I explain my absence?"

"Would Gina notice it?"

"I suspect so. She's accustomed to having me about."

"More's the pity."

When the carriage stopped, he disembarked, then handed her down. With his arm around her, pulling her in close against him, he escorted her up the steps. She retrieved her key, only to have him take it from her, and use it to unlock the door. She closed her fingers around it when he extended it toward her. She needed something solid and firm to hold on to, something that reminded her where she needed to be.

He leaned down, she tilted up her face, welcoming the brushing of his lips over hers.

"Let your sister know that I'll be taking her rowing this afternoon," he said quietly, before shoving open the door.

It was ridiculous how much she didn't want to leave him.

"Be certain you're her chaperone."

Nodding, she slipped through the doorway, held her breath as the door closed with a hushed click. She locked it, then leaned against it, and waited, listening for the sound of his retreating carriage.

When it came, she headed for the stairs, wondering how she could possibly sleep, knowing that she'd be seeing him in only a few hours.

Chapter 14

Gina Hammersley was beginning to suspect she was the one serving as chaperone on these outings. While she was very much aware Rexton wasn't courting her, she was beginning to suspect he might well be courting her sister. She'd noticed the attraction simmering between them during their first outing to the park. But it seemed they were no longer striving to ignore it or to pretend it didn't exist.

Sitting beside her on the boat's bench, Tillie was wearing a pretty pink frock and holding a matching parasol that kept the sun off her face. While she appeared to be searching the water for tiny fish swimming about, her gaze continually flitted over to Rexton and her cheeks would turn a bright rosy hue as though the man had leaned over and whispered something naughty in her ear. Meanwhile his eyes darkened, the muscles in his bared forearms would flex all the more, and the boat would travel a bit faster. It was fascinating to watch.

She didn't quite understand how this exercise was going to garner the opportunity for her to meet and talk with men. When she expressed her concerns, Rexton assured her it was all about being seen. But anyone who saw them all together was going to know she wasn't holding the marquess's interest.

She feared by Season's end she'd be in the same position she was now, with no one to call her own.

*T*illie did wish he hadn't removed his jacket or rolled up his sleeves so slowly, so provocatively, revealing those lovely forearms upon which he'd rested the night before while dipping down to kiss her shoulder after one of their passion-filled rides had come to an end. It was ludicrous that she should find hair on the forearms so masculine, that the way the ropy muscles bunched as he rowed should be so intoxicating. No wonder he was so strong, had been able to carry her as though she weighed nothing at all.

It was a lovely cool summer afternoon, yet she felt as though she was walking in New York with the sun beating down on her and no air to be found.

Before falling into slumber, she'd convinced herself last night had been an aberration, that she'd misread the intensity of his attentions because she'd gone so long without a man's interest. She'd been desperate for it, and so she'd imagined it to be far greater than it was. Although at the moment, she was surprised the little boat didn't ignite into flames from his heated glances.

She read promises there, precious vows of what he would do with her when next he had her. Dear God, but being a man's mistress was far better than being his wife. Perhaps it was because affairs were illicit and therefore brought with them a greater temptation.

Perhaps it was because they were renegades, breaking the laws of God and man. Perhaps it was because they were fully aware their time together was finite. That they wouldn't be together until death so each moment was more precious.

Whatever it was, she feared that everyone in the boats surrounding them knew what they'd done last night, what they would do again. That they could see him branded upon her, knew exactly where his mouth had been, where she longed for it to be once more.

"Perhaps we should discuss your efforts where Gina is concerned," she said as much to distract herself from her wandering wicked thoughts as to ensure he did indeed have some plan for securing a husband for her sister.

"I believe there is some sort of affair tomorrow night," he said laconically as though he hadn't given it any thought.

"Yes, the Ainsley ball. Gina will be there. It's well attended." She lifted a shoulder, dropped it back down. "At least it was some years back when I was welcomed. I've no reason to believe that's changed." She'd read nothing in the gossip sheets to indicate the duke and duchess had lost favor. "How will you proceed while there?"

He glanced behind him, no doubt striving to ensure he didn't ram into anyone. Several boats were being rowed along this stretch of river. "Continue to introduce her about, shower her with attention, dance with her."

She hated every aspect of his plan. It struck a chord of jealousy within her that she didn't much like. She wanted him to dance with her, to shower her with attention, to escort her among his peers. Impossible, all of it. Yet still she wanted it. Where had he been when she'd been open to courtship?

"I like the way you both converse as though I'm not here," Gina said, a bit testily.

Reaching out, Tillie squeezed her hand. "Sorry, sweeting. That was rather rude of us."

"Won't people find it odd that you're suddenly attending balls, my lord?"

He directed his attention to Gina, his smile warm, not nearly as wicked as the ones he bestowed on Tillie. "With rare exception, I do avoid them. The mamas are all a bit too pushy for my tastes. That's to our advantage now, though, as people will believe I'm truly smitten with you. Why else would I go if my heart had not been captured?"

"If you appear too smitten," Tillie felt compelled to point out, "others may steer clear out of respect for you."

"I shall display the proper amount of attention to indicate I'm interested but not yet fully committed."

"You seem rather good at these games." She hated that she sounded out of sorts by the thought.

"I have friends who have fallen. I had the chance to observe them as they made fools of themselves. I'm determined to go down with a bit more dignity."

"You're open to love then?"

"I am. When the right woman comes along."

"What would make a woman the right one?" Gina asked.

"Gina, don't be so bold," Tillie chastised.

"Why not? He asked what I wanted in a husband. I'm curious as to what qualities he seeks in a wife."

He laughed. "We're not looking to match me up, Little One."

Tillie was selfishly glad he wasn't yet ready to marry. Although he would be and soon.

"Why not?" Gina insisted. "You're getting up in years. If you wait much longer you might not be able to produce an offspring."

Gina was correct. He required an heir. Strange how if Tillie had been married to him she didn't think she'd find fault with his mother for reminding her that she was to get with child quickly. She would have wanted to present him with a son, had the insane notion she could give him one now. *That* would be disastrous. But if she were to find herself with child before leaving for New York, she would have no regrets. She would claim herself to be a widow—

What ludicrous thoughts.

He scowled as though deeply offended by her sister's words. "I'm not yet thirty."

"Close, though, I'd wager. I could help you find someone while you're helping me."

"A wife for me is not on the table for discussion. Concentrate on yourself. You don't need the distraction."

"But—"

"He's right," Tillie interrupted, knowing when Gina latched on to an idea she was not one to let it go easily. "We haven't much time. The Season is already half over. We need to focus on getting you wed."

"So you can abandon me and return to America?"

"So I can get on with my life, yes." She wasn't going to feel guilty about it. She'd already sacrificed so much for Gina, stayed here when she desperately wanted to move on.

She was aware of the oars going still, silent, no longer moving through the water. Rexton's gaze was on her, studying her as though he were searching for something important.

"Do you miss it?" he finally asked.

"New York? Yes, of course I do. Dreadfully."

His jaw tightened as though he didn't much like her answer. "What of the balls? Society? Being welcomed here in London?"

More than she'd thought possible. In her youth, she'd thrived on the excitement, the festivities, and constantly being in motion. Her nights had been filled with balls, dinners, theater. Her days had included museums, art shows, morning calls. She'd visited with people; they had visited with her. "What I miss or do not miss is of no consequence."

"Would you stay if you were accepted back into Society?"

Stay and watch him take another woman to wife? A man in his position did not marry a woman of Tillie's circumstances. If she were welcomed back, no man of any consequence would ask for her tainted hand. He watched her with such intensity she felt as though she were once again in court, aware of all eyes on her, as her sins were leveled against her. She'd endured it because she'd known that at the end she would gain her freedom. She couldn't give it up again. "Our entire focus should be on Gina. So the ball, and then what plans have you?"

He seemed less than happy with her response, but he had to be aware of the reality of their situation, the truth of hers: acceptance would never be full and complete.

"Then we see," he said.

"You don't seem to have this planned out."

"I was under the impression love could not be planned."

"But some action must be taken."

"We are taking action."

"I just don't see that our current activity is proving fruitful."

"Oh, ye of little faith." He brought the oars out of the water, set them in the bottom of the boat, and looked once more over his shoulder. "Oy! Somerdale! Noticed you stopped. Having trouble, there?"

The earl, one of Rexton's contemporaries, turned a bright red. "No, old chap. Just taking a bit of a rest." He leaned forward slightly. "Is that Miss Hammersley with you?"

"It is. And her sister, the lovely Lady Landsdowne."

The man seemed surprised by that pronouncement. As was Tillie. Lovely? If she didn't know better she'd think he was striving to foist her off on someone. He should have used the descriptor for Gina. Still Somerdale swept his hat from his head. "Lady Landsdowne, Miss Hammersley. May I say you look incredibly fetching today?"

Tillie didn't think he was talking to her. Gina must have had the same thought because she smiled brightly before saying, "Thank you, my lord. I noticed you rowing by us earlier."

"I tend to go in circles."

"Especially when pretty ladies are serving as scenery, eh, Somerdale?" Rexton asked easily.

"Indeed. Seems hardly fair that I have none and you have two."

"Care to take one off my hands?" Rexton asked. "The extra weight in the boat has tired me out."

She and Gina both squealed at the insult. Tillie would have reached out and smacked his shoulder if it weren't for the fact that the action would do Gina's reputation no great service. She would, however, have a go at him later.

"Well . . ." Lord Somerdale suddenly looked as though he wished his boat would spring a leak, sink, and he would drown.

"We could flip for it." Rexton removed a coin from his pocket. "Heads you take Miss Hammersley, tails Lady Landsdowne. Truly you'd be doing me a great service."

"Of course, my lord. Flip away."

She watched the coin spinning through the air. Rexton grabbed it, slapped it onto the back of his hand, uncovered it, and showed it to Gina.

"Heads it is," she announced with a wide smile.

Somerdale looked as though he'd just been invited to an audience with the queen. "Splendid!"

"Draw in closer." Rexton repocketed the coin, stood. The boat rocked. Tillie and Gina once again squealed but this time it was fear and not indignation that caused the exclamation. He extended his hand to Gina. "Rise up very slowly."

Her sister did as ordered. With only a bit more bobbing of the boat, Rexton expertly transferred her to Somerdale. "Stay within sight. Lady Landsdowne is acting as chaperone and she'll have my head if she thinks I allowed anything untoward to happen to her sister. Just down to the next bridge. My carriage is awaiting us there."

"Yes, my lord. Not to worry. I'll be on my best behavior."

"See that you are." Rexton settled back onto the bench, and Tillie watched as the beaming Lord Somerdale rowed off with her sister.

"You took quite the chance," she said. "He'd have been horrified if he'd ended up with me."

"I wasn't going to let him end up with you."

The words made her feel warm, special, *liked*.

He flipped the coin to her. She managed to catch it quite easily. She studied one side then the other—which was identical to the first. Her eyes widened as her jaw dropped. "You cheated."

"Shh." Snatching the coin from her, he winked. "Don't say that too loudly. We wouldn't want it to get around that I sometimes fix the outcome."

"But you do! All the time."

"Not all the time. Depends how badly I want something. And I wanted some time alone with you."

As though he hadn't said something that had the power to turn her world upside down, he reached casually for the oars, dipped them back into the water, and with a powerful movement, set the boat back into motion.

"Did you arrange for Somerdale's timely arrival?" she asked.

"I did not. But I've been looking around for someone who was expressing an interest. His sister is married to Drake, so I have it on good authority he is fascinated by American heiresses and on the hunt for a wife."

"I thought you were simply striving not to crash into anyone."

"That was a consideration. Pity people are about as I'm rather desperate to kiss you."

The look he gave her caused her lips and other areas he'd kissed to tingle with want and anticipation. "It would undermine our efforts regarding Gina."

"Indeed." He wasn't rowing with nearly as much effort as he had before. "You didn't answer my question from before."

Slowly, she removed her glove, noting the muscles at his throat working as he swallowed. "Oh? What question was that?" She dipped her fingers into the cool water.

"Would you stay?"

She studied the sun-dappled water. "It's a moot question. I shall never be fully accepted here. And you're very much aware of that."

"Do you miss the balls?"

"I'll attend them every night when I return to New York." Lifting her hand, she flicked water at him, taking delight in the way he ineffectually jerked back to avoid the droplets. "That's the only answer you'll get."

"Careful, Countess. Bait the tiger and you may find yourself serving as his meal tonight."

She flicked at him again. "Tomorrow. Per our terms I come to you the day after an outing. You didn't escort her anywhere yesterday."

"I should think after last night you'd want to amend those terms."

She did. She wanted to amend them so she had to go

to him whether or not there was an outing. "I think it best if we stick with the original agreement."

"Have pity on me, witch. Surely you'll not leave me to ache all night."

Never had she possessed such power. It lifted her to such heights that she felt dizzy. She'd long yearned to be so wanted, so desired. "My absence tonight will ensure our time together tomorrow is all the more appreciated."

"I'm more than willing to show ample appreciation tonight."

The bubble of laughter that burst out of her had her slapping her wet hand over her mouth. She couldn't remember the last time she'd made such a joyful noise. Lowering her hand, she stared at it as though it might explain where the sound had come from.

Suddenly his hand was beneath her chin, tilting up her face until their eyes met. He was leaning toward her, as though drawn, captured, and snagged by the sound. "You don't do that often enough," he said quietly.

I never do it. Not in years. Not since I married. She'd catalogued everything Downie had taken from her, and somehow she'd overlooked this. She'd once been as joyful and carefree as Gina. He'd turned her into something withered and old.

"Tomorrow night you're going to do it again, longer, louder, if I have to tickle you from head to toe to make it happen."

He would, too. She was rather certain of it. But she couldn't let him have that, not so easily. "Good luck with that. I'm not ticklish in the least."

His grin made her wish they had indeed altered the terms of their arrangement, that tonight she would see him. "You've never been tickled by me."

The promise in his words both terrified and excited her. *Don't*, she nearly pleaded, *don't change me, don't do anything to make me lonelier than I already am.*

But she feared it was too late to beg anything of him.

Chapter 15

$\mathcal{R}$exton didn't know why he kept searching for her, why every time he spied silky black hair out of the corner of his eye, he turned hoping to see her. Tillie wasn't at the ball. He understood her reasons, hated that they existed.

He escorted Gina around the ballroom, enticed a few gents into signing her dance card, spoke flatteringly of her, hinted she'd make a wonderful complement to any lord's arm—without insinuating she'd spend the remainder of her life on his. He waltzed with her, then left her in his sister's keeping, asking Grace to see that she was partnered for other dances. Being in the overstuffed ballroom made him feel as though his waistcoat was too tight.

Walking through the ballroom, he'd never in his life wanted to be anywhere else so badly. The odd thing was he'd be more content sitting in a parlor sipping whisky with Tillie, asking after her day, talking books, weather, or horses. Or simply enjoying her company in silence. It was strange, how often he thought of her, how he wondered what she was doing now, how he wished she was with him. He wanted her near, fully clothed, smiling up at him, her hand resting on his arm. He wasn't quite sure when he'd begun spending as much time envisioning being with her outside his bed as in it.

It was an unsettling realization. Their association was going to be short-lived. She'd set a time for it to end. Even if he could convince her to extend it—which he was fairly certain he could do with a bit of tender persuasion—she deserved more than an illicit affair. She could find a permanent relationship in America, but here, her scandalous past limited her opportunities. Even if he overlooked the scandal of her divorce, he couldn't guarantee it wouldn't taint their children. He knew what it was to be the offspring of a woman not completely embraced by Society. Even when it appeared everyone loved his mother, he'd still heard the ugly whispered words, been the recipient of snubs. He wouldn't wish it on his children.

Stepping onto the terrace, he inhaled deeply the cool evening air and wandered over to a darkened corner. If Tillie were here, he'd kiss her in these shadows or perhaps they'd stroll into the gardens, eventually wandering off the path for a secluded seduction. She seduced him as ferociously as he did her. He'd missed her the night before, missed not having her in his bed. After only one night with her, how was it that a night without her had loomed like a great gaping maw of emptiness?

He would have her tonight and tomorrow. And the night after that because he was not going to allow a single afternoon or evening to pass without escorting Gina somewhere: to the park, to a museum, to a ball.

Even if for only an hour. He would meet the minimum terms so Tillie was obligated to come to him.

Hearing the strike of a match, he looked over to see Landsdowne standing nearby lighting a cheroot, the flame illuminating features Rexton was of a mind to rearrange. He was surprised by the absolute abhorrence of the man that skittered through him. The earl had failed to appreciate what he had, and in so doing, he'd effectively ruined Tillie's chance for happiness. At least on this side of the Atlantic. Perhaps she'd find happiness on the other. But she'd find it without him, and he was no longer certain he could find it without her.

Landsdowne extinguished the flame with a rapid waving of his hand, inhaled deeply, and blew out a stream of smoke. "Care for one, old boy?"

Only then did Rexton realize he'd been glaring at the man since he became alerted to his presence. "No."

"I see you're still hanging on to Gina's skirts. Without Mathilda in tow tonight."

"As you're well aware, she's no longer invited into parlors, grand salons, and dining rooms."

"As well a woman of her low moral character shouldn't be. I did hear you were seen rowing with her."

"Your point?"

"If you have any hope of having Gina accepted, you'd do best to keep her disgusting sister in the shadows."

Rexton moved swiftly, grabbing Landsdowne by the lapels and giving him a shake. The cheroot went flying. "You will cease your disparaging remarks regarding Tillie."

The earl's eyes went wide. "Dear God, it's not Gina

who truly holds your attention, but the tart I married. She's spreading her le—"

The jab was quick and hard. He heard the snap of cartilage despite the earl's groan. He took satisfaction in it. "Watch your words where she is concerned."

"She's a cunning—"

Another quick jab, another groan.

"You're not listening, Landsdowne."

"She's not worthy of your devotion, Rexton. She won't return it in kind." His sentiments were muffled because he was holding a handkerchief to his nose, trying to stem the flow of blood.

Rexton hadn't earned her devotion. She was with him because she wanted his assistance. But that didn't mean she wasn't worthy of devotion or respect. "I have to ask myself, Landsdowne, what failings in you caused her to turn to another man, a footman for God's sake?" No longer able to stand touching him, he shoved the earl back. Then took a step nearer. Landsdowne flinched. "My mother taught me if I had nothing good to say about a person, I should hold my tongue. Heed the advice and heed it well. Because if I hear you have directed a single unkind word in Tillie's direction, rumors regarding your lack of . . . virility might begin making the rounds. I have enough friends and family to ensure the speculations travel very quickly. Mark my words, there won't be a place you can appear where you won't feel judgment. Damnation, I might just do it anyway so you have a clearer understanding of how your former wife feels."

"She deserves to be snubbed and gossiped about."

"No, Landsdowne, she does not. And I think you damned well know it."

"She wanted a divorce. She didn't care about the damned scandal."

"And again, I must wonder why. I know you were unfaithful. But I suspect there was more to it than that. Pray, if I ever find out the specifics, that I don't have a need to strike you again."

Spinning on his heel, he left Landsdowne blubbering some sort of unintelligible sounds. The man had been unfaithful. He had divorced his wife. Yet he moved about in Society with no consequence while Tillie was denied the opportunity to waltz in a crowded ballroom, to waltz in Rexton's arms. He'd never considered the unfairness of it. He was certainly considering it now.

*W*earing her nightdress and dressing gown, sitting in a chair, Tillie looked longingly out her bedchamber window, miserably waiting for Gina's return from the ball. She thought of Rexton waltzing with her sister, waltzing with any number of young ladies, and she longed to be the one in his arms. She imagined flirting with him in the ballroom, strolling through a shadowed garden, sneaking in a kiss behind a trellis.

Her first Season, while she was unattached to a man or scandal, she'd enjoyed herself immensely: laughing, discussing various gentlemen's attributes, and gossiping. She sighed. She'd never again gossip and not just because she wouldn't be welcomed into a ballroom, but because she now understood how much it hurt and how often there was more to the story than anyone truly realized.

A thrill shot through her as she saw the carriage pulling into the drive, illuminated by the gas lamps.

Jumping to her feet, she positioned herself behind the drawn aside curtain so she could peer out without her silhouette being visible—she didn't want to look like some child with her nose pressed to the glass of a sweet shop—and watched as Rexton climbed out through the door the footman had opened for him. His movements were so smooth, so dashing. Even something as simple as the sight of him disembarking from a conveyance caused her stomach to flutter with anticipation.

He handed Gina down, said something which Tillie couldn't hear. Her sister tossed her head back and laughed. She envied her the ease of her laughter and the fact she'd been fortunate enough to have the marquess elicit the sound from her. They seemed extremely comfortable in each other's company.

The maid followed. Tillie lost sight of them as they neared the front door. Not even a minute later, Rexton was approaching the carriage. He stopped, swept his hat from his head, and gazed up at her window. Perhaps she wasn't as invisible as she thought or maybe he felt her watching him. Her mouth went dry as a shiver of delight raced through her because he'd taken the time to look up.

Then he clambered aboard and the vehicle took off. She knew it wasn't going to go far: just to the end of the drive where it would wait for her in shadows.

Schooling her features to show none of her anticipation, she settled into her chair and opened the book that had been keeping her company or might have if her mind hadn't wandered so many times this evening. She'd left the door to her bedchamber open wide so she wasn't surprised when Gina passed by, stopped, and walked in.

"Oh, you're still up, I see."

Tillie set the book aside. "I can't sleep until you're home safe. How did your evening go?"

"Splendid. A dozen dances with various lords. Much tittering with ladies. The Duchess of Lovingdon has taken me under her wing—no doubt at her brother's behest. He disappeared for a bit."

She didn't want to think that he might have secreted some lady away for a tryst in the garden. They had an understanding. He wouldn't break his promise not to spend time with another woman. But then Downie had made the same promise before God, and he'd broken it easily enough. "Did he dance much?"

She hated that she'd asked, that she sounded like a possessive wife.

"He waltzed with me, of course. Twice. But other than that I didn't see him circling anyone else about the ballroom."

"I wonder where he went then."

"To play cards perhaps." Gina sat on the edge of the bed. "I think he's secretly courting you."

"What a silly notion."

"You are the only thing we talk about."

Tillie wasn't going to let on how much that pleased her. "That must have been a short conversation."

"On the contrary. He is unrelenting in his inquiries."

Tillie furrowed her brow. "What does he want to know?"

"He asks a good deal about our life in New York."

"Well, then, you see he's asking after you."

Gina smiled. "No. He wants to know about our residence there. If that's where you'll live when you return to the city. What do we do in New York? Do *you* go to the theater, the parks? What do *you* like to do for enjoyment? It always comes back to you."

She looked at the book in her lap, ran her finger over the spine. "I suppose I should be flattered."

"I think you're going to meet him in secret once I leave you."

Tillie jerked her head up so quickly that she heard a little pop in her neck. "Don't be ridiculous. I'm dressed for bed."

"Of course. I forget one can't change one's clothes after midnight."

"Gina—"

"It's all right, Tillie." Her sister slid off the bed, came toward her, and looked down on her with a serene smile. "I want you to be happy. He makes you so, doesn't he?"

"I do like him." That was the most she'd admit. "However, nothing permanent can come of it."

"Why not?"

She pushed herself up and began to pace. "Because I'm scandal-ridden."

"He obviously doesn't care. People see the two of you together—"

She swung around. "They see the three of us together. They know I'm acting as chaperone. I suspect many are questioning that. I'm not good for him. Not in the long run. And it doesn't matter. That's not what he wants." He was clear up front. He wanted an affair only. She wanted the same. She had no desire to be tied here.

Crossing over to her sister, she took Gina's hands.

"Don't worry about me, sweeting. This is your Season. We need to ensure that you're happy, that you find the right man."

"You're right. I believe a couple of gents are going to call on me tomorrow. I'll want you there to observe, to share your insights."

"Yes, of course."

Gina yawned. "Now I must be abed. It wouldn't do at all for me to nod off while they're trying to woo me."

"Sleep well."

Gina gave her a saucy smile, a twinkle in her eyes. "You, too."

As her sister wandered out, Tillie settled back into the chair, picked up her book, and pretended to be reading. What she really wanted to do was dash out of the residence and to the waiting carriage, the waiting man. Although, he might not still be there. He might have given up on her ever appearing. But she had to give Gina time to retire before slipping out of the residence. Even if her sister suspected the truth, Tillie had no plans to confirm it. Still it was difficult to wait when she wanted to be with him so badly. The extent to which she was drawn to him was unnerving. So she forced herself to wait a full half hour simply to prove she could.

Then she grabbed her cloak, drew it about her, and stepped into the hallway. All was quiet. Gina was no doubt asleep by now. Tillie made a mad dash down the stairs and out the door. On slippered feet, she raced along the drive—

Her progress was abruptly stopped as an arm snaked around her and brought her up against a hard body. Her squeal was cut off as a warm, seductive mouth blanketed hers. Wrapping her arms around his neck, she melted against Rexton, grateful she hadn't needed to go a minute longer without being pressed against him, surrounded by his fragrance, enjoying his taste, his enthusiasm, his nearness.

Drawing back, she held his gaze. "What are you doing here?"

"I wasn't going to have you traipsing in the dark to my carriage." His gaze dipped down. "What the devil are you wearing?"

"My nightclothes. I assumed we'd be going straight to bed once we arrived at your residence."

He gave her a slow, wicked grin. "We are now."

*F*rom her window, Gina watched as Tillie was snatched up by Rexton. She felt guilty not looking away as the marquess kissed her sister. Their bodies practically melded into one. Then they were dashing down the drive, no doubt to his waiting carriage.

For a tryst.

She sighed. While she was glad the marquess had taken a shine to her sister, this was not the outcome she'd hoped for. She'd hoped Rexton would see Tillie accepted again. Her sister deserved better than an affair. She deserved marriage.

She obviously wasn't going to find it here. Gina was going to have to redouble her efforts to get herself wedded so Tillie could return to New York where hopefully she'd find a man who recognized her worth.

Chapter 16

$\mathscr{T}$he following morning, Tillie felt the nudge on her shoulder and squinted up at her maid.

"It's time, my lady."

She'd asked to be awakened for luncheon. Stretching languorously, she admitted that last night her body had been well and truly used—in the most glorious of manners. Dear God, but Rexton was a man of such talents that he would make a fortune if he were a male tart. She furrowed her brow. Was there a name for a man who sold his services? Did men sell their services? Perhaps she'd ask him. He no doubt knew. He seemed to know all manner of wicked things.

When she was prepared for the day in a simple navy frock that buttoned to her throat and her wrists as befitting one serving as chaperone, she headed down to the dining room. Gina was already there. She glanced up from her plate.

"Well, you slept rather late."

"I was in need of some additional rest after waiting up for you last night." After filling her plate at the sideboard, she took her seat.

"Something arrived for you," Gina said rather mysteriously.

"What would that be?"

"I don't know. It's all wrapped up. Griggs placed it on your desk. I was tempted to take a peek but I refrained."

"Do we know who it's from?"

Gina shook her head. "No, no marking whatsoever. Griggs said the gent who delivered it wasn't wearing livery so no clues there. Perhaps you've a secret admirer. Or not so secret."

"Honestly, Gina, you're reading too much into our outings with Rexton."

"Would you marry him if you could?"

She shook her head. "I'm a failure at marriage. All of London will tell you so."

"Does Rexton believe that?"

"It doesn't matter. I'm going back to New York."

"I suppose then that I need to ensure my husband is open to traveling across the ocean blue."

"Indeed."

Tillie didn't know if she'd ever eaten so quickly. She was anxious to discover what the package contained. It seemed Gina was equally anxious as she kept skipping ahead down the hallway, then stopping and giving an exaggerated roll of her eyes. "Hurry!"

"It's not going anywhere."

It was larger than she expected. Perhaps a foot tall, a foot wide. She untied the string. The paper fell away. Tentatively she lifted the lid from the box, gasped in surprise, and lifted out a stone sprite with a mischievous grin, legs crossed beneath her, holding a folded note in her lap. Setting the statuette aside, she read the scrap of paper.

What is a whimsical garden without a bit of faerie?

Smiling brightly, she clutched the parchment to her chest.

"Is it from Rexton?" Gina asked.

"It doesn't say."

Gina jabbed at her arm. "But it is, isn't it? Otherwise you wouldn't look so besotted by a piece of stone."

"I'm not besotted and it's not just a piece of stone. It's for my garden."

"Jewelry would have been better."

No, it wouldn't have and he knew that. He'd accurately determined what would bring her joy. He didn't find her little garden demeaning or a ridiculous waste of her time as Downie had. Rexton never belittled her, never made her feel that she didn't measure up.

Tillie changed into her gardening clothes and took the sprite into her garden to make a space for it among her flowers. She wanted it positioned so it was clearly visible but also partially hidden behind the blossoms, as though shy, not meant to be seen.

Kneeling, she moved it a little to the right, a tad back, a smidgen forward, searching for that perfect placement—

"Mathilda."

With a start, she glanced up at the man towering over her. He removed his hat, the sunlight hit him, and she gasped. "My God, Downie, what the devil happened to your face?"

She shoved herself to her feet, reached out, stopped herself just shy of touching his grossly misshaped nose and swollen eye. He'd never been one for offering or receiving comfort.

"Seems you have a champion," he said quietly.

Rexton. She was at once thrilled and appalled by the notion that he'd inflicted this damage. Unlike the gent at the club, Downie hadn't attacked her. "What did you do to deserve his wrath?"

"You think I deserved it?"

"I don't believe he's one to go about willy-nilly hitting fellows."

He looked down at his shoes as though striving to determine if they needed to be polished. "I might have said something untoward regarding you." He lifted his gaze. She couldn't recall ever seeing him looking guilty or remorseful. He did so now. "Might we walk for a bit?"

They'd walked often before they were married. Not once during. Once the vows were exchanged, so much between them changed. "Yes, of course."

He didn't offer his arm. She hadn't expected him to. So much of their relationship had been based on obligation rather than desire. She hadn't realized it would be so until after she married him.

"I miss the gardens," he said wistfully.

"They're my favorite part of the residence," she admitted.

"I never appreciated you laboring in them."

"It's not really laboring, Downie, when it brings me

such peace and joy." Digging in the earth calmed her, arranging her plants brought ease. They never judged, never found fault with her.

"Are you involved with him?"

Interesting that since his arrival he'd avoided calling Rexton by name. "That's not really any of your concern."

"He can't offer you marriage you know. Those of our station do not wed *divorced* women."

He emphasized the word as though her condition were entirely her own doing. "Having been married to an Englishman, I assure you I have no interest in being married to another. It was a remarkably cold and lonely existence."

He nodded. "I was wrong to marry you, but I needed the funds."

"I'm well aware. Perhaps my dowry will allow you to marry for love next time." Since apparently the state of divorce didn't attach itself to men quite as unflatteringly.

With a long slow sigh, he shook his head. "The woman I love is married to another."

She was taken aback by the knowledge that he actually loved someone other than himself. "Is she the one you met at the Nightingale or are you unfaithful to her as well?" He'd never provided any details on the woman. Only admitted to the affair when she confronted him.

He stopped and faced her. "It's the only way she'll come to me. She fears if we meet elsewhere, we will be spotted, she will be recognized. The Nightingale makes me feel as though what we have is . . . cheap. She has three children. I look at them and wonder if any of them might be mine."

He averted his gaze, looked up into the trees. For the briefest of moments, she thought she saw a welling of tears in the corner of his eye. He cleared his throat.

"If you're asking me to forgive you, I can't," she said softly. "I deserved better. I deserved your fidelity."

Another clearing of his throat, a straightening of his shoulders before turning back to her and giving her his full attention. He looked at her squarely, more squarely than he'd ever done when they were married. "You did. I was a cad. Weak. Caring only for my own happiness—reaching for it and yet it was always beyond my grasp. I suspect if I had devoted myself to you that I might have come to love you in time."

If he thought he was making her feel better, he was gravely mistaken. She had an urge to make his right eye match his left.

"I don't suppose you want to give it another go."

Her unexpected bark of laughter was loud and harsh. Abrupt and forceful enough to cause an ache in her chest. "No. Dear God, no."

"I didn't think so but I thought nothing lost in asking."

Except maybe a bit of his pride. She rather hoped so. Not very charitable of her, but he had managed through his selfishness to ruin her life.

"Since the discovery of you with the footman I've not spoken very highly of you," he said. "That will cease. You're not deserving of it."

"Why the change of heart?"

"Rexton questioned why you might turn to another man. I am forced to admit that I might have played a role in your misbehavior. I do wish, however, that you had traded up."

"At the time, I rather felt that I had."

He blanched. "I deserved that cutting remark, I suppose."

"You broke my heart, Downie. Yes, my mother wanted me to marry someone titled, but don't you think if that was what mattered to me, I'd have gone with a duke?"

Another sigh, another study of his shoes. Finally, he met her gaze again. "Should our paths cross again in a social situation, rest assured that I shall be cordial."

"I shall reciprocate." Although she couldn't imagine any social situation where they'd cross paths.

"Very good." He settled his hat on his head. "Good day to you, Mathilda."

He'd taken only three steps from her before she called out, "Downie?"

He faced her.

She damned her inability to be cruel. "I only ever kissed the footman."

He blinked, opened his mouth, closed it, blinked again. "You didn't deny having an affair."

"I wanted a divorce more than I wanted a sterling reputation." She'd been wilting like flowers left without water.

He chuckled low. "Well played, Mathilda. I'm afraid, though, m'dear that I won't be striving to set *that* record straight. It might make me appear more the fool."

With that, he walked away. She didn't need him to set the record straight. She was divorced. Nothing was going to change that or the shame that went with it.

Chapter 17

A week later, without thought, Tillie periodically turned the pages in the book she held in her lap, striving to give the impression that she was lost in the world the author created when in fact she was very much aware of every breath, sigh, and clink of teacup hitting saucer that occurred within the parlor where she sat a discreet distance away from Gina and her gentleman caller—the Earl of Somerdale.

He'd been unable to contribute much to Gina's treatise regarding Mr. Darcy's true identity. Apparently, Somerdale was vaguely familiar with Jane Austen—enough to know she was in fact a female author—but confessed to not being a devotee of books. He preferred activities that pushed the limits of the body—such as rowing, riding, and dancing. With him, Gina would no doubt have an active life, but Tillie couldn't imagine a duller sort than a man who did not exercise the mind with reading.

Still, the gent seemed somewhat devoted to Gina, describing his family's estate as though he would one day share it with her. Gina seemed happy enough to be in his company, smiling broadly and never taking her gaze from him.

It was odd. Tillie had known from the beginning that Rexton wasn't right for Gina. She felt the same way about Somerdale but she was having a devil of a time identifying exactly why she didn't feel he suited. Perhaps the fault rested more with her, and her desire that Gina not settle on anyone too soon, for once her sister was situated, Tillie's time with Rexton would come to an end. And she was enjoying him far more than she should.

Hearing the faint knocking echoing through the foyer, she fought to calm her accelerating heart. It could be another caller for Gina, but when the man strode into the parlor without being announced, she fairly leaped to her feet with gladness, then squelched her smile because it was intolerable to be so happy to see Rexton. Besides, Somerdale needed to be convinced that the marquess was here for Gina. To reveal otherwise, could undermine their plans.

Apparently Somerdale was convinced as he, too, jumped to his feet, evidently forgetting that he'd been successfully balancing a teacup and saucer on his thigh because both went flying. "My lord." He glanced down, glanced up, looked at Gina, turned to the marquess, guilt washing over his features as though he'd been caught pilfering valuable family jewels. "My calling on Miss Hammersley is quite innocent, I assure you. I'm not attempting to steal her away—"

"It's quite all right, Somerdale," Rexton said. "I've not yet stated my intentions nor asked for her hand. Besides I appreciate competition."

Somerdale visibly relaxed. "I shall strive to offer

some that is worthy of you." He turned to Gina. "I must be off."

"Must you?" Gina asked. "I do wish you wouldn't allow Lord Rexton to chase you away."

"Oh, it isn't that . . ."

Although Tillie suspected it was exactly that, and in her mind, it made him unsuitable for Gina.

"I'd dearly love for you to take me on a stroll through the park," Gina said, boldly, batting her eyelashes at him. "My sister and Lord Rexton could serve as chaperones."

"I very much doubt—"

"Splendid notion," Rexton said before the earl could finish. "Perhaps you can teach me a thing or two about courtship, Somerdale."

Tillie knew it was impossible, but if it weren't, she was fairly certain Somerdale's chin would have touched the carpet, his mouth was so agape.

"To be honest, my lord, I would like to take the lady to the park."

"Then let's be on our way, shall we?" Rexton bowed slightly toward her. "If you don't mind accompanying me, Lady Landsdowne?"

"I was beginning to wonder if I ever was going to be included in this conversation and my opinion sought on the ridiculous notion of you allowing Somerdale to escort a lady in whom you've been showing interest."

"Oh, Tillie, don't be a spoilsport. I'd love to have a bit more time with Lord Somerdale." Her sister reached out and patted the mentioned man's arm. He preened. "Then I'll have a spot of tea with Lord Rexton. Until I make a decision, I don't see why I can't have more than one swain. Besides, you could do with a bit of sun. You're looking far too pale these days. I'll snag our parasols, shall I?"

She considered objecting, but in the end, decided it couldn't hurt for Gina to be seen with two gentlemen in tow, even if the second was walking beside Tillie while she followed her sister and Somerdale. They'd ridden to the park in Rexton's open carriage, so Tillie suspected he had planned to bring them to the park all along, but for a ride, not a walk.

"I don't know why we didn't remain in your carriage," she muttered.

"My presence intimidates Somerdale."

She could see that, suspected his presence intimidated everyone.

"Give me your arm," Rexton said quietly.

She didn't. She skewed her face into a moue of displeasure. "You could at least show a measure of jealousy because a man is infringing upon your interests."

"But he's not."

"He should think he is."

"I don't want to overplay my hand. If he believes I've staked a claim, he's going to scurry away." Reaching down, he closed his fingers around her wrist.

She tugged. His hold tightened.

"Don't make a scene," he ordered. "It will do harm to Gina's quest."

Narrowing her eyes, she relaxed, allowed him to tuck her hand into the crook of his arm.

"Much better," he murmured.

His look of pure satisfaction made her want to laugh and smack him at the same time. During the past week, she'd laughed more with him than she could remember laughing during her entire time in England before him.

"I want to see you tonight," he said.

"You didn't take Gina anywhere yesterday," she reminded him.

"Surely it's time to let that little rule go to the wayside. Besides, if I'm correct about Somerdale's interest, I'm not going to have that many more nights with you."

And she wouldn't have many with him. She didn't want to be in the habit of sharing every night with him, because it would be so dreadfully difficult to face all the nights that awaited her without him. "I have plans for the evening."

"Such as?" His tone was low, flat, curt. For a moment, she almost believed he might be jealous.

"I began a new book this afternoon. I want to finish it this evening."

"You can finish it at my residence."

She shook her head. "I don't think it's a good idea to spend every night in each other's company."

"It's not going to be *every* night. There's a finite number, and Somerdale is likely to make that number a small one." He didn't bother to disguise his disgruntlement.

"Today is the first day he's called. He's not going to ask for her immediately. Please, let's not argue about this."

He gave a brief nod, and she took it as his acquiescence. If she didn't care for him so much she would go to him tonight. The problem was that her heart was becoming much more involved than it should.

"He seems rather besotted," Rexton said.

"Yes, he does, doesn't he? But she doesn't."

"She hasn't taken her eyes off him."

"I know, but . . ." Unable to pinpoint what exactly bothered her, she nibbled on her lower lip.

"Keep doing that and I'm going to drag you behind a tree and kiss you."

With a start, she looked at him. He appeared deadly serious. "Doing what?"

"Nibble on that enticing lip of yours. If there's any nibbling to be done, I should be the one doing it."

Heat rushed into her cheeks. "Oh, the things you say." They made her feel incredibly powerful and beguiling.

"The things I do are better than those I say. And oh, the things I'd like to do with you right this moment."

She could see in his eyes what a good many of those things entailed. Naughty, incredible things. "Behave."

"I love when you blush."

She imagined she was blushing even more. The day seemed unbearably hot all of a sudden.

"Come to me tonight and I'll make you blush all over."

He would. She knew it without reservation. She needed to change the conversation. "Tell me everything you know about Somerdale. Is he capable of great love, do you think?"

"Where your sister is concerned, I suspect any man is."

She couldn't argue with that. Gina was lovable. Tillie had once considered herself so, but now she was brittle and cold, afraid to trust any man with her heart, even Rexton. The reason she couldn't go to him every night. She had to protect her heart. How did other mistresses do it? she wondered.

At least in her relationship with Rexton, she held some power. Still she didn't know if it would make things easier when their time together came to its conclusion.

*R*exton was a selfish bastard. He didn't want her returning to New York, didn't want the Season to come to an end, didn't want his association with her to be finished.

He wanted more of her laughter, her smiles, her company. He wanted people to see her walking with him and to know his interest was in her—not her sister. He no longer cared that she'd been seen kissing a footman, that she was divorced, that she wasn't suitable for a man who would one day be a duke.

"Did you enjoy the carousel?" he asked casually, knowing he should be paying more attention to the couple in front of them, ensuring Somerdale did nothing to compromise Gina, nothing that would result in a rushed marriage that hastened the ending of his relationship with Tillie.

She smiled, the soft, gentle curling of her lips that filled him with a sense of satisfaction and joy unlike any he'd ever known. "You know I did. It was marvelous."

"Then I won the wager, and you owe me another night."

Her lips shifted into a straight line, but he didn't think she was truly irritated with him because her eyes remained warm, sparkling with merriment.

"And you want to claim it tonight?"

"I'd claim it this very moment with an enthusiastic kiss if I didn't think you'd go off in a huff afterward."

Her smile returned, her laughter tinkled around him. "You're incorrigible."

"Only where you're concerned." He slowed his step, allowing more distance between them and the strolling couple. "Rather than coming to me tonight, give me tomorrow."

The smile disappeared completely, her brow furrowed. "Tomorrow?"

"During the day. I want to take you somewhere. Just the two of us."

She shook her head. "We can't be seen going about without Gina."

"No one of any consequence, of the Marlborough House Set, will see us."

Seeming uncertain, she slid her arm away from his so they were no longer touching. He didn't like the separation. Perhaps she was right, perhaps some time apart would do them both good, but he knew they were rapidly approaching the mark where they would forever be apart. Somerdale's wooing of Gina could quicken its arrival.

"Are we going to see the carousel again? Is it finished?"

"No. I want to share something else with you."

Appearing uncomfortable, she moved her parasol to the other shoulder, back again. "Our arrangement was for the nights only."

"What are you afraid of, Tillie?" That he might come to mean something to her, that she wouldn't want to part ways at the end of the Season? He already knew he didn't. One night with her was all it had taken. It hadn't happened the first night he'd bedded her, but the one before, when he'd first caught sight of her smile.

"I just don't think it's wise for us to do things beyond the parameters of our arrangement."

"You'll enjoy it."

She shook her head. "You say that with such confidence, as though you know me."

"I was correct about the carousel, wasn't I?"

The corner of her mouth tilted up slightly and he knew he had her. Only she shook her head. "No. Please don't ask again."

Frustration hit him. She was afraid of something—or at the very least hesitant. He wondered if it had anything to do with Downie, with the way the man had disappointed her. He might have asked if it weren't for the fact that Gina and Somerdale were walking toward them.

Smiling, they seemed very much at ease with each other, standing close but not scandalously so. Gina seemed quite enthralled by whatever Somerdale was espousing. Although glad to see her enjoying the attention, Rexton couldn't help but wonder if perhaps he might be on the cusp of finally making progress, if their need for him might end sooner than he wanted. He should have insisted their time together would last as long as Tillie was in the country—and would recommence anytime she returned for a visit.

They took his carriage back to the residence where Somerdale immediately took his leave.

Gina smiled at Rexton. "Will you be joining us for tea now, my lord?"

"No, but I will escort you to the door."

"I rather like Lord Somerdale," Gina said as they walked up the path.

"I'm glad to hear it," Rexton said, although the

words were false. He wanted the girl happy but not when it meant shortening his time with Tillie.

"Having an inheritance is certainly a double-edged sword," Gina mused. "I wonder how the lady is to ever know if a man truly wants her instead of her money."

"A man would be a fool not to want you more than he wanted your money."

She gave him a bright smile. "You're kind to say so but I would say the same is true of Tillie and look how things worked out for her."

"My past is a cautionary tale," Tillie said, "and I shall use the experience to keenly observe Lord Somerdale and anyone else who comes to call. No reason for you to settle on the first gent to call."

"I like him well enough."

"Well enough is not necessarily good enough."

Just as she reached to open the door, he said, "Gina, I was hoping to take your sister on an outing on the morrow but she has declined my invitation. I'm hoping you might convince her otherwise."

Gina's eyes were wide and glowing with pleasure. "You mean just the two of you?"

"Precisely."

"Which is the reason I declined," Tillie said sharply. "We need to spend our time ensuring you are out and about and seen."

"One day wouldn't hurt," Gina said. Reaching out, she touched his arm. "Never you fear, my lord. I shall ensure she is ready and enthusiastic when you arrive for her tomorrow."

Taking her hand, holding her gaze, he pressed a kiss to her knuckles. "I was rather certain I could count on you. I shall be here at dawn."

"Dawn?" Tillie echoed.

"It is to be a full day, Countess."

"It shall be a day you spend alone." She retreated into the house.

Gnawing on her lower lip, Gina said, "You like her, don't you?"

"Very much so," he admitted, not only to her but to himself.

"She may be a bit grumpy to start, but she will go with you. I promise."

With a wink, he leaned in. "See that she wears something simple, with few petticoats, as we'll be doing a bit of traveling."

As he headed back to his carriage, he was rather certain Tillie would see his enlisting her sister's assistance as cheating. But where she was concerned, he was willing to do whatever necessary to spend as much time with her as possible.

*I*t was too early for whisky, yet Tillie stood at the window, full glass in hand, watching as Rexton and Gina—her traitorous sister—talked. She was rather certain if she spent too much time alone with him that she would be setting herself up for heartache. She liked him far more than she should, more than was wise when she realized her heart might be on the mend. That made it so much more vulnerable.

When she saw Rexton walking away and Gina heading for the door, Tillie moved away from the window and settled into a chair, striving to appear calm when she was anything but.

"Why won't you spend the day with him?" Gina asked without preamble as she marched into the parlor.

Tillie took a slow sip of her whisky before saying, "It serves neither of us any good."

Gina dropped into the chair opposite her. "He wants to court you, Tillie."

Tillie's heart somersaulted to the floor. "Did he tell you that? Did he use those exact words?"

Shifting in her chair, Gina averted her gaze. "No, but why else would he want time alone with you?"

For another frolic between the sheets. She wouldn't have minded, but her fear was that he did want something more, something that could never reach fruition. "I don't know," she answered honestly.

Gina brought her gaze back to Tillie. "Aren't you curious?"

What if it was something like the carousel, something designed to touch her heart? She was going to leave England when Gina was situated, and she had no desire to leave her heart behind. She feared with Rexton, she was very much in danger of doing that.

Her face earnest, Gina scooted to the edge of the chair. "I think you should do it, Tillie, if for no other reason than simply to find out what he's about."

She was afraid. She'd been swept off her feet before, and she'd landed hard on her backside. It would be so much worse with Rexton. So much worse.

On the other hand, he'd already given her so many warm memories that had begun to shove aside the horrid ones of her past.

"If you're not curious," Gina said, "I am. I will die if you don't go with him and report back to me what sort of outing he planned that begins at such an ungodly hour. If you don't go, I'm going—simply because I must know what sort of deviousness he arranged."

"I doubt it's devious."

"Then what's your excuse for not going?"

She couldn't admit her fears, her doubts—not to her baby sister. She was supposed to be older and wiser. "I suppose there's no harm in it."

"Splendid."

Although she would have a few choice words for Rexton because he'd involved her sister. It seemed the man had no qualms about doing whatever necessary to gain what he wanted. While she knew she should be miffed, she couldn't help but feel a bit of joy with the knowledge that it appeared one of the things he craved was time alone with her.

$\mathcal{H}$e could not have been more thrilled to see Gina standing on the steps with a self-satisfied smirk on her face while Tillie stood beside her. He leaped out of the carriage before it came to a complete stop, not bothering to wait for a footman to open the door. The sky was lightening, but it was still dark enough that he wasn't likely to be recognized.

"It took some convincing," Gina said gleefully, "but I did it."

"I owe you a dance at the next ball," he said.

She laughed. "You'll give me that anyway."

He held out his hand to Tillie, closing his fingers around hers when she placed her palm against his.

"We're going to have a discussion about your underhanded means of using my sister," she said haughtily.

Any chastisement he endured would be worth it. He had her for the day.

"I'll have her back before nightfall," he promised Gina.

"Take your time. I'm off to get a new frock." She fairly skipped into the residence.

After settling Tillie into the coach, he sat beside her.

"Seriously, Rex, I don't want her knowing about the affair."

He understood her reservations. People didn't usually boast about their clandestine meetings. "She's not oblivious, Tillie. She's known from the beginning I have an interest in you. She won't think anything more of our daytime outing than my wanting some time with you." Leaning in, he kissed her temple, lowered his voice. "Which I do. You must wish for the same or you'd have not agreed. I doubt anyone can convince you to do something you're averse to."

"There are times when I find you insufferable."

He might have been wounded if he didn't hear the smile in her voice. There was little he liked more than her lowering her defenses enough to tease him.

Placing his arm around her, he nestled her up against his side, turning slightly so her head could be cradled within the hollow of his shoulder. "We'll be on the road for at least two hours. Try to get some sleep."

She snuggled up against him, far too easily and comfortably to be too put out by his underhanded means to get her to join him.

"Where are we going?" she asked.

"I'd rather not say, but I do think you'll find it a delightful way to spend the day."

"How many women have you shared such delights with?"

He suspected her relationship with Downie caused her to think that nothing special would be shared with her, that she would be the recipient of what he gave to everyone else—in spite of the fact that he'd shared far more with her than he'd ever shared with anyone else. "As with the carousel and my residence, you will share with me today what no other woman has."

Holding her near as he was, he was aware of her going very still, very quiet. He wondered if she had an inkling regarding how much he treasured her, how much he wanted experiences with her that he'd had with no other. He doubted it, as he, too, was finding it difficult to comprehend how much she was coming to mean to him in so short a span of time. When he'd first met her, he noticed the outer trimmings, been drawn to them, but he'd also been aware of an inner steel, a fortitude that appealed even more. She was strength and courage and determination.

She was willing to do whatever necessary to gain what she wanted—no, what she *needed*. She'd needed a divorce in order to survive, to avoid a pit of despair. She'd taken actions most would consider drastic in order to obtain it.

Now she wanted her sister wed and, again, she'd taken unusual measures, had become his temporary mistress.

Temporary, however, no longer suited him. It was his turn to take drastic measures to ensure temporary no longer suited her either.

Chapter 18

*S*he hadn't meant to fall asleep, but she'd slept fit-
fully the night before, so she'd welcomed his arm
closing around her and the comfort of his shoulder.
She didn't much like how much she looked forward
to being in his company. Their arrangement was for
night hours only. Extending their time alone to day-
light hours was dangerous, might cause her to wish for
more than what they could have together. She would
indulge him—and her interfering sister—today, and
then she would make it clear that they would return to
the original terms.

She didn't want him romancing her. The lie sat
heavy on her heart. If she were a debutante, in her first
Season, she would want all he offered. But she wasn't.
She was used goods. A man in his position had to consider his place in Society, his legacy, and the respect
given to him by his peers. She might be a foreigner, but
she had learned in short order that marrying into the
aristocracy came with exacting expectations. Exhaust-
ing ones because its members were always on display,
their actions scrutinized and gossiped over.

Gina wanted it. Tillie did not.

Rex closed his hand over her shoulder and gently gave her a nudge. "Sweetheart, it's time to awaken. We're almost there."

She loved the endearment, the gentleness of it, the warmth it carried. Slowly, she opened her eyes, forced herself to move away from him, and stretched as best she could within the confines of the conveyance. "Where are we?"

"Kingsbrook Park."

"You brought me to a park?" she asked, leaning toward the window and gazing out. She saw rolling fields, occasional trees, green.

"Not exactly," he said. "It's my personal estate."

She glanced back over her shoulder at him. "Personal?"

"Not entailed. I have my own income from investments and such. I bought this place a couple of years ago."

Turning her attention back to the window, she spied the manor, simple in its design. Rectangular, brick, three stories. Then the enormous stables and numerous paddocks came into view. The excitement thrummed through her, and she couldn't keep it from echoing in her voice. Not that she would have tried. She wanted him to know how much this moment meant to her. "It's where you keep your horses."

As Rexton helped Tillie out of the coach, he felt like a young lad sharing a new discovery. Her smile was incredibly bright, larger than he'd ever seen it, and her eyes glowed with enthusiasm. She was fairly bouncing with anticipation as he led her toward the largest paddock where a dark bay munched on flowers. He'd known the outing would please her. He should have made a wager on it. He could think of a thousand things he wanted with her, things she might be reluctant to give.

He nodded toward the trainer and a couple of the stable boys who were at work nearby. When he and Tillie reached the enclosure, Rexton whistled and the horse trotted over, making quick work of snatching up the carrot he'd removed from his pocket and extended toward her. He patted the mare fondly. "Lady Landsdowne, meet Fair Vixen."

"Hello, beautiful," she said with affection, rubbing her hand beneath the forelock. "I've seen her race. Up close, she's gorgeous."

"Would you like to ride her?"

Tillie's eyes widened, her jaw dropped. He knew it was a sight he'd never forget.

"Are you serious?" she asked in a near whisper. "Or am I asleep, still dreaming?"

"Why do you think I asked that you dress in something simple?"

"You should have told me to wear my riding habit."

"I feared that might give away the surprise." Leaning in, he brushed his lips over hers. "I do so like it when you're surprised."

Tears quickly welled in her eyes, were blinked back. "You're dangerous."

He didn't take offense because he suspected she'd just delivered a compliment. At least, he was hoping so. "Not so much so that you won't accept the offer to go for a jaunt on my finest mare."

Laughing, she shook her head. "No, not that dangerous."

He called to the head groomer to ready Fair Vixen and Naughty Boy, his favorite stallion. Tillie had burst out with laughter when she heard the name. He'd not yet raced the beast so it wasn't known. Because Grace sometimes visited, they had a sidesaddle, although Rexton wouldn't have minded if Tillie had sat astride. He didn't think she could do anything with which he'd be offended.

Before long, they were galloping over the hills. He let her take the lead, enjoyed watching her graceful movements. Her affection for horses matched his own. He had a wild thought that he could spend an eternity racing with her, enjoying the movement of the horse beneath him.

When Tillie brought her horse to a halt at the top of a rise, she was breathless and glowing, and he wanted to do all in his power to keep her looking that joyous, that happy.

"She runs like a dream," Tillie said, patting the horse as he neared. "You will certainly get a winner off her with Black Diamond."

"That's my hope."

He dismounted, walked over to her, and brought her to the ground. By now, he should be immune to the pleasure it brought him to touch her, to curve his palms against her sides, to have her hands curling over his shoulders. As Tillie walked away, he tethered the horses to some low-lying shrubbery. He joined her, put his arms around her, and brought her back against his chest. She folded her arms over his.

"It's lovely here."

He pressed a kiss to the nape of her neck. "We'll let the horses rest for a while, then we'll head back to the manor for luncheon."

"Do you come here often?"

"Once a month or so. I like spending time with the horses."

"I'm considering having a horse farm when I return to New York. Perhaps I'll ask you for some advice."

He didn't want to think about her leaving. Moving away from her, he removed his jacket, spread it over the ground, and assisted her in sitting on it. He dropped down beside her.

"This is the perfect spot for a picnic," she said.

"Perhaps we'll do that next time." He didn't know why he needed the words, why he needed to believe there would be a next time, why he was grateful she didn't indicate that this would be the only time she'd grace his small estate with her presence. Cupping her face, he turned her toward him. "For now, there's something else far more delicious than anything my cook can prepare that I'd like to nibble on."

$\mathcal{T}$illie welcomed his mouth blanketing hers, his tongue sweeping possessively across hers. It frightened her a little—how easily she could see herself spending her days here with him, walking the grounds, riding, laughing. But that honor would go to some other woman, someone with a sterling reputation. She wondered if he would allow his wife to ride Fair Vixen or if his memories of her on the mare would be such that he wouldn't want them replaced.

She selfishly wished for the latter. When their time

came to an end, she wanted some aspects of what they'd shared to be unique to her so he could never forget her. She wanted him to watch Fair Vixen race and to remember this day.

Smoothly, his mouth never leaving hers, he lowered her to the cool ground. Grass tickled her cheek. The fragrance of the wildflowers grew stronger, but not strong enough to drown out his purely masculine scent. It had somehow woven itself into the fabric of her being. No matter what colognes other men in her life wore, they would never smell as good as he did.

He skimmed his hand down her side, over her hip, and clamped it around her thigh, positioning her leg so her knee was raised and bent. His hand slid further down to circle her ankle, over the leather of her shoe, and he gave a gentle squeeze, before gliding those lovely fingers up her calf. Over her knee, down her thigh, lifting her skirt back as he went. The cool breeze wafted over her skin, causing little chill bumps to erupt everywhere, even where the air didn't touch her directly.

Breaking off the kiss, he raised his head, captured her gaze, held it in a manner so sensual that he made it impossible for her to look away as his hand advanced through the slit in her drawers to conquer her heated flesh with a caress that was at once gentle, but demanding. He wanted her surrendering to pleasure, here on the grassy knoll where nature looked on. She didn't know if she could do it, but when his eyes darkened with determination, his lips parted slightly, and two of his fingers entered her while his thumb stroked, pressed, teased, passion roared through her, tearing away any sense of propriety, of civilization.

"That's it, sweetheart," he murmured. "Scream for me. No one will hear."

He would hear. She wanted him to. How was it that he could so easily turn her into a wanton? She curled her hand around his neck, scraped her fingers up into his hair, held him there.

The glorious sensations built and built until she couldn't hold back, until she was screaming his name, her voice mingling with the flutter of wings as birds took flight from the boughs.

His hand stilled; leisurely he lowered his mouth to hers, taking only a small nibble before moving to her throat where he planted a series of kisses. "I love watching as pleasure overtakes you." His voice was raspy and low as though he were the one who'd shattered the quiet surrounding them.

"I enjoy watching you watch me." She couldn't use the word love as easily as he did. She'd misjudged it before. To admit to herself that her feelings toward him might be that strong would make her vulnerable. Theirs was an arrangement based on need: hers to see her sister comfortably situated; his to see that his baser needs were met.

He rose up. His gaze roamed slowly over her face as though he were memorizing each facet, every dip, curve, and line. Finally, his eyes came back to hers, held there. "I want more, Tillie. I want to waltz with you."

The joy that whipped through her with his simple declaration was terrifying. She shouldn't be this happy when what he desired was the impossible. "We could waltz here."

"I want to dance with you in a ballroom."

"If you ever come to New York—"

"Attend the next ball with Gina."

Shaking her head, she fought not to look away from him. "I'm not invited."

"You could come as my guest."

"No. You saw how it was at the theater, how men view me as loose and accessible—it will be far worse in a ballroom."

"Not if I'm at your side."

He underestimated the cruelty of Society. "It will serve Gina no good. I must see to her happiness."

"Why? Why must you accept the responsibility for it?"

"Because I'm the elder, because my mother dragged her over here, forced her to leave all her friends behind—because of my ambitions."

"You said your mother wanted the title."

"She did." She shoved herself up to a sitting position, flung her skirts back over her legs, and drew her knees in close, wrapping her arms around them, staring out at the fields that appeared untouched by man. "But so did I. There was a boy I fancied in New York." She laughed darkly. "A boy. He was twenty-four; I seventeen. He wanted to marry me but his mother wouldn't have it. He acquiesced to her demands to stop stepping out with me. His mother saw to it that we weren't invited to dinners or balls or welcomed because we were newly-moneyed and as such we were beneath them because they were old money. So when my mother hatched her scheme to put them in their place by marrying me off to nobility—I was not nearly as against the notion as I claimed. But poor Gina was eleven when she was up-rooted, brought here."

"She seems to have adjusted well enough."

Turning, she wasn't surprised to find him so near. It would take her swaying only a couple of inches to place her lips against his. "Not before she shed a good many tears. She released far more than I ever did. Eventually, yes, she accepted our move and became enamored with the aristocracy. She deserves to find here the happiness I never did. I am determined at least one of us will benefit from the upheaval in our life."

"This bloke in New York—"

"Anson."

"Anson," he repeated as though it left a sour taste in his mouth. "Is he the reason you're returning to New York?"

"Heavens no. He's married. I've heard he's unhappy. I can't take satisfaction in it. I was a silly girl to think revenge was the answer. I doubt he cared at all when I married."

Rexton suspected the bastard had in fact very much cared. But he also knew she would not have been happy with him—not in the long term. It was one thing to honor one's parents. Quite another to allow them to dictate one's life, whom one could love and marry. He couldn't imagine his parents wanting anything for their children except to be happy. But then his parents had defied convention. Dukes did not marry bookkeepers.

Still he couldn't imagine Tillie remaining infatuated with a man who wouldn't stand up for what he wanted. The thought of her leaving once her sister was married left a pain in his chest as though his horse had wandered over and kicked him.

She tugged a flower from the earth and began plucking off the petals. He'd done the same when he'd fancied himself in love with Emmaline, tearing a petal in two to ensure he ended the childish litany that accompanied his actions with "She loves me."

He almost told Tillie she didn't need to go through the ritual, that he could provide the answer. But he wasn't fool enough to reveal his heart when he wasn't certain it would change the future. She was determined to leave. Perhaps he would go to New York.

With a sigh, she flung the petal-less stem away.

"Not the outcome for which you were hoping?" he asked.

Her smile was self-mocking as she glanced back at him. "I think the horses are rested. We should probably go now."

"I'm not Anson," he said. "While I respect my parents and their opinion, I am no longer a child who follows their dictates when they are in opposition to what I want. Nor am I Downie. I would never be unfaithful to my wife, nor would I cause her misery."

Staring at him, she was as still as a statue. He wasn't even certain she breathed.

"If I say I will stand by your side in a ballroom, stand by your side I will. Anyone who crosses you crosses me. And trust me, sweetheart, no one would dare cross me."

"But you cannot be at my side forever. Your life is here and mine is in New York."

She was correct. He couldn't promise her happiness here, not when she wanted to leave so desperately.

Chapter 19

Once a month, Rexton joined his entire family for dinner at his parents' residence in St. James. He always looked forward to the family gathering. This particular evening, a week after he'd taken Tillie to Kingsbrook Park, his father sat at the head of the table with his duchess to his right and Rexton opposite him. Grace sat beside Lovingdon. Drake was whispering something to his wife, Ophelia. Seeing their intimacy made Rexton long for Tillie's nearness.

"So how is your courtship of Miss Hammersley going?" Grace asked, from her place beside their mother.

His mother perked up. "What's this then?"

"Did you not know?" Andrew asked. "Rex has set his sights on an American heiress."

"Hammersley," his mother repeated softly. "The name is familiar. I can't quite place it."

Not unusual. His mother cared little for the social scene. As his father's eyesight had deteriorated they'd attended fewer balls. But then she'd always been more interested in orphans, the poor, and her charitable works than impressing London's finest, except when she could entice them into donating to her causes.

"Her sister, Mathilda Hammersley, arrived from America and made quite the splash several years back," Grace said. "She married Landsdowne."

"Ah, yes. She got mixed up in some sort of scandal, didn't she?"

"She had a very public affair with a footman," Ophelia said.

"Sounds as though she likes a bit of the rough then," Andrew said in a tone that clearly labeled her a whore.

"She doesn't," Rexton stated succinctly, grateful the butter knife he was presently clutching couldn't do much damage if he jabbed it at his brother.

"How would you know that?" Lovingdon asked.

"I've spoken with her about the particulars."

"Oh, my God, Rex," Grace said softly, slowly, trance-like. "Your interest doesn't reside with Miss Hammersley at all, does it? It rests with Lady Landsdowne, the notorious heiress herself."

Grace had always been too sharp by half. "Don't refer to her in that manner. She's not deserving of it."

"Bloody hell, Grace has the right of it!" Andrew fairly crowed with glee.

"Andrew, watch your language at the table," their father chastised. "There are ladies about."

"Grace uses profanity more often than I do."

"That does not excuse your behavior." Even with his eyesight nearly gone, their father could deliver a formidable glare designed to keep his children in line, no matter their age.

"Sorry, Father. Ladies, if I offended I apologize. Can we return to the important issue here? Is it Lady Landsdowne who holds your interest?"

Taking a slow swallow of wine, Rexton was aware of the thick silence stretching between him and the others, everyone waiting on tenterhooks. He wasn't even certain anyone breathed. "I will admit to being fascinated by her."

"So you're escorting her sister about," Grace began hesitantly as though deciphering a complex problem, "so you can . . . what exactly? Have an excuse to cross paths with Lady Landsdowne?"

"It's a long story. Suffice it to say their uncle, Garrett Hammersley, thought if I gave a bit of attention to Miss Hammersley, it would make her more acceptable to Society and other gents would take an interest in her. In the process I met Lady Landsdowne."

"What is the benefit to you in this arrangement if not to acquire a wife?" his father asked. He'd forever questioned their motives and behaviors, insistent they set a good example.

Rexton couldn't very well tell the present benefit without earning his mother's wrath—and his sister's and no doubt Ophelia's as well. "Hammersley offered me Black Diamond for stud." Once upon a time.

His father's eyebrows winged up. "That's a fine stallion."

"Precisely."

"Still, rather unconventional trade there."

Especially the one which had replaced it. Although it was far more valuable than the original . . . and he feared in the end it would be far more costly. He'd gone into it as a business arrangement. Now it was anything but cold and calculating. At least from his perspective.

"He wants the girl married," Rexton felt obligated to say.

"So she becomes someone else's problem," Grace announced indignantly. She was far more independent than most ladies of her station and often found fault with how men overall viewed a woman's place in the world.

"It is not my place to judge," he said.

"Yet you brought me in on this ruse, asking that I approach you at the park to give some legitimacy to this endeavor, then having me escort the girl around the ballroom as though I'd taken her under my wing expecting her to become part of the family. I do wish you'd been honest about the reasons behind your seeking my assistance. I thought I was helping *you* to secure a wife."

He grinned at her. "Which was the only way to ensure your compliance. I would appreciate it, however, if you would continue to make Miss Hammersley feel accepted, and Lady Landsdowne as well, should your paths cross."

"You're not seriously considering marrying a divorced woman." His sister, who was usually so accepting of people, sounded horrified by the notion.

"I'm not certain those around this table should be casting stones regarding questionable behavior."

"But to be divorced is beyond the pale. I know no one else who has done such a thing. It's quite ruinous to one's social standing."

"So you can well imagine how desperately she wanted to be rid of Landsdowne, knowing the censure she would receive. Would you think more highly of her if she'd poisoned him or she'd spent her life in misery honoring vows that meant nothing to him? I find her courageous and admirable and spirited. You would as well if you took the time to get to know her."

Grace and everyone else at the table stared at him as though he'd lost his mind. "My apologies for the outburst, but I find her to be the most extraordinary woman I've ever met. As soon as her sister is situated, she'll return to New York and we shall be the poorer for it." He stood. "If you'll excuse me, I need a bit of air."

When he reached the terrace, he was still trembling with indignation on Tillie's behalf. He took several deep breaths, and tried to imagine how it might have been for her when she'd told her family she was to be a divorced woman. Gina had stood by her but what of the others? He'd never seen Tillie with her uncle. He recalled the night he'd asked Rexton for his help. He'd certainly not used flattering language where his elder niece was concerned.

When he heard the quiet footsteps, he blew out a gust of air before turning to face his mother. "My apologies. I didn't mean to ruin dinner."

"It's been a good long while since I've heard you speak so passionately," she said softly. "You care for her a great deal."

Leaning forward, he placed his forearms on the railing and gazed out into the darkened gardens. "Before I met her, I judged her as harshly as everyone else did. As I came to know her, she defied all my expectations. She is not cowed by life, by circumstance. She's incredibly strong and resilient, devoted to family. You'd like her."

"You've always had admirable taste so I'm certain I would."

Straightening, he faced her. "How much do you adore me?"

Reaching up, she brushed the hair back from his brow. "Abundantly. What do you require of me?"

He didn't know if he'd ever known anyone more generous. "You and Father haven't hosted a ball in years. I know he is no longer comfortable in crowds, and I feel like an utter ass for asking but if you were to host a ball, all of London would come. And if you were to invite Lady Landsdowne, welcome her in to your home, it might go a long way toward Society accepting her again."

"You want to see her accepted."

He wanted her to see that she could be received again, that she didn't have to be an outcast here in London, that she didn't have to return to New York to gain the happiness she deserved. "She's a remarkable woman who's been unfairly judged."

"Do you love her?"

He looked back out over the gardens. What he felt for Tillie couldn't be condensed into one word, one emotion. It encompassed every feeling he'd ever experienced. It scared the bloody hell out of him at times. The only thing that frightened him more was the thought of losing her. "I need her to know I can make a place for her here."

"And if she doesn't want this place?"

Turning back to his mother, he saw the profound sadness and immense knowledge in her eyes.

"I didn't want it," she said quietly. "I didn't want to be part of the aristocracy, to move about in this world."

"Yet here you are."

"Yet here I am. Love can be both wondrous and wicked in turn." With a tender smile, she gently patted his shoulder. "You shall have your ball and your lady shall have her invitation."

$\mathscr{A}$ week later, sitting behind her desk, Tillie stared at the vellum envelope she held gingerly between her fingers, her name written on it in precise and delicate script.

"It's not going to explode," Gina said impatiently. She'd been curled in a nearby chair going through the most recent invitations she'd received when she noted the one addressed to Tillie and handed it over with a great deal of excitement.

"I'm certain it's a mistake . . . or some sort of prank." All invitations had ceased arriving after she'd been caught with Griggs. Her eventual divorce had cemented no pen ever again scratched her name across a vellum envelope. Yet here it was, when she'd never thought to see it again—at least on this side of the pond. ,

"Open it," Gina urged. "See who it's from, at the very least."

Picking up the letter opener, she was surprised to see her fingers trembling, just a little, just enough to be embarrassing. It was ridiculous to place so much merit on a scrap of paper. Once she'd made use of the opener, she pulled out the embossed invitation. It was for a ball, hosted by the Duke and Duchess of Greystone.

She couldn't recall the last time she'd seen any mention of them hosting an affair. The same script that adorned the envelope prettied up a personal note.

My dear Lady Landsdowne—

> *It would please our family greatly to welcome you into our home.*
>
> > *The Duchess*
> > *of Greystone*

She stared at the words. Read them again. The invitation was truly for her.

"You've gone as pale as someone who's seen a ghost," Gina said, snatching the vellum from between her fingers and reading it. "Oh my God. This is wonderful! You're being welcomed back into Society."

"I'm being welcomed into one home."

"But it's a start. You're going of course."

She couldn't imagine it. Walking into a ballroom. All eyes would be upon her. The guests would stare in silence and then the whispers would start. Just as they had at the theater. The duchess might welcome her, but others would turn their back on her. She shook her head. "No."

"Why ever not?"

"I'm occupied that night."

"With what? Jane Austen? Mary Shelley? Charlotte Brontë? Honestly, Tillie, you can't say no to the Duchess of Greystone."

She could and she would. She rose and walked to the window where rain splattered the pane. She needed to be in her garden, digging in the soil, nurturing the blossoms, listening to the bees humming. She'd lived the life of an aristocrat and found it to be a very uncomfortable fit. Once was enough.

*E*xcept for the nights when there was a blasted ball that went into the wee hours, Tillie always met him at eleven, precisely, on the dot. His carriage parked at the far end of the drive, out of sight, he waited in the shadows of the trees and hedges near the front steps. Every night. Even if he hadn't taken Gina somewhere the day before. That part of their arrangement had flittered away, much to his delight.

Sometimes she wore only her nightclothes, sometimes she came to him in evening gowns, sometimes in plain frocks. He determined how they would spend their night based upon what she wore. The night she'd been attired in a simple dress with lots of buttons, he'd taken her to a tavern in Whitechapel where he'd known they'd not encounter anyone of consequence. They'd sat in a corner, he downing ale, her sipping on it, and had speculated about the people within and their happiness. The tavern was a place he enjoyed because it lacked pretense. With Tillie that night, he'd imagined a lifetime of going places with her where they could be themselves.

But if she were not accepted by Society, they would only be able to visit places on the fringes of it. While he enjoyed it on occasion, it wasn't his world and it shouldn't be hers. He didn't want it to be theirs.

When the devil had he begun thinking of never letting her go, of never being without her? He couldn't pinpoint the exact moment. She'd simply become part of his plans, his thoughts. He couldn't imagine going a day without seeing her, having a night without her in his bed. Hence the request of his mother.

Half an hour later, he began to think the request of his mother was the reason he still stood alone near the hedges. She had told him the invitation had been delivered today. Perhaps he should have warned Tillie it would be arriving, but he'd thought she'd appreciate the surprise.

An hour later, he was fairly certain she had not.

Unfortunately for her, he was not one to be so easily or quickly dismissed. He bounded up the front steps and used the knocker for all it was worth. Waited. Pounded his fist on the door. Waited. Pounded with a bit more ferocity.

The butler, Griggs, opened the door. Before he could say a word, Rexton shoved past him. "Where is she?"

"Her Ladyship has retired for the night and left orders not to be disturbed under any circumstances."

So she'd expected a disturbance, had she? He headed for the stairs.

"Sir, I must insist you leave."

He swung around. "Try and stop me. Give me an excuse to introduce my fist to your teeth." The man might not have bedded her, but he'd bloody well kissed her, had moved his mouth over hers, knew her taste, her—

"Rexton."

The word sliced through the thickness of the air, through his temper. She stood on the landing in black, buttons up to her chin, past her wrists. Every aspect of her spoke of her displeasure with him.

She started down. He waited. Perhaps he'd mis-

judged, perhaps another reason had delayed her joining him, but the fact that she didn't smile, her eyes
didn't sparkle told him that he wasn't wrong in his
assumptions.

"You may retire now, Griggs," she said as she swept
past Rexton and carried on into the parlor.

The butler hesitated. Rexton took pity on him. "She's
safe with me."

"My concern, sir, is you might not be safe with her.
She has quite the temper on her."

Rexton wasn't pleased the servant knew her so well,
but then he had been in her company for years. He
wasn't certain what his face might have revealed, but
the man offered a distinguished bow before leaving.
Spoiling for a fight, Rexton strode into the parlor.

No whisky had been poured. Apparently she was
spoiling for a fight as well.

"Were you intending to leave me waiting out there
all night?" he asked.

She angled her chin, a bit higher than he'd ever
seen. "I assumed you'd leave after a while."

"Why would I when I'd been given no hint anything
was amiss?"

"You had your mother invite me to her ball!" she
blurted, clearly agitated, her hands clasped so tightly
in front of her that he could see her knuckles turning
white.

"I did more than that. I implored her to have the
damned ball to begin with."

She swung away from him, marched to the sideboard, poured whisky into a glass, and downed it like
a seaman who'd just come into port after years at sea.

She spun back around and glared at him. "We should have discussed this before you took any action."

"I told you I wanted to waltz with you."

"This is about more than a waltz. I declined your mother's invite."

"Why?"

"Because I don't want to be part of that world again. It's haughty and cruel and pitiless. Intolerant of those who don't adhere to the strict rules that are as ancient as this country. I abhor it. I'm glad not to be part of it."

"It is my world."

"Yes." She shook her head. "I cannot—will not—make it mine again."

He considered walking over and pouring his own whisky. He was in need of it. "I know it won't be easy, but you won't be alone. I'll be there. My family, my friends—"

She moved her head from side to side with more force, more speed. "They spit on me, you know. Ladies of quality. When I passed them on the street or crossed paths with them at the dressmaker. They hug their children close as though I am a leper. Do you know why I wrested this house from Landsdowne, why I made him an offer so generous he would be forced to take it? So I could lord it over them that they may be petty and small but I have the means to live like a queen."

"But is it not lonely in your castle?"

She turned her back on him, and he suspected at that moment she hated him with every breath she drew. He walked over to the table of decanters, poured two glasses of whisky, strode to where she stood so stiffly he feared she'd shatter.

When he held a glass out to her, he wished she hadn't looked at him, that he hadn't seen the deep pain and hurt reflected in her eyes. Still, she accepted his offering and took a long swallow.

"I know what it is to bear the brunt of unkindness, Tillie."

She scoffed, following that ugly sound with an even more hideous laugh. He didn't blame her for lashing out at him.

"I was only twelve, new to being away from home, new to Eton. Perhaps if I'd been older, I'd have not felt the pain of not being accepted so sharply. Certainly now I could care less what a man thinks of me. But then it meant everything. They thought me unworthy of being in their presence because my mother came from the streets. I suffered at their hands. I hid from them—in attics and bell towers and among the foliage. But the escape was only temporary because one must get on with life. It was only when I stood up to them that I showed myself worthy. And I developed a good right jab."

Her mouth gave the tiniest of twitches but it was enough to offer him hope. "I am not saying that a boy's hurts cannot run deep, but they can't compare to a woman's when she is cast out and cast aside," she said softly.

"You're right, of course. I don't mean to imply my experience in any way equals what you have suffered, but I do have an inkling regarding what you are going through," he offered quietly. "I always had my family and my friends to lend me their strength and support, to be there when I was in need. I don't believe you had that—not family or friends who stood beside you— except for Gina, and she would have been too young to carry any sort of weight. How could you lean on her? Even now that she's grown, you don't. For all intents and purposes you've been on your own, alone, to face the dragons. You no longer have to be. I will stand beside you and so will my family and friends."

"Because their loyalty is to you. How easily they can remove their support if they are not pleased with me or you ask them to cast me aside."

"Once they get to know you, you will have their loyalty."

"I don't need them. I don't want them."

"But perhaps they need you. How better their world would be if you were in it. You've been strong for so long. Lean on me, trust me to take care of you."

*S*taring into those imploring blue eyes, she couldn't help but believe he was saying he needed her, that his world would be better if she were in it. But she had loved before and been betrayed. If her sister suffered because of her misdeeds, how could her children not?

Life had taught her to trust only herself. She turned away from him before she fell into those blue depths, before she promised her heart and soul to him, before he made her forget how humiliation at the hands of those she'd once considered friends could be.

She walked to the window, gazed out but she could see his faint reflection in the pane, watching her, waiting. "I've had others promise to take care of me. Promises can be broken."

"Mine won't be. I love you, Tillie. With every beat of my heart, every breath that I draw."

She slammed her eyes closed. Not fair, not fair, not fair. Not when she knew her past actions had the power to bring him to ruin. "You can't."

"But I do."

She shook her head. "I will not move back into Society, regardless of your words or promises."

"To hell with Society then," he said. "We'll live at Kingsbrook Park. Avoid the social scene altogether. Raise horses and children."

Children? The word was like a blow to her midsection. Was he implying marriage? She wanted nothing more than to give him children—but how might they suffer because of her scandals? She couldn't bear the thought of being responsible for any unkindness they might endure.

Opening her eyes, she forced herself to stare at his wavering reflection. If she turned to face him, saw him with clarity, she might fall into his arms. "The terms of our arrangement were for an affair. While it has been a glorious undertaking, I have no wish to extend our relationship beyond that."

A lie, but he didn't need the likes of her in his life. His birth gave him responsibilities and obligations. She couldn't imagine him casting them aside in favor of her. He might believe he could do it, but he was a product of his upbringing—and she wouldn't ask him to be less than he was.

"It seems I misjudged your affection," he said quietly.

To see him happy, she had no choice but to rebuff him, to free him of her scandal, her past. "It is an easy thing to do, my lord."

"Goodbye, Lady Landsdowne."

His reflection in the window was no more, but she didn't look away. She tormented herself by listening to his retreating footsteps, the closing of the door. She watched his solitary figure walk down her drive, his head held high.

Then she sank to the floor and wept for all the dreams—hers and his—she'd just shattered, for the loneliness she knew she would experience without him, for the sorrow she'd brought him, for how desperately she wanted to rush out after him and beg him not to leave her.

Chapter 20

The next morning, she awoke with eyes gritty and swollen. If she could bring herself to look in the mirror, she'd no doubt see they were red as well. In between bouts of restless sleep, she'd wept.

She couldn't recall her heart ever hurting this much. And she'd brought it all on herself. She'd thought he understood the terms of their relationship, that it would never be more than an affair.

Although she probably should have made certain her heart understood the terms as well, because damn it all to hell, she'd fallen in love with him. How could she not when he made her smile, made her laugh. When he gave her sprites for her garden. When he kissed her on a roundabout.

She rang for her maid and then took great pains to avoid her reflection in the mirror. She didn't want to see the sad and wretched creature she was. Sometime before the day was done, she was going to have to explain to Gina that she was on her own when it came to finding a husband. Tillie could no longer help her. She was going to return to New York.

When she was dressed, she made her way downstairs. Feeling as though she were slogging through mire, she headed to the dining room for breakfast. Griggs stopped her in the hallway.

"My lady, the coachman sent word up that a horse has been delivered to the stables. The lad who delivered it told him you are now its owner."

"No." The word escaped as a horrified whisper.

Before Griggs could respond, she hiked up her skirts and ran, through the residence, out a rear door into the gardens, past the pixie and roses and trellises until she reached the stables near the mews.

The coachman, a groom, and the stable boy were standing about admiring the proud and beautiful mare. Tillie staggered to a stop, gasping for breath, her heart feeling as though it were being rent in two.

The coachman turned to her, his face splitting into a wide grin. "She's a beaut, m'lady. The lad what brung her said she's to be called Fair Vixen." The mare whinnied and tossed her head. "Seems to know her name, she does. I thought to have one of the lads here ride her, see if she's as gentle as she seems."

"No," she said, "no one is to ride her. We won't be keeping her."

"That's a shame. I 'spect she runs right fast."

She runs like the wind. "Someone will be picking her up this afternoon," she told him. "Give her great care and keep her comfortable until then."

"Yes, m'lady."

She'd intended to walk away then, but she seemed unable to stop her legs from moving forward. The horse lowered her head as she approached, and Tillie found herself stroking the muzzle before pressing her forehead to it. "He values you. Why did he send you here?"

Because their arrangement was at an end. Gina was not betrothed. He was paying the forfeit for his failure.

"*I*'m not taking your horse. You can send someone to pick her up."

It seemed the problem with having an affair with a lady in his own residence was that she learned her away around it and apparently didn't think she needed the butler to announce her but was perfectly comfortable storming into his library in the late morning hours, with no regard for what a man might be doing.

Behind his desk, Rexton shoved back his chair and stood. The three men gathered in front of him also came to their feet, obviously perplexed by the intrusion to their weekly meeting. "Gentlemen, we'll leave matters there and take it up again when next we gather."

They mumbled their goodbyes to him, tipped their heads to Tillie as they passed her. He forced himself not to be gladdened by her arrival, to remain where he was rather than rushing forward, drawing her in, and begging her to reconsider a future with him.

Somewhat abashedly, she walked forward. "I apologize. I didn't mean to interrupt your discussion."

"Why are you here?" He was rather proud of the fact he had kept his tone flat, uncaring.

"You don't owe me Fair Vixen."

"Of course I do. Those were the terms of our *agreement*. If I abandoned the quest before the end of the

Season, my prize mare was forfeit. I have abandoned the quest ahead of time, completely and absolutely. With no regret or remorse. Fair Vixen is yours."

"But you didn't abandon it after taking me to your bed. The arrangement has ended because of my actions. You are not at fault."

He came around the desk, because he needed to ensure she heard and understood what he said. She took two steps back. He advanced. She took three steps back, then held her ground, chin coming up. He stopped when they were toe to toe.

"Our arrangement, madam, was that I would forfeit the horse if I did not see things through to a satisfactory conclusion. The terms of forfeiture have been met. The damned mare is yours."

"You're angry."

"I'm bloody furious. That you would come here and presume to tell me what I do or do not owe you? I am a man of my word. I honor my vows and my promises. I could marry a woman I despised and if I swore before man and God I would forsake all others then I would be true to her and never stray. I do not take words given lightly. I am not Landsdowne."

She blanched. "I am well aware of that." She lifted her hand as though to touch his cheek. If she touched him, he would go to his knees and agree to have her in his life on her terms. He didn't know what was reflected in his eyes, but she dropped her hand. "You come from a respected and noble family. You are a marquess. One day you will be a duke. You cannot be associated with a woman of scandal."

"You have told me Americans are not favored here.

I will admit I have found many of them to be rather crass, boasting about their wealth. And yes, madam, you judge the English just as harshly. Lord knows you've been ill treated by an Englishman." He gave his head an impatient jerk. "By several, by all accounts. But by all? My brother did not turn on his heel and leave my box when he saw you sitting there. He was a gentleman, kissed your hand. My sister approached you at the park. Did you think her insincere? My mother who has not hosted a ball in years, whose husband is nearly blind, is hosting an affair that will no doubt be well attended so she can show all of London you are welcomed in her house. I would hold your hand in public, yet you want to limit what we share to the shadows. I am even willing to live away from Society, but that seems not to suit you either. Yes, madam, I am rather put out."

He spun on his heel and headed for the double doors that led into the gardens because he feared he was very close to howling out his frustration. "The horse is yours, Lady Landsdowne. Mate her with Black Diamond. Get yourself a winner."

*S*he was sitting on the settee in the parlor sipping her third glass of whisky when Gina walked in.

"Oh my God, whatever is wrong? It's early afternoon and you're drinking."

"I made him angry," she said, her tone devoid of emotion.

"That's wonderful! That's what you're supposed to do." Gina sat on the settee beside her, smiling joyfully.

Tillie stared at her; her sister had gone mad. "I beg your pardon?"

"When you were giving me advice, you told me at some point I needed to make the gentleman courting me angry so I could see what he was truly like."

Had she said that? She had a vague recollection of it. "I am not one whose courting advice you should follow."

"So what is he like when he's angry?"

"Cutting." She shook her head. "No, that's not quite accurate. His words are clipped but there is a vibration in his voice, like the lingering thrum of a chord struck on a piano. It sounds like hurt. And his eyes were those of someone wounded who was trying to pretend he wasn't hurt." She knew that look. She'd seen it often enough in her own reflection while she was married to Downie.

"Did he strike you?"

"No." As angry as he'd appeared, she'd never feared him. Well, she'd had a brief moment of apprehension when he'd come around the desk and advanced on her like a soldier determined to rout out the enemy, but then she'd remembered how well she knew him and had known he wouldn't hurt her. "He would never strike a woman, no matter how angry she made him or how much she disappointed him."

"Do you love him, Tillie?"

Closing her eyes, she took a deep breath. "So much, Gina. It's frightening how much I love him."

"Then you should be with him."

She looked at her sister imploringly. "I can't. Because I love him so much, I can't. I can't put the burden of my scandalous past on him."

"He has awfully wide shoulders. I expect he could manage any burden just fine."

She almost smiled at that, at the thought of his shoulders, the little hollow where she would rest her head. "But he shouldn't have to. And neither should you. I'm going back to New York. I'm going to leave you here alone to sort out your own love life."

"I suppose I can't blame you for leaving. I know it's been difficult for you to remain with me. However, it's high time I took responsibility for myself and my own happiness, isn't it?"

Suddenly Gina seemed more mature than Tillie had given her credit for. "You don't feel as though I'm abandoning you?"

"Absolutely not, dear sister. I've learned a great deal from you, and I shall put it to good use. You needn't worry about me."

"I love you, Gina."

"I know you do, but it's time you got on with your life. And speaking of getting on—as you won't be here for much longer, what say we do something special together?" She took the glass of whisky from Tillie and set it aside. "The Royal Tea Palace is supposed to be the place to be seen. Let's go for high tea, shall we?"

"Gina—"

"Oh, Tillie, we never go out as sisters are wont to do. We'll ask for a secluded corner table. No one will bother us." She squeezed Tillie's hand. "Let's have a bit of fun and get your mind off Rexton."

Tillie doubted anything would ever accomplish that goal, but she did admire Gina's determination to make the best of things. How she was going to miss her! "Yes, all right. We'll have a jolly good time."

* * *

"*H*ave you a reservation?" the gentleman standing at a rather high desk beside the door asked.

"No, we don't," Tillie said quietly. "But I can see there are empty tables." Round tables, covered in white lacy cloth. It was the sort of place where one spoke in hushed tones.

"Many of them are reserved. Let me see if one is available." He dragged his finger along what looked to be a ledger of names. "Yes, it appears—"

"I do hope you are not considering admitting them, Mr. Wadsworth," Lady Blanford, Downie's sister, announced in the exact opposite of a hushed tone, standing there like the prow of a ship, staring down her nose at Tillie. She'd put on considerable weight since Tillie had last seen her. No doubt because Tillie's dowry allowed the woman to purchase all the confectionaries she could eat.

"Good afternoon, Lady Blanford," Tillie said politely.

The countess sniffed. "Mr. Wadsworth, this woman is not the sort to whom you should permit admittance. I daresay if word gets around you even allowed her in the door you will find yourself tossed on the street by your employer. Her sister is just as despicable."

The anger shimmied through Tillie. "Say what you want of me, madam, but don't you dare disparage my sister."

"Like breeds like. I have seen your sister sniffing around our gents, and I assure you I have ensured no mother will allow her son to give her so much as the time of day. She is on a fool's quest if she expects to marry into the nobility. The rumors I can spread—"

"Be forewarned, madam. I do carry a pistol in my reticule. I wouldn't kill you, of course, but I might leave you with a scar designed to ruin the line of that wonderful décolletage of yours."

Lady Blanford inhaled sharply. "Do you see, Mr. Wadsworth? Do you see why you cannot allow this vile creature entry, that she would threaten me so?"

"Yes, my lady." He gave Tillie an apologetic look. "I'm sorry, madam, but—"

"Oh, Lady Landsdowne, Miss Hammersley. There you are."

Tillie turned to see the Duchess of Lovingdon coming around from behind Lady Blanford. Smiling brightly, she was the picture of calm. She placed her hands on Tillie's shoulders, bussed a kiss across her cheek, then did the same with Gina. "We've been waiting for you."

"Your Grace . . ." She didn't know quite what else to say. The duchess took her hand, tucked it into the corner of her elbow as though she were creating an unbreakable chain. With a wink, she patted Tillie's hand.

"Mr. Wadsworth, Lady Landsdowne and Miss Hammersley are joining me for tea. You should see them written down as sitting at my table."

"Surely you jest," Lady Blanford stated emphatically.

"I do not," the duchess replied calmly.

"I'm sorry, Your Grace," Mr. Wadsworth began. "I don't see—" He looked up, caught sight of the duchess's determined expression, glanced back down. "Ah, yes, here they are. I must have overlooked them."

"I thought so. I admire your tenacity in continuing to persevere until the matter was satisfactorily sorted out. I shall sing your praises to the owner."

"Thank you, Your Grace."

"Come along," the duchess said to Tillie and Gina.

Lady Blanford had the audacity to step in front of them. "Mr. Wadsworth, I must insist you prevent this rabble from entering."

"Come now, Countess," the duchess said, her voice tight but controlled, "do you really think he is going to adhere to your wishes when doing so will mean that my party immediately leaves to never return? And let's not forget Lady Landsdowne's pistol. Scars can be a symbol of courage but I'm not certain that would hold true in your case. Now step aside and do not make a further fuss or you will find yourself being the one escorted out."

Glaring at Tillie, the countess did as ordered.

"This way, ladies." The duchess indicated they should precede her into the dining area.

As Tillie was walking past, she heard the duchess say, "Lady Blanford, you may have heard my mother is hosting a ball tomorrow evening. You might have even received an invitation. If so, disregard it. My mother does not tolerate nasty people."

Then the duchess was ushering Tillie and Gina to a table near the window.

"Duchess, I appreciate all you've done, but we don't want to impose," Tillie said quietly.

"No imposition." The duchess smiled softly. "We all have moments when we have to deal with her sort. Such a bother, but there you are." She indicated the table. "Do you know everyone?"

She did indeed. The Duchesses of Avendale and Ashebury, the Countess of Greyling, and Mrs. Drake Darling. Yes, Mr. Wadsworth would have been unhappy indeed if the duchess and her friends had left.

Once they were all seated, Gina said, "This is such an honor, to be enjoying tea with all of you."

"So, Miss Hammersley, we hear you are on the husband hunt," Mrs. Darling said. "There is nothing we like better than matchmaking. Perhaps we can assist."

"Lord Rexton has been trying to help me. We've had little luck."

"A man who has been avoiding marriage is probably not best suited to helping someone else acquire it," the Duchess of Ashebury said. "Let's discuss strategy."

While the ladies began peppering Gina with questions regarding her likes and dislikes, the Duchess of Lovingdon leaned toward Tillie. "I understand you declined my mother's invitation."

"I thought it for the best."

"My brother cares for you a great deal."

"That is why it is for the best."

"Because you think Society will not forgive your actions nor accept you."

Tillie nodded.

"Yet, here you sit with three duchesses, a countess, and the wife of one of the wealthiest men in London. I think, Lady Landsdowne, that there is another reason for your reluctance. Maybe you should consider that."

She bit her lower lip while her heart pounded. "I misjudged before," she whispered. "I fear I will disappoint him and he won't be able to love me always."

"Always. That's what we want, isn't it? Love for always. Do you know my husband nearly tossed me over because there is a chance I will die before we are old and he could not stand the thought of losing me? For some always is a short time. For others it is long. What matters is that we had a chance at it at all."

Chapter 21

Two nights later, Rexton was still in a foul mood. He'd considered going into Whitechapel, hoping to run across some ruffians upon whom he could vent his frustrations but he feared he might take matters a bit too far and find himself dancing in the wind at the gallows. And he certainly didn't want to wake up on the floor at Jamie's again. So he'd come to the Dragons, where he'd known he'd find a private game with high stakes taking place in a secluded room. So far he'd lost every hand. He had no interest in cheating, in winning. He was here merely for the company and the whisky that the appointed footman continually poured into his glass.

Perhaps he shouldn't have been so selfish as to want to spend so much time alone with Tillie. If he'd brought her here, where he often played cards with family and friends, she'd have known acceptance. No one within this room would have stared at her or accosted her; she would have been welcomed, simply because she was on his arm. No, that wasn't quite true. She'd have been welcomed because of herself, her strength, her charms, her confidence. Those within this room never judged on gossip, but rather on merit. Tillie would have proven herself worthy of their regard in short order. Perhaps then she would have recognized the potential permanence for what they shared together, instead of relegating it to a short-lived affair. Even if in the beginning that was all he'd expected of it as well.

He downed the little bit of whisky that remained in his glass and waited impatiently for the footman to fill it. Damnation but he missed her. His residence seemed quieter, more lonely at night. He could hardly stand to be within it.

"I ran across Lady Landsdowne the other day at the Royal Tea Palace," Grace said, her tone reflecting the same casualness with which she tossed away two of her cards, yet still with the mention of Tillie he stiffened as though his sister had prodded him with a hot poker, torn between wanting to know every minute detail and begging Grace to say no more. "Threatening Lady Blanford with a pistol of all things."

A week ago he would have laughed, taken pride in her actions. Damn it, he couldn't help but still feel a measure of satisfaction at her boldness and wished he'd been there to see it.

"She appeared as miserable as you," Grace went on. "As you didn't bring her here tonight, am I to assume that whatever was between you has come to an end?"

While everyone seemed focused on the cards they were holding, he knew the others at the table— Lovingdon, the Duke and Duchess of Avendale, Jamie, the Swindler twins, and Drake—well enough to sense they were very much aware of the conversation. "We decided we didn't suit."

"Pity. I rather liked her."

He glared at his sister. "From a few words at the park?"

"No, from our visit during tea. I invited her to join us at our table. You asked us to be welcoming to her, so I was." After cards were revealed, Grace scooped the chips in the center of the table into her ever-growing pile. She was the most skilled cheater of the lot. "Although I would have done so anyway. Lady Blanford was being an absolute beast. I can't tolerate bullies."

He almost smiled at the thought of Tillie and his sister together. They'd make a formidable pair. "I'm sure she'd have put Lady Blanford in her place and handled the matter satisfactorily."

"Without question. But still it's always nice to know you have someone at your back."

Cards were dealt. Rexton studied his, sighed. Grace could no doubt turn it into a winning hand. The problem was he didn't care if he lost a fortune tonight because he'd already lost the only thing that mattered: a life spent with Tillie.

$\mathcal{H}$aving purchased her passage for the steamer, Tillie knew she would be back in New York by the end of the month. She didn't know why she wasn't more excited by the prospect of leaving this city and its ghastly people behind. Perhaps because she would miss Gina so much. And she would worry about her.

Just as she was now worried because Gina was not bubbling over with excitement at the prospect of attending tonight's ball. She sat still as a statue at her dressing table while Annie pinned her hair up into an elaborate style that somehow managed to make her look older, wiser.

"I do wish you would reconsider attending the Greystone ball," Gina said, capturing Tillie's gaze in her mirror's reflection, even though Tillie sat in the far corner of the room. She didn't usually watch her sister's rituals as she prepared for an evening out, but knowing their time together was dwindling seemed to make every minute more precious.

"No good would come of it." It would simply rekindle hope that she would have to dash with the truth: she was more scandalous than Rex's mother and, therefore, their children might be made to suffer more than he had. She'd thought long and hard on his revelations. Children were indeed cruel, and their own might find themselves less accepted than she was.

"I disagree, Tillie." Gina swung around on the bench and faced her, while her maid scurried behind her to finish the preparing of her hair. "During the past five days you've been absolutely downtrodden. Defeated, so remarkably sad that's it very difficult to be happy around you."

Joy sparked for the first time since Rex had walked out of her parlor. "Are you happy?"

"No, of course not. You're leaving."

"You always knew I would."

"I was hoping if I married a man who embraced you that you would stay."

"Do you think you might marry Somerdale?"

Gina shrugged, sighed. "I don't know. I like him well enough but courting is rather like sampling chocolates, isn't it? You don't know if you ate the best one first until you've sampled the entire box."

Tillie leaped to her feet. "It's nothing at all like eating chocolates. A lady doesn't sample the entire box of . . . of men."

"Then how does one know?"

Unsure as to how to best explain, Tillie began pacing between the wardrobe and the bed. "You know because of the way he makes you feel when he is with you and when he is not. When he is with you . . ." Stopping near the bed, she ran her hand along the intricately carved post. "Your entire body seems to be smiling. You long for his touch, his nearness. You welcome the accidental brushing of hands. And you're desperate for him to get you alone so he can kiss you." Her bed had never felt so large, so cold, so unwelcoming as it had once she was no longer spending her nights with Rex. Each night, she dreaded crawling beneath the covers, lying there alone, staring at the window, the canopy, the shadows, missing him until it was a physical ache in her chest.

"And when he isn't with you?" Gina prodded.

"You wish like the devil he was." She dropped onto the edge of the bed, not at all surprised when Gina joined her there.

"You miss Rexton, don't you?"

So terribly much, but she didn't want to think about that. "Will you dance with him tonight?"

"I suspect so. As it's his mother's ball, he's bound to be there."

Looking incredibly handsome in his evening clothes, speaking with other ladies, smiling, flirting. He was done with her. He'd move on easily enough. Perhaps someday, she would move on as well, although she couldn't envision herself with anyone else.

Gina took her hand, squeezed, as though she knew

the melancholy path her traitorous thoughts traveled. "I was only thirteen when you married Downie," her sister said musingly. "Even in the very beginning, when I would see you with him, I would think, 'Love isn't such a grand thing after all.' I thought love was supposed to transform and fill one with gladness. I began to think perhaps I didn't want it, would be happier without it."

"Gina—"

"Let me finish," she said sharply, more tartly than she'd ever spoken to anyone. "I have a point to make. I know you think me naïve and innocent in the way of things, and perhaps a bit flighty on occasion because I refuse to take the world seriously, but I watched you, Tillie, watched as you became this sad creature who was so foreign to me. Your smiles became rare, your laughter nonexistent. I was glad when you divorced him, when he was no longer in your daily life; it was as though I could feel a great weight being lifted from you. And I thought, 'She merely chose poorly. And I shan't. I shall choose a love that will elevate me.'"

"Is that Somerdale?"

"Perhaps. Or perhaps not. Because I have now seen you in love—and more importantly, I have seen a man in love with you. I know how love makes a lady's eyes sparkle and a man's smolder. I know how it makes one's footsteps light as air when she's rushing out to a carriage at midnight for a bit of naughtiness—"

"Oh, Gina, you were never supposed to know about that."

"I don't know why you're blushing so deeply. But don't you see? You gave me glimpses into a world I want. I don't want to simply be part of the aristocracy.

I want to find someone who loves me as deeply as Rexton loves you—someone I can adore as much as you do him."

"But I am so wrong for him. He needs a wife who is welcomed into a blasted tea room."

"I thought you handled yourself with an amazing amount of grace." She tilted her head to the side, skewed her mouth. "Although I do rather wish you'd removed your pistol from your reticule. I certainly would have liked to see Downie's sister scurrying away. She wouldn't have stood up to you."

Tillie couldn't help but give a half smile. "No, she wouldn't have."

"I think Rexton would have been proud of you, Tillie. What does it matter what others say or how they act when you have people who love you?"

"But others' actions and words reach beyond me." Tenderly she touched her sister's cheek. "They touch those I love. They touch you. Look at this Season. You should be the belle of the balls, with suitors streaming through our front door every afternoon, and flowers filling the entryway every morning. But you aren't, because of me."

"Maybe you're not the reason I haven't had an abundance of suitors. Perhaps I'm to blame. Perhaps I'm not lovable."

"Don't be ridiculous. Don't doubt yourself. All the lords want heiresses, Gina. When I'm gone you'll have a dozen men from whom to choose. Just don't *sample* them."

Gina's lips curled up teasingly. "Not even a kiss from each of them?"

"Absolutely not."

"Without you here, I don't know that I'll have it within me to restrain and behave."

"I shall be hiring a proper chaperone before I leave." An older woman with a keen eye and sharp tongue to keep the gents in line.

A rap sounded on the door just before it opened and a maid stuck her head inside. "Mr. Hammersley has arrived."

"Tell Uncle I'll be down in a moment," Gina said, before turning back to Tillie. "Are you sure you won't come?"

"I'm sure."

"I hate that you're letting them win." She pushed herself off the bed, gathered her wrap and fan, turned for the door, stopped, and looked back at Tillie. "Although perhaps if Rexton can't have you, he'll settle for the sister."

Tillie felt as though Gina had picked up the poker and stabbed it through her heart. "I don't think you'd suit."

"You might be right, but whatever you're feeling right now, imagine how much worse it's going to be when you read of his betrothal in the papers."

"You're a little witch."

Gina smiled brightly. "I can be. Just think about it, Tillie."

She wasn't going to think about it—about Rexton with someone else. She wanted him to have the happiness he deserved. Even if it wasn't with her.

Following her sister to the stairs, she repeated that unsatisfying litany. She watched as her sister descended the steps, maid in tow to serve as chaperone, watched as her uncle greeted Gina before glancing up at her and giving her a put-upon nod, watched as they walked out of the residence. Without her, as it should be.

She wandered into her bedchamber and came up short at the sight of the lavender ball gown spread over her bed, the gilded invitation lying in wait in the center of the bodice. Her sister was dastardly in her ploys. "Oh, Gina."

Carefully she picked up the vellum as though she expected it to burn her fingers. Perhaps she should attend so Gina—and Rexton—would finally understand exactly why it was impossible for her to stay. What did she have to lose? She'd already lost the only man who mattered.

Chapter 22

*R*exton had the right of it. Within his parents' residence, the grand salon—as well as other nearby rooms—were stuffed with an assortment of people swarming through them, while other guests spilled out onto the terrace and into the gardens. He was reminded of a beehive he'd once watched in fascination as a boy. Only this was not nearly as entertaining.

Because he had requested the affair, he was obligated to stay in the ballroom and partner up with ladies for conversation and an occasional dance. But even he required a respite now and then. This moment was the first he'd had alone, without conversation. Sipping the champagne, he fought not to think of Tillie, of how he'd wanted this night to show her the past could be forgotten—or at the very least not whispered about as loudly.

He'd seen Gina arrive with her uncle, the blasted maid in tow to serve as chaperone. But then he was aware of everyone who'd accepted the invitation because they were announced at the top of the stairs before beginning their descent into what for him was rapidly becoming the bowels of hell. No conversation intrigued him, merely reminded him of the countless discussions he'd had with Tillie. Every word they'd ever exchanged was emblazoned on his memory. No dance partner satisfied him. While he'd never danced with Tillie, he'd held her in his arms and they literally ached to hold her once more. He couldn't quite envision it: never again inhaling her fragrance, never again gazing into her eyes, never again hearing her voice. Never again making love to her.

It was quite possible he'd die without issue as he couldn't imagine any other woman stirring his desires, igniting his passions. She had spoiled him, and he couldn't quite work up the enthusiasm to be with any other woman.

Even preparing for tonight's venture had been an exercise in fortitude not only for himself but for his valet. Rexton hadn't shaved since the evening he walked—no, stormed—out of Tillie's residence. He might not have taken a razor to his face earlier if his valet hadn't warned him he looked like a wild beast. He'd straightened himself up only because he didn't want his mother to worry, when in truth, he didn't give a damn about his appearance or much else for that matter.

"Are you drinking champagne?"

Supposing he should be grateful for the intrusion into his downwardly spiraling thoughts, he glanced over at his brother. "It was all I could find."

"You used to live here. Surely you know where to locate the better stuff." Andrew took Rexton's glass and tossed the bubbly contents into the fern's pot.

"It's likely to kill the plant."

"Purchase Mother a new one." Andrew removed a flask from his jacket pocket and filled the flute with amber liquid before handing it back to Rexton. "You look like you're in desperate need of something stronger."

With a nod, he tossed back a good portion of the whisky, relishing the burn. Yes, the sharp bite was exactly what he'd needed, a kick to the system that might carry him through the night. "It's unusual for you to be at a ball."

"It's Mother's ball. Besides, she gave me a rather stern lecture on the importance of attending and making Lady Landsdowne feel welcomed. So I know what tonight was supposed to be about. I'm dreadfully sorry all didn't go as planned regarding the ball and your lady," Andrew said. "You seemed to fancy her quite a bit."

Rexton almost touted all her exceptional qualities, but he knew once he began traveling that path he'd be holding his brother captive for the entirety of the evening, so he merely shrugged as though his disappointment was of no consequence. "Perhaps I'll meet someone tonight who I'll decide to court." *Not bloody likely*. He couldn't imagine courtship being in his near or distant future. "How's your actress?"

Staring forward, Andrew pursed his lips, took a sip from his flask. "We've parted ways."

"Then I don't suppose I'll be finding you in my box anytime soon."

"I might make use of it yet. Are you truly not interested in Miss Hammersley?"

"Not in the least." Then the tone of his brother's

question hit him and he stared at Andrew. "Don't tell me you are?"

Andrew shifted his stance. "She doesn't seem a bad sort and these Americans are a bit more daring than our English roses."

"Somerdale has shown some interest in her." Although as far as he knew he'd only called on her the once.

"Ah, she won't be happy with him."

"You don't know that."

Andrew merely chuckled. "I know a good many more things than you give me credit for."

"You'd best not hurt her," Rexton admonished.

"I thought you were done with her."

"She's no longer under my protection—" Damn it all to hell. "She's under my protection. Her uncle is worthless. Besides, apparently Grace and her friends have taken up her cause and intend to see her well matched."

"You don't think I'd fit the bill."

"Only if you think you can love her." He finished off the whisky, set the glass aside. "Be aware I shall warn her about you during our waltz."

Andrew grinned. "I'll convince her you lied when I dance with her after you."

"I'm serious, Andrew. I know you have no plans to marry so don't go anywhere near her."

"Surely a dance can't hurt."

He'd thought the same thing the night he'd first danced with her. It had taken him on an unexpected journey. "Drake warned me things never go as planned. Steer clear of her." Leaving his brother with that bit of sage advice, he went in search of Gina.

He found her engaged in conversation, smiling, and laughing with three gentlemen, who seemed to have a keen interest in her. Looking past one, she widened her eyes and her smile. "My lord."

He was grateful she was having a jolly good time, that tonight's efforts wouldn't be completely wasted. He did want her to find happiness, and the right man. While he liked Somerdale, he couldn't help but wonder if Andrew was correct. "Excuse me, gents, but I'm fortunate indeed that this dance belongs to me."

Once they reached the dance floor, he swept her into the fray of dancers, trying not to recall how he'd longed to do the same with her sister. "You look exceedingly lovely this evening, beyond compare."

"You're kind to say so, but I know it's not me with whom you wish to dance. I'm dreadfully sorry she didn't come. I tried to convince her otherwise, but she'd have none of it."

"No matter. I don't know that this residence could hold one more guest." Although he'd kick the lot of them out to make room for her—which he supposed would defeat the original purpose of even having the blasted affair.

"For what it's worth, I think she's a fool."

Perhaps he'd been the fool, for not wanting to marry sooner, for not being here when she was younger, for not meeting her before Downie. But he didn't want to think about what might have been. What would never be. "You seem to have drawn the attention of quite a few gents tonight."

Her smile rivaled the stars. "Your sister and her friends are powerful allies. Every dance is claimed. I rather wish no gentleman decides to court me seriously as I'd like to have an entire Season like tonight. It was like this for Tillie. Everyone wanted to be with her, to be her friend . . . and then they didn't."

"Their loss." In the end. And his.

"She's purchased her passage back to New York."

So soon? He stopped whirling her over the floor as though she'd placed a brick wall in front of him. He'd known Tillie was going to leave—but now that the moment was upon him—

"When?"

"End of the week."

There wasn't much time. "Are you going with her?" he asked.

"No. She's planning to hire a chaperone for me, which will leave her with no one." Her brow was furrowed. All the joy she'd exhibited earlier had dissipated.

Lifting her gloved hand, he pressed a kiss to her knuckles. "Don't worry, Little One, she won't be going alone."

"What are you going to do?"

What he should have done all along.

"Mathilda Paget! Countess of Landsdowne!" The majordomo's voice boomed through the room. Rexton could have sworn he felt it shimmering around him.

"What did he say?" He looked toward the top of the stairs. He wasn't the only one. The music ended and the murmurings began, but he didn't care about any of that. None of it mattered.

"She came," Gina breathed out on a rush, clutching his arm. "She came. She told me she wouldn't."

Standing there in lilac, looking out over the ballroom. Bold, gorgeous, defiant.

And then the woman he loved more than life began her descent.

*S*he had never been more nervous and terrified in her entire life.

After her name was announced, she swore the room became so quiet she could have heard a pin drop. It also became incredibly still. People no longer danced. The music ceased to play. She told herself it was because she had arrived unfashionably late, and people were surprised by a guest's tardiness.

But then she became aware of the quiet murmuring, the whispers. This was no doubt a mistake, a huge mistake. But she'd recently made a much larger one: she had let him go without a fight.

With a deep, shaky breath she began her descent into the ballroom. She'd managed only a half dozen steps when she saw Rexton charging up them, his long legs taking them three at a time, his devilish smile making her smile.

Dear God, she'd never been so glad to see anyone in her life, and not because it meant she wasn't going to have to face the crowd alone, but because he was simply there and looked so bloody marvelous. And so glad to see her. Perhaps she hadn't lost him completely.

But then he stopped, one step below her, within reach. All she had to do was extend her fingers to cradle his jaw, flick them through his hair, curl them over his shoulder to steady herself.

"You're here," he said quietly as his gaze drifted over her face, before settling on her eyes, holding them as though if he claimed them he could claim her.

"It seems so, yes."

"Why?"

Such a short word, a simple word, for an incredibly complex question with an even more complex answer. But in the end, there was too much to explain and she suddenly realized this wasn't the place or the moment. "Because I wanted a memory of sharing a waltz with you."

"Do you think there will be but one?"

"I don't know. I'm not even sure there will be that one."

"Where men are concerned, it seems you continually misjudge. I promise as long as you are willing, you will have a good many waltzes with me."

He was the one who misunderstood: why she was here and the point she was striving to make so she could leave England behind with fewer regrets, but she realized even they would forever haunt her.

She shook her head. "Do you not feel the stares?"

"Because they are unaccustomed to gazing on one so beautiful."

She couldn't help herself. She rolled her eyes at his compliment. It couldn't deflect the truth. "Do you not hear the silence?" His approach had quieted the crowd, but she knew at any moment the mutterings would begin anew.

"It's just as well. Their conversations are boring. I've nearly nodded off at least a half dozen times this evening listening as they waxed on about nothing of consequence."

"Rex—"

"Let's have our waltz. But first we must greet my parents."

He extended his arm. She wrapped hers around it,

relishing the sturdiness as he escorted her down the miles and miles of stairs that ended at a polished floor where surely at some point people would once again begin dancing. But at that moment they seemed content to merely watch the drama unfolding before them as she approached one of the most powerful and beloved couples in all of England. Even remembering the words relayed in the duchess's handwritten note did little to assuage her worries that in the end she would be rebuffed.

Releasing her hold on Rex, she curtsied deeply. "Your Graces."

"My dear," the Duchess of Greystone said kindly, taking Tillie's hand and squeezing her fingers. "We're so glad you were able to attend after all. I can see your arrival has pleased my son, and that pleases us no end."

"I appreciate the invitation."

"You'd have received one sooner, but we've not hosted a ball in years."

"If I still danced with anyone other than my wife," the duke said, "rest assured you'd find yourself on my arm."

"I'm honored. I can't thank either of you enough for the kindness."

"Posh. I never understood the appeal of not being kind. Now off with you, have your waltz."

Rex again offered his arm, and she took it. As he led her across the floor, people moved aside, although she wasn't quite certain their drifting back had anything to do with her, but rather the determination on his face. When they neared the balcony where the orchestra waited, he called up, "A waltz!"

The first strain had barely sounded when she found

herself in his arms, held improperly close, as they glided over the floor.

"Why are you truly here?" he asked.

"As I said: to have a waltz before I leave."

Out of the corner of her eye, she saw the Duke and Duchess of Lovingdon step onto the dance floor, followed by Drake Darling and his wife, then Gina and Lord Andrew. Then the Duke and Duchess of Greystone were dancing along the edge of the crowd.

"You told me your father was losing his eyesight," she said quietly.

"He is. If you watch them closely enough, you'll see she's leading. That's what love is, Tillie, making the most of a bad situation, doing what one must to ensure the other is happy. You want New York? You can have it. I'll go there with you."

She'd been on the verge of looking at his parents more intently but his words had her gaze coming back and crashing with his. "You mean to visit?"

"I mean to live. To raise horses and children with the woman I love."

She shook her head. "But you're heir to a dukedom. Your life is here."

"The estates are here. My life is with you. I can manage them from New York. I could manage them from the North Pole if I had to."

"You can't give this up for me." More people were waltzing around them now.

"Isn't it our choice to make, Tillie? Whether we're in each other's lives, if we're happier together than apart? The people standing at the edge of the ballroom, with their noses in the air and their snickers, what do they matter? I don't care if they approve of us or not."

Tears began burning her eyes. "You don't understand what it will truly be like. It'll be much worse than when you were a boy. Don't ask me to stand by and watch as you become miserable."

"I'm asking you to stand by me and make me happy."

Then they were no longer waltzing. He'd gone down on one knee. "Marry me."

The music had again halted; the couples had ceased dancing.

"You have gone mad."

"Madly in love with you."

"But my reputation. I'm notorious—"

"I don't give a fig. I love you, with my heart and my soul and my body. I will go wherever you will have me, wherever you will be happy."

The tears rolled onto her cheeks. "I love you so much. I'm afraid to love you this much."

"Don't be. For however much you love me, I shall love you more. I shall never be unfaithful. I shall go to bed each night deciding what I can do the next day to make you even happier."

She saw the truth, his devotion, his belief in the rightness of their future mirrored in his eyes. "I shall go to bed each night doing the same. Never in my life have I wanted anything more than I want to be your wife. Yes, I'll marry you."

He rose to his feet, cradled her face, and kissed her tenderly. Then he swung around, took her hand, and lifted it.

"She has agreed to become my wife!" he announced, then brought her fingers to his lips. "A more fortunate man there has never been."

Nor, she thought, had there ever been a more fortunate lady.

*T*illie was surprised by all the congratulations and well wishes. She'd expected them from Rex's family and her own, but there were a few people she'd not spoken to in years who offered her their best. She didn't know if it was because her sins were forgiven or they didn't want to risk falling out of favor with such an influential family. It didn't matter. None of it mattered.

It was an odd thing to realize how much she'd allowed her past choices to influence her actions, to cause her to view herself through the lens Society held when in truth all that mattered was how she viewed herself. She'd never been ashamed of what she'd done but she'd retreated. No more.

Rex held her in his arms and swept her over the dance floor, his gaze never leaving hers.

"I don't know that I've seen you look so happy or smile so much," he said now.

"Love does that, doesn't it? Makes all right with the world?"

"I think that discovery calls for a private celebration. Care to be scandalous and slip away with me?"

"What notorious woman worth her reputation wouldn't accept such an enticing proposal?"

Although she arrived in her own carriage, she left in his. As soon as the coach door closed on them, he drew her onto his lap and kissed her enthusiastically. She had missed this so much: his nearness, his passion, his devotion. How had she ever thought she would be happy without him in her life?

"Dear God, but I've nearly gone mad with missing you," he rasped, trailing his mouth over her neck to her shoulder and back up again.

"You've missed the sex."

"I did, but it was more than that. It's always been different with you—more intense, more frightening, more demanding."

She leaned back. "Frightening?"

He began removing the pins from her hair, scattering them about the vehicle. "I always worried when you left me that you might not come back, that I may have failed in communicating exactly how precious you are to me. Justifiable concern based on the past few days and nights."

Her hair tumbled around her, and he gathered a good portion of it up in one large hand. How she had longed to have those hands skimming over her again. She cradled his face. "Let's focus on moving forward from this moment and not thinking on the past."

"From this moment on." Then he again took her mouth, his taste rich and decadent. His tongue slid deliciously over hers and she knew very soon it would be sliding elsewhere, creating wondrous sensations as it was wont to do.

The coach slowed, turned onto a drive, came to a halt outside his residence.

"It would be ungentlemanly of me not to give my mistress a proper farewell," he said wickedly before disembarking from the vehicle and handing her down.

"She would be disappointed indeed not to have time with you before you marry," she teased as he swept her into his arms and carried her up the steps, into the manor, and up the stairs.

Once in his bedchamber, he set her feet on the carpet and took her mouth with fervent passion, his hands skimming over her.

"Ah, this room has missed you," he rasped when he finally drew back.

"I missed it. You spoiled me. Nights without you were the loneliest of my life."

"You shall never have another."

"When will we marry?"

"As soon as possible. In the meantime—"

In spite of the numerous kisses, touches, gazes, they made short work of removing each other's clothing. The bed beckoned and they answered the call, racing to it and falling on it in a tangle of arms and legs.

How had she ever thought she could find this with anyone in New York or elsewhere?

"I don't want to go to New York straightaway," she said as his heated mouth coated her throat in dew. "I want to be here for Gina, help her find someone who deserves her."

Lifting himself up, he gazed down on her. "As you wish."

She combed her fingers up into his hair. "Attending the ball wasn't as awful as I expected."

"High praise indeed for my proposal."

She laughed. God, she did love him and his teasing. "That part was absolutely wonderful. No, I meant the people. I received many more congratulations than I expected. Perhaps we'll just take it a day at a time."

"We'll take it however you want." He gave her a devilish grin. "Speaking of taking it . . ."

He rolled over her, clasped her to him, rolled some more until he was on his back and she was straddling him. "You once told me you wanted me to be your slave." He stretched his arms over his head. "Do with me as you will."

He looked so gloriously decadent lying there, completely at her mercy, giving her the freedom to do as she would. "I was a different woman then." Lowering herself, she ran her tongue around his nipple, relished his groan. "I wanted control, thought I needed it." She suckled the turgid tip. He growled. "With you, I never seem to give it up. We're equals in the bed. Equals out of it. I love you, Rex, more than I thought it possible to love anyone."

With a feral snarl, he captured her mouth while plunging his cock home, filling her, stretching her. She cried out with the joy of it, the sensation of closing tightly around his length, owning him while he possessed her. The beauty of being with him was that even when he took, he gave. He made her powerful, confident. He erased all her doubts.

Those wonderful hands of his kneaded her breasts, pinched her nipples. Moving his hands around to her back, he rose up slightly and stroked his tongue over the taut peaks, soothing them even as he caused excitement to run rampant through her. Arching her back, riding him hard and fast, she felt the pressure beginning to build in her—in him. His arms tightened around her as his mouth journeyed up to hers, capturing her lips as effectively as he'd captured her heart. They would have a lifetime of this—of moving in tandem, of seeking pleasure together, of cries, and gasps, and God's name softly taken in vain.

She did love when he growled out profanity like a debauched libertine discovering unexplored aspects to ecstasy. It made her feel as though what he experienced with her were things he'd never experienced with another, that for all his vast knowledge when it came to women, she was still able to surprise him, to take him off guard. To please him, thrill him, and make him ever so glad that she was the woman in his arms, in his bed.

With a feral growl, he clutched her close, rolled her over so her back hit the mattress and he was looming over her, holding her gaze as though it were the anchor in the storm. "Scream for me, Tillie."

"Make me, my lord."

His deep laughter echoed around her as he thrust into her with purpose and determination. As she dug her fingers into his firm buttocks, she clasped her legs around his hips, holding him as tightly as possible while the sensations coiled and spiraled, propelling her into the realm of cataclysmic pleasure.

She did scream—for him, for herself, for the pure joy that rocked through her body.

He followed, plunging deep and sure with his final thrusts as his back arched and he bellowed her name through gritted teeth, before collapsing on top of her, covered in dew, pressing his forehead to hers.

"We shall no doubt live a short life," he breathed out on a warm chuckle, pressing a kiss to her nose, her chin. "Making love to you as often as I intend is likely to kill me when all is said and done."

"Oh, but what a life it shall be."

"The very best, Tillie, I promise you that. Whether here in England or in New York, I shall do all in my power to ensure you awaken every morning glad to find me in your bed."

She had no doubt whatsoever that she would always be glad to find him in her bed, to have him in her life.

Four Years Later

*M*arriage the second time around was so much better than the first that there were times when Tillie could actually look on her marriage to Downie as not a complete catastrophe because it had eventually in a roundabout way led her to Rex. Sitting with him in the grandstand at Epsom Downs, surrounded by his family and hers, she could not have been happier or known a keener sense of satisfaction.

"Lady Rexton, upon whom should I wager?" Bertie, Prince of Wales, called out to her as he passed.

Wherever she went these days, people greeted her with fondness and respect. Oh, there were a few who held on to old grudges but since she now counted the wives of some of the most influential families among her friends, she took any snubs she received with a grain of salt. She knew there was nothing she and Rex couldn't weather together.

"If you wish to win, Your Highness, you should place your money on Notorious."

"Not biased are you?"

"Terribly," she assured him.

With a laugh, he turned to a man following him, said something, and the young gent rushed off.

"Dear God, I do hope our stallion wins," Rex said sotto voice, "or we may find in a few years I have no title to inherit."

"How can he not win when he is the progeny of Black Diamond and Fair Vixen?"

"Here he comes," he said with pride, ducking beneath the broad brim of her hat to buss a quick kiss for luck over her cheek.

She watched as Notorious, gorgeous with his shiny dark brown coat, was paraded before them on his way to the starting gate. The odds were against the three-year-old winning his first race. But then that was to be expected when Rex hadn't let anyone outside of those who resided at Kingsbrook Park see the colt run. Tillie had a feeling the servants had made wagers on the outcome. She did hope they wouldn't all resign from their positions based on their winnings.

She and Rex spent most of their time at Kingsbrook, only occasionally going into London, even though she was now comfortable moving about the city and attending all the various and numerous social affairs to which they were invited. But they both loved the horses so much that they were happiest spending their days in their company, even taking a hand in training them now and then. Although truth be told, as long as Rex was with her, she was joyful to be anywhere. He was her home.

They'd traveled to New York. It wasn't as she'd remembered—or perhaps it was just that she'd changed so much she no longer felt as though she fit as comfortably as she once had. But she'd certainly enjoyed forcing those who once snubbed her mother to address her using her title. She'd even run into Anson. A sadder looking fellow she'd never seen, and she found it difficult to believe she'd once pinned her hopes for happiness on him. Much better to be responsible for her own happiness, to secure it through her own efforts, to be with a man who wasn't at all threatened by her independent nature, who encouraged and took pride in it.

"Notorious doesn't seem bothered by the noise or the crowds," she said now to her husband.

He smiled down on her. "For one so young, he has an amazing amount of confidence. He knows he's going to win."

"I hope so, for your sake. You're going to lose a small fortune if he doesn't."

"Not to worry. I married an heiress. She has the means to see me well taken care of if need be."

Laughing, she wound her arm around his, squeezed. He'd yet to touch as much as a penny. Still, she no longer considered her inheritance as hers, but she saw it as theirs. Everything they possessed was theirs. They shared equally in all aspects of their lives. She'd always dreamed of having this sort of marriage. The reality of it was so much better than anything she'd ever imagined.

As Notorious entered the starting gate, Tillie drew a sharp breath.

"He's going to do fine," Rex said.

The pistol report echoed around them. She was torn between squeezing her eyes shut and watching. In the middle of the pack, the horse was magnificent, his muscles bunching and stretching—

Moving up until he was in third place.

Then when the finish line came into view, he poured his heart and soul into his efforts, passing the other horses as though they stood still. Tillie was shouting and crying as Notorious crossed the finish line well ahead of the others.

"We've got our winner!" Rex shouted as he drew her against him and kissed her with as much enthusiasm as Notorious had exhibited completing the race.

She might have blushed, except she'd grown accustomed to the ease with which he kissed her in public, and those who knew them came to expect it. The Marquess of Rexton was known to be madly in love with his wife, and never missed an opportunity to show her and the world how much he adored her.

When he drew back, he shook hands with his brothers and brother-in-law, hugged his sister and sisters-in-law. Tillie embraced Gina. "I'm so glad you could be here today."

"I wouldn't have missed it."

Rex slid his arm around Tillie and drew her up against his side. "Come, my lady. Let's go down and thank our winner, shall we?"

She smiled up at him. "We have another winner on the way."

His brow furrowed. "Fair Vixen hasn't recovered from the last foal she delivered. I don't see how—" He stopped, dropped his gaze to her belly, then lifted his eyes to hers. "You?"

Nodding, she held back the squeal she wanted to release. She'd been holding the secret for a while, waiting for the right moment. "Finally, I'm with child."

His smile was so tender and loving that she felt lighthearted. After all this time, he still had the power to make her feel giddy and young, to let her know without words that nothing in his life was more precious than she.

"With you as the mother, he—or she—will most certainly be a winner."

Dipping his head down, he once again took her mouth. She reveled in the way his arms closed protectively around her, the way he announced without words that nothing in his life was more precious than she. But then it was only fair because she felt the same way about him. He had pieced back together her heart and would forever hold it in his keeping.

Epilogue

From the Journal of the Marquess of Rexton

I had always wanted to marry a woman above reproach. But like my father, I discovered what I wanted was not what I needed. What I needed was Tillie, always and forever.

The love the aristocracy eventually bestowed upon her was unrivaled. Her sympathy and compassion toward anyone who suffered through difficulties was unparalleled. Our world was changing and many turned to her to lead the way. Divorce became more common and while not wholly accepted, people did become more sympathetic toward those who chose that route.

Notorious was a champion in England and abroad. He, in turn, sired future champions.

As did Tillie. Our children were our pride and joy. They made our life so much richer. At the family estate, we would sit in the garden and watch our children riding the roundabout, their laughter echoing over the green, mingling with that of their cousins. As our children grew toward adulthood, the wooden creatures eventually sat idle, waiting for the next generation. The wind and sun and rain took their toll.

When we were blessed with grandchildren, Tillie and I stood in the garden and watched as the workers dismantled the roundabout, so it could be repaired, painted, and made to look as it once did. We knew the sons and grandsons of Mr. Durham would take great care to make it right again.

While they worked, I held Tillie close, snuggled against me, her head pressed to my chest, so I could easily reach down to kiss her temple. When I think on that moment, I see it and hear the words as clearly as if all had happened yesterday.

"Are you going to ask them to bring you the notes hidden inside the horse?" she asked.

"No, I don't think so. If they find them, let them make up stories about them. And if they don't, perhaps they'll be discovered a hundred years from now. Do you remember what you wrote?"

Turning in my arms, she dropped her head back to hold my gaze. "Do you remember what you wrote?" she asked.

"I do."

"I'll tell if you will."

"Shall we flip a coin to see who goes first?"

She laughed. The years had been filled with her laughter. "No, you'd only use one of your cheating coins." She brushed the hair back from my brow. "I wrote: I wish I'd loved him first. And you, what did you write?"

"I wish I'd loved her first." I bracketed her face between my hands and looked into the blue depths of her eyes, feeling as though I were once again falling for her. I was constantly falling for her. "But all that truly matters, Tillie, is that we loved each other last."

Then I kissed her as I have these many years, with my heart and my soul and all that I was.

Coming August 2017
A novella from Avon Impulse

Gentlemen Prefer Heiresses

Gina Hammersley survived her sister's
scandal, but as the Season nears its end the
question becomes: can she survive her own?

NEW YORK TIMES BESTSELLING AUTHOR

LorraineHeath

FALLING INTO BED WITH A DUKE
978-0-06-239101-8

Miss Minerva Dodger chooses spinsterhood over fortune-hungry suitors. But at the Nightingale Club, where ladies don masks before choosing a lover, she can at least enjoy one night of pleasure. The sinfully handsome Duke of Ashebury is more than willing to satisfy the secretive lady's desires. Intrigued by her wit and daring, he sets out to woo her in earnest.

THE EARL TAKES ALL
978-0-06-239103-2

One summer night, Edward Alcott gives in to temptation and kisses Lady Julia Kenney in a dark garden. However, the passion she stirs within him is best left in the shadows as she weds his twin, the Earl of Greyling. But when tragedy strikes, to honor the vow he makes to his dying brother, Edward must pretend to be Greyling until the countess delivers her babe.

THE VISCOUNT AND THE VIXEN
978-0-06-239105-6

Desperation forced Portia Gladstone to agree to marry a madman. The arrangement will offer the protection she needs. Or so she believes until the marquess's distractingly handsome son peruses the fine print ... and takes his father's place! But because she begins to fall for her devilishly seductive husband, her dark secrets surface and threaten to ruin them both.

LH2 0617